For all of my friends and family who kept on reading snippets and never complained.

Innocence Lost

by

Altany Craik

Chapter 1

As usual, the de-mister was taking a long time to clear the inner frost on my windscreen. A high pitched squeal, like a kettle boiling in the next room, wasn't irritating enough to make me switch off the fan. Tonight was the first time I had been called back to Gleninch, the town of my childhood. Sure, I had visited my sister who still lives there, but not for a few years. I had never been called back on business. Business, like most things, was slow in Gleninch.

The journey across the Forth Road Bridge, a masterful piece of engineering with near continual resurfacing work, into the Kingdom of Fife had been uneventful and the new dual carriageway meant it was less than forty minutes since I had locked my front door. I had paid the entrance fee of one pound sterling. Fife, an exclusive land, where one pays to get in. Tolls on the entry bridges from Tayside in the north and Lothian to the south; made Fife the only place one has to pay to get into. It might have been better to charge the denizens of Fife to get out.

It was now slightly after three in the morning and bloody freezing as I drove speedily along the empty road. The recently completed regional dual carriageway meant that I wouldn't need to drive through the villages that had made up the bulk of Fife's industrial heritage. The new road would take me to the New town. It was new just after the war; tired would be a better description now. The landscape looked quite nice with a blanket of frost. Darkness hid most of the details. It was probably just as well.

I had not been freezing when my vibrating, screaming phone had woken me. A brief message from the Home office and I had been summoned. No niceties either just a summons. A warm bed had been deserted in favour of a trip to St Margaret's in the Fields, whose priest was decorating the car park with his cooling

1

body. They only call me when it's a religious matter. A murdered priest was a religious matter, apparently. So here I was. A homecoming I neither wanted nor needed. The prodigal son returns. Maybe not.

The blue strobe lights and radio chatter give an unearthly feel to even the most mundane of situations but a murder scene seems even more bizarre. Vehicles parked, in what seems like a random order, tape flapping yellow and black and sometimes red, and uniformed and plain clothes all jumbled together like a flash mob. The noise of radios and half barked orders like a hubbub before the curtain rises; now that I was here, I supposed the curtain was about to go up. Another opening of another show.

I pulled my red Nissan Sunny in to the kerbside and waited on the uniformed officer to approach. Thankfully the screeching had subsided to a little ringing noise. He was young and cold, and mist clouds erupted when he spoke. Like puff the magic dragon, no flame just steam.

"Move along, Sir. Nothing to see here." He waggled his torch hand, indicating that I should piss off. His disinterest was written all over his face. His bulky high visibility jacket clearly identifying him as in charge.

I turned off the engine and stepped out of my car. It was bloody freezing and a shiver ran through me. His face was a cross between non comprehension and incredulity as I had totally ignored him. I pressed the lock button in my key fob and a solid clunk-kitty-clunk rang out behind me. His mouth opened but I cut in.

"They are waiting for me, I believe." I spoke calmly, telling the nice policeman nothing.

"Excuse me." He tried the hard ass. All frown and forward leaning, wielding a unibrow of impressive bushiness. I am only five ten and slim with it. This would be fun. A no contest. He might need that stab vest to protect him.

"They are waiting for me officer. I am the reason you are all still waiting in the cold." I smiled pleasantly and watched the

2

lights come on in his empty head. He was a little slow to catch the words but he was trying.

"Who's in charge and where is the body?" I asked as I walked past him. He followed like a good fellow. He didn't have any choice, really.

"Inspector Brotherton. Rear car park." He managed to splutter not knowing what to do. He stopped, a little worried about leaving his post. He let me go on alone.

He hadn't even asked for ID; he must be new. I have identification and official looking passes for what I do, and sometimes they even get checked out. It might as well read 'God Squad'. I am a servant of the Church and empowered by the state. What a combination. When it's my area, I'm in charge. Who's the Daddy?

Turning the corner of the old white church I can see Brotherton and his detectives standing around, waiting. Waiting for me. All they will know is to touch nothing until I say so. They look so miserable and unhappy; I am sure that won't change. I am not renowned for spreading sunshine on my travels. I have difficulty making a good impression and even more difficulty giving a shit about it.

"Inspector Brotherton? Father Andrew Steel." I smile as I introduce myself, he takes the proffered hand and shakes it. No games just a handshake. I don't look much like a priest. I'm a bit untidy, I don't wear robes, need a shave and in the middle of the night my hair sticks up at the back. A combination that is guaranteed to earn instant respect and cooperation, obviously.

"Glad you could make it Father," not a trace of sarcasm, "the body is just over here." He motions onwards and starts to lead the way.

"Have you taken photos?" I expect they will have but always better to ask. He nods allowing me to pass him and go first as we get closer. Brotherton didn't seem too keen to go near. It is always this way when the body is a Priest, I don't know why that should be. A body is a body, isn't it?

Oh well, time to do my Thing. My Thing is like a gift from

3

God, only much less impressive. I get impressions from things. I usually touch them and see what I see; I have always been able to do it. If the supernatural is involved I can feel it. If the priest was simply battered to death by a thug, then I could leave this one and go back to bed.

I was hoping for bed, most often the outcome is negative and the Police handle it. The body, I don't want the name, is face down in a pool of blood. The pool seems to emanate from the head area, like a big treacle circle. I'm going to have to move the body a little to see the wound. Wearing my long dark overcoat was a bad choice. It would get dipped in the pool of blood unless I took it off. So off it came and the sub-zero temperature caressed my back like the hand from Hell. Now I understood why it gets called the wind chill factor, all heat almost instantly blown from my skin. I handed the coat to Brotherton and squatted by the corpse. My knees protest a little but I manage not to groan like a creaking gate.

I teased the grey shot hair back from the forehead hoping I could see a bit of the face. I couldn't so I rolled him over, away from the pool. I've been splashed a few times; experience is a great teacher. I try to keep my face neutral as I see the front view, wouldn't want the provincial cops to think I was a rookie at this. I have seen a few interesting bodies.

It was not pretty, a head wound above his right eye had been the cause of death. Well his skull had been bashed in killing him pretty quickly I would expect. Bludgeoned sums it up pretty well, but I'm not the pathologist. Sometimes I wish I could just look at bodies and use my Gift. I can't, so, I have to touch. I pull in some of the chilled night time air and resist the urge to cough as my lungs protest. I don't smoke but sometimes the cough sounds so similar.

Dead bodies have a feel all of their own. Like cold feet but worse, much worse. Clammy and almost like raw chicken that has been lurking at the back of the fridge. I was chittering a bit as the wind drove the last of the heat from me. I was well and truly wind chilled. I decided the hand would be better than

4

touching the head. I took his right hand gently and hoped for nothing. When my gift kicks in it can be a bit uncontrolled. Tonight was totally uncontrolled; I got a jolt like an electric shock. I dropped the hand like it had grown spikes and promptly fell from my squat onto my ass. Shit. I missed, by a few inches, the pool of blood. Last thing I needed was a blood stained ass. It was so undignified and credibility destroying.

"I'm sorry Inspector I'll be staying a while with this one." I extended my hand and he helped me to my feet. Not a happy look on his face and he barely knows me. I really wanted my coat, but I appreciated the help. I was still puffing a bit as I tried to catch my breath and buttoning up the coat with the fiddly buttons was a trial but I managed. The shivering becoming severe until I stuffed my hands deep in my pockets. I am aware that they are are watching expectantly.

"I need to look inside the church. Is it locked?" God squad efficiency coming to the fore. I really wanted a coffee. However out of the wind would be a start. I should really work on small talk but tonight, like most nights, I didn't make the effort.

"Can we process the body?" Someone behind me asked. I nodded, nothing to see that couldn't wait. They asked so nicely. The crew springing to life behind me was efficient looking and very little chit chat filled the night.

"The church is open, Father." Inspector Brotherton led the way back round. The houses that overlooked St Margaret's had poltergeists twitching the curtains. One or two hardy souls stood in their doorways looking across at us as we crossed the threshold. I almost waved. That's me, the celebrity. Where were the paparazzi when you needed them? What did they expect to see? I wondered if they knew the Priest well.

It was dark inside the doorway, like the mouth of Hell, dark and gaping. I never feel afraid entering a house of God. I always feel safe, whether the lights are on or not. God lives there and we should always remember that. Brotherton didn't feel the same as he fumbled around for the light switch. He managed not to panic but he certainly wasn't comfortable. I wondered if he was scarred

5

by early Sunday school stories or teenage horror movie experiences. Might be both.

A solid clunk and the lobby basked in a clean white light, so bright our eyes squinted in self defence. The worn red carpet showing signs of where the congregation walked, the pile flat in the middle and like new at the edges. To the right the doors into the Church itself were closed. I opened one and stepped in. The light of Christ burned steadily in its holder. God was here. So was I. No comparison really.

Why I was here was a question beyond me. The jolt from the dead priest outside called for my continued presence. Supernatural bludgeoning? I didn't think so. Traces lead to questions that lead to more questions. I was going to wander through the church and see what that turned up. Scientific method or what?

"Father." Brotherton called me back to the present. He has a deep manly voice, lucky bastard. Although he still didn't sound comfortable.

"Yes?" I'm still not that with it. I am bloody freezing. He seems to expect me to be doing something. Perhaps if I had waved a crucifix around or chanted he might have been more impressed.

"I'll get uniform to cordon off the area and place men for the rest of the night and tomorrow." His voice was almost steady. Not the religious type. No, definitely not. He had barely finished his statement and the door closed behind him. He might be tall, dark and have a manly voice but he was behaving like a chicken.

I sat my ass down on the front pew, waiting for some inspiration. Modern churches are much more informal, and it doesn't often feel that spiritual to sit in one. I prefer the old style with high stained glass windows and stone. I let my eyes wander around the church picking out the mandatory elements. I looked at the rail and wondered 'What was going on here?' New Town Scotland, with drink and drugs all around. A precinctular heaven, designed and built for modern living in the fifties. Now it was a bloody soulless dormitory town near to arterial roads and a daily massed exodus to jobs somewhere else. Town and country planners had pretty much failed to deliver on their vision. Now something else was going to blight the lives of the poor sods that lived here.

I let out a slow puff of air to see if it misted. It did. I'd be better off in the car. After a heartfelt sigh I put on my 'Best get on with it' face. Start with the obvious, the rooms at the back, after that, the office and lastly the house of God. I was hoping that I got no more impressions so I could get a place to sleep and get warm. I hate being cold, it makes me cranky. Or should I say crankier?

I hate surprises, too. Christmas presents are always opened early and I don't remember the last Birthday present that I got. Poor me. My life has been a series of little disappointments that have left me a soured middle aged grumpy man. My face was beginning to show it too.

I wandered up the red carpeted hall and felt like visiting royalty. The corridor echoed under my feet as I walked into the darker recesses of this church. The Office was a picture of efficiency. Everything had been filed correctly and not a thing was out of place. No letters in the 'in' tray, no pending items and nothing to go out either. In fact it was the most sterile Priest's office I had ever been in and I've seen lots of them. I wasn't so cold now and my brain was beginning to work; well sort of.

"What are you hiding? Come on, what is it?" I speak to myself, often. Usually its drivel but sometimes I amaze myself. I looked under the desk and slid my hand across the dark floor. I got a jolt that made me bang my head on the underside of the desk. It was the sort of thing that I was happy not to have an audience for.

"Ow. Shit." What the hell had I touched? Under the desk was dark and I could see nothing. I reached in slowly waiting to touch something solid. Nothing, another sweep and a knot of hair was the source. It seemed to be mixed with a herb of some sort. Smelled like sage but I might be wrong. I scooped it into a bag for evidence. Like I give a rat's ass about evidence. I could hear it now.

"M'lord this hair knot gives off supernatural vibes leading me to the accused." Oh yeah, that would be a winner. I can see the old fool in his wig already. Red nose supporting half lens glasses. Too much wine at lunch and a totally befuddled look covering his face.

I still had no clue as to what was going on here. Then it hit me, was the body outside waiting to be killed? Had he put all his affairs in order? I'd check that out later. I would be here in Sunny Gleninch, the land of my youth, investigating the unimaginable. That's me, supernatural sleuth. More like secret squirrel.

Pulling on my coat and closing the door behind me I set off to find a Travel Inn and a bed for a few hours. Then I'd phone in. I couldn't wait, what a great conversation that would be. Priest bludgeoned to death and a vibe from a knot of hair. Joy of joys. The Bishop would be so impressed.

Chapter 2

Travel Inns, motels, call them what you will; they are a modern necessity. I'm in them all the time, a connoisseur you might say. The church like me to be frugal and boy are they frugal. I have to make good use of the congregation's donations. No four star hotels for me. Gleninch has about four different brands of cheap motels. I picked the nearest one. A few raps on the glass doors had brought a sleepy looking night porter to the door. He wasn't impressed with me either. It got better when he got my credit card and realised my holy status. It was 'yes father', 'no father','anything you need father?' On and on. Behaving like a extra from Father Ted.

Amazingly in less than twenty minutes I was back in bed asleep. No longer cold; asleep. The heavy, hollow-fibre, thirty tog duvet wrapped tightly around me. I'd love to say I don't dream but I do. Sometimes in colour, sometimes in glorious technicolour. It all depends what the dream is about; nightmarish images are always colour and childhood memories are always black and white. Odd? Probably. Maybe it's because we had a black and white television when I was young. I never had enough toys either. We were poor in those days. Although in the town of my younger years, everyone was poor but we just didn't know any different. The rows of newly built post war houses were filled with overspills from all over the place and by the time I was born they were full of working class poor folks.

Around nine the constant beep-beep of the phone dragged me from the warm cocoon I had made on the bed. It must have been beeping for some time to rouse me from a deep and dreamless sleep. I pulled myself across the king size bed to put my mobile phone to my ear.

"Steel." I managed to sound mildly grumpy, not pissed off.

My face enough to curdle milk. The escaping yawn covered by my hand as I faced away.

"Andrew, did I wake you?" Bishop Michael tried to sound apologetic, his deep voice rumbling. He wanted to know what was going on. Me too. His manners were just so much better than mine and he was obviously a morning person. For him the day was half over by nine o'clock whereas mine rarely ever started before then.

"Yeah. I'll be here a while." I pulled the quilt closely and yawned again quietly away from the phone. I didn't want to let the cool air inside, my bladder would rebel. I hoped that this would be a quick call.

"Oh, I see. Terrible business I hear." His voice sounding like a shocked old lady at a tea dance or high tea. I could almost imaging him fanning himself in shock. I smiled a little at my own humour.

"Beaten to death." I didn't really want to go into it now. I was disinclined to elaborate and the silence began to build. He is a patient man, the Bishop, and he out waited me. He knows me too well.

"I'll mail you a preliminary in a few hours. I don't know what's going on yet. Something is though." I just stopped and waited. So did he, the fly old bugger. It was a return to the cat and mouse we often play.

"Andrew, try and play nicely with the police this time." Bad press was so difficult to explain. A point he never tired of reminding me. Although he never spoke of the event in question, we both knew what he was referring to. I had been recalled for not playing nicely with the police. "They need evidence. Try to get some. I'll call you later." He hung up. No chance for dissent nor reply. Probably just as well, all things considered.

"Okay, bye. Thanks for the wake up call." I spoke to the dead receiver, I was pissed off now. Might as well get on with it, I had received my orders. That's me, non-morning person, filled with the joys of life. At least the room had a shower. And the shower had hot water; oh the sins of the flesh.

It just looks like an ordinary modern church. There is nothing particularly clever about it. White render, mesh over the windows and a close cut well-maintained grassy trim around it. There are probably hundreds of buildings like this all over the central belt of Scotland. Imagination in construction was at a premium at the time, I suppose. This one was an Anglican one. Makes no difference to me which denomination it is. I investigate them all. Funny how ecumenical they can be on this front and bugger all else. Maybe it's because I'm not actually a Priest as such. Well I am, but not really in the traditional way. As I have the gift; I was kind of recruited for this role. Head-hunted as it were, five hundred years ago I'd have been burned at the stake or head-hunted in an entirely different way. Progress. I have been ordained by all the main groups so that I can cause little offence to all sides. I do my best to cause offence as often as possible to anyone who'll listen. Maybe I'll get fired. Yeah right, I wish.

Police tape flapping everywhere. Two police cars and a handful of nosey, bored, spectator-ghouls. I parked behind the yellow luminous stripes of the police car and hoped I would be able to slip in unnoticed. I ducked under the tape and made for the front doors. The polite uniformed bobby intercepted me smoothly and asked what my business was here. His high visibility yellow jacket looked like it had seen better days; cleaner ones too. He didn't seem to be dialled in to my presence here.

"Where's Brotherton." No attempt at civility on my part as I just want to get inside. The grey weather feels like it will bring rain, just like every other day in Fife at this time of year. I tried not to look too irritated and I don't know if I pulled it off. Not that I care overly much either way.

"Inside. Are you Father Steel? He's expecting you." Deferential and competent, I was beginning to feel less peevish. He managed to ignore my irritation. He had probably had a decent night's sleep though.

"I am. Good morning, Officer. I know the way." I bare my

11

teeth in an attempt to smile at the young man. I'm never really sure how much teeth to show, don't want to look stupid. I just go for something in the middle, enough teeth but not the whole goofy. Smiling should be part of church PR training.

He stepped back and let me pass into the house of God. My domain. The door closed with a solid thud and silence fell heavily in the foyer. I made for the office where I expected to find Brotherton. I was right. Psychic or what?

"Morning." I spoke first and scanned the room. The small office had been searched thoroughly and was a lot less tidy than the last time I was there. You just can't get the staff these days.

"Father Steel. I have been ordered to extend any assistance to you, that you might need." He paused and caught my eye. His hostility was simmering under the surface of those cop eyes. He didn't know why he had to extend anything to the scruffy priest in front of him. Life is full of little mysteries. I serve up my best bland face giving nothing away.

"I don't see why we need help with a fairly straightforward mugging that's lead to murder?" He let it out. He had been holding that one a while. He was not happy at this situation. Orders from on high with no explanation. I wouldn't take kindly to 'do as you are told' as an reason either. I caught his eye and held it for a moment, not challenging just pulling his attention to me.

"I'm not here to walk over your turf Inspector. I'm here to walk on God's turf. Neither of us want to piss Him off now, do we?" I smile, I am so irreverent. The smile reached my eyes, briefly, but at least it got there. I hoped that would break the ice a little.

Brotherton's eyebrow shot up as he tried to decide how serious I was. He had been given orders and would follow them. Good dog. He didn't like the not knowing why, however. There was no sign that my smiled had penetrated his irritation.

"It's not about turf." He managed to squeeze the words out; sullen but not teenager sullen. He was keeping a tight rein on his emotions. He was well trained on that front.

"Whatever, Brotherton. We have to work together to resolve this situation. What have you found out?" That's me, reconciliation personified. The sooner we found out what was going on the sooner I would piss off. It seemed he had grasped that too.

"Not much. The late Father MacPhail was hit on the head and died in his car park. Nothing was stolen. No sign of any attempt to break into the church or the Rectory next door. Nothing suspicious in here." Brotherton paused and glared. He was reporting like a rookie, not an Inspector of twelve years experience. He wasn't happy.

"Go on, you're doing splendidly." I couldn't resist. I am often the oldest child in the room. Sometimes I try not to be but not very often. A deep breath and a bite on his tongue and Brotherton continued.

"We have not entered the Rectory yet; we were waiting for you. I have the keys to the rectory and his car. Not a lot to go on yet. He was well liked, apparently." He concluded his update and waited. Apart from the person who caved his skull in, obviously.

"Inspector, I'm a pain in the ass. I'll try to make this as painless as possible. Let's go take a look. Generally, Priests don't get beaten to death. This is Gleninch, though." My mouth twitched a little, well I tried to look friendly.

"It's the fifth murder this year and it's only February." Brotherton shook his head. He was getting hammered and it was beginning to show. The relentless stream of horrors he would have seen obviously taking its toll.

"How many do you normally get? A year that is?" I asked, five sounded a lot to me. I had grown up here and I remembered a church pianist being beaten to death when I was about ten but no others came to mind. Gleninch wasn't that dangerous or violent.

"Less than five for a year, not five in five weeks." He didn't look very happy, but then again maybe he had been run off his feet. He looked a little ragged at the edges.

13

"Solved any yet?" It didn't come out right but you know how it is. His face darkened as he turned towards me. Stony would be the right description of his look. I had touched a nerve with my big foot, which was firmly in my mouth.

"We have successful outcomes on each one so far." He was not amused, he probably felt I was questioning his competence. Well I was, in a way. He didn't need to take it personally, though. I was just asking.

"Excellent. Then we'll have this sorted out in no time." The smile I made definitely did not reach my eyes. I led the way, the Rectory was waiting for us, locked up and intact like a virgin waiting to be deflowered. Its secrets to be discovered by the dynamic duo.

We went forth like a couple after a row, all front but with an atmosphere that fooled no one. Mum and Dad had definitely not kissed and made up. The uniformed kids didn't look directly at us as we made our way to the Rectory. The trees, skies, bushes and houses much more interesting than us apparently.

Brotherton handed me the key to the door and I did the honours.

Chapter 3

A little push was all it took to open the door. Welcome mat smiling up at us, 'Jesus Lives..Here'. Interesting choice, I thought. Parquet flooring in a lovely herringbone design leading up the hall just begging to be walked on. A mirror on the wall and coats hanging along side; stairs up on the left. This was so normal looking. Why was it anything but normal? What should have been a sanctuary had my gift tingling my skin and screaming warnings to my brain. We were most definitely in the right place.

I stepped over the threshold and knew then that the problem was mine to solve. I stopped dead in my tracks and Brotherton shunted me forward. I hoped he didn't drive like that. His mumbled apology almost missed as I felt power washing over me. Like a rising tide clambering up my legs and across my torso. The wave of nausea that ran through me was sharp and brought a trickle of bile up my throat, the burning sensation making me cough.

"Sorry Father, I …" He mumbled another apology. I still hadn't moved forward and he was blocked in the doorway. He could tell something wasn't right.

"Brotherton, no one else comes in but us for a while." Orders from the tufty-haired priest. My voice the most grown up one I could muster in the circumstances. I hoped I didn't sound too shaky,

"No problem." He shut the door behind us, and spoke quickly into his radio. The double glazed door closing out the traffic noise with a clunk.

Something flapped over my shoulder, blue latex gloves. Brotherton was interested in the integrity of the evidence, apparently. I pulled them on without too much fumbling and only a few hairs plucked from my wrist. I felt like I was in a cop drama or that forensic one on Satellite television. More like

Inspector Clouseau than Inspector Morse. Maybe by the time I had silver hair I'd be good at this although the grey was beginning to make more appearances these days. A silver fox in the making.

I wandered up the hall, every fibre of my being thrumming, some shit was going on here. I did not like the feel of this one little bit. The parquet flooring didn't squeak under our feet, it amplified the sounds of our footfall. MacPhail may have been popular and a pillar of the community but his rectory reeked of supernatural activity. Ahead of me the lounge looked inviting and friendly; a soft sofa and two leather chairs. Books filled a bookcase, and DVD's filled another bookcase. The carpet was an old Axminster style rug, like my granny had owned years ago. Varnished floorboards surrounded the rug. It all looked so normal and yet I knew it was anything but. The working of magic in this place had been frequent and spanned many years. How had this been kept secret? Surely someone must have suspected at some point? Secrets always find a way out.

Sliding double glazed patio doors led outside to a nice town garden. Sunlight was peeking through a gap in the heavy velour burgundy curtains. I stepped over to them and opened them wide, sunlight had power over the Dark. One fact that the movies never seem to get wrong and it didn't just destroy vampires. It worked on almost anything.

My skin was crawling on its own, trying to get off and run away. A bad case of the hebe-geebees. The room looked like it should, no neon signs pointing to clues. A selection of framed photographs adorned the wall. One or two pictures with Bishops and the like, and one with the First minister of the new Scottish assembly. A right hob-nobber. A few ornaments from Africa on the wall unit among other odds and ends. I walked round the sofa, still tingling. I sat in his seat; the seat of power as it were. It enveloped me as I sank in to its arms.

I felt him then. His presence was filling the room, a malignant, evil, mean and cruel spirit. Priest, Pastor, Minister whatever title suits your flavour best, usually these titles bring a certain expectation of the work of God. Usually, love, faith, charity, compassion that sort of thing can be expected. Father MacPhail was definitely reading from a different scripture. I could feel his essence and he was an utter bastard. This was a room of tears. The emotions in this room were raw and stark and I could feel them. How many had he hurt in here? I felt tears tickling the sides of my face. It happens, I cry. Live with it. Sometimes the tears come unbidden as I feel some of the memories laid down and fed back to me. Experiencing them as if my own. I have long since stopped trying to control them.

"Father, are you all right?" Oh bloody marvellous. Brotherton chose now to look in. He looked a bit confused, it might have been embarrassment. How often do grown men cry for no good reason? I do it all the time.

"I'm just peachy." I do nothing about the tears. I act like they are not there, it works for me. Most people just play along and ignore them too. The 'Don't stare' training we give children always seems to kick in.

"There will be some evidence here. I'll find it." I stated. Brotherton looked a bit bemused. He had no idea what my way of working might be nor why I was the empowered pain in the ass. He seemed to accept my statement at face value though.

"I've looked upstairs and the kitchen and all is neat and orderly. I don't think the killer was in here." His words sounded a little too matter-of-fact for my liking. Of course the killer wasn't in here, that's not really in question. Never argue with a psychic, I always want to say. It always comes out differently though.

"Brotherton, I'll check out the upstairs. I don't like this at all." I was so glad to get out of that seat. Just like that MacPhail left me, thank God. What a bastard he had been. He had enjoyed inflicting the pain both mental and physical.

Three rooms upstairs and a bathroom. Over specified for a single man, if you ask me. I start in his bedroom. I dislike the décor immediately, jealous of the high standards that MacPhail lived in. The dado rail splitting the vertical striped paper from the,tonally matching, painted upper section. The pile on the carpet was deep and soft, and new. No doubt it felt lovely between the toes. I didn't think the colour matched the wallpaper.

"You can't hide from me you bastard." I state flatly to the room. I could feel the carnality like a breeze in my face. A parade of partners had warmed the bed. Both genders and a mixture of ages I was sure. I know corruption when it kisses my skin. Brotherton would need evidence. Fuck that. I remove the latex glove and lean forward. My hand lightly touched the sheet, Egyptian cotton no doubt.

A mixed patina of essences flew through me and I get a totally unwanted view of the most recent bed warmers. This bed is a busy place; there had been a few recently. I screw my eyes shut and get a picture of MacPhail and his depravity. A slim form face down, followed quickly by a rather fat older woman on her knees. I open my eyes quickly to dispel the image. Not an image I want to keep. Vivid and strong it had been burned into me and was so difficult to unsee. I need brain bleach to get that out but it will be stuck there for all time, it's just the way my memory works. Total flash recall and never what I want to remember.

I can't miss the mixture of lust, pain and cruelty that fills the bedroom. I can feel that this is no ordinary rectory. I've seen, and felt, some hairy stuff but this is right up there. A mixture of sex, pain and supernatural power fill the whole bloody place. Like a cocktail of all things debauched and dangerous. I open the bedside drawer and find nothing. It is empty, nothing. My bedside cabinet is full of letters, junk and all sorts of oddments. MacPhail has an empty drawer. The tidiest priest I've ever seen. What the hell was he doing? Tidying up before I got here? Or did someone else do it? Shit. I am a bit slow, sometimes.

"Brotherton." I call, without barking. Although there might have been a growl buried in there somewhere. I hope I don't need to shout again because invariably that is a bark. I hear him on the stairs and I start speaking before he gets into the bedroom.

"Who called this in? Everything has been tidied up or removed." I state quickly. He flipped out his notebook and flipped through the pencil scrawls until a name jumped out.

"Anonymous caller I'm afraid." Brotherton shook his head. He wasn't even surprised, just disappointed. Modern times and no one wanting to get involved. This time I think the caller was involved.

"Surprising isn't it?" I can be a little sarcastic on occasion. This was one of those. I had that near sneer on my lips that is one of my best looks.

"Not really. Most 999 calls are anonymous. People don't want to get involved." Brotherton explained. At least he looked apologetic. It was something.

"Who can blame them eh?" I try not to look too sour but not really pulling it off. I do understand there is nothing to be done about it now.

"Doesn't explain the tidy up job, though. Why would the rectory need tidied up? What needed to be hidden?" Brotherton frowned. It seemed to me that he didn't like it either. His blue eyes looked cold and serious, first time I noticed anything about him. We might need to get along for a while. I am not good at getting along, apparently.

"Well we'd better go through the motions." I smile to myself. I always liked the double entendre. Okay, I know it's a disgusting idea but whatever gets me through the day.

In all the rooms there are essences and vibrations that make me feel pretty woozy and I feel almost a little tipsy. Even the bathroom. I mean the bathroom for fucks sake, what supernatural shit takes place in the bathroom. Well I had to find that out. There was a strange looking bar above the shower, I decided that I knew what it was for. There was no way I was touching it. After having touched his sheets I didn't want to watch his pornographic life any further. I decided to check out the sink.

I made a bit of a mess. I became a plumber for the morning and hauled off the sink trap expecting evidence and clues to be contained in the gooey sludge that lived there. Brotherton wasn't entirely happy at the mess I made of the floor but he was impressed that I thought of it. The sludge was bagged and tagged.

I couldn't reach under the bath panel so I left it alone. The trap under the bath could wait.

His home office was a bit more like it. It wasn't totally tidied up. The beige computer sitting proudly on the desk was begging me to touch its keyboard. It was probably a good idea to leave that to the specialists. The last time I had tried to interrogate a computer on a case I had set us back months in terms of evidence. I moved the mouse with the back of my hand and the screen leapt to life. A lovely view of the countryside and the dreaded password request. Bloody typical. It already had a sticker on the top, asking for it to be taken for analysis. Brotherton had been through this room.

"I have an address book from the desk." He chimed from the doorway, seeing me scanning the desk. I didn't turn round, I just let my eyes rove across the surface waiting for inspiration to strike.

"That will be useful." I meant it but probably sounded a bit sarcastic. I would be looking through it later hoping that someone or something jumped out at me. I pulled the top drawer out of the desk and looked inside. If it was anything like my desk, things fell down inside at the back. I couldn't really see so I reached inside. I felt something and pulled it out. Like little Jack Horner I had pulled out a plum. It was an envelope with Polaroids in it.

"Ah ha." I couldn't resist. Of course I had left fibres from my sleeve all over the edge, hopefully no one would notice this minor contamination but I had put my gloves back on earlier so no prints. I waved the envelope in the air. Brotherton was over in a flash. We looked at the photos together, all six of them. If I wasn't so sex deprived I would have been upset but I was simply envious. MacPhail, I presume, was the male in the photos and there were three different women in them. Not a face in sight, though, but it might be fun trying to identify them.

"I wonder who these ladies might be?" I mused, aloud. I think I sounded a bit of a sanctimonious prigg but too bad. I couldn't keep a little smirk from twitching my lips.

"Members of the congregation?" Brotherton was catching

on. We might sort this mess out after all. We both knew there was much more than the beating to death about this case.

"Probably. Not the usual activities of pastoral care. MacPhail was busy." I smirked wider this time, I just couldn't help it. The inner juvenile escaped in time to dispel my grown up success of finding evidence.

"I'll have forensics tear this place apart and that computer. We'll have a better idea once we have done that. Maybe a jealous husband or lover?" He was getting all efficient on me just like a proper detective. I didn't feel the need to say that neither of those were likely.

"Let's go. I need to report in." Things were going to be very interesting.

We were standing together at the foot of the stairs about to leave. Brotherton had locked the back door and had radioed the forensic crew to proceed. I looked up and saw it. A loft hatch. Upstairs hall and a loft hatch. All these houses had them. I looked at Brotherton and flicked my eyes upstairs. Did I need to spell it out? Apparently, I did.

"What?" He was confused by my clue. Maybe it was the untidy eyebrows that did it. Perhaps I had over estimated how efficient he was as a detective. Maybe both.

"There is a loft up there. I want to look." Direct I think it is called. Abrasive, it certainly is.

"Hold off on that crew." He sighed into his radio microphone. He was following his orders to the letter, extend all aid as required. The little sunshine had stopped peeking out from his cloud and he was back to grey and brooding. He obviously felt that I was going to be a burden that he alone would have to bear. Just like Eeyore.

"After you." I gesture up the stairs.

Moments later we have found the rod used to open the loft and pull down the stainless steel ladder. B&Q's finest loft ladder kit installed by a professional not some botch of a DIY job. Brotherton produces a large torch and turns it on. Where he had it

I do not know but I want to call him Pockets. Probably not the best idea as we are still in the getting to know you phase, only our second date as it were. It is time to ascend into the inner sanctum. Now we were making progress, the loft would tell us all we needed, I hoped. I was betting that MacPhail hid all his shit in the loft. I know I did as a kid.

Chapter 4

Lofts are amazing places. When I was young I spent ages in our loft. It was floored and carpeted. It was a cool den, of course, it was bloody cold in the winter. My friends and I used to hang out up in the loft and read girlie magazines and lie about our prowess with the ladies. Those were the days, gone and never to return. I doubted MacPhail had any girlie magazines up here. His was into a more hands on kind of lifestyle.

It came as no surprise to me that Macprise's loft wasn't cold. It was lined with board and carpeted and had an interesting skylight window in the roof. No, it was positively luxurious. No spiders, nor webs for that matter, to make me cringe. It did, however, have a telescope and lots of star charts. Apart from being an utter bastard, who obviously got my ration of sex, he was an astronomer. Stargazer of a serious vent, if the telescope was anything to go by, it looked very pricey. Not a forty nine pounds starter from Argos but a great big round one with all sorts of attachments. Cost was no object, apparently, when it came to his toys. This was a toy with a purpose and I was betting I wouldn't like what he did with it. Brotherton whistled under his breath, he was impressed too. Like some things, size matters.

"Good call, Father." He was warming up to me. Everyone does, eventually. Yeah right. We stood looking, not really wanting to touch anything, until we both set off at once our fingers reaching for clues.

"I had a train set in my loft. He obviously kept his toy in the loft, too." I didn't want to be too smug. I think I got the balance just right. Two in a row and all that. The smirk that played around the edge of my mouth wasn't juvenile in the least.

"There is some very expensive stuff here." Brotherton was on the money. A statement of the obvious is a good way to start. He was scanning the room looking for obvious clues, poor soul. I

23

doubt any of the clues here would be of the obvious variety. Police training is probably not big on occult or astronomy.

"Let's see what he was looking at." What I know about astronomy you can write neatly on the rear of a postage stamp, and not one of the big ones either. I can bluff with the best though. I look at the telescope and see a power cord, which I switch on before I put my eye to the eyepiece. Luckily for the amateur that I am, it is not pointed at the sun. Or it would have been curtains for my eyeball, it would have been fried. It's daytime so I have proven my lack of knowledge, better to do this after dark. I will come back later. I move away from the all-seeing eye. It sits on some sort of motorised thing. Well I dunno what it is called, like a track that it would move on. Looks complicated.

"Does it matter what he's looking at? As long as it's not someone's bedroom window?" Brotherton was looking round, inspiration failing to strike. The training at Tulliallan Police College is very much an inside the box style of thing.

I opened the drawer of his immaculate desk, it even felt expensive. Usually priests are recipients of hand me downs but MacPhail appeared to be well to do. Nothing in the whole house contradicted this. Smoothly it slid open, inside some star charts with lines on them. I hoped these were what we, in the business, call clues. I picked them up.

"Inspector, I'll need these examined." I spoke with certainty I didn't feel. I tried to look like I knew what they might mean.

"Examined for what? Fingerprints?" Poor man really had no idea. His face was showing that very fact. I was pleased that he indulged my search of the house, after all the body had been found outside.

"I was thinking more by an astronomer. What do these lines mean?" I waved them about a bit.

"Will it be related to the murder?" His scepticism was really unbecoming. After all I had found the photos. To say I was a little disappointed by his lack of seeing the wider picture would be an understatement.

"Probably not, but it will help me find out what's actually going on." I could have explained but I didn't. He just had to do as I asked him.

"I'll see what I can do." The ubiquitous plastic evidence bag appeared in his hand waiting for my deposit of the clue. I am sure they are just freezer bags with printing on them. I duly dropped them inside, knowing that they were probably meaningless.

"I am sure I know someone at the museum if you need help." I was trying to be helpful, I hoped he realised that. I don't always offer up my experts. Sharing my toys was one thing I never learned at nursery school.

"Shall I let the SOCO boys in?" I nodded. It was unlikely that I would get my hat-trick of clues. This house was giving me a headache anyway. Way too much monkey mojo for this time in the day. Besides my grumbling stomach was telling me that breakfast was the most important meal of the day. Pity I had missed it. Well it was seven pounds fifty. Bloody rip off, if you ask me.

"Bishop Michael please." I managed to be polite, just. The gatekeeper didn't sound all that friendly nor deferential.

"Can I put you on hold?" No time to say no as the music began, Gregorian chanting. For goodness sake how bloody predictable. Never mind I was almost humming along when it stopped to be replaced by my boss.

"Andrew, how are things going?" He was way too cheerful, disgustingly, cheerful. The absolute opposite to how I felt after the visit to the manse.

"Well Bishop, I have searched his house and it stinks of activity. Sex and depravity all over it." Why was I so coy about saying supernatural? I always feel embarrassed as I say it, so I avoid it. It just sounds idiotic.

"That is not good. I need you to wrap this up quickly if you can. I have something else for you to deal with soon. Are you getting help from the local police?" He asked. What he really meant was 'are you playing nicely?'

"They have been very good. Inspector Brotherton has extended every courtesy. They are looking into MacPhail's computer and some star charts. He was an astronomer as well as a dabbler in something." I swigged from my coffee cup and it was cold. Cold coffee is an acquired taste, one I have never acquired. I almost spat as my tongue recoiled.

"Send the charts on to me and I'll get them examined by our people for any religious significance. Oh and Andrew, keep the news of his behaviours out of the press if you can." It would be a PR disaster if word got out about a shagging priest and his flock. Maybe years ago but not these days, it was almost expected. Besides, didn't shepherds have previous with their sheep?

"I'll try Bishop. Do you want Brotherton to destroy the Polaroids?" I knew I was pushing my luck, especially after the evidence reminder.

"I don't think that will be necessary. Just don't want them appearing in the Sunday papers. Or any other paper for that matter." He was getting bored. I can tell when I bore people. It is like another side to my gift. Let me be anything but a bore.

"OK will do my very best. I'll call tomorrow." Sarcasm was beginning to creep in. Best not to antagonise the Bishop, after all, he sends me out to play.

"All right Andrew. Good luck and you be careful." The phone call was over. I had reported in. I also had not made it sound like I was totally clueless. One back for me.

What the hell was I going to do now? I couldn't exactly go round the congregation asking who was sleeping with MacPhail. I should probably start with the members of the Vestry, the committee that run the church at a local level. I'd get the names from Brotherton.

"Inspector Brotherton? Steel here. Can you give me the names of the members of the Vestry at St Margaret's?" Straight in at the jugular, no messing with small talk. I find the less I say the less chance that I'll piss someone off.

"Yes I have a pen. OK, go ahead." And just like that I had a list of possibles. One of them at least knew what was going on.

Time to put on my Spanish inquisition robes and go biting the guilty. Well more a subterfuge over the tragedy. The lamp in the eyes could wait till later. I wondered if Brotherton had a lamp all set up. He didn't strike me as the type.

Chapter 5

There is a reason that I am not a regular Priest. Well actually there are loads but the main one is that I am a lousy conversationalist. It's true. I really can't feign that much interest and after the pleasantries are exchanged then that's where the difficulty starts. I ask you, what do I have to say to an eighty year old woman who thinks the world is a den of iniquity? She has a point, of course, but it gets a bit wearing. Then there's the apologising for every bloody or damn that passes their lips, like I am fragile and will faint at a little swear word. Pisses me off. However, the main issue I have is the tea. Cups and cups of tea. Plates of biscuits brought out especially for the visit of the priest. Small wonder so many of my brothers are portly.

"It's terrible these days. Who would do such a thing to a man of god? It's just terrible." She was obviously in shock. It was a bad world out there, one which she obviously didn't understand. Her scrunched up hankie dabbed at her nose, a sniff as vocal accompaniment. What the hell was I going to say now? I am really crap at the pastoral empathy bit. Maybe while she was a bit unsettled I could pump her for information. What a callous bastard I am. There was no hint of anything in my area in this house. I waited for a hundred. A slow hundred before I opened my big mouth.

"Well Mrs McLaughlin, you must have seen a few Rectors in your time here?" I thought I might as well let her ramble on a bit, who knows what might turn up. She was, after all, the longest serving member of the vestry committee. If there were any skeletons buried in the congregation, she would know where, when and who. Probably even the why.

"Oh well, Father Andrew, that's true. I have been a member of St Margaret's since it was built for the new town in the early fifties." She smiled proudly. A long association made her one of the Holy.

"You've seen many changes then?" Just priming the pump, as it were. Or avoiding putting my foot in it too quickly. I smiled gently to the old dear, encouraging her to recount the stories of the past.

"Oh yes. From such a small congregation we've grown until there are more than four hundred on the roll and more than two hundred on a Sunday." Stats like a football commentator, next she'll be telling me what they've won. We did the double in 1995, perhaps a treble and a European cup too. She was off and running. The achievements were remarkable, if you like that sort of thing.

"That's a big crowd for a Sunday, how do you manage it?" I sounded suitably in awe. After all attendances had been dropping, at worship, like a stone and this one bucked the trend.

"Father MacPhail, Lord bless his soul," she paused to cross herself and take a breath to avoid more tears, "was very popular among the younger members of the congregation." I almost choke on my digestive crumbs. Was she telling me something?

"Scripture union? Youth fellowship? That sort of thing?" Just giving her some rope to hang herself with. The rope I hoped would tie up a few loose ends about MacPhail.

"Well those too. He was a very handsome man after all." So much left unsaid. Just a big enough hint for me. I don't think she meant it though. It might just have been me projecting a meaning into her words.

"It always helps attract new people to the church. His sermons must have been very modern too I suppose." Hopefully she didn't approve. Some parishioners dislike change with a passion.

"Well I suppose so, but he always remembered the more traditional messages too. He was good for the parish." A maudlin look began to settle on her face. She obviously liked the man. I wonder how much she knew. Probably nothing but I'd bet she could guess plenty. The faraway look passed to one with tears at the edges, her front was cracking.

"I'm sure he was." I'd decided to let her get her equilibrium back a little before I asked her for the minutes of the meetings. A moment passed.

"The Bishop sent me over as soon as the news broke this morning. I will be with you until something more permanent can be arranged." I shifted slightly in my seat as I got ready to make my request. If you ever play poker against me, I am in trouble. I have too many tells apparently. The old dear barely noticed. She nodded her understanding.

"'Be tactful Andrew, it is a time of great shock' he told me, and of course I understand how many of you must feel." I paused, all sincerity and sympathy, "So that I can get up to speed with Father MacPhail's duties I need to look over the vestry minutes. It will be so much simpler than bothering the members at this sad time." I smiled softly all full of concern that I didn't feel. I needed a flaming clue as to what was happening and had to start somewhere.

"Of course, I have copies. Let me get them for you." She painfully hoisted herself from her chair and ambled from the room. No doubt she had a folder going all the way back to the fifties.

The second she closed the door behind herself I stood up and looked at the pictures inside the dresser cabinet over by the window. Inside the frames were a variety of pictures, some obviously family, others with Father MacPhail and assorted others. I have a good memory for faces and stared hard at the group photos, hoping that later I might see some of these people again. Names are a little more difficult. I had just re-parked my backside beside the biscuits when she came in with a handful of typed minutes for me.

"These are the minutes of the last three Vestry meetings Father." She handed them to me without any further explanation. She was obviously distracted. Why the last three meetings I wonder? Who knows but maybe I was over thinking it. A few more minutes of banality and I was on my way through the door offering platitudes of consolation and sympathy.

Interesting reading they were not. Dull, dull, dull. The minutiae of the details of these vestry meetings was telling me bugger all. Finances look fine. Points made at the meeting bore little resemblance to anything sinister. Total waste of time, the lot of it. The good people who participate in the running of churches give a lot of their time to make it work. Why did it have to be so very boring? Probably because they were generally older men and women who longed for control of something. It was a sad place to try and gain fulfilment. I was a little grateful that Mrs MacLaughlin had only given me three doses of this drivel to read. After all she could have given me years worth. I had just decided to go to the police station and see Brotherton when the phone rang. Not my mobile phone, but the room phone. I hadn't given the number to anyone except Brotherton or the Bishop.

"Yes." Neutrality achieved. No clues that this was a surprise.

"Stay away. Or you'll regret it." A voice heavy with malice rolled down the line towards me. Sounded like one too many old gangster movies had influenced the caller. I was betting he wasn't a really bad man. Just a wannabe.

"Piss off." Didn't expect that, did he. A click and the conversation was over. I smiled. It usually took me a couple of days to alienate the locals, I had managed it in less than an afternoon. I laughed to myself. Progress. The phone rang again

"What?" I snapped. I was just pretending though. I hoped he was calling back for round two, after all I had knocked him off his stride.

"Father Steel? Brotherton here." He sounded confused. Doesn't everyone snap down the phone?

"Sorry I thought you were someone else." I was smirking like an idiot now. Poor Brotherton having to work with me.

"Preliminary post mortem report is in. Do you want to come down to the station? I am at Rowan Road local station. Do you know where it is?" He was trying to be helpful, bless him. I grew up in this town and knew where it was.

31

"I'll be there in ten minutes. I know where it is." It was less than four hundred yards from where I grew up. I could find it in a blackout.

"I'll put the kettle on." Brotherton was extending an olive branch. He must want to know something. Well he'd better be patient because I am not the sharing kind. I pulled on my coat, it was raining again. Actually it hadn't really stopped. Yep that's what I remembered about Gleninch, pissing rain and grey skies. Oh yeah and a bloody cold wind off the North Sea. Why do the natives stay? I had no idea.

Chapter 6

Fan belt screaming like a banshee, it was better than a siren. I couldn't really see much through the misted windscreen but that was just too bad. I could find the Rowan Road station in the dark with a blindfold. I used to lust after a girl called Helen who lived just around the corner from it. I smiled as I remembered her. A priest should not be having these impure thoughts I chastised myself. Well actually, I just enjoyed the reverie. She was pretty, after all. We had a great time for a while, amazing how much fun you can have at fifteen.

The houses had changed very little, the trees a little bigger, and the cars in the streets more modern. Overall Gleninch was like the Eternal City, unchanging. It was still a dormitory not really sure what to be. The new town experiments after the war were not really the success that was hoped for. Overspill populations from the west coast transplanted to the east coast. A recipe for success, I don't think.

Rowan Road Police Station, was the headquarters in Gleninch for years, but had since been replaced by a newer building further from the town centre. It was a masterpiece of utilitarian design, dull and functional in the extreme. I had been here a few times before. The first time, I was eight, on a school trip. I had freaked out in the cells after the kind policeman had locked me in, 'to let me see what it was like'. An early form of aversion therapy I presume. Unfortunately I could feel all the ills that the many inhabitants of that cell had perpetrated on their victims. It gave me nightmares for weeks. Not a nice experience for an eight year old psychic sensitive.

I drove into the rear car park beside all the luminescent yellow chequered traffic cars, enjoying my exalted status. I was hoping to meet unibrow boy, but that was wishful thinking on my part. I got out, pressed my remote locking as I turned away and began to march towards the service entrance. I had my dog collar on, in uniform, I looked the part apart from the stubborn sticking up tuft at the back.

Brotherton met me at the back door. He was looking a bit too friendly for my liking. He had a smile on his face, all white teeth. I bared mine back at him as best I could and he ushered me inside. He marched past the various offices until we came to an interview room. He sat facing the door and I had the perp's seat. The report was in a manilla file. All official looking. Brotherton slid it across the desk to me. I opened the report and read it. The silent waiting doesn't bother me but I expect Brotherton uses it regularly.

I have no real idea what half the words actually meant but the best I could do was work out that blunt force trauma was what killed him. I didn't need the report to tell me that. I had seen the dent in his cranium. I took a while to flick through the rest, I said nothing. I just waited and then after, what I hoped was long enough, put it down on the desk. I looked at Brotherton.

"What do you think Father?" He asked me, like I should know. He seemed a little too smug for my liking but I was still waiting for his great reveal.

"What? Skull stove in? A mystery isn't it." It was a little too sarcastic. Never mind eh? Must try harder next time.

"The Toxicology report, I meant." He was unflappable. Bloody detectives. He was dragging this out and I was not really sure where he was going.

"Oh sorry, I never looked at that bit." I looked a little sheepish, I had been found out.

"He had a hell of a cocktail in his blood. I am amazed he could stand." Brotherton opened the report and handed me the toxicologist report. More chemical stuff, I had no idea.

"Tell me what I'm reading Inspector. I don't know what half this stuff is?" No point in bluffing and bullshitting. He would need to spell it out for me. My degree was most certainly not pharmacology.

"Ketamine. They use that to sedate horses. It also has

hallucinogenic effects. On the streets it's called Vitamin K. Heavy stuff." Brotherton looked at me. All was clear now then, apparently.

"So he took drugs?" I am a bit slow sometimes, maybe if he had given me coffee and biscuits I might have been better placed to keep up.

"The amount of Ketamine in his blood, he probably couldn't stand let alone walk. Pathologist thinks he might have even been in a coma before the blow to the head killed him. Might even have been from his head hitting the pavement." Brotherton, looked a little bit happy. Now I knew why. If it wasn't murder then I would be out of his hair.

"Could the Ketamine have been administered later?" All CSI now, like a pro. I knew he had been murdered, no doubt about it. I also knew that there was something hinky going on, regardless of his report.

"Doc says no chance, well and truly through his system. It was inhaled." Brotherton was hanging on to misadventure like a terrier to a rat. After all, the most obvious reason is usually the right one. Brotherton seemed keen to not look too far past the end of his nose.

"Brotherton, he was murdered. End of." I was getting a bit bored with this and my shirtyness seemed to be on the increase.

"'There's evidence to suggest he may have fallen over, banged his head in a drug induced haze and died where he fell. On K you feel next to nothing that happens to your body." He was being patient with the new boy.

"Did we find an inhaler? Any Ketamine in the house? Better have a look then." I moved on as he shook his head. To leap to assumptions about what killed MacPhail was just sloppy police work. Brotherton didn't strike me as the kind who was sloppy. Maybe he was, who knows. The happy demeanour had evaporated like stink off a turd. He shut the file and stood up, looked like we were going back to the scene. I noticed the absence of the cup of tea and Rich Tea biscuit. Probably best not to mention it. Don't really like Tea that much anyway.

We would be going in his car. Suited me fine. I wondered if he would crack first and start up a conversation. I gave him a minute tops, once we were in the car. I was right.

"Just what are you doing here Father?" Curiosity had got him at last. He had to know.

"I am here because the Home Office called me the other night." I was being bland and obtuse. Skills I have in spades. I was going to make him work for an explanation. Well he started it with the Ketamine stuff.

"Why was I ordered to give you anything you need?" Brotherton's hands were griping the steering wheel quite tightly. I noticed the tension filling his voice and his large frame.

"Good manners maybe?" I laughed gently and then went on, "I deal with crimes against religion. It's my area." Everything and nothing.

"This isn't hate crime. This is a simple death by misadventure or a murder. What do you need to be involved for?" He wasn't happy at my evasions. Life is so hard.

"Brotherton, all crimes against the Church are checked by me and if I deem it necessary to stay for a while, I do. If I think that the local police can manage I let them. It is really that simple."

His brows lowered a bit further. He was not happy. Luckily we were almost there. The psychic realm of terror that was the home of the dead body we had on ice. Ketamine my arse. We would find nothing supporting drug use and I knew it. A little smile was failing to stay off my face.

Chapter 7

"No sign of any drug equipment." Brotherton's faith in misadventure was wavering. I smiled to myself. I am usually right. It's a trait that gets on everyone's nerves eventually. Sometimes that eventually can be measured in minutes.

"I'm not saying he didn't take it, but he was murdered." I tried not to be too smug. Another failure in my many flawed character.

"Why would he take it? He's a pillar of the community? Responsible and well respected." Brotherton was thinking aloud.

"He was also a sexual predator who would sleep with anything that moved." Oops did I just let that out. Yep I did and I meant to. Now whatdya think Inspector?

"What?" Brotherton had a stunned look on his face. He hadn't expected that series of words to fill the air between us.

"Sit down Brotherton and I'll tell you why I am here." He sat on the couch. I wasn't sitting down in here again.

"What I am telling you is covered by the official secrets act 1989 and following and failure to observe the tenets of that act can lead to prosecution." I paused, I like doing this bit. I have had a bit of practice. "Of course you'd lose your job, pension and employment prospects if you decide to ignore my warning." I went on. He nodded, good boy.

"I am an instrument of the Church and the Home office. I am psychically gifted and can feel things." No emotion on my face. He knew I wasn't pissing about.

"Really? But how?" He was a bit babbly but otherwise he believed me. His acceptance was a promising start.

"If the supernatural is involved then it's my area. MacPhail, as it turns out, was a bad man involved in something even worse. I am not sure yet what it is." I paused to let him catch up. He was silent, obviously thinking.

"Are you a religious man Inspector?" I looked straight at him and waited. He shook his head a little. He obviously didn't want to say no.

"Not really. Not been to church in years. It's the job." He seemed apologetic. I am not surprised though, five murders in as many weeks would be awfully hard to reconcile with a good god.

"Find some faith. You'll need it." I smiled. I knew he was one of the good guys. Only problem was that he could see evil all around and could never see any evidence of God. Admittedly I have to look hard to find him too, sometimes. I knew Brotherton was going to be vital to me if I was to work out what was going on. So we needed to be on the same page.

"Why would he take Ketamine then?" He asked, his voice just not getting it. The small things, it seemed, bugged him too.

"Did you not say it had hallucinogenic qualities? Maybe he was looking to see the spiritual world? Or maybe he was given it when unconscious and on the ground?" I thought the first more likely than the idea of post-mortem addition. Now I was thinking out loud. Wasn't really helping.

"What are we missing here? Something is going on behind the façade of normality and we need to work it out." I was pacing around the room. One thing was for sure there was more than MacPhail in on it. I scratched my head, making the tuft at the back stick up. I was managing to keep the room's mojo out but it was tiring.

"What do we actually know?" Brotherton spoke quietly. Back to basics seemed a reasonable place to start. Of course, sometimes it can be a very short list.

"MacPhail is dead. Murdered by someone or something." I began as I paced about. Sherlock Holmes time. I stared out the patio doors looking into the well manicured garden. He must have had a gardener; it was so well kept and tidy. He certainly would not have had any energy left over for gardening.

"We also know someone tidied up after the event." Brotherton added from the couch. He was right but how he could sit there and feel nothing was beyond me.

"I don't like knowing the square root of fuck all." I growled to the room. I saw Brotherton's eyebrows shoot up. He obviously had not heard a priest swear before. He caught his face quickly and looked away.

"Let's get SOCO to pull this place apart." That's the spirit. I smiled to Brotherton and nodded. Let's just turn the place over and see what was under every stone. Let us shine the light into the dark corners and see what scurries out.

"Great idea. Can we keep it quiet? I have had a warning call already." I told him, now we were best buddies and all.

"You should have told me." Brotherton gave me the cop look filled with disappointment at my lack of full disclosure. I shrugged.

"I just did." There we go, obtuse as ever. Brotherton just shook his head as he called in the crime scene forensics team.

Bloody amazing what technology can turn up. I might get an impression here and there but hi tech gizmos are truly amazing. Who would have seen the outline of a pentagram drawn in blood on the polished wooden floor? With an ultra violet light all became apparent. MacPhail was indeed a follower of the Dark. No wonder the living room made me feel queasy. Of course we were really no further forward. I already knew he was bad to the bone. The revelation of the pentagram made little real difference. What he had done with it was something else. A blood pentagram suggests a real practitioner not merely a dilettante.

So now I knew that this was some serious shit. Shock and horror. No idea what flavour of course. That would come later.

Chapter 8

When I decided to visit all the members of the vestry
committee I thought it was a good idea. However, after three
visits and no progress, I was beginning to change my mind. I had
sat on three very uncomfortable couches and tasted a variety of
teas. I had learned nothing. It was like a normal congregation so
far; an annoyingly bland congregation that loved its priest. All
good except the priest in question was a Satanist and all round
bad guy.

I was getting a bit pissy, as I usually do when things are not
going to plan. Which probably makes me pissy most of the time.
However, my luck was about to change. It's funny how these
things happen. I don't usually get much of an impression off of
people when they are alive but when I shook hands with Angela
Brookes, wife of David Brookes the treasurer, I got a surprise.
She was a rather attractive thirty something. Not that being
attractive was unusual. It was the image I received from her. She
was one of the last bed partners of MacPhail. I could see her
fucking the living daylights out of him like a lioness in heat. It
was all I could do to be coherent. She didn't notice.

"Come in Father, my husband isn't home." Did I catch just a
hint of a possibility? I hoped not. I know that I am not
irresistible to women. I might like to be, just once, but the reality
is that I am so very average in looks and a bit too slim to be all
that manly. Her smile was full of potential, or at least I thought
so.

"Will he be long?" Great line eh? Spent hours working that
one out, the delivery was lame too.

"Unfortunately not Father." I hadn't been imagining her
willingness after all. "Would you like some tea?" she seemed
disappointed.

"Thank you." She led the way into the, rather sterile, modern furnished living room. She obviously had a lot of spare time on her hands. The laminate flooring was cleaned and held a lovely polish. There was little to identify who might live here. A couple of photos stood upon the mantelpiece. One was a loving family portrait, Angela, David and a lovely younger female version of them. She looked about fourteen. It was a picture like millions of others on mantelpieces the world over. The other was a church outing of some sort.

"Milk and sugar Father?" Her voice came from the kitchen as the kettle began to boil. I couldn't care less actually, with or without, it was probably tasteless. "Both please." I walked over to look out the window. This could be an opportunity. Not to get laid but to get some serious information. If she thought I was one of MacPhail's ilk she might just let something, other than her virtue, slip. I hoped so.

"There we are." She smiled sweetly as she placed the tray on the table. A plate of biscuits accompanied the tea. Nothing too fancy just digestives and hobnobs.

She sat down demurely lifting her tea, a picture of the women's institute if ever there was one. Skirt at the knee and a pressed blouse with two buttons undone. Not a hint of what she hid beneath. From where I was sitting, she looked in very fine shape.

"Terrible business." I shook my head ruefully, imply everything say nothing.

"Oh yes, poor Father MacPhail. He will be sorely missed." Funny how there was little sadness in her voice. I wonder what she would be missing. I kept the smirk contained and sipped once more. It was tasteless.

"I will be helping run things for a while." Okay it was a little fib, but it backed up my hunch. It was true to a degree. After all the Bishop had sent me to deal with the interregnum.

"I am glad. What happened? To Father MacPhail, I mean." She wanted all the gory details that I could share that with her. I could feel her interest rising.

"He was beaten to death outside his home, in the car park. A

41

random mugging apparently." I made it sound so ordinary. So unremarkable. So new town.

"Oh how terrible." She paused, a little catch in her breath " Was it bad?" She was a blood thirsty one.

"Very bloody. Repeated blows to his head and face." I lied smoothly, who would ever find out. I was just playing to my audience. I could tell what she wanted to hear and what would help me find out more.

"Oh my goodness that is awful." It was almost erotic to her. Her eyes sparkled and her lips parted just a little. A flush beginning on her neck and her cheeks pinking a little.

"Yes it is. Who do I need to meet in the congregation, to let me find my feet as it were?" It was suitably vague and might just do the trick. If she was sleeping with MacPhail she was in on it. Her eyes sharpened a little before she answered.

"Let your eyes guide you in your search." Fuck, it was a password. I looked back as I sipped my tea. That was it buggered. My plan hanging in tatters.

"Mom!" A shout from the front door as their daughter arrived. She had saved my bacon, I hoped. The living room door opened and a rather pretty young lady in a school uniform burst in. A tornado all on her own.

"Mom, can I go to a sleepover at Hannah's tonight, please?" She wasn't really asking. She was all grown up in all the wrong places. If she was fifteen I would have been surprised. If she were my daughter, I might just have been locking her in a tower. I doubted the local boys were safe with her around; their little hearts broken repeatedly I expect.

"Your father will be home soon, you can ask him." Angela smiled sweetly. I wondered what she really thought. A huff of displeasure exploded from the daughter.

"Michelle, this is Father Andrew. He will be at St Margaret's for a while." The look that I received was a very strange response to a simple statement. She looked a little wary of me. Not what I expected at all. Was MacPhail a predator on the youngsters too? I kept a straight face nonetheless.

"Pleased to meet you, Michelle." It was as neutral as I could make it and not give myself away. I hoped I was wrong. I could feel the anger inside begin to burn at me like acid reflux. MacPhail was lucky to be already dead or I might have helped him along that road.

"Nice to meet you, too, Father." She smiled, it had a speculative quality about it. She must have learned it from her mother. God help her father, and anyone she used that smile on.

"Wait until your father comes in and ask him. I have no objections to you staying overnight.' Angela sounded so reasonable. So very Mother's Union.

"Speak of the Devil." The front door opened and in walked the head of the household, a weedy little man, who seemed as down trodden as Horace wimp. I could see immediately who wore the trousers in this house. He was at least third in the pecking order.

"Hi Honey, I'm home." A greeting spouted forth in many a household. He walked in to the living room to be immediately harassed for permission. Which he duly gave. Resistance was futile.

"Darling this is Father Steel. He will be at Saint Margaret's, after what happened to Father MacPhail." As if that said everything; well it did, kind of. He finished hanging up his jacket and crossed towards me.

"Good to meet you Father." He took my hand, he was a little limp. I looked into his eyes as I returned greetings.

"I wanted to chat to you about the vestry, trying to catch up and cause as little disruption as possible." I smiled. I was getting very slick at this particular set of untruths. Practice making perfect.

"Of course. Good idea, shall we go through to my office." He was an archetypical accountant and he wittered on for ages about the finances of Saint Margaret's. To be honest the finances were irrelevant. I just wanted to see what he was going to let slip. I struggled hard to focus and ask pertinent questions. In a gap in his explanations his wife appeared with more tea and biscuits. A warning look to me was meant to be a hint. What was she trying to tell me? Her husband was in the dark?

"Will you stay to dinner Father?" She made the offer like it was the most natural thing in the world. I had no option. She was definitely trying to tell me something.

"Thank you. I'd be delighted." Well maybe I'd find out something worth knowing. David Brookes talked on and on, oblivious to my growing boredom with the facts and figures. Then again he had a lot to go through and his professionalism was not in question.

As we sat around the table, the three of us, all seemed normal. David, the genial host, talked about everything; from politics to the economy and the social breakdown of society. All the while his wife was giving me tantalising looks and caressing my leg with her stocking covered foot. If I were inclined I could have made her flirting easier and moved forward to enjoy her caresses. It appeared that her husband was oblivious to her extra marital fucking of priests. I hoped it would stay that way.

"Father MacPhail, was an excellent Rector for the parish." David was saying, I looked at him distracted by the rising foot. I nodded my agreement. Trying to concentrate on his words.

"He was a bit of a ladies man, so I hear." Perhaps the wine was loosening his tongue or maybe he knew about his wife's infidelity after all. She however, never even skipped a beat. Her foot teasing as she turned disapproving to her husband.

"David, the man has been murdered for goodness sake." She sounded shocked. Her delivery was flawless and he recoiled a little before her.

"It might have been the reason, you never know." He had a working hypothesis after all. Maybe he was the Hercule Poirot of Gleninch.

"It was a mugging, or so the police have said." I tried to divert everyone. I was learning very little. Perhaps he was about to drop something in my lap. I just hoped it didn't collide with his wife's insistent foot. I am such a tart. A man's a man for a' that as Burns would say.

"I am going out for a cigarette. Do you smoke Father?" He pushed his seat back and stood up. I shook my head. Never did understand why anyone would want to smoke. I just drink instead. One vice less to keep track of.

"Won't be long." He smiled and left me alone with his horny wife. I nodded. She sat there looking like the image of a faithful wife. Loveliness personified.

"He has no idea." She whispered like I understood everything. She was telling me that the treasurer was not in on MacPhail's sins. I wondered if she meant the sex or the Satanism. Going by her actions it was hard to tell. He probably had no idea about any of her extra-curricular activities.

"I see." I looked straight at her, picking up on her arousal. "It might be better if it stays that way."

She smiled, thinking that she would soon be warming my bed as she had warmed MacPhail's. "Where are you staying?" It was hurried now, her husband might be back any second. She wanted the details.

"At the Holiday Inn." This act was working just a little too well. She might end up in my bed and then what the hell would I do. I am not a celibate priest. Oh fuck. Just then the flight of the Valkyrie's began to howl from my phone. I was about to be saved. Saved from myself and the erection that filled my trousers.

"Steel." I answered strongly, looking away from my temptress and placing the phone against my ear. I needed to clear my head quickly.

"Brotherton. We have access to his computer. I thought you might like to come and see what has turned up." He sounded pleased with himself.

"I'll be there in ten minutes." I hung up as my hostess cleared the table and her husband walked in from outside. I quickly made my apologies and left seeking the sanctuary of the Police station. It would, thankfully, keep me busy all night.

Chapter 9

"Well Inspector? What have you found on his computer?" I asked. I knew it had to be juicy or he would have left his call until the morning. Maybe it was just wishful thinking.

"Well, it took a little while to get past the password but that was all that held us back." He paused, sending the constable from the room. He didn't want the facts to leak out. It certainly piqued my interest. A conspiracy was about to be unmasked. Progress was about to be made.

"Why would you put a password on a totally blank computer?" Brotherton's cop mode was in full flow. He looked up from the computer, his face not sitting on the happy spectrum.

"Doesn't make any sense to me. I take it that the computer still has windows on it?" Wow, what a techie I had become. I knew that most PC's used windows but I knew little beyond word and email. It was the telescope all over again.

"It does. But there was nothing else. It has been scrubbed." He spoke with finality, like they had tried everything. I might have used a more industrial description.

"No church records or sermons or anything?" That's what should have been on it. Priests were usually a bit predictable. If nothing was on here then where was it? He certainly didn't have piles of handwritten sermons lying around and Priests don't freestyle every week.

"Not a damn thing. What the hell was he doing?" Brotherton was obviously irritated too. So was I. We were like a pair of wasps caught in a kids jam jar, and someone was shaking us.

"What was his password?" I asked, with no real reason why. I just did. I am always surprised by what comes out of my mouth. It's often a random explosion.

"His password was Jehovah." Brotherton looked at me, missing the irony. What was so unusual about a priest using God's name as his password?

"Really?" Incredulity seeping out. I'll bet the bastard had another computer somewhere. Was this computer left for us to find?

"Seems logical enough to me." Brotherton said. Well, it proved that comprehensive education was successfully producing cultural pygmies, after all. Or perhaps he hadn't been forced to go to Sunday School.

"I doubt that MacPhail would have used THAT as his password. After all he is batting for the other side." I was trying hard not to be dismissive. I had another brainwave. "Can you tell when it was last used? Like a log or something?" Maybe a star-date like the captain's log on Star Trek?

"Maybe." An overwhelming endorsement from Inspector Brotherton. I was touched. His fingers began a tango of love as he did something technical. It looked very impressive to an amateur like me. Menu after menu flashed by as he picked his way to the answer.

"The user account was made yesterday." He looked disgusted. The irritated shove of the keyboard and the accompanying noise matching his expression perfectly.

"What does that mean, exactly?" Trying hard to keep up. I knew what I thought it meant but it was better to check.

"MacPhail has never used this machine. It's been planted to replace the original." He pushed his chair back from the computer and stomped around the room. I could see that the swearing would follow soon.

"Now that is interesting." I meant it. Brotherton stopped his march of the grumpy bastards and looked at me. I don't think interesting was what he thought this was.

"We are so far behind on this case it is ridiculous. Did they really think that I wouldn't notice the machine was a plant. God they must think I am stupid.' His face was a wonderful contortion. Now he was pissed as hell.

"Someone tampered with the scene or swapped it before we were called in." Statements of the obvious never really go wrong. I liked that he was pissed off. I spend most of my life pissed off and it works for me.

"Who? What the fuck is going on?" He might as well have growled at me. Like I knew the answer to that one.

"Let's get some air." I motioned with my head. I didn't want to be overheard. Brotherton was taking a few seconds to catch on. I put my finger to my lips. A silent shh, he got it. We walked out like it was the most natural thing in the world. Two men going outside for a fag. No smoking buildings gave a great excuse to take some air and get some privacy. It wasn't raining but it was cold. Our breath misting as we spoke. We were in a little huddle.

"Who else knows we have the computer?" I had a plan. Perhaps it was even a cunning plan. We needed to use this to our advantage.

"Anyone who looks on the evidence log, the neighbours might have seen us remove it. SOCO and some of the constables here. Why?" He looked at me after a long pull at his cigarette.

"Put in your report that the computer has been examined and nothing was learned from it. Nothing more." He nodded, catching my thinking. A tight little grin beginning to form on his lips.

"We don't need to let them know we know. Someone is fucking with us." Shocked him again. His eyes widening at the F word.

"Who?" His question deserved a good answer. An answer I didn't have. I wanted to have the answer but it would have to wait. We would find out eventually.

"There is a group, of which MacPhail was one, within St Margaret's. They obviously have friends in a few places." I carefully avoided the usual buzz words; sect, cult coven. I didn't want to scare the good inspector.

"Fuck." There, he let it out. Welcome to the F users Club, free memberships available.

"Exactly. I have a lead that I am cultivating. One of MacPhail's bed warmers. Perhaps I can pump her for information." I tried hard not to smirk. Childish and juvenile but

I just had to. Brotherton's face split into a smile.

"Pump away. Let me know how it goes." That's my boy, getting into the swing of it. Just because it was serious didn't mean that we couldn't laugh.

"I will, but we need to be careful about what we say. Phones are particularly easy to bug aren't they?" I have seen movies and it looks too easy.

"Yes. Be careful what you say and we will avoid letting anything out. If it is being covered up then they will be watching us." Brotherton stated the obvious beautifully. Our conspiratorial team of two had been born.

"Right then. I will just call your mobile and we can meet up whenever we have anything to discuss. I will report to the Bishop and take over the day to day services at St Margaret's. Time to be vigilant. They will slip up." Confidence filled my voice like I knew what I was talking about.

"Okay. We'll proceed quietly and see what turns up." Brotherton was getting good at agreeing with me. I was beginning to like him. If he kept this up we might even end up friends. I don't have many of those.

"Keep everything to yourself Brotherton, your pension and career might be on the line." He had things to lose that I didn't. He needed to remember that.

"I'll be fine." He sounded like he had felt the heat from above before. Good luck to him this time.

"I am going back to my room, I have to make a report to Bishop Michael. Joy of Joys." I looked heavenward, no inspiration was forthcoming. I think I am meant to help myself.

"Nite then." Brotherton went back inside knowing that he was alone and surrounded by potential spies and enemies. A true Daniel in the lions den. I had a short drive to make to a warm comfortable room. A phone call that loomed large ahead of me. How can I spin out 'I have no idea what is happening on this case.' My whore red car squealed as the fan belt began to slip a little. My little car didn't like the cold and to be honest, I don't like the cold either.

Chapter 10

I plugged the slim plastic card into the slot. I am used to this kind of lock. It came as no surprise when it failed to work first go. A slower attempt and the door unlocked letting me inside. Although not palatial, the room was warm and comfortable. A far cry from some of the budget places I was often sent to. I flicked on the lights and there it was. On the bed, a manilla envelope. It had my name typed on it. Someone had been inside my room and left me a message. I didn't think it was a thank you card from the congregation welcoming me to my temporary stay with them.

I checked the rest of the room before I approached the letter. The shower room and toilet were clean and empty. No psycho moments for me tonight. Shower curtains just give me the creeps. I looked closely at the typing and smiled.

"Dozy bastards." I like my enemies to be able to spell my name at the very least. It brought a smile to my lips to be called Father Steal. I picked the envelope from the bed and peeled it open gently avoiding covering it in finger prints. Well you never know, might yield another clue. After all, the inability to spell might mean that the delivery person was dumb enough to cover it in whorls and whirls. I poured the letter on to the bed and picked it up by a corner.

The letter, on white A4 folded in three sections, was brutal in its simplicity. It had one line across the centre.

"Leave now, you have no place here. Only pain will come to you if you stay." I read aloud. I dropped the letter and envelope on the dresser shelf. Heard it. Got the tee shirt and seen the DVD. Who are these people? They have obviously been watching far too many B-movies. I shook my head and looked in the mirror. It was then I saw the lightest smear, so I huffed on it. The misting on the glass revealed a point of a pentagram. Point down. The twin points upwards representing the horns of Satan.

They at least knew that much. Perhaps they were a bit more committed than I had realised.

I checked the bathroom mirror and there was another mark. On the inside of the window another mark had been made. Okay they were pissing me off now. I was beginning to feel the hairs on the back of my neck stand up when I realised that a working had been conducted in my room. There must be other pentagrams one of which would be the focus. If I could find that one I would be able, maybe, to see what the enemy had in store for me. I managed to avoid getting too frantic as I scanned around.

"Fuck, fuck fuckitty fuck!" I was surrounded by little pentagrams. The television had a big one, the bedside lamps a little one each, on the brass plate of the door handle another little five pointer, the metal ceiling lamp had another. This was getting serious. I touched the right hand lamp shade, it's brushed metal surface cold. I got a tingling in my finger tip. I closed my eyes. I tried to see the mark being made, I couldn't. All I could feel was a crowded room. A room full of people with faces I couldn't see.

I searched more thoroughly finding an interesting one on the toilet seat lid and another in the shower. I had lost count of how many there were. I was beginning to feel the net closing in. Everywhere I looked there seemed to be the sign of the horns. The power was growing with each little discovered servant that I found. A tight band was beginning to squeeze my head like a vice. I had to get out of here. Soon or I might be kissing the carpet. I reached the door and realised that the pentagrams weren't random. They had sealed the room. I was trapped in a room of malice. Whoever had laid this trap was a sorcerer and not an apprentice either. I could not get out. The door, windows and even the water way from the loo were sealed. I could feel my gorge rising. I was going to vomit my dinner all over the place. Oh the embarrassment. I made it to the sink only to see the taps caressed with a star. Too bad, my mouth was filling with saliva, without water it was inevitable. My head thudding as the grip of the vice made me feel dizzy and weak, I closed my eyes and let go. I made most of it hit the sink, not in the sink but in that general area. The rest went into the toilet. The splash radius was contained but some splattered the bottom of my trousers and my shoes. The retching and coughing went on for a few minutes as I tried to get my equilibrium back. My nose had delivered a fountain of it's own and the residual smell was making me want to retch again. I blew my nose hard and the remaining sickness sprayed across the tiled floor. Almost in the style of a professional footballer. I almost laughed, but not quite. I needed to get out. Hysteria was beginning to want its moment.

The phone. I staggered to the bedside phone, it was adorned too. They had been very thorough and I was beginning to feel the panic pulling at me. Now that I knew I was inside the seals of my enemy to touch the pentagrams would probably make me pass out. Sometimes there are downsides to feeling things. A vibration in my pocket pulled my mind into focus. A fucking text. I put my hand in my pocket and pulled out my mobile. My salvation was from Korea. Samsung had saved the day. I dialled the front desk and asked for some assistance. The night porter said he would be along immediately.

I stood staring at the door waiting. It was all I could do to keep the room from swirling round me. It was like I was drunk as the room canted from side to side. I held my head together with both hands, one at each temple. The door opened and a very confused young man asked me if I was all right.

'I need another room.' I managed as I got into the hall. 'I have been sick all over the bathroom. I am sorry, it was something I ate.' He looked at me sceptically, but led me to another room down the hall. The poor guy would have to clean it up. He brought me a key-card a few minutes later.

'Do you need a doctor?' I obviously didn't look very healthy. I shook my head and waved him away as nicely as I could manage. He deposited my bags inside and left me to it. The pain in my skull was lessening, thankfully. There would be a reckoning for this. Anger filled me taking over from the fear I had felt just moments ago.

I staggered to the window and opened it. It barely opened,

just in case I was prone to jumping. It is only the first floor for goodness sake. I needed air. Clean, cold fresh air. I stood like a gasping fish drinking in the cure to my malady. I looked down at my vomit decorated trousers and shoes. Very tastefully done. I needed a shower. My report would need to wait a little while. Making a call to Bishop Michael needed working up to. Besides he was probably in bed by now. It was past eleven and I was about to disturb my neighbours by standing in the shower until I used all the hot water. Too bad, my need was greater than theirs. Bite me.

Chapter 11

It's like a hangover for me. When I get too much stimulation the next morning can be a little difficult. Add to that projectile vomit and a sense of danger and I am in for a fragile morning. I didn't set the alarm, preferring the organic method of waking up. Bladder pressure is the limiting factor and eventually it will wake me up.

"House keeping." A cheery female voice reached my ears. I managed not to be offensive, I think, when I sent back the 'later' response. The heavy curtains had kept the room quite dark. Probably just as well as I had strewn my stuff about in my efforts to recover from my incident.

I rolled over thinking that I could escape back to a dreamless sleep and a long lie in bed. No rest for the wicked apparently. Buzzing and ringing my mobile phone began its call for attention. It wasn't that early, but it still pissed me off. I picked it up and looked disgustedly at my saviour of last evening. On the display it was Bishop Michael. I'd better answer it then.

"Steel." A winner of a start. A bit neutral not really giving too much away.

"Andrew, how are things in Gleninch?" He was such a morning person. At least he had waited until nearly ten. This was late by his standards.

"Well, things are progressing I think." Master of the say fuck all, that I am. I took a deep breath but Bishop Michael beat me to the next bit.

"In what way?" He wasn't letting me flannel him today. He still sounded relatively cheerful. That would be changing soon I thought.

"I don't know what is going on. I have, however, had a threatening phone call and a mystical attack on me in my hotel room. Oh yes and a warning letter.' I paused. I like to get things out in the open early.

"That sounds dangerous. Are you all right? How about your police assistance? Is it forthcoming?" Way to go a bombardment of questions. I took a breath.

"It is. Yes. The police inspector I have assigned is a good man, considering there is evidence of a bit of pressure to hush the lot up." Conspiracy theory too, what a delivery from me. The hits they keep on coming.

"Keep your eyes open Andrew. I have made arrangements for you to take over at Saint Margaret's for the coming weeks till we clear this up." The Bishop's desk phone started to ring. It was time to let him get on with running things.

"I will be fine. I'll call in later today. This looks like a long one." Tell him what he wants to hear.

"Okay Andrew I'll speak to you soon. Be careful." And a final click and he was off the line. No hanging about with Bishop Michael.

"Thanks for your call. Bollocks." I was well and truly awake now. I staggered to the toilet trying to get my fuzzy head to function. I popped a couple of aspirin and swigged from the tap. After an extended seat in the bathroom I got dressed. Jeans and a baggy sweat shirt, I would be in plain clothes for the day. I needed to get my official uniform cleaned. Oh the joys. I might even need a new one, I would be so embarrassed putting it in to be cleaned.

After an extended apology and offers of financial restitution I was able to keep my room at the inn. No stables out the back. It had been a little embarrassing trying to feign food poisoning as the reason for the projectile vomit. I know that priests have a reputation for the imbibing curse of whisky. I have been known occasionally to hit the bottle with a vengeance. I am sure the manager was thinking that I was of the alcoholic brotherhood. Too bad, I wasn't going to try and change his mind. Someone here had allowed access to my room. It might even have been him so I just let it go and went out.

I migrated to the heart of the matter, the white church that was Saint Margaret's in the fields. I was a nice church for its type. Well, it was in decent nick at any rate. I had been here on a few occasions; most notably school Christmas carol services. It was close to my old high school, a place that was a source of torment for those of academic persuasion, unless of course, you were good at sports too. I was naturally disinterested in sports and made little effort to get involved with the Luddites that wanted to kick my head in. Well, I had no interest in a return visit for old time's sake.

I opened the doors, which were unlocked, like every house of god should be. I always like the feeling of being alone in a church. It is like a warm familiar blanket that surrounds you, making you feel safe. I needed that, this morning, especially after last night's escapades. I sat on the front pew, with its crocheted kneelers and heated panel. Devotion to God need not be uncomfortable in the winter. The heating wasn't on at the moment but the cold air wasn't too upsetting. I knelt and let myself pray. It is more like a meditation experience as I let my brain wander after I give thanks and beg forgiveness for the sins I have and am about to commit. I have a very personal arrangement with the almighty, and it seems to work well for us both. It is simply a no blame culture. I don't criticise his actions and he doesn't blast me into oblivion with lightning strikes. I don't push my luck too far though, just in case.

It was while I was kneeling at prayer that I heard the outer door being opened and soon I had company in the pews. I looked round, a middle aged woman had joined me near the front. I nodded to her and smiled. It was returned after she crossed herself and settled down to pray.

After about ten minutes I left her to her reflection and went into the vestibule. I was looking over the church notices when she emerged. Her eyes were a little moist. A sadness had settled on her features, she obviously had a burden to carry.

"Are you looking for someone?" She asked politely. I obviously didn't look like I should have been there. I smiled to her. I decided that levity was not the right response in this case.

"I am Father Andrew Steel. I will be covering here for a while until a replacement can be found for Father MacPhail. Pleased to meet you." I extended a hand and she took it. Nothing happened thankfully. I could feel her sadness, didn't need to be a psychic to do that. Sometimes normal is what I need.

"Christine McLeod. I am pleased to meet you too, Father." Her smile was one that had more than a tinge of relief. I could have been anybody. A member of the press, a vagrant or just the psycho who had killed their Priest. After all I wasn't exactly dressed for the part.

"Would you like a cup of tea?" I can be taught. She accepted and looked like she needed to share with someone. A stranger would be just perfect. I doubted that MacPhail would have been much help to her. Maybe I was wrong. In a few minutes we were ensconced in soft seats like old friends as she began to tell me her tale of woe.

Her son, John, was on active service in Iraq. She was terrified and could barely watch the news. It was filled with bombings and deaths, and increasingly hostile news coverage about the legitimacy of the war. She was fraught and her nerves were frazzled. He was due home in a few weeks and while she was glad of that, she felt a mounting panic that something terrible was going to happen. It always seemed that fate cruelly snatched those on their way back to loved ones. She carried the worry that all service families do, but for her John was all she had left. Long divorced her son filled her thoughts.

I let her speak for a while until she ran out steam. I made all the right noises and then asked her about the congregation. She was relatively alone in the church, surrounded by those who never really took the time to include her. She had been coming for almost two years but still felt totally isolated. I got the impression that MacPhail was too busy for real pastoral care. How many others had he neglected as he fornicated in his little coven. My face grew a frown. My face often gives me away , a direct line to my thoughts.

"I've said too much Father I am sorry." She began to

apologise. I stopped her with a smile and reassurances that I had just remembered that I was to go to the police station this morning. I really wanted her to be okay and I let my sincerity escape like a beam of goodwill.

"I hope you will come on Sunday. It will be nice to see a familiar face." I wanted her to be comforted in her time of need. She seemed to accept my excuse, but the time was over and she had to go too. Perhaps I needed a little reminder of what was and what wasn't the lord's work. We left together. A communion of sorts.

Chapter 12

MacPhail's funeral was not mine to officiate over. There are limits to my hypocrisy and that would have been one step too far. I did, however, attend the service at 'the Crem.' It was the crematorium in the nearby town of Kirkcaldy. A simple service with three hymns and a few readings. The singing was particularly tuneless. I did think the turnout for the service was quite good. There appeared to be a good mix of family, friends and parishioners. I wondered how many had been intimate with the man in the coffin and how many were part of whatever was going on. I sat at the back and watched. Once or twice I caught a few sidelong looks in my direction. The plot thickened before my eyes. A collection was made for a charity supporting missionary work in Africa. I didn't want to support his message being exported.

As the final tortured verse of 'Abide with me' was being completed I looked at those who sat nearest the front. They were my prime suspects. The blessing sent us all on our way. After a few silent moments of reflection that I used to think of what I might say in response to any questions that came my way we were told of a buffet lunch being held at the Salazar hotel further into Kirkcaldy. I looked up and caught the eye of Angela Brookes. A mischievous smile almost made it to her face as she winked to me. I could feel my ears beginning to heat up. That was most definitely a problem in the making.

"Good morning Father." Angela let her presence be known as we moved from the hand shaking line to the car park. I had expected to get some sort of indications from the line up but I didn't. Of course the pain and loss that filled the Crematorium had been laid down by thousands, if not millions, of mourners over the years. I thought I might have been able to escape without the Complication that had just called out to me.

59

"Angela, lovely to see you." I managed to smile. Not a hint of salaciousness in tone or face for that matter. I was in public and didn't need a hint of scandal this early in the day. She, however, was an expert at clandestine flirting. Her eyes flashed intent as she made a seemingly simple request. She was a good looking woman.

"Can you give me a lift to the Salazar? David dropped me off for the service. He had to work today. He was so disappointed." All sorts of information had just been passed. She looked very tidy today, make up understated, clothes giving no hint of the, undoubtedly, sexy lingerie that was hidden underneath. Perhaps I was projecting what I hoped was hidden.

"Of course, no problem at all." I was committed now. If she was involved, I was heading for trouble. If she wasn't then she was simply a sex mad adulteress who fucked priests as her partner of choice. Oh the sins I would probably be committing. I led her over to the red chariot that waited unobtrusively in the car park. I could almost feel the tension in the air as we got to the car. Even the clunk-kitty click of the central locking felt anticipatory. A moment later we were inside and buckled in. I had no idea what to say. Like I said, I am not great at small talk.

"Do you know how to get there? The Salazar, that is?" Angela asked. I replied in the negative, although I knew where it was. It would keep her busy until we got there. Perhaps it might prevent things getting out of hand on the way. Not that my fantasies were getting to the surface of my brain.

"I make much better tea than the Salazar. Do you want to come back to mine for some?" She said it like she was discussing the weather. Damn she was good.

"Sounds like a better idea." I was in, deep. I didn't actually care. The prospect of sex with this, rather fine, woman was the over riding thought. She smiled a wicked little smile. She had me and she knew it. Worse still, I knew it too. I started the car and in a few moments we were driving towards Gleninch and an illicit encounter that I, certainly, would never forget. You can't be led anywhere you don't really want to go.

As I drove I was checking her out. She was a pretty thirty something. Not perfect by any means but a woman a man would be proud to have on his arm. She had great legs and had regained her figure after the birth of her one child. Her eyes were a greeny-blue augmented by mascara and eye shadow that showed them beautifully. I liked what I saw. I was on tenterhooks as I drove along, expecting a caressing hand to reach for my loins. I was disappointed and the journey passed without any inappropriate actions. After a battery of small talk about the service I pulled up outside the Brookes' house. It looked so ordinary looking, a priest dropping off a member of his congregation and coming in for a cup of tea. The reality would be so different.

She walked up the path and unlocked the door, welcoming me to her house. I wondered how it would go. I, after all, am not MacPhail; maybe she liked her priest to take charge and treat her badly. Punishment scenarios that sort of thing. If that was what she liked I was fucked, literally. I can play along but I have no idea how that sort of thing goes.

"Just milk isn't it Father?" She called from the kitchen as she clicked the kettle on. Maybe I was imagining too much. She came to the kitchen doorway and smiled sexily. Leaning against the door frame and managing not to look like a clique or a bunny boiler.

"Or should we just skip the tea?" I tried to look unsurprised but failed to pull it off. I tried to smile back but probably looked scared. She walked slowly towards me and kissed my lips gently. Taking my hand she led me upstairs. I should have resisted but I didn't really want to. I hadn't had sex for months, at least, not the kind that involved someone else. She looked delicious as she led me up the staircase. Her bedroom looked so very normal. This was anything but.

Its not that I haven't had sex in the daytime with a married woman before. It is simply that I haven't done it with someone who could easily be on the other side. I know that it was stupid and totally lust driven, but it was damn good. All my worries about her desire for kinky sex were unfounded. She was simply a very sexual woman who got off knowing she was fucking her priest. Deep rooted issues I think. I managed reasonably well, I think, considering it had been so long. I left after about two hours giving her time to tidy up and make like nothing had taken place in her marital bed. I went back to the Holiday Inn and showered. The hot water was so very welcome. I noticed that my cheeks were ruddy and I looked younger. Amazing, one good session and the years fall off. From inside the room my phone was calling me to action.

"Steel." I almost sounded cheerful. I'd better stop that before anyone thought I had been replaced by a doppelgänger

"That's much better." It was Angela. Her voice seemed much huskier than I remembered it being. However, that wasn't what I had been paying attention to.

"Hi, everything okay?" I asked her, a little too quickly. Worry clutching my gut that I had been compromised and the fan was about to be covered in the brown stuff.

"Couldn't be much better. Thank you for today. Anytime you feel like dropping by just drop me a text. I can't wait." She spoke like a naughty teenager. Maybe she was. I was joining in.

"I had a great time too. Thank you." I have no idea what to say in these situations. There is no real protocol for it in the Canon Code.

"Gotta go. I will send you something as a reminder. Later." She was gone just like that. I was surprised and I sat down on the bed, the towel round my waist parting to reveal the only part of me that had been thinking today. I shook my head in disappointment at myself. The phone rang again.

"Steel." I still didn't sound like the grumpy man that usually answered my phone.

"Brotherton, can you come down?" He sounded a bit put out. He wouldn't be saying any more over the phone.

"Of course, I'm just out of the shower but won't be too long." I wondered what he wanted. Hopefully something had come up.

You never know. It might even be a clue.

"Father Steel, I am glad you could make it." Inspector
Brotherton met me in the car park. He was still smoking a
cigarette. He looked irritated and it wasn't my fault this time.
"No problem. Developments?" I asked quietly. He nodded.
I could have been saying anything if we were being watched. I
am not that clear a speaker at times and prone to the odd mumble.
"We have a confession. He is sitting in the cells right now.
Claims it was a burglary that went wrong and that he didn't mean
to kill the priest." Disgusted Brotherton flicked the butt of his
cigarette away. It bounced a few times before rolling to a
remnant of yesterday's rain. There were always puddles to be
found in Gleninch. It lies right in the rain passage of Fife,
planners eh?
"Really, wow. Has he managed to keep his story straight?"
Fake confessions wasted a great deal of police time. I tried not to
swear and succeeded, a whole new me.
"He has the details and a murder weapon. Looks like a
closed case. At least that's what the Fiscal's office is calling it.
We're done." He looked me in the eye. His face holding a blank
look that wouldn't give him away.
"You know that its bollocks, and so do I." I paused, "I have to
get to the bottom of the situation at St Margaret's regardless of
the Procurator Fiscal's office. I might need your help anyway."
"I'll do what I can but I'm being reassigned to another case
tomorrow. We are six for six on murders this year." Brotherton
didn't like the smell of it either. A confession would mean his
talents would be allocated elsewhere and I was going to be on my
own for the most part.
"I got a threatening letter trying to scare me off, and a call.
Best keep our eyes open. This isn't over by a long way."
Brotherton's eyebrows shot up in response. He was surprised at
my calmness, I expect.
"Be careful Father, this is a dangerous town." His tone
telling me that I had no real idea how dangerous it had become.

"Oh I will. I am always careful." A bravado that I didn't really feel filling my voice. I left him then. I didn't need to meet the patsy. He would get off with manslaughter and out in a few short years. Who was he hiding? Fucked if I knew, yet.

Chapter 13

"The blood of Christ, given for you." I tipped the chalice forward, a little wine passed the lips of the elderly woman kneeling at the rail. Her stick was protruding past the rail and I stepped around it, carefully. Repeating my phrase as I delivered the communion wine to all comers to the feast of Christ. They had already had the wafers that some felt had been transformed into the actual body of Christ. This was my first Sunday service at St Margaret's Only the prayer and dismissal to go. I was determined to depart from the norms and have a special prayer for those who risked their lives for their country. A few eyebrows would rise at that.

"Go in peace to love and serve the Lord." I sang out and the joyous flock sang back the response "In the name of Christ, Amen." And my ordeal was over. Only the coffee morning to navigate and it would be over. A grateful look came my way from Christine McLeod, it was all worth it. I had carefully avoided too many looks at Angela, she was a disaster in progress. I didn't need to make it obvious.

I took a deep breath as I removed my outer robes and made my way to the door. Hand shaking and 'lovely to see you's ' to go. No feelings flooding me as I took their hands. Some limp, some firm, some clammy and all of them on their way out the house of God.

A few moments later I was accepting the plaudits of a wonderful sermon from an old bloke who had served his country in the War, I didn't ask which one. The procession of faces that had disappeared out the door left only the hardiest of core congregation members inside having coffee. It seemed strange to me that so many had left, I had expected more to stay. Maybe all had not been so great after all. Perhaps the outsiders just didn't feel welcome here. Lord knows I didn't feel welcome either. I walked in to a hall full of conversation. It missed a beat, almost.

Maybe I am a bit paranoid. Here am I, Daniel in the lion's den, about to chat and glad-hand my way through a nest of vipers. Some of those in this room are definitely involved in some sort of supernatural naughtiness. Maybe I should just make my own coffee. Some of the faces I recognised, some I didn't. Didn't appear to be that many kids around today. I would have expected to see more of them. Still maybe they'll come to the youth club tonight. No doubt I'd find out.

"Lovely sermon this morning, Father.'" A white haired, well turned out elderly gentleman grasped my hand and shook it vigorously. His eyes sparkled a little too much for my liking, why I have no idea. I didn't think it was that moving. I had slipped in a few double entendres that might have given an impression to the shadow flock that I was one of them. Maybe that was what had made him well up? I nodded conspiratorially, but didn't want to be too obvious. Quicksand all around.

"Coffee Father?" David Brookes extended a brown liquid filled white cup. His other hand held his own. They say that if you need milk and sugar in coffee then you don't actually like it. The bitter taste that met my lips questioned my belief that I liked coffee. David smiled as my face registered the taste. He was the only one I knew wasn't on their side, and I was shagging his wife.

"It takes some getting used to. It is amazing what you can get used to." He began to steer me to a table with some other middle aged professional types. You know pillars of the community and all that. I wondered about them, they were probably safe-ish.

"I'd like to introduce you to the Thursday night gang." It was obviously an in thing. The explanation of their weekly card game and an informal invite to come and lose my money were forthcoming.

"With my poker playing skills I would lose my stipend in no time at all." We laughed together. I noticed a little symbol in some spilled sugar on the table. It was slowly wiped away by John something, I really should pay attention. It was a funny little loopy squiggle that I was meant to recognise. I nodded slowly while catching his eye and moving on to another group. Another one identified in this motley crew.

"How are you settling in Father?" An elderly lady fired from across another table. There was a whole gallery of them sipping from cups and jibber jabbering to each other. I had no idea which one fired at me but I smiled and professed that I had been made most welcome and was very pleased to be here. I told them all how nice the Holiday Inn was, I can fib a little.

I can feel my spidey senses going off all round me as eyes are following me round the room. Acting as natural as I can, I try to scope out the congregation and split them into them and not them. Thankfully, I am just about finished the first chalice of brown cooling sludge. There appears to have been a thinning out of the coffee drinkers and only a few remain, including Angela Brookes. Her Husband is busy and her daughter is talking animatedly with her friend Hannah, when Angela gives me a look that would give a statue an erection. I look away quickly hoping no one has noticed. She is an expert at this surreptitious flirting. I am out of my league. I turn in time to be approached by a middle aged man, whom I have been introduced to, whose name is a blank.

"Father, it is a pleasure to have you with us at such an important time." He speaks quietly but not a whisper. Another one, perhaps? I add him to the mental list of Them.

"I serve wherever I am needed." I go for cryptic and ambiguous. I leave my face schooled and give nothing away. Or at least I hope I pull it off.

"And you are needed here. Welcome to our little group." He pats me on the shoulder as he makes his way from the hall. Like all Churches the same few do the tidying up and putting away. In St Margaret's it seems it is the Brookes's turn on the rota. I make my goodbye's and escape before I get into any more trouble. One last look from Angela was worth it. Smokinnn.

Chapter 14

"Andrew, how are things....progressing?" Bishop Michael was always so circumspect when he had to call. I hadn't been checking in regularly enough, obviously. Progress would be an overstatement. I knew that there were bad guys here and they knew I knew. Other than that there was 'eff all progress made in the last week. I couldn't pretend otherwise.

"Slowly Bishop, slowly." I paused, I like to irritate him if he calls, rebel that I am.

"Such as? Any more threats?" Since they hexed my room at the inn, all had been quiet. I'm not complaining either. I didn't need another night like that. Ever.

"No, fortunately. Anything on the star charts?" It's a bit like tennis, our conversations. I am more a John McEnroe style player or I'd like to be. The bishop is a steadier Swedish style. Maybe a Borg or an Edberg.

"I will have something for you tomorrow. It has our friends in a bit of a tizzy. They are very interested, can you make it over tomorrow around four?" It wasn't really a request and we both knew it. I know a summons when I get one.

"Of course, I'll see you then." Dismissive compliance at its best, could just have said 'whatever'. I didn't let out my inner teenager.

"Andrew, be careful." He sounded worried and that was a rarity in itself. What did the old fox know that he didn't want to say over the phone? I would find out in his time and no other. Not that he was a control freak or anything. He could just have spit it out and saved me a trip.

"I will." Click, check up call over. No blood spilled, no arguments; just a passive-assertive 'Get a move on!' I glower at the keypad of my phone and drop it with a sour look into my jacket pocket. I am on my way to dispense communion to a few of the older, house-bound members of the congregation and then a hospital visit. Probably explains my grumpiness, either that or I am generally a miserable sod. If I were a celibate I'd blame my moodiness on that. However, in the last week, I have had more rumpy-pumpy than in the last two years so that most certainly isn't the problem. I think I am looking younger.

As if in response to my thoughts, my phone vibrates. 'Answer me' it seems to scream. I frown and fumble about until I look at the small screen. A text, all that for a bloomin text. It is more than a text, a full graphic close up of Angela Brook's bits; and a come and get me message. The woman knows she can have me any time and I need to put a stop to this and soon. It is so getting out of hand. I'm not that great at it, I'd say she is though. A smirk covers my face as I look at the picture, again, and text back 'On my way'. I told you, I am a bit stupid at times. A spring in my step in anticipation of a brief social interlude and I am underway in no time.

Angela Brookes, is stamped with a health warning. Or at least she should be. I know I should not be in her bed, lying back as she gives me the most toe curling sensations. Under the duvet her mouth is trying to give me the punishment heart-attack that I deserve. I push away the duvet and see her in all her luscious glory working up and down me. How beautifully decadent; her red lipstick and perfect white teeth almost hypnotic as she relishes my flesh. In the middle ages she'd have been burned at the stake as a succubus and a temptress. In this century she's just a bored housewife with a thing for priests. Progress.

A sunny Sunday post Eucharist tumble is certainly not how I expected this day to go. I didn't resist, even though I might indeed be sleeping with the enemy. How deep was she in? probably right up to my neck. I know that MacPhail had certainly enjoyed her sinful wiles. Why on earth didn't that stop me? Like I said, stupidity shouldn't be ruled out.

I am pulled back into the here and now as she has released me temporarily and climbed aboard. Tight, hot, wet and energetic I am drowning in a sea of her making. Time flies past and soon I am kissing her goodbye. An unforgettable experience, hopefully it won't get me killed. I whistle softly to myself as I head out to take communion to the elderly. The sun is smiling down on me. Either that or God is glaring at me.

Gleninch is a town of roundabouts; they provide a level of entertainment and conflict between those who know which lane to be in and the idiots who don't. I happen to know which is which, being a native. I was, however, distracted by a ten foot Tyrannosaurus Rex that was meant to pass as roadside art emerging from the foliage in the middle of one. So I went round again like a tourist. Not the sort of thing you see everyday. Although Gleninch has hippopotamus cast from concrete scattered around the place. I don't think it is hippopotami, might be wrong though.

The flashing blue lights that caught my attention moments later didn't prepare me for what came next. The local traffic police were pulling me over. Oh the shame, tourist driving gets you pulled over and me a born a bred native.

"Is there a problem officer?" Why do we all say that? "No, I want your autograph" isn't going to be the response is it. Well maybe for some it might be.

"Step out of the car and turn off the engine please, sir" No nonsense, he might well have added. His tone was officious, if I am being kind, intimidating if I'm not. I look like a problem motorist of course, a bit stubbly (I shaved in a hurry this morning after I slept in), hair as usual and a dog-collar. Priests are such bad boys.

I do as the nice officer asks and reach in my pocket for my ID. He looks like he wants to hit me with his night stick. It usually takes time for me to illicit this level of hostility. Did I piss this one off at the crime scene? I don't think so but who knows. I do it so often and indiscriminately.

"Ease down, I'm just getting my Id." I'm trying to diffuse the situation for a change. He doesn't present the 'protect and serve' persona; more a 'I'm gonna kick your head in' one reserved for Saturday nights.

"I know who you are. This is your third warning" he's moving forward, his voice low and full of menace. "We are watching you. Its time you just left. This is none of your affair. Understand?" He is in close now and it looks like he wants to hit me. He's fervent, all shiny eyes and barely hanging on. No numbers on his epaulettes either. Needs a mint, too.

"I hear you." I manage to stay calm. He's within head-butting range and I have nowhere to step back to. This might get very painful. I prepare for the inevitable.

"You and your chums can fuck right off." Great line eh? I never know what is going to escape my lips at moments of tension. Apparently the head butt that I expect turns out to be a knee in the groin and I am kissing the tarmac as his boot caresses by ribs. Air is in very short supply as I gasp like a landed fish. The shooting pains coursing through me are almost unbearable.

"You've been warned Fucker." He stomps back to the traffic car and the warning has well and truly been delivered. I manage to pull myself up and back into my car. Excruciating pain filling my core and bile rising in my gorge. My ribs feel like they don't want to expand as I try to get air into my lungs. The burning sensation brings tears to my eyes, that and the crushing pain from my groin. I don't know whether to rub them or count them, if you take my meaning.

"Body of Christ, given for you." I practically stuff the wafer into her mouth. I need to concentrate. I keep thinking about earlier. Her croaky 'Amen' the prompt for me to proffer the chalice and present it to her lips. The salvation giving body and blood of Christ has passed her lips.

Communion for the infirm and elderly can take a large chunk of time. I had already brought solace and nurture to three old souls and had a hospital visit to follow this one. Being the parish priest is a busy job, how did MacPhail manage it with all the extra-curricular activities he was engaged in? No idea but I was running about like a headless chicken. Perhaps the post-Eucharist tumble should have been avoided.

"The Blood of Christ, given for you." At least she was ready this time. I gave her the contents and tidied up my things. Her eyes closed as she prayed. I suppose its natural to be closer to God the closer one gets to going.

A blessing to conclude and I am ready to go. The ache in the pit of my stomach is still there, but subsiding, and the tenderness of my ribs growing. I just want to get finished so I can self medicate with Glenfiddich. At least it will help me sleep. Just the hospital to go. It was this last stop that I dreaded most. Bedside manner is not my thing; I never know what to say. Long pauses, usually uncomfortable, and banal blethering about the weather or the news fill hospital visits. Trying to sit for any length of time will be excruciating.

A polite refusal of a cup of tea and I reach the sanctuary of my car. No flat tyres, no broken windscreen, no key-scratches and no further warnings then.

The Queen Mary General Hospital, as it was in my day has changed beyond all recognition. What once was a forbidding old building of dubious design has been transformed into an architectural modern beauty of glass and steel. Of course, in Fife, all the investment goes into Kirkcaldy and not Gleninch but it doesn't stop me admiring the building. A multi-storey car park to the rear with lots of spaces and clear signs directing non-locals where they need to go has replaced the old gravel park that passed as parking in years gone by. Although it is dark, it is busy with lots of coming and going. Visiting time is flexible these days, apparently.

Following the new blue signs, which are easy to see and understand, I find myself at ward Nine, post surgery convalescence. How helpful they even tell you what the ward is for. No starchy Sisters or Matrons but a helpful receptionist who smiling asks me who I am here to visit. Luckily I remember without referring to my scrap of paper. Jimmy Anderson, not the cricketer, has a visitor – me. It is logged in the register. All very efficient, I am directed to his room. Room! All of the patients have their own private room. The NHS has come a long way from the four-bed common spaces of the past with the pull round drapes. Money well spent if you ask me. Privacy and dignity when you are ill, not being on show to the whole world.

Jimmy Anderson is around sixty, grey hair and of a basically sour looking demeanour. Grumpy would probably do. Mind you, if I had just my liver transplanted then I might be a tad crabbit too. Very little jaundice and he looks like it might have been a success. Liver failure is a terrible thing, I've seen a few taken in the past. It is not the way to go.

"Mr Anderson, I'm Father Steel. I'm Father MacPhail's replacement." I smile (well twitch my face a bit) and extend my hand. His other hand has a drip connected but his handshake is firm enough. He isn't leaving this mortal coil anytime soon; he is too stubborn I expect. Hale is how he might have been described in years gone by.

"Pleased to meet you father. Terrible business, MacPhail, I mean." His face gives nothing away. I try not to give much away either. Although the throbbing inside has me a little off my game.

73

"Indeed, the congregation is still reeling at the shock of it. His funeral was a lovely service." Black tongue time has commenced. Will I burn in hell for lying? No, I only lie to the bad guys, honest.

"So, how are you holding up?" I venture, a little sympathetically but in a manly way. It's a start. I don't think he wants the soft soap, syrupy stuff that some need.

"My back is killing me but other than that I'm fine." He isn't comfortable with talking about it, I can tell. Oh well, I plough on anyway.

"You'll be up and around in no time I expect." I'm doing my best but the ache from my nether regions is reminding me of its existence. I shift uncomfortably on the hard plastic chair. Visiting time may be flexible but I can't imagine visitors sitting on this for an hour; sore bollocks or no.

"I bloody hope so." He grumbles giving away nothing. He shifts on the bed, it probably isn't any more comfortable than the chair.

"I have communion with me, if you'd like." I say this in as ambiguous a fashion as possible, looking for a clue that may or may not be there. Baiting the hook.

"Ours or theirs?" He winks a little humour lightening up his crabbit features. Bingo, he's one of the opposition. A slow reeling in needed, I might even get something useful.

"Only ours." I wink as I say it. I hope they just take a wafer and don't have special phrases to say, or I am well screwed. Hoist by my own petard, as it were.

He nods as I reach into my pilot case. I fumble about before coming up with a bit of a holy wafer, hoping that they use the same one's as I do. I put my finger to my lips, in a keep quiet signal. I surreptitiously look over my shoulder to the door as I lean forward to deliver the wafer into his mouth. Cleverly I try to keep it out of his line of sight. I think I've managed to pull it off. He swallows it quickly.

"Curse the Nazarene." He whispers. He's bought my cover. I have a positive ID on another one of the enemy. Another one down loads to go, no doubt. He closes his eyes to savour his unholy communion, a tight smile of satisfied rebellion on his face. I want to punch him. Probably better not.

My phone vibrates and buzzes in my pocket. Maybe I can escape without giving myself away after all. I frown, letting myself look irritated at the interruption and then raise my eyebrows in apology. My hand fumbling into my pocket.

"No rest for the wicked eh?" Anderson manages to croak out, a small smile playing on his lips. His yellowy stained teeth creeping into view. Years of nicotine sticks have left their mark on him. His fingers bearing similar mementoes of his habit.

"Apparently." I manage to look like I was in on his witticism. It's obvious I am going to leave and I close up my case and pull on my jacket. Anderson wants to ask something. Something delicate I expect as he beckons me forward. I lean in, hoping he's going to drop another gem for me. His voice low and gravelly he drops the bomb.

"Father, this was a white liver wasn't it? I was promised a white liver. I don't want any dirty black's organs in me. Not for twenty thousand I don't." His grip on my sleeve is fervent. His eyes searching mine looking for the reassurance he needs.

"Relax, all is as you requested. Get well and I'll see you soon." I extricate myself smoothly and leave him with a gentle pat on the shoulder. He leans back against the white pillows with the blue 'property of' peeking out.

"Dark is the way." He whispers waving me away. Time for a quick exit. I close the door behind me and leave, with more clues than I know what to do with. It is like doing a jigsaw from the back with no picture.

What on earth was that old goat on about? Didn't want a black liver? Like I knew what he meant. It was like a secret I was supposed to know. I must have bluffed well enough because he seemed to accept my words.

"A black liver?" I muse out loud; sometimes it helps, not often but you never know when it will. It's my excuse for talking to myself and I'm sticking to it.

"A black liver?" Just in case I wasn't listening to myself or didn't hear first time. I am pacing around my generic motel room, whisky glass in my hand and my bollocks still aching. It really isn't big enough to pace being about six steps by about four steps. It is beginning to bug me, I am asking the right question but have no idea what the answer is.

When in doubt put the telly on. After all, noise seems to help me think. Honestly, it does. I don't think well in silence. Anyway, BBC news 24 is a good choice, I can argue with the news presenters. Has anyone noticed that there are always two of them nowadays? Changed days. Is it now an anchor couple rather than the anchor man?

After sections on the economy, which I don't understand, and a section on the Royal family about whom I don't care. The sport is due up after a special report on Africa. It's a load of drivel about changes due to charitable relief and Medicin-sans-frontiers. It did, however, make me watch for a moment and in that moment, I get an idea. A terrible idea about MacPhail and his nasty little cult. He went to Africa every year. Collections were made for a village in wherever the fuck was it. Damn, I couldn't remember.

"It's about organs!" I blurt to myself. A smirk plays across my lips as I think the double entendre. Juvenile, yep, sorry. "So that's where the black liver's comes in."

Of course I have no idea how they do it but at least I have a working theory, (a first), which needs to be looked at. It's too late to call Brotherton with my revelation.

Chapter 16

About four, Bishop Michael had said, so four on the dot is what he meant. A very precise man, the Bishop. So five past four saw me pulling in to the neat grey gravel drive and parking my red smear next to the four black cars that were parked neatly in a row. A rose among thorns.

The Bishop's mansion is a very grand affair, not exactly a mansion but more a manor house large and solidly built. The lintel stone bears the Roman numerals for the eighteenth century, a time when buildings were made to last. The double doors are oak studded with iron and you wouldn't want to try to shoulder them in. A good first-line of defence from the days of angry mobs. Scars in the stones on either side evidence of the past.

Clunk-kitty-clunk and I stuff my keys back into my pocket. I have made an effort, though. I have shaved, have clean clothes on, polished my shoes and brushed my hair. My dog collar is nice and white. I am, after all, staying to dinner. Gravel crunching under my feet as I approach the door and, as if by magic, it opens. Magic in the form of a young priest, standing aside and waiting for my entry. Aren't they getting younger these days?

"Welcome Father Andrew. His Eminence is ready for you, in the Library." He smiles but it doesn't reach his eyes, like a server in McDonalds. I smile back with a similar lack of sparkle.

"I know the way, thank you." I hand him my coat, even though he didn't ask. Butler training is not what it once was, apparently. His smile evaporates; obviously no-one told him that he was the butler. Still, better a butler than being a lackey. I hear the heavy door close behind me as I walk smartly along the corridor to the library. I ignore the portraits of previous residents, their disapproval not needed today. I knock, a little too, forcibly on the door.

"Come in." Authority voice being projected, he obviously has an audience to impress. I smirk inwardly 'If he has on the full regalia I will wet myself.' A little twinkle settles in my eyes as I go in. There is humour everywhere, if only one looks for it.

"Andrew, so glad you could make it. Come in, come in." He seems in a good mood. Too much sherry, perhaps, his cheeks are a little ruddier than I expected. Another priest gets up from the chesterfield club chair and waits to be introduced; an uninspiring kind of fellow by the looks of him. A bit weedy and bookish, says the manly priest.

"This is Father Jeremy. He's very interested in your charts." He nods, no handshake. He looks about fifty, but it might be the grey hair, dark spectacles and mandatory sense of humour bypass as evidenced by the deep frown lines. No wonder numbers are down across the board, too many like him and not enough Robbie Coltranes.

"Father Jeremy, pleased to meet you." I nod back, poker face doing the bland. I hope it wasn't the unfriendly face, I can't always get them right.

"Let's sit gentlemen. Sherry?" Bishop Michael is the convivial host. I sit in the chair farthest from him, old habits die hard. Soon the tinkling decanter has filled a trio of glasses and we can begin. Sherry is a great start.

"The charts are most fascinating." The voice soft and smooth, escapes father Jeremy's lips. No fags or excessive booze in his past then. "They depict an alignment of stars that suggests adherence to a set of writings from the fifteen-eighties." He pauses. If he's expecting rational comment he's sorely disappointed. We're all agog and waiting. Is Santa Claus real?

"Vincenzo de Pedastalli, was an astronomer of the Left Hand Path and his writings talk of celestial sabbats that can open portals to places we are not meant to go." Oh fuck, this isn't good news. Bishop Michael has finished his sherry and so have I.

"His writings perished, allegedly, soon after his excoriation and recanting. It seems that the Vatican wanted them made safe for the future." Father Jeremy didn't quite let the sneer reach his lips, but there was a definite wrinkling of the nose. Was it due to shit that hit the fan four centuries ago and had percolated into a coming shit-storm? Probably.

"These star charts are modern, not ancient." I point out, helpful wee soul that I am. Best not have any misconceptions.

"Indeed, but they have been copied from a very credible source, showing one or two minor errors that existed on the original charts." Rolling out the charts Father Jeremy points to three transparent little post-its. I look up smartly.

"How do we know what was on the originals? Weren't they destroyed? Made safe?" I try not to let my incredulity fill my voice and fail. No wonder we are in the shit, regularly. Making things safe obviously does not mean what I think it means.

"One set of his works still exists in the Vatican Library vault. The originals were burned on the orders of, the then pope, Gregory the Thirteenth." Father Jeremy has been digging hard, it seems. We should all be thankful to Gregory the thirteenth.

"If one copy exists, why not another eh? Is that it?" The Bishop has caught on pretty quickly and he doesn't look happy and he's very slow to refill I notice. Maybe if I waggle my glass a little more?

"So our Friends have seen a copy. Or perhaps a copy of a copy of a copy. So?" My patience is wearing thin due to blood infiltrating my alcohol stream. My frown lines are deepening by the moment.

"There is a Celestial Sabbat soon, we think." Jeremy drops his bombshell and stops. Cue the dramatic music and ominous looks.

"Do these actually exist? Do they really open portals?" Lots of mumbo-jumbo gets written and because it's old some people believe it. Look at some of the stuff included in the Book, not exactly literal or credible at times.

"Perhaps. I have been tracing back through de Pedastalli's works and have discerned various dates on which an alignment may have taken place." He sipped his sherry before flipping open his notebook. His handwriting looks like chicken scratchings or hieroglyphics and is totally unintelligible upside down. I can usually read upside down writing. It has gotten me out of trouble regularly.

"Four times in the nineteenth century, three times in the twentieth and the next one is within five years, as near as I can tell. Of course it may already have occurred. Calculations of this type are notoriously difficult and unreliable." He concludes looking over reading glasses.

I love information like this. I try not to be sarcastic but it does tend to seep out. However, sometimes I don't actually try very hard and this was going to be one of them.

"Do the portal's actually open?" Which, after all, is the important bit. At least I think it is the important bit.

"There is evidence to suggest they do. However, the portals let things in, they don't let mankind out." He raises his hand to stop me butting in, "The Summa Exorcisma lists events that roughly correspond to these Celestial Sabbat. It appears Vincenzo di Pedastalli was correct."

"Not exactly good news then. Within the next five years all hell breaks loose." I get in past the raised hand.

"Quite, Andrew, quite." Bishop Michael was reaching for the sherry. Personally, I think, scotch would be more appropriate. Sherry just doesn't cut it sometimes. He has noticed my empty glass though.

"How do they open these portals? A specific ritual? A location? A sacrifice?" I head to the land of the practical, after all I am on the ground and will probably be deployed to assist.

"We don't know." Father Jeremy's frown deepens, "There have been accounts of all of those. There is no clear pattern emerging from the histories."

"This might cause us a problem then. What if a whole bunch of Satanists decide to open portals all over the place? We'd be in trouble if it worked." The drama queen in me is getting out soon to be followed by the screaming panic merchant.

"Only one portal opens at a time, and only opened for the minute at midnight. According to Vincenzo, and he's been right about everything else."

"Well we've got to be thankful for that." Bishop Michael looking for the upside. An upside which I doubt, very much, there will be. His sherry has evaporated.

"So the portal is open for a minute and what happens to the visitor? Do they get pulled back or are they our guest until we send them on their way?" See a sensible contribution. However, I am self-interested, it'll be me or someone like me who'll have to do the sending. Happy bunny, I am not.

"It would stay until despatched." Father Jeremy looks smug, knowing he's not holding that bag. Bollocks.

Driving home to sunny Gleninch in the dark, and probably over the legal alcohol limit due to a few sherries and claret inside me, I start to replay the dinner conversation. It was all 'what if' and supposition, with the odd 'according to Vincenzo' thrown in for good measure. Father Jeremy wasn't nearly as dull as I had expected; his dry sense of humour appealed to me. My sense of the ridiculous didn't appear to sit too well with Bishop Michael. His loss.

I didn't share my recent run in with the local traffic cops nor did I share my latest lead on organ trafficking. Not sure why I didn't but it could wait. Besides if I had mentioned progress Michael would want it all wrapped up quickly. And I was no where near that yet.

It's funny how the mind starts to play tricks. After one hard knee in the nuts every pair of headlights coming up behind had me worrying if a second instalment was going to be delivered. Not fear, exactly, more trepidation. It was interrupting my Sherlock Holmes routine. I just wanted to be back in my room with the door locked (after checking for hexes). I had a few nagging questions. Organ smuggling, how does that work? And how did the bad guys kill MacPhail? I should probably add why to that list too. The answers I had were all beginning to sound the same; I have no fucking idea.

What a rigmarole, keeping my room door open with one foot while checking for hexes on the inside handle. Just because they have done me once already doesn't mean they won't do it again. No hexes that I can see or feel, so I step in and let the door close with a click. Paranoia has set in, flicking the lights on I check the shower curtain for a Norman Bates-a-gram. The room is safe, apparently. As untidy as I left it; no tidy up elves here then. I smile to myself, more in relief than anything else, and pour myself a large one. It helps me sleep. Drunken stupors do that, you know.

The smile, incongruous at best on my face, slides off as I see an A4 manilla envelope lying on my pillow. The fucking fairies have been in again. Not impressed is an understatement, pissed off is much, much closer.

"Secure room, what a fucking joke." I snarl as I snatch up the envelope. Fuck the evidence trail, there won't be a fingerprint anywhere on it. They are too bloody careful for that.

Where I was expecting a composite newspaper letter message, I am surprised to find some sort of shipping manifest and other documentation. Obviously someone wants to help me. A text would have been fine. My anger dissipates leaving a ridiculous look on my face, which I have just seen in the mirror. I am puzzled. These documents are trying to tell me something but I can't actually discern what exactly. It looks like it might be important though.

Chapter 17

The following morning as I collected the mail, from the 'knocking shop' as I had taken to calling MacPhail's old house, the phone rang. I considered ignoring it but, call me weak, but once I hear a phone ringing I need to answer it. After all it might be God eh? Anyway, the point is, it was ringing and I picked it up. I was totally unprepared for what happened next.

"Hello" I can answer the phone like an adult, sometimes. The delay, you know the empty pause, told me it was an overseas call, quite a way overseas, if the reception was anything to go by. Who would be phoning a dead priest? I started thinking about how to break the news. I'm not great at this sort of thing.

"Father MacPhail, please." Accent was a bit British but not quite. The caller was about to get some bad news. I drew a breath and tried my solemn voice.

"I'm afraid, Father MacPhail is no longer here." I began, best priest voice. I didn't want to just blurt out 'He's dead', although given his practices I maybe could get away with it.

"Give him a message for me yeah? The container has cleared customs in Johannesburg without any problems. Got it yeah?" It was a South African accent. What effing container? A container of what?

"Who will I say called?" Pumping time. Any info would be a help.

"Den Beer, Marc Den Beer, got that yeah? Den Beer." The reception was so poor, he could have been saying Mars bar. I didn't let on that I wasn't sure of his words.

"I've got it thanks. I'll let him know the container has passed customs. OK. Bye." Best to keep it simple, lessens chance of giving myself away. I put the receiver down and let out the breath that I'd been holding. This tied in nicely with my clue present from the other night. If only I could pull them together.

Serendipity, that's what it is. A chance happening that gave me a clue. And like all usual clues, I had no idea what the hell to do with it. There's a funny thing about clues. They seem to be like buses, never there when you want one then two or three turn up at once.

This case was beginning to make my head hurt. Permanently. I had been here three weeks and had made next to no progress. At least now I had a workable hypothesis. Murderer? No idea, something supernatural certainly. Victim? Bad, bad man who had more sex than anyone had a right to. A cult in the congregation? Yep, but no idea who they were and how they operated. A sorcerer, who knows what he's doing making the whole thing very dangerous. I was totally screwed. Now this clue may indeed be a fresh impetus to my bumbling. I would be guarding it like a squirrel hoards nuts.

South Bloody Africa, a new focus on MacPhail's extra clerical activities was most definitely called for. I suppose I'd best go back to square one, a place I know well, and look for African clues. The manse was littered with artefacts after all.

"Brotherton, How are you?" Start off normal, it helps you know, breaks the ice. Probably a good idea to build up to my great unveiling of a combination of clues.

"Good thanks. You?" That's my boy, no clues to those around him. Secret squirrel eat your heart out. Next we would be having a secret handshake or password.

"Good. I need 5 minutes with you, today if you can manage it." Keeping to the point and allowing him the opportunity to say very little in public,.

"Great idea, say 6pm at yours?" By mine he means the hotel that I had been incarcerated in. It was functional and anonymous and perfect for a clandestine-in-plain-view-drop.

"No probs, I'll see you in the bar." A priest in a bar, a cliche if ever there was one. Not that we all have a drink problem you understand. It was public but fine for a handover of information. I plan to give him my thoughts on the organ trail and the call from

Den Beer that morning. He would be best placed to pull out a narrative that we could explore and pursue.

His professional detective skills would be needed to bring down the ring. My skills would be needed to deal with the dabblers and their master. Bishop Michael would be needed to hush it all up afterwards. What a team eh? Practically the X-Men. So what did I actually have? A phone call, a manifest and a 'black liver' comment from an old racist. What did I not have? Any real idea how it all hangs together or who the hell was hanging it all together.

It's a pretty poor excuse for a bar but at least it has tables and sells food. Okay, I admit it, I am a snob at times. The food is limited to something and chips or chicken tikka ding. However, I won't starve and the beer is not too bad. The padded stools and red velour booths have seen better days and no doubt conform to the contours of some regular's arse. I am a little fidgety as I await Brotherton. My large manilla envelope gets moved around and fondled like the Precious. If I start saying 'Gollum' I will be beyond any chance of recovery. I swig the remnants of my first pint; it didn't last long. I am about to get a refill when Inspector Brotherton makes an appearance. He gets the refills, good man. Thirsty work this detective thing.

"I know what's going on!" I blurt out, all pretence of being cool, discrete and secretive gone. No one in the bar seems to have noticed my outburst. Which is probably just as well.

"Keep it down, man." Brotherton remembered where we were. I had been bouncing about all day, excited at my breakthrough and needing someone to tell. For a man who can hear secrets and keep them under the seal of the sacrament of the confession, I should be able to manage you'd think. Apparently not.

"Sorry. It's true though." I slide the manilla envelope across the damp copper topped table. Evidence now in the hands of the authorities, as it were. I have copies just in case. I lean forward, all secret-service like, careful not to knock over my pint.

"It's all about organ trafficking. MacPhail is just part of the chain; stretching from here to South Africa and beyond. In that envelope is the start of the proof, the smoking gun." I'm too earnest when I am excited, and Brotherton is edging away, trying to escape the crazy man.

"Proof? In here? But why did they kill MacPhail then?" Pockets asks the bit I don't bloody know. Bloody police training. I slump like a burst balloon that has had its air seep out. I reach for the pint of reviving lager.

"I don't know that bit but he was in it up to his neck. I had a call from South Africa telling me the container had passed customs with no problems." As if that proved my point. It does sort of. Well, it helps at any rate.

"That doesn't prove anything, though." Brotherton raises his hand to stop me interrupting, which I was about to do. "But it does suggest a course of enquiry. We'll need to be careful not to spook the horses. If we do they'll close up shop and move on to somewhere else." Brotherton swigs his pint, the foamy moustache disappears quickly as he wipes with the back of his hand.

Time to play my trump card. "I had an interesting visit to a member of my congregation in hospital the other day. He let slip that he'd paid for a liver and he didn't want a black one." I smile, see told you. Letting the narrative build one piece at a time.

"Well, we have a link to follow. What's his name?" Brotherton seems more interested now. He has a tangible witness and accomplice with reach and a line of enquiry. I expect to see a happy cop face, soon.

"All in the envelope." What a pro I am, prepared and everything. "He's also in their little cult, so I'll be pursuing my own enquiries on that front."

"Be careful then. And keep me posted. There's big money in organ trafficking. They've murdered one priest, I doubt they'd baulk at making that two." Mr Doom and Gloom strikes again and no sign of happy cop.

"I'll be careful." Thanks mate, thanks a lot.

Chapter 18

Evening Prayer was always my favourite service; it set me at peace as a teenager each night before going home to a somewhat chaotic home life. My father having left years before and mum's boyfriend, well least said about that the better. The beautiful simplicity of the words, even now, brings me calm. When I was a teenager at evening prayer, it was often just me and the priest. I bet he thought I was a strange kid but he was always kind to me. A real man of God; dead now, of course.

I needed some peace tonight. This morning news came through, on the BBC no less, that the Gleninch Priest Killer had hanged himself in his cell, whilst on remand. A note was left on the floor and he was found hanging. Piss dripping off his shoes, eyes bulging and mouth agape he wasn't a pretty sight apparently. Didn't get that on the news. Of course with his demise they thought I would, no doubt, be recalled from Gleninch. It was over, or at least it was meant to be. A fit of swearing had taken over my usual grumpiness and it wasn't helped when Brotherton dropped by after mid morning to fill me in on the details.

"The note looks iffy to me." He started with the obvious. My peevishness was writ large on my face, so he soldiered on. "He was barely bloody literate when I took his confession and now his suicide note reads like Dan-bloody-Brown." Way to go, Brotherton. He is beginning to sound like me. Imitation being the highest form of flattery.

"Of course, there'll be no investigation. Open and shut case. They want this to go away." He concluded, didn't even use his notebook. He was as frustrated as I was, apparently. My disgust at this turn of events was obvious and normally my responses would be calm, measured, erudite even.

"Fucking Bastards." Was the best I could manage. I stomped into the Vestry to get out of my outfit. Inspector Brotherton followed me in and shut the door quietly. I was still growling under my breath as he waited. The staccato nature of my movements adding a level of violence to my anger culminating in a tear of my cassock. I manage to grind my teeth rather than let out another high volume expletive.

"The shipping note you gave me was for a consignment of organ transplant boxes." He was speaking quietly forcing me to stop stomping about. Making me stop and listen, once the purple chasuble was over my head.

"And?"

"They were for onward shipping through a few different import-export companies until they ended up in Kenya, a little town called Lamooro." He paused again to see if I was keeping up. I was.

"MacPhail's little friends in Africa. Why would they need a whole container of organ transplant boxes? A few maybe, but a container load?" I was folding my vestments,badly, and trying to stow them neatly. A task that seemed beyond me at that moment.

"Exactly, they wouldn't." Brotherton knew in his gut we were on to something. I just wasn't quite there yet. The dates on the manifest were way before the Den Beer call and didn't match up with the clearing customs comment.

"So what the fuck do they do with them then?" I knew that expletives were building up in direct proportion with my lack of understanding. My mother always said it was a weakness of vocabulary to swear so much, I was such a disappointment.

"There's been a civil war in neighbouring Mozambique or Somalia. I think they are harvesting them there. There's very little control in that whole region. It's like the bloody wild west." No notebook for this either. We were well and truly off the record. I wondered what he had done with my evidence.

"And then they sell them all over the world? That's a heck of a big job. Wouldn't someone notice?" I like a good conspiracy theory but this would be huge. And all from a casual statement from a racist bigot. Ain't Karma a bitch.

"Proof, that's the problem. We haven't got any." Inspector

Rain-on-the-parade stated making sure I wasn't getting ahead of myself.

"I have that problem regularly. This organ traffic is funding a satanic organisation and its many contacts, and you want proof. Do you think MacPhail was about to blow the whistle?" My musing out loud often helps if someone else is listening and can make some semblance of sense of it all. I look at him, perhaps a little too expectantly.

"It gives us a motive. Still we need to work this further. I have a forensic accountant working on the flows of the money; hopefully that will turn up something." The old team back together, but this time Brotherton couldn't afford to get caught.

"So the MacPhail murder case is closed then. No one will be looking any further. What did you do with the manifest?" I sounded disappointed even to me but I needed to know in case Brotherton was ever removed.

"That ship has sailed but let's see what else we can do. They got Capone for tax evasion after all. The manifest is filed in the shoplifting file for David Graham, only we know it is there. A classic misfiling." Inspector Brotherton the optimist. Me? I'd stick to complaining about the unfairness of it all.

Chapter 19

It is probably not a good idea to tell the nice policeman that the reason I want access to MacPhail's manse is to perform a working. You know, magic. They might take a dim view of it after all. I used the 'I need to gather some congregation details that Father MacPhail has in his (that is our) manse. It worked so much better after all. No tricky questions just a simple smile and nod of assent. A well mannered policeman keeping watch over my back should have been reassuring but after my traffic cop meeting I was somewhat wary. I locked the door from the inside, quietly.

So anyway, I wanted to remove and disperse some of the power of Darkness that still resonated from the house. Well, in particular, from the circle on the living room floor. It had been etched many times and as such held a deep rooted nexus, the darkness of the enemy. Just sitting in his armchair had brought tears and pain to me, so God knows what rolling back his circle would be like. A picnic in the sunshine it would not be.

After turning the key in the lock and locking out the rest of the world, I stepped forward to a place I'd rather not go. The sun, however, bolstered my spirits. I wouldn't want to be doing this after dark. It was almost noon, so I had plenty of time to complete the working and be on my way before Dark-rise. Or True Dark if you prefer.

Funny how unoccupied buildings have a smell. Not a damp musty smell but simply a smell; as if to say 'this is not a place of the living'. How very appropriate for this place. MacPhail was certainly gone but his vibrations could still be felt, or at least I could still feel them. I left the key in the lock. The door was secured; no one would be interrupting me. The last thing I needed was someone to walk in mid-incantation as it were.

"I come to cleanse this place with the Host of our Lord. In

the name of the Father, The Son and the Holy spirit." My voice full of authority. No explosion or supernatural phenomena in response, so I began the Walk. The Walk. The steps of Our Lord Jesus Christ along the streets of Jerusalem, around him enemies, scorn and hatred. In this place I could feel the air tight with anticipation. The sun was high in the sky, this is my time.

"I hear your taunts, your jeers, your curses but the blood of My Lord was spilled to redeem me. His steps, filled with pain, cleanse these stones as once they trod the paths of Jerusalem." I stepped up each step making the sign of the cross, bringing the blessing of the Lord to each space in the house. It took less than an hour. I did think the bedroom might need special attention as the whiff of corruption seemed to have seeped into the very fabric of the building. I cast open the windows and scattered the essence that pervaded the bedroom. Like the casting down of the money lenders in the temple, the throwing open my arms scattered the sexual residue of magic built up by the many sessions of MacPhail.

I walked every room except the living room where the circle was etched. The knocking shop that was the bedroom, the main event so far. When I reached the front door again I took a moment to open my spirit. This was always a bit hit or miss, any residual trouble might strike now.

I walked each room again 'open' to the psychic or supernatural forces that may have been present. I sought out the little pockets of the Dark that could have been missed as I walked before. If I had started this way I would have been swamped and overwhelmed by the darkness and pain that had been present. The blessing and the walk of Our Lord had washed away the malignant residue of MacPhail and his cronies. This house felt a much more wholesome place, with only a passing memory of the darkness that had filled it.

I felt a darkness at the edge of my vision, as I passed the meter cupboard. I had not opened this space and had missed a possible hiding place. It was a strong sink of Darkness, being probably the darkest spot in the whole house. I blessed myself and the door before tugging the handle. Inside, beside the Vacuum cleaner and the dusters, blackness seeped from the floor. No carpet covering the floor, I could see the dark sigils of power warding against me. A magical booby trap on a floorboard, what lay beneath I had no idea but it worried me that someone had felt the need to ward against the powers of light. I wondered, which is like hesitation or dithering but much more meaningful. I finally decided. I would trust my protection and I pulled it up. Good eh?

When I have the host in my pocket and unction on my forehead, I feel bullet-proof. Experience would suggest otherwise as often I have been caught out a bit. The jolt that fired up my arm was strong and left me lying half upright against the opposite wall. A stunned moment passed as I caught up. Breath rasping as I sucked it back into my lungs.

"Bastard." A single swearword to encapsulate my feelings. The dark sigils remained intact, although invisible to the human eye. They had acted like a sharp rebuke, and a casual reminder that these were no fools. Why this had been missed when they had cleared out the evidence? Had MacPhail been keeping secrets from his own side? I would be finding out soon. The sigils emanating a 'nothing to see here' may have kept the untrained eyes away.

A prayer of cleansing and the sprinkling of Holy water should render the sigils powerless this time. I reached out and pulled up the floorboard. The Hammer house of horror creak that accompanied my pulling was startlingly loud in the confined space. There in the space below was a black velvet puddle. Inside the velvet was something vaguely rectangular, I presumed so anyway. I squatted there and looked into the secret hiding place. I opened my spirit to feel around the edges. I felt a depth to this darkness far further than the foot or so it seems in the physical world. Deep inside this little place was a pit of pure darkness, a well into the Otherworld. Which came first? The well or the manse? Or was this manse deliberately sited here because of the well? If that were the case then every single Priest in this parish had been of the enemy and the fingers of Evil had spread widely indeed.

A horrible thought struck me. I looked round as the worry began to build in my imagination. If the Manse was specifically put here what of the church itself? What about it? Was it compromised and unsanctified? Desecrated? It didn't feel that way but then again I hadn't been looking for that.

"In the name of Our Lord Jesus Christ, and of Saint Michael and his Angels, I abjure your Evil. Feel the cleansing power of Our Lord in the purity of this Holy Water and let it wash away the Evil contained within. Blessed is he that comes in the Name of the Lord, Hosanna in the highest." I put forth my hand and sprinkle more holy water before pulling forth the velvet package. It is heavy and feels almost as if someone is holding it and trying to pull it back in. With a wrench I pull it free. From the velvet material power ripples across my hands like a static charge or pins and needles. I move back into the sunlight carrying it before me. The kitchen is closest and filled with sunshine.

I dump the package on the kitchen island and flick open the velvet wrap. A book was protected within the folds of, very expensive and old, velvet. The air is still but inside my mind I hear the hissing of the sunlight as it caresses and cleanses this evil artefact. The leather is old and well worn. The red, almost a burgundy, leather is etched and tooled with a fleur-de-lys edging. In the centre a tiger's eye stone sits in a well and around the whole a leather tie passes on three loops. It is sizzling still as the power contained within resists the sunlight and the power of light.

"Fuck." I manage to gasp as I stare at the shadows running over the surface. This is a major Arcana. I don't know what I should do with it. I want to open it but I know that is hazardous. I really should leave it alone and call in for some support but I am the Johnny on the spot. I drip some holy water onto the leather tie and then after blessing myself I slip the leather tie off and pull it free. My hands shake a little as I avoid contact with the book itself, although I know I will open it in a moment or two. I wet my lips and give a little cough, readying my voice should it be needed. I flip the page.

Inside on an ancient creamy page a pictorial representation of the satanic Goat covers the first page. The baleful scowl as it looks up at me, not quite so terrifying as I expected. The tingling in my finger tips is fading away. I turn the page gently, and realise I am holding onto a breath. I let it escape my lips slowly. I scan the next page, covered in dire warnings of disaster for all who have no right to look upon these words. My usual joviality has evaporated and this book has my fullest concentration. Outside, in the real world, the sun marches on across the sky.

The book is written in what looks like Latin, but there is something slightly off with some of the spelling. I can't really translate it, and shouldn't get too interested in trying to do so. I will pass this back to Bishop Michael and he can get it to the right place. This is a dangerous tome and needs to be studied and locked away. It appears to be the scripture and order of service for the worship of their Dark Satanic master. I close it and bind it shut. I am weary and my eyes feel gritty, somewhat like the morning after the night before. I sprinkle more Holy water and offer a benediction to ward and contain the dark words and evil intent contained inside. I have a working to do on the living room. The sun is slanting in now as the afternoon has passed in a blink. Fuck.

Leaving the tome in the kitchen and warding shut the door under the stairs, I need to hurry or it will be dark before I am done. I announce my presence and push open the door. I am Daniel and I enter the mouth of the beast. I speak the words of our faith in Latin and then in English as I cross the threshold. I fear not as the Lord is with me. I am a tool in his hands.

"Begone, in the Name of the Father, Son and Holy Spirit. I command thee in his name.'" I step to the heavy drapes and throw them back. Sunlight floods in but a full third of the room is not touched directly. If only I had left the book until later.

I look around the room, my spirit eyes scanning and seeing the blood circle on the floor. It is deepest of black from the many old rituals performed here. I walk my way to the tip of his left horn and begin the walking back. Anti clockwise each step is a challenge to my authority. I feel the resistance like a thickening in the air. I can feel the hurt, the pain, the sex, the abuse and most of all in this room of tears I can taste the salt and hear the cries of anguish.

"Wash clean this dirt of sin, as our Lord washed the feet of the sinners. My service, oh Lord, is yours let these memories be washed away and cleansed from this place." I walk round and am at the horns again. This path has been worked many times. Not just by MacPhail but by his predecessors. The circle is strong and is resisting still. The power laid down time after time.

"I walk the many steps to Golgotha, let me carry the burden of these sins as you once did, oh Lord. Let me be the unworthy vessel to break these bonds of evil." I passed round once more. I feel the evil tendrils gripping and tugging at my feet as I pass. They are powerless to prevent me but still they resist. In the shadows I feel a malevolence gathering, and its eyes bore into my back as I pass round time and again. Impotent and angry I can sense its frustration. The afternoon sun is running away and soon the circle and pentagram will be out of the direct rays. Things may get a bit interesting then.

The walking back of such a strong and well used pentagram was always going to take a while and I can feel the progress as the power seems to be fading at each turn. I am hopeful that I can complete the ritual before nightfall. The afternoon sun still strong is no longer on the floor and almost imperceptibly the mood in the room starts to change. I walk back another turn and am startled as I hear the cries of pain that once filled this room, echoes of a torment in the past. Memories of pain and tears, of hurt and torment, flood over me. Heart rending sobs burst from me. I am sharing their fates. I walk round again, more of a stumble as my eyes stream with tears. Tears that were shed years ago are relived by me as I pull myself around and around in the gathering gloom.

The feeble overhead light casts a dull yellow glow in the room as the sun has long since disappeared from the inside. The dark garden hedge casting a shadow over the garden shows the passing of time and the nearing of night. I am wrung out, as my emotions are shredded again and again. I know that each one I feel is set free forever, it is my pain to bear and just an echo of a great wrong.

I am shuffling now, and a new feeling begins. I can feel the change in the air. Lust. Before this room was filled with tears this circle was imbued with blood and sex magic. I lift my eyes and see flashes of another priest in MacPhail's chair with a succession of partners fellating, fucking, and masturbating in a frenzy of flickering images. My senses are overwhelmed and my body responds to these memories. I feel like a total slut in moments as I am at once one and many sexual servants to this man. My mouth recalls his taste, my body feels his penetration, the desires and releases flood me as I spurt and spurt incapable of resisting. I am spent as I complete this circle. A mocking laughter fills the room. I need to get out of here, like Douglas MacArthur 'I shall return.'

Outside, with the door closed behind me I try to catch my breath. I am gasping like a landed fish. Looking down to my groin the mess of my trousers is evident and feels totally icky.

"Fucks sake." I manage to walk like John Wayne to the kitchen and snatch up the now, hopefully, inert book and velvet. Sunlight is a hell of a thing.

Chapter 20

Outside of Gleninch there's an old tower, monument thing. Well, actually, it's on the other side of the Lomond Hills which are sometimes called the Paps of Fife. Although to be blunt, they are the most misshapen pair of boobs on the planet and if you include Largo Law then there are three of them. Go figure.

Anyway, a message to meet my reluctant informer at a remote monument was just too irresistible for me. So I had set off at lunchtime in my happy, little 'here I am' red car and was almost there when a chained forestry commission gate barred my way. I thought, wrongly, that there was a road all the way and no outside walking would be needed. Pulled up short in a tight pine forest (plantation not a real forest) and feeling hemmed in, I have to reverse up the road to a wide bit. It's all relative but there appear to be something like passing places along the track. Ahead of me, beyond the gate, a hard core track of mud and grey aggregate leads onwards and upwards to the monument. The gate must be new-ish as I have walked here a few times when youthful exuberance made me tramp over the local hills. I didn't remember this track nor the gate.

I looked down at my footwear and held out little hope that I could pick my way through without falling on my arse. As for the gate, I hoped not to fall off as I swung my legs over. Ordinarily I would have walked round but the quagmire to the sides looked like a disaster waiting to happen. It would be bad enough with mud covering my shoes and new trouser hem, the older pair didn't survive the vomit coating, but I didn't want to meet my informant plastered in grey mud from arsehole to elbow.

I was almost half a mile from it, clouds overhead didn't look that bad, so I left the brolly and pulled up my collar. Ah the country. Why is it always bloody freezing? Perhaps that is a question that is only asked in northern climes. Even in the summer it isn't actually hot, I personally would settle for warm occasionally. Now I know traipsing off into the wilds is like a trap from a horror movie. I can almost hear myself snorting at the screen. I am not that stupid. I've left a note for Brotherton and I have a few weapons with me. Holy water, unction, Magnum 357- probably the most powerful handgun in the world (not the last one). I also have a slick torch that I bought, with batteries, at the garage this morning. I've even tested it, maglite apparently, LED and bright as hell. So I'm all prepared, obviously.

Black leather Gibson shoes are so not for tramping along forestry roads, as my slipping and stumbling attests to. The mud is all over them and lines the bottoms of my trousers; it's a brown-grey clingy, clumpy mud that will be an utter pig to get out. Anyway, I tramp along with indelicate language spilling from my lips. At least no-one can hear me. Or at least I hope no one can.

Some minutes of tip-toeing and swearing later, I break through the trees as the tended grass of the monument comes into view. On my right a large stone tower, with a cracking view out over the Howe of Fife, looms up above me. A view that is well worth the walk if not the mud. Farms and fields sweeping away to the mountains in the distance and the wind cutting through my clothes. Bracing, I believe, it's called. Apparently my clothes are totally unsuitable and offer next to no protection from the wind at all. Wind Chill factor; if it gets any colder my tonsils will have company.

Is this a wild goose chase or a trap? I have a quick recce round the tower with a casual look inside the open doorway, while trying not to look like a pratt. I now know that it was erected in honour of Onesipherious Tyndall- Bruce in 1855, and is called the Tyndall Bruce monument, so not a wasted trip then. There is no one inside, I checked with my new torch, but it was very dark. I am suspicious by nature and am beginning to feel set up. Checking my phone I discover that it is a zero bar zone and no phoning for help will be happening anytime soon. Stooging around the monument, I feel exposed. My early bravado at agreeing to meet here has evaporated to be replaced by a nagging ache in the pit of my stomach. Not quite fear but might build into it given time.

On about my third lap, I notice something blue at the foot of the viewpoint. Well, on the ground below the rail to be precise, it looks like a rain jacket. Funny how the human brain refuses to recognise some things, broken bloody bodies at the foot of a large drop being one of them. I was staring for, what seemed to me at any rate, ages until it dawned on me. This might be my anonymous ally. Bloody hell of a coincidence that the site of my secret rendezvous, should come with a body.

Slowly, my brain started to work and I whirled round away from the rail fence. Don't want a helping hand, as it were. I can feel the shaking begin as I fumble for my phone. Shock makes the brain slow and body problematic. I can't get my pocket zip open. I'm pulling and tugging and finally it gives up spilling forth its contents. Luckily the ground is soft and springy which prevents it smashing to smithereens. I am clumsy enough without shock and you'd think I was picking up a bar of soap as it takes three goes to get it into my hand. Using both hands I manage to steady the screen enough to realise there is no signal.

"Fuck!" fear is setting in. Will I be helped over the edge too? I can feel the saliva gathering in my mouth. For god's sake I am going to hurl. I spit and spit, trying to stave it off but soon the heaving starts and my cookies are well and truly tossed. I am an easy target. If they wanted me out of the frame, now it would be easy to facilitate it. I decide to leg it. A stumbling, stagger of a run but with my footwear it soon turns into a knee scraping, muddy fall down and stagger up kind of thing. I am covered from almost head to toe. I am a mess. A terrified, soggy muddy mess.

Obviously my description, garbled as it was, is sufficient. Before long two police cars and an ambulance have filled the road behind my car. The gate is in the process of being unchained. Some constable has my keys and is behind the wheel of my Nissan. I have recovered some coherence. Now I just look a state. Where is Brotherton? I don't trust any of this mob, I am surrounded in the countryside but the ball kicker isn't among them. A nice young sergeant is trying to get me to sit in his car, in the back I notice. I sit on the bonnet, all cold and shivery. I'm sure he is waiting on an answer. He asked something a moment ago. No idea what it was though?

"Father, are you all right?" He uses his best solicitous tone. He probably thinks it helps. It doesn't, by the way.

"Do you know the person who was killed?" Pushing, hard but not too hard. He may have been asking that for a while but I wasn't really with it.

"Yes, well actually no I don't." I manage to blab. Bollocks. No was the answer. Shock making dissembling difficult either that or the cold and mud.

"Which is it? Yes or no?" His patience has evaporated, and he now starts looking less than certain of my role in the event. I can see he isn't sure that my hands didn't do the helping.

"I don't." Better and firmer this time. I'd probably best not mention my rendezvous. Otherwise a whole new line of difficult questions might start to need answering. A bit like Pandora's box, once it is opened the trouble starts.

"What brought you out here, father?" His suspicious mind is working overtime. Hardly surprising. What are the chances of someone falling to their death in a remote place to be discovered before they are cold?

"The view." I am a bit surly and it doesn't sit well with the nice policeman. He has obviously had the sense of humour bypass that all uniformed officers get at the Police training college. He gives me the look, one from which I am immune. I look blandly back. He waits. He isn't sure if he wants to get in trouble for detaining the witness or for letting the killer escape.

A sigh escapes him, recognising that I am not saying anything else. His radio bleeps into life and a 'Two-six receiving' is swiftly spoken as he turns away. I can hear every word but I am not surprised when words like accident and instantaneous are decipherable. Perhaps I won't have to flash my card after all. I wonder if I will need Brotherton as a character witness. It might be better to leave him out of it, for now. Protect his pension for a little longer. His shoulders seem to slump as more information is relayed. Obviously I will be going soon; he has no need to keep me here. You never know, he might want to interview me anyway. Such is my sparkling line in wit and repartee. Perhaps the lamp in the eyes and wring a confession from me is on the menu.

"Father Steel," he turns round slowly, obviously having come to a decision. 'Can you come down to the station and give a statement?' He manages to make it sound optional.

"Now or later?" I decide that he'll have to work. Never get into a car with a strange man I was always told. Policemen count as strange men.

"Now would be best. Get it done and let you get on your way." Ooh a fencer. I bet he's just going to want a full search and check under the nails of the body. Stalling for time and trying to keep his options open.

"Sergeant, I want to go home and change my clothes. I can give you a statement here and now if that will suffice?" See, me the height of reasonableness. I am bloody freezing and have had just about enough of this nonsense. My inner child might escape and a tantrum ensue.

Before he can answer, the radio interrupts again. He's walking away a bit. I see a smile playing on his lips. I bet he can see a promotion coming as he makes a collar on a murder. Purposefully he walks over to me, a new spring in his step, a grim little smile on his face. His cuffs come out as he slaps one on my wrist. The steel colder than I am.

"I am detaining you on suspicion of murder." He turns me round and cuffs my wrists together. He's doing the blah, blah, blah that he needs to do. He isn't very gentle either, his excitement getting the better of him.

"Do you have anything to say?" He pauses. I snort derisively but he thinks he's Taggart, with a dodgy Fife accent, obviously. We are going to get along famously, I imagine. At least he ducks my head as he puts me in the back of his nice car.

Oh well its going to be one of those days. I wonder if I'll get a cup of tea. Maybe a couple of digestives?

Chapter 21

I am being, what is called by the police, 'processed'. I wonder at which point I should whip out my get-out-of-jail-free-card. The smug bastard with the cuffs is going to be disappointed. I look forward to that moment, you know the 'get it right up ye' moment. However, at the moment I am looking at the messy state of my clothes. I think there is a mud free bit somewhere. They are getting a bit uncomfortable as they stick to me and the hard plastic chair I have to sit on. I suppose it could be worse, no full body search yet. No hosing down or rubber hose treatment. I wonder if these things ever really did happen. No tea yet either.

The door opens and two plain clothed chaps wander in. I wonder if they are from the same mould as the arresting officer. I suppose I am about to find out. I compose my face in the blandest look I can manage. But I really struggle as I can still smell and taste my own vomit from earlier. It just makes me look like a sour puss. I hope they can smell it, too.

One presses down the record buttons on the two cassette recorder. His spotty cheeks a hangover from his unwashed youth and the sneer well practised in front of the mirror in the mornings. He tries to glare at me but I am distracted by the burgeoning carbuncle on the side of his nose and the creamy pus beginning to present itself. The tone denotes the race has started. Time and date stamps are blathered at the machine as well as the names of those present. He looks at me, all stern and serious, he's seen Taggart too,

"Father Steel?" Starts Tweedledum. They join me at the table, a manilla folder in front of them with lots of contents. Photos, I expect. Lurid and close up of the impact of a rapid descent onto rocks. I guess I'd better confess quick.

"I am Detective Sergeant McKay, this is Detective Constable Davidson." He nods at his partner. So they aren't called

Tweedledum and Tweedledumber? Shocking. I don't offer anything, just let him go on. Why interrupt his preprepared speech? Wouldn't want to throw him off into a series of ehm's and ehs.

"I am going to question you, before I do so I must caution you, you are not obliged to answer any of these questions but any answers you give will be noted and may be used in evidence against you." The preliminaries are over. Worst foreplay ever.

"Do you know why you are being detained?" He pauses, waiting for me. I suppose I'd better take part in this farce. I sigh, heavily, and regret it smelling again the vomit from earlier.

"I am being detained because your officer on the scene has a very vivid imagination and the inability to think past Taggart.' I didn't mean that to come out, oh well. Here we go. There won't be tea anytime soon after that.

"You are a murder suspect chummy, so cut that lip or you'll regret it." DC Tweedledumber barks out. Ooh he is so terrifying. I smile, a smug 'Fuck off Spotty' if ever I saw one. I should stop pissing about but I am now entrenched and not letting this pass easily.

"You must belong to the same school of pointless police training I suppose." I love the colour that flushes his face. It might be called puce.

"Murder is a very serious matter Father Steel. I suggest you answer the questions properly." Much better, DS Tweedledumb is quite calm.

"Why did you shove him over the rail?" dumber leans forward, all attempted menace. Comical stuff really.

"I didn't." I snort, and instantly wish I hadn't. That little moment of having to swallow down the remnants of back-of-the-nose sickness and trying not to heave again was upon me. I hung in there, just.

"Why were you out there?" DS Dumb, tries from his side. "His number was on your phone?" Really, I wonder about that. It said withheld when the call came in.

"Sight seeing." I might as well have said 'fuck off'. His

gambit had failed. I moved in my seat eliciting a squelching noise from the muddy trousers sticking to the plastic.

"Father, this is serious and you are in the frame for murder." He pulls out a picture of one of my parishioners, all broken and bloody. It is the still from first arrival at the scene. Pretty Gruesome. "Tell me what happened, it will save us all a great deal of time." Aww bless he is trying to coax me into blabbing.

"Who is this?" DS Dumber blurts from his side. He really needs to re-attend basic training and learn the art of shutting up.

"Colin somebody, Patterson I think." I can be helpful. He lives alone though so unless they are going to inform his cat, I can't point them anywhere else. Anyway it clears up who was helping me.

"So you knew each other then." I missed which one of them uttered the words as I looked at the wreckage of a decent man lying before me in glorious colour. It saddened me that he had been killed for trying to help me solve the mess. Another victim of the MacPhail gang. Retribution would find them, all of them. My face took on a stony look which the illustrious detectives took to mean something.

"He is one of the congregation of St Margaret's in the Fields, in Gleninch." I try hard to keep my voice even. I can feel the anger churning inside me.

"So why were you out there together then?" DC Dumber, again.

"We weren't together." I have just about had enough of these clowns. Will I ask for Brotherton or pull out my God Squad ID? Decisions, decisions.

"Pretty fishy both being there at the same time. Middle of nowhere. Stinks Father, totally stinks. Why did you kill him?" DC Dumber continues. He would be out of his depth in a puddle. I look at him, like the thick shit he is.

"Pfft." I make a noise but not a snort after last time. I have learned that lesson the hard way.

"A lovers tryst gone wrong?" He soldiers on obviously unaware of the old adage 'better to remain silent and look a fool than to speak and remove all doubt'.

"You may fancy him but he's not my type." My smart mouth designed to get me in to bother. DC homophobe jumps to his feet, all flushed and angry. Go on, I dare you my face screams at him. My arrogance designed to elicit a response. His boss gets him in check with a look. Good doggie, sit. He has decided something.

"We are formally detaining you and will need DNA samples and your clothes for analysis. Perhaps afterwards you'll be prepared to cooperate." DS Dumb, flaps the folder shut. He doesn't look happy.

Fuck them, let them waste their time. Not surprised so many crimes are unsolved. This lot couldn't find their arse with both hands and a team of sniffer dogs. More processing then. Still no tea.

After a brief interlude in the stupidity a uniformed officer comes in with a paper onesie for me and a big poly bag for my clothes. It will be a pleasure to get the muddy mess off and be in a nice clean outfit. White is so fattening, I look like I have gained three stone since Christmas. Never mind, I am sure I can get back to my fighting weight for the Olympics. Not very likely though.

"Press that buzzer when you are changed Father." What a polite young fellow, He leaves me to the task in hand. So I spare him some of the more acidic responses in my repertoire. He is just getting on with his job.

"I will. Thank you. Any chance of tea?" If you don't ask, as they say. He smiles, maybe he has heard about the interview.

"I will see what I can do. NATO standard?" He seems utterly lacking in hostility. Milk and two is fine and I nod, although hot and wet would do. Stripping off muddy, vomit encrusted clothes is a task for celebrity jungle programmes, not one I had really wanted to try out personally. Vomit splatter is bad enough but the heavy clumpy sticky mud has stuck my hairy legs to the inside of my trousers and is worse than a band aid being pulled off. I am wincing like a woose as I get myself disentangled. Fun it is not. Anyway, the buzzer is well and truly pressed.

A few minutes, spanning an eternity, pass and a mug of tea arrives as my bag of mud-cakes is taken away for processing. I only get a sip when DS Dumb (or dumber) arrives in a somewhat unhappy mood. He slaps my wallet on the table. He has run a check on my ID. Oh dear, the disappointment must be crushing.

"Why didn't you tell us who you were?" He manages to spit out. I am sure there were spaces for expletives in there. He really isn't trying. I smile antagonising him further.

"You didn't ask." All pretence of giving a shit gone. I sip at the sweet tea that the nice Duty constable brought me.

"By wasting our time the real killer is getting away." He is exasperated. Poor wee lamb.

"You lot couldn't fall out of a boat and hit water." I sneer, it isn't really an attractive look. "Get me a lift back to Gleninch, and I wont mention the level of ineptitude you managed to display."

He is going red to purple from the collar upwards. Probably a stroke waiting to happen. He is trying to hold himself together but I am sure I can goad him past the point. Probably better not to.

"You are free to go. Your belongings will be returned to you." What a massive effort to retain control. He stalks from the room like Kevin the teenager.

"Thank you." I slurp my tea. I am so childish at times, it is embarrassing. They started it defence is probably not going to wash. I expect the Bishop won't be happy either.

Chapter 22

It was making me feel sick. The air was charged with mojo but whose it was I had no idea. After being vomitous when my room was attacked, I was wary of being so exposed. Of course, I was armed and not with mundane protection either. I had some Holy Unction in my pocket for my direst need. A little pukey feeling wasn't direst need, yet.

"I can feel you, you bastard." I mutter to myself. I try to keep the hostility to myself but I'm sure I just look like a grumpy git. The civic reception is to celebrate sixty years of new town status is not the place for a bun-fight. It is only three days since I had a run in with the Police in Falkland, and I don't think I am quite recovered from the ear bashing that the Bishop gave me over the rank stupidity of the situation. Worse still I had been fending off the attentions of Mrs Brookes and was running out of excuses, finally giving in to a meet tomorrow.

In the new council building, showing no end to the public money to be squandered is a gathering of the great and the good of civic society. Why on earth was I invited? Must be the dog-collar-factor. It gets me into all sorts of places. Some of them quite entertaining. Despite the nausea, I have a flute of fizzy white wine in my hand as I am introduced to the Lord Lieutenant of Fife and the Lady Provost. 'My, what a big gold chain you have Provost' is what I want to say but I stick to playing nicely with the other children.

"I'm a native." I pause to allow the Provost time to keep up and nod. "I went to school here and my sister still lives here." I sip, giving her a chance to chime in.

"Really?" She fakes interest so well. She is destined for high office, if her insincerity is a measure. Of course she isn't a native being from another part of Fife, Dunfermline. It might as well be another planet. Fife is a bit like that; if you aren't local then near enough isn't good enough.

"Oh yes, it's changed quite a bit over the last twenty years." Always helps to establish one's local pedigree and credentials. Prevents one looking like a total junket hog.

"What brings you back here Father Steel?" Oh dear, I knew someone would ask. I could get into a helluva trouble with this one. I will play it with the official line; a straight bat as they say.

"Sadly, Father MacPhail's demise brought me home. It has been a while." Look at that. Bland drivel and so in keeping with the occasion. Funny how that seems to work so well. I still don't know why my spidey-senses are working overtime. The room is full of the suited and booted and the addition of alcohol hasn't really worked. Although maybe I should try having more?

"Oh yes, a real loss to the community, so involved with everything. A real man of the cloth." The Lady Provost spouts the commonly held belief. Oh how little they really know. Of course, some in here really knew MacPhail for what he was. There are enemies all around, hidden in plain sight. Am I Julius Caesar surrounded by knife wielding plotters? I wonder if the Enemy knows that I am here. I manage not to splutter in my flute. I mumble platitudes to pass off my agreement with the accepted public image of the departed.

"Will you be staying long Father?" She asks as she sips her wine. She has piercing eyes, I finally notice. A lovely shade of blue, she must have been exceptionally pretty as a young woman.

"Not too long, I expect, only until a permanent replacement is appointed. Then my path will take me onwards again." Was she too interested? Or was it just politeness? The Provost's chain looks heavy but is obviously not real gold, just gilt. A veneer just like the town itself. New and civilised but underneath a whole different ball game; drugs, drink, satanic cults – you know, the usual 21st century problems. Luckily, an aide takes her elbow and steers her away from Tufty the Priest. "Lovely to meet you" exchanged with smiles. Yet neither smile reaching the eyes, what a pair of phoneys we are.

I drain my flute and turn to the conversation on my left where the Lord Lieutenant has been engaged by a sycophant of some sort. My head is still thudding dully and I am still no closer to identifying the source of my pain. I scan surreptitiously as I snag another cheap plonk from the drinks waiter.

This feeling of 'something not right' turns into a full-blown 'turn-the-fuck-round-now'. I always like to see the white of my enemy's eyes. Like a western gunfight, it's the eyes that matter. Easier to catch the bastards eh? I slowly look round, there at the far side of the room, a pair of eyes is boring holes into me and he's just too slow to look away in time before I clock him. Gotcha.

He's a normal looking bloke, pretty nondescript, is he a flunky or a dignitary? Nice suit though, grey with a shadow stripe, his tie is a blood red from a power dressing manual. Gold watch peeking out from French cuffs and natty cufflinks, thirty something so probably not a flunky. I keep an eye on him and those he is in conversation with. He knows I have clocked him and keeps trying not to look in my direction. Quite amusing really, or it would be if this wasn't serious.

Fuck it, I'm going in. Red leader standing by, I'm making my run now. I extricate myself from the Lord Lieutenant and the ass kissing that is going on. I can't exactly charge over and put the cross on him or drag him before the Inquisition, so I meander with purpose. Finger buffet and a fresh glass of wine (red this time) and I toddle over. Like a lioness stalking a gazelle, I am closing in and I can see his panic beginning to mount.

He tracks my progress and knows I'm coming. Better still he knows I know he's the enemy. He knows he might be up shit creek without a paddle. I can almost hear the jaws theme playing as I glide through the gathering. Above his collar a flush is starting to show, his discomfort becoming evident. Funnily enough I no longer feel nauseous, the feelings of moments ago have gone. Was he just being used as a channel for someone else? His master perhaps? The mojo has gone for now.

"Father, let me introduce you" a calm voice moves alongside me, pulling me into the group containing minion-of-the-dark-in-the-nice-suit. Here we go, chocks away and all that. I look round to see who's doing the steering, one of the faces from my flock apparently. The name escapes me as I let him lead me in. At least I hope he's one of mine.

"This is Councillor Gray, Councillor McIntosh, Councillor Swan and Councillor Dempster." He allows me time to shake each hand in turn and I look for my enemy but he has melted away. Shite and buckets of it. I know what he looks like, I'll get him.

"Councillors, I am pleased to meet you." I manage to keep disappointment hidden from my voice. Next time I'll get the slippery little flunky, nice suit and all. My vibrating pocket extricates me from a long, tedious conversation around planning objections for a new housing estate to the west of the town. Thank you, I almost mouth to the ceiling. Bishop Andrew is identified as the caller.

"Steel." I can't help myself, voice flat and neutral. I'm in public and giving nothing away. He is used to it, however.

"Andrew, that book is very important, can you come over this evening?" Wow, that is direct by any standard. For Bishop Michael, it is positively rude.

"Of course, I can be there by seven." I am interested to know what it is for, so my usual surliness is put on hold. It is a classic quid pro quo or something like that.

"See you tonight." He hangs up, no love and kisses or anything. I return to the function room, realising that I am probably marginal for being over the limit for driving later. I'd better eat some of these delicious looking sausage rolls, and the rather dubious looking wrap things with unidentifiable contents.

At the appointed hour I am pulling in to the gravel drive of supreme crunchiness at Bishop Michael's residence. I managed to have a little nap, later in the afternoon and let the three glasses of wine make their way through and out of my system. The stone building, housing probably, the most important Bishop in the UK (at least in the war against evil) is somewhat unremarkable but

111

very old. The stone a welcome home for much of the lichen and moss that adorn the surface. The windows, old and leaded are very pretty but a bit too Gothic for my tastes. Anyway, I am here, as summoned.

Leaving the orange flashing hazard lights in my wake as the immobiliser kicks in on my hot little red number, I walk swiftly to the large door to the Bishop's mansion. It opens as my feet reach the steps. Like magic, I am easily amused, the personal assistant with the sour expression welcomes me to the residence. I bare my teeth at him. Apparently, I am to go right on in. A feeling of deja-vu settles upon me as we have meeting round two with Father Jeremy and his Eminence. I knock and enter in response to the bellow from within.

"Andrew, so glad you could make it. I have taken the liberty of having dinner prepared and plated for you." He motions to a wooden sideboard, upon which sits a dinner. With some sort of decorations around the edges, oh they are green beans. Far too healthy looking but I will have no choice but to devour it. I make my way over to the table where Jezza and the Bish are already ensconced.

It all looks so civilized, like three clergymen meeting for a meal. Well, on the surface that is what it is, it looks ordinary. It's not like this scenario is played out all over the world whenever a few dog collars are gathered together. Father Jeremy seems to be a bit more sociable as he sips a half-full goblet of claret. I look down at my plate, I know I will need to make an effort. Some meat substance in dark gravy, spuds, green beans, it is proper food. The Bishop smiles at me as I start to eat, I have no idea why. I notice he hasn't poured me a glass of the wine yet.

"Andrew, Father Jeremy has been looking at the book. Wherever did you find it?" Bloody pointless question as I have already done this with him on the phone. I manage not to let my sarcasm genes kick in. It must be for Father Jeremy.

"Under a warded floorboard, in the stair cupboard in the manse wrapped in velvet, Bishop." Perfunction at its best. No add ons. Sticking to the facts as I force down the green beans. I

112

hate vegetables and I blame school dinners of the seventies. They were boiled to death until only a tasteless pulp was left; no wonder kids left them most of the time. A glass of Claret has appeared as if by magic.

"Andrew, it is a Grand Grimoire. Only a few of these have ever been recovered." Father Jeremy seems quite excited. I would have been concerned as it proves these guys are serious.

"Which means?" Bishop Michael, gets in before I do and I keep eating. Playing catch up without looking like I am gulping it down. 'Chew Andrew' my mother used to chide me about the rate at which food disappeared.

"It means, your Eminence, that the book gives us an insight that we rarely get. These cultists are no amateurs but a well established and very powerful group." Full of good news I see.

"It seemed to me that there was a dark well of power underneath the manse." Bombshell dropped as I shovel in some more green beans. Both of their heads spin towards me, any faster and they would have had whiplash injuries. I chew on, keeping my mouth tight shut. 'Andrew chew with your mouth closed' was another one I heard regularly.

"There was also a blood worked circle in the lounge, which I started the walk back on. There have been a few pieces of work in that manse." I pick up my claret to have a swig, helps when giving bad news I suppose.

"Andrew, you need to share these things earlier." The Bishop doesn't look impressed. First he doesn't want detail and now he does. Seems picky to me. I do wish he would make up his mind.

"Bishop, I need to visit this manse. There is so much we can learn there." Father Jeremy is all bright eyed and bushy tailed it seems. The bishop is refilling his glass, me too I almost add but think he might not be too happy. Wait until he offers I think.

"Andrew?" He's asking me if I want to take Jezza on a field trip? I decide that I might as well go with the flow and assent. If the Bishop decides I need help I won't be able to refuse.

"Not an issue for me, as I need to complete the walking back of the circle. It isn't a nice place though." I try not to make it sound exciting. Jezza is licking his lips. I hope he will mop up the drool.

"I can come through at the end of next week if that works? I will need a few days to check the previous incumbents and the records. I should be back from Canterbury by then.' I shrug, I don't really care as long as he tells me when he wants to visit.

"It is settled then. Father Jeremy shall visit the manse and we shall take it from there." Bishop Michael tinkles his bell and the dinner fairies will be on their way. Better get on with my dinner and the claret. Have I been stitched up? Probably.

Chapter 23

Sometimes, I don't know why but I get a hankering to just check. You know, personally. That is why I am standing, in the cold, outside the back door of St Margaret-in-the-fields, checking that it is locked. Funnily enough, it isn't. The night is quiet as a tomb and so is the church. So why am I anxious? This door is not overlooked by any of the nearby houses and has easy access without being seen. A thick beech hedge runs down to the main road, offering good cover. An army could march up here and no one would be any the wiser. Okay, maybe not an army but you get the point.

I turn the handle and silently the door slips open. More a case of secret entrance and well-oiled hinges. The hairs on the back of my neck start to stand up, screaming a warning. A heavy drape blocks out any light from inside. I push the drape aside and let the door close behind me. This short passage runs along to the priest's dressing room, funny how I missed it. Hidden in plain sight and all that. It is always surprising what is missed by familiarity or just not seeing it as important. I don't usually have any qualms about entering the house of god but tonight it feels somewhat different. Yes its late, yes I'm sneaking in and yes some shit is going on. Oh for Brotherton and his pockets, or more specifically his torch. I can see the mat but that's about it. At least it doesn't say 'God lives here.' I smirk at my own humour. I should know better but with a dimple in my cheek I slip past the drape and step inside. Shutting the outer door behind me I drop the snib and let Yale guard my back. I may be suspicious but I don't like unlocked doors at my back. I've seen way too many Hammer House of Horror films. I am still not taking any chances, however.

A deep breath later and its time to go. I am a peeker. I like to peek first. I am not about to announce my presence until I know what or who else is here. It always pays to know what kind of shit you are about to step into. The hair on the nape of my neck is caressing and telling me to leave; or at least be careful. I am stuck in that minute between the moments that define everything. I take a breath and pulling up my big girl panties, move into the house of God.

The short corridor, which I am standing at the end of, turns after a few steps. I know this because the office is on my left. I can see light around the corner. Well, I can't see round corners but I can see that a flickering light is round there. Candle apparently. So, with my good sense running for the hills and my inbred stupidity taking over, I sneak like a ninja into the office. It is empty, thank goodness.

I consider calling Brotherton on my life saving cell phone but what would I say 'Brotherton, come quick I'm hiding in the office because there's a candle in the corridor?' Best not, I suppose. Maybe later.

It really takes no time for good sense to evaporate. I sneak, sidle, wall hug and crab-step along the carpet. Not a sound escapes my movement. Chuck Norris, eat your heart out. Wetting my fingertips, I reach down and snuff out the candle. It's a fat black one on a sturdy metal holder, another one further on lights the way. Awfully kind of them. I count the steps, just in case I have to run for it. Wouldn't want to crash into the wall after all.

As I get closer to black candle number two, I hear it. A low murmuring of voices, the words are indistinct but voices nonetheless. They are coming from inside the chapel itself. Is there a little ex-curricular evensong? I think not. As the incumbent, I most certainly do not approve. I could phone now but, like I said, stupidity should never be ruled out as a reason for doing something. Ninja-peeker that I am, I'm going to see who and what is going on. Although I could probably guess. Dennis Wheatley has furnished many a dullard with enough Satanist material to have a fairly good wild stab at it. Remarkably, they wouldn't be far wrong.

I should have run but I peeked through the partially open doorway. Safe in the darkness I have time to get a really good view of the proceedings. I'm a details kinda guy but usually miss the big things. Usually later I can re-picture and recall the whole thing but in the moment I can miss plenty.

I couldn't miss the fact that there is a whole gang of hooded and black robed folks in God's house. I didn't miss the fact that there has been some redecoration. Crux Ansata front and centre, altar has had a make over, its like a satellite TV house doctor show in here with faux fur throws and scatter cushions all over the floor. Oh yes and a pale skinned, rather fit, naked woman is spread eagled on the altar. See, I told you I miss things. Her head is hanging off the far end so I will have to wait to identify her. The incoherent mumbling still fills the air, no idea what is being said, probably Latin though.

"Brothers and Sisters" I practically jump out of my skin. One of them, with a phantom of the opera mask on, steps up behind the altar. It's show-time then. I hadn't expected a front row seat at the Satanic gathering of the month. My mind was rolling through significant dates on the calendar but I could hang this service on no saint day or significant day in the year. Perhaps this is just a weekly or monthly thing. It certainly doesn't fit with the known Satanic dates.

"Tonight we are gathered to feast. Before us is an offering to sustain us in our cause." He scans his little gang. I try to count them and get to about ten but there might be another one. A right dirty dozen. I wonder if he is the one who spiked my room. We'll see but I can't feel anything mystical or supernatural yet. Seems to be a load of middle class wannabes who want to dabble and get a little thrill. That and eternal damnation, obviously.

"Our Sister offers her flesh to bring us power; Our Master blesses us in our cause." He sweeps a hand over the altar and bows his head at the 'Our Master' bit. I find myself a little distracted by the view, she obviously waxes. I don't think it's cold either.

"Tonight, Our Master" (another nod), 'will fill us with power.

The power to smite and drive away our enemy.' I presume he means me. I have never been the object of a special Satanic ritual; makes me feel kinda important. I doubt that he will be listening to their pleas. I am a little rapt by the show unfolding before me.

"Through lust give us power. Through Blood give us power and through deception make us strong. Let us erode the Latin Plague on the people of the Horned God." He has a powerful voice and a sense of theatre; he draws a curved blade across his forearm dripping blood all over her breasts. A sinister sight in the candlelight. With a swift tug at a cord his robe falls away. His mangy little flock do the same, hoods and masks still cover their faces.

Some images etch themselves indelibly on the mind, for me its nude women that have that effect. There are four I can see but now they are all moving around the altar. Car crash viewing at its best. I should leg it now but all my good sense left the building ages ago. They are moving round the altar counter clockwise, left hands entwined.

Their glorious leader, erect now, stands at the head end with his arms raised like horns as they pass round him. Like an adult game of ring-a-roses. They are mumbling again. If this were a Hollywood film then all the bodies would be toned and buff. It isn't and they aren't. Beer bellies and cellulite adorn the players. I am sure I have a Polaroid of a few of them somewhere. Are these just middle aged swingers with a twist? A new thrill? Well they're following enough clichés to be playing at it.

The smell of incense, same as I use, fills my nostrils as they start to caress the female offering. The excitement is building, if the male members are anything to go by, as they continue to circle. They bob (the men), and wobble (some of the women) as they build up pace, moving faster around the offering. The stroking and touching smears the blood all over her breasts, a mimic of a real sacrifice. Their symbolism is consistent, whoever is organising this is no fool. I feel a tightening band around my head. They are raising power, lots of power.

118

Through a gap in the flesh I see the Offering's mouth is filled with the Celebrant's member. Around the altar the pace picks up once more, they are circling faster and faster as he thrusts in time deep into her throat. One by one they genuflect and place their mouths on her freshly waxed genitals, her writhing testament to their facile tongues. I am distracted, never having actually observed a working, and should have left ages ago. St Margaret-in-the Fields has a satanic cult as a lodger. This has happened to churches before but this cult is for real. They are not playing at it, these aren't petty dabblers. This is a long established cult residing in the, rather ordinary, New Town Church of St Margaret's in the Fields.

I can feel the power of the sex magic thickening the air. It's almost like drowning or trying to breathe underwater. Closing my eyes and gulping in some air, I try to get control. They seem to be nearing a crescendo, only one of them is being filled with power I think. The Circle will get only earthly pleasure as a reward. The power is heavy and potent; making the darkness around me deeper and the pressure in my head feel like a vice.

I notice that they each stop to plant kisses on their master's behind as their circle spins. I like sex, I find it fascinating but this magic, sex and blood, is making me ill. I can't identify any of them and unless we have a naked Eucharist on Sunday, their identities are safe for now. I need to leave but I know I have waited too long. My feet feel like they are rooted to the spot and my legs like wood. I cannot leave now, even though I want to.

"Master" his supplication fills the room with power as he splatters the Offering's chest with his seed. It's like a thunderclap inside my head and I know I'm fainting. Fuck. Fuck, fuckitty-fuck.

I am so foggy this morning that even the opening of my eyes is a Herculean task. I ache all over like a stampede of hairy highland cows has passed over me. Perhaps I had fallen asleep, or passed out pissed, on a drovers trail. I can't have been that pissed as I am undressed and in bed as opposed to the more traditional fully-clothed collapse on top of the sumptuously-soft motel bed. I have no recollection of anything, however.

The curse of whisky is the blackouts. The gaps in the memory and the inability to recall precisely what happened. Going by the strength of this hangover, a good night was, certainly, had by all. In fact, the lassitude that I feel would suggest a very late night was had and a further spell in slumberland is the order of the day. I blink at my wrist to find my watch has escaped and is just a few feet away adorning the bedside cabinet. I must have been utterly gone because I rarely take my chronograph off. Why I am so obsessed by knowing the time is a deep rooted psychological problem from childhood, I expect. That, however, would be the tiniest issue a psychologist would find if rooting around in my mind. It is not a place to explore for the uninitiated.

Everything feels so heavy as I seek to move across the bed to get my watch. My pubes are matted and my balls sticky. Not a pleasant sensation, so there was sex too? What a night to have no recollection of. This is so unfair, I am paying the consequence and I can't enjoy the sin. My bladder is telling me to move and if I know one thing, I know that it pays to obey. A few groans escape me as I lurch to the bathroom. The harsh strip light over the mirror lancing into my eyes and spearing my brain. My head feels like a split may occur any second. I am wrecked.

I sit on the throne, head in my hands and bemoaning my misery. Keeping my eyes shut is a good idea, I think. This is the emperor of all morning afters. What was I thinking? I readily admit I, probably, wasn't. What a bloody idiot. Even in this state I try to work out what appointments I have and what I can reschedule. It is now that I realise a piece of information is truly eluding me. What day is it?

Ablutions over, I look, through slitted eyelids, in the mirror. I look pale and this light isn't helping. Covering my chest is a series of bruises, and lower down too. There are more, low on my stomach and around my groin. Bruises? Love bites, what a blooming mess. A hungry vampire has suckled all over me and I can't recall a second of it. I have never had such a complete blackout covering events that I might have enjoyed. Something feels very wrong. Sharp, I am not.

The moment when realisation starts to dawn, is a horrible time. If I wasn't pissed then what the fuck happened to me? I need a shower, perhaps that will clear some of the aches and defog my brain. I doubt that it will but I will give it a go. A hot shower cascading and pummelling on my head as I stand immobile is slowly reawakening my cognitive functions. My arms are braced against the wall like Atlas I am shouldering a massive weight; the weight of ignorance and fear. A million what-if scenarios are buzzing around in my fevered imagination. My body has been used. How, exactly, I am unsure but spent would describe it pretty effectively.

Eventually I turn off the hot water and allow a moment of cold to caress me into life. Shock is a better description. It works and I step out on to the tiles, with the attendant little slip. I see my reflection and it is not a pretty sight. Neck hickies above the dog collar line, for fucks sake. I look down my reflection to assess the extent of my hickification. I count twelve on the front and one just at the base of my spine. Thirteen in all. Thirteen! A working, most definitely. How the fuck did that happen?

"Oh fuck." I start to check my body for aches, more specifically puncture wounds. I hope they haven't taken my blood. If they are amateurs then I might be lucky. They aren't and I'm not. I find a hypodermic puncture in my right arm. The size of this calamity is growing by the second. How on earth I will explain this to the bishop I have no idea. Impressed he will not be. I think that might be the least of my worries.

"You get me into so much trouble." I say addressing my penis and giving it a waggle. I notice a bald patch in the now de-matted pubes. Blood, semen, pubes – what else have they got? The shit-meter has gone into the 'very-deep' shit category. Meaning totally submerged in the shit storm to come. My demeanour is one of totally pissed-offed-ness as I scowl at my reflection. My phone ringing draws me from my staring contest. I shamble through to answer the call, my legs and hands not quite working but after only a few excruciatingly painful rings I manage to answer.

'Steel.' Just about, anyway.

"Andrew? Are you all right? You sound different." A pause, "Have you been drinking?" Bishop Michael worries that I will backslide again, bless him. He has every right to worry. When he rescued me, I had a whisky tolerance that would stun a rugby team and was heading to the very early exit from this life. With it would have gone the gift that God gave to me. Bishop Michael cleaned me up, well he had others do it but you get the idea.

"Yes, no, no." I am being unhelpful. It was three questions wasn't it? I could barely stand vertically as I slumped beside the bed, using it to stiffen my backbone and keep me semi-upright.

"What has occurred?" Bishop Michael continues. You or I would have said 'What has happened?' but Bishops aren't like the rest of us. They really aren't.

"I have been worked. I have no idea how or by whom. I need help." I sound tired, even to me. The words are slow and slightly slurred at the edges.

"Oh good gracious." He sounds shocked. See I told you they aren't like us. "Andrew are you safe?" An odd question.

"Well I have just woken up and had a shower." I begin at the beginning. "I am covered in love bites, have had multiple ejaculations, am missing a patch of pubic hair and have had blood taken." I pause. "Apart from that and no recollection of events whatsoever, I am just peachy." Too much detail? Probably. Now he knows as much as I do.

"Oh Dear Lord, Andrew. You might be in terrible danger. What can I do to help?" Wow, no questions about it being my fault. Supportive, I am unused to.

"I need purged and cleansed. Can you arrange it? Tomorrow, if possible." I need serious help, I need whatever they have done to me cleared up. I need the equivalent of 400cc of penicillin to clear the clap, and I need it soon. There is no shortcut to getting me out of this mess. There is no sure-fire way to break any hold they may have established over me.

"I will get it organised. I'll call you back." And he's gone, A Bish on a Mish, I laugh at the idea. I stop quickly as my head reminds me how much of a hangover I have. I flick on the television, in a vain hope that I can reconnect with the current date and time. A few flicks and the BBC tell me it is Tuesday and after one in the afternoon. Don't care about any of the headlines to be honest. I am blank on all of Monday and can only vaguely remember the Eucharist on Sunday. Well and truly wiped, then. Almost Men in Black standard, I haven't looked at any pens recently. I smile at my own humour.

Waking up naked, in a hotel room, covered in love-bites and having no memory of it sounds so rock and roll. Not exactly the sort of thing that the seminary prepares you for. My buzzing, noisy friend calls me back to the here and now.

"That was quick." I am almost happy sounding. Relieved probably.

"Listen Nazarene, we have you. We own you. Get out now, or else." Menace successfully delivered. I feel a cold chill run over me. Goosebumps and my hair standing on edge evidence of a change in temperature. Being naked and slightly damp may be a factor but I doubt it. I am in deep.

"Who is this?" When in doubt, be indignant. A very British response. It often throws people off their stride, not today though.

"Feeling cold Priest? What about now?" I feel a flush of

heat emanate from the centre of my back and roll round my body. A cruel laugh bursts from the phone.

"You are ours. Leave or die." The final words spat out and full of malice. I am truly worried now. I can just about see the sadistic sod playing with his effigy of me. Coated in my blood, semen and hair. What's next? A pin in the doll making me scream in agony. I pick up my rosary, wrapping the beads around my right hand. I need to respond, last word syndrome. It has often gotten me into trouble but I need it now.

"I don't think so. Do your baddest." Anything can happen now as I await a pain that doesn't come. Instead a stiffening in my groin as my flaccid friend starts to grow. I can't believe it. Whatever he is doing controls my very function. In a few heartbeats I am at full mast. I need to break this link. I hang up.

"Like hell you will." I am not giving in to these bastards. I begin to recite the creed of Nicea, the core articles of all our faiths. I regain control of my body. Now I am truly worried. The Bishop better hurry the fuck up.

Chapter 25

It sounds so nice, Cleansing. Like some sort of new age tai-chi bollocks. It isn't. It leaves me drained and emptied out. I don't know what they did to me and after this I will know. Well, actually, I will get the joy of re-experiencing it again. I haven't needed a cleansing in the last decade. It's not like a nice cosy confessional with an 'Ego te absolve' kind of thing. Oh well, the car is here and the roller coaster ride is about to begin.

When I told Bishop Michael to hurry up, he was as good as his word and the car has taken less than an hour to turn up here. It is a big black Volvo, all utilitarian and efficient. The leather seats look nice though. It isn't the Bishop's official car, more a workhorse for days like this. The driver nods as I get in and we are off. He says nothing as I sit and mumble my way through a few prayers. I want to keep control until I am safe. Bastards have really spooked me out. While I might look calm to the outside, my innards are doing a tango.

I feel a caress over my skin. I am alone but know they are trying to reconnect the link. Sex magicians then. They seem to know how to work inside my defences. I have faltered in my recitations of holy creeds and they have reconnected. Fuck. I bite my lip and the sharp pain clears my mind momentarily, just enough to begin again. The fact that I am moving is probably helping me escape their grasp.

I mumble louder and it seems that my mumbles are connected to the accelerator as the car speeds along the new link road, no screaming fan-belt, more a powerful growl as we pass car after car. We seem to be doing about a hundred miles an hour. I appreciate his candour but I want to get there alive. The bridge over the Forth is under our tyres and the attempted link is gone. Rivers, it seems, are a barrier that works on more than vampires. I take a deep breath, hold then let it out. Relaxing one-oh-one in action. More like a knackered Thank God that's over but you get the idea. I collapse back against the leather every muscle sagging, seat belt holding me roughly in place.

It feels that in no time we have pulled in to the gravel drive and I am being escorted to the door. Magically the door opens as I put my foot on the bottom step, who knew it was magic. I smile at my own idiotic thoughts. The flunky holds the door for me. Even he looks worried.

"Father Andrew, you are to proceed downstairs immediately, all is ready for you." Proceed, what a formal load of nonsense. Go for Fucks Sake, Go. What are you a fucking policeman? I almost scream at him.

"Thank you." I so can't be arsed flunky-baiting. I have been through this before, so there are no surprises. The stairs down are stone and unadorned, a nice little spiral stairway to the underworld. Perhaps another world would be more accurate. Medieval looking and solid, they have seen many a priestly traveller and offer only a reminder that the Church is old and has many, many secrets.

As I reach the bottom I step into the modern world. A fully fitted out secret lair resides beneath the palace. The stone walls the only real reminder of the age of this place. In front of me a dark haired thirty-something Lady Doctor in her pristine white lab coat waits for me. This is very different from the last time.

"Father Andrew, remove all your garments then step over here, please." No small talk then? No screen either. Modesty it seems will not be required. She is new, to me at least, and she is all efficiency. She is pretty, however, and that always helps. The unpeeling of my clothes begins. I notice it isn't cold in the room, funny that. I am glad, for lots of reasons. She is waiting and studying my manly physique as I get undressed, she shows no emotion as I finally remove the boxers that cover my bits. Hands are designed specifically for covering one's bollocks when naked.

"Where do you want me?" A little levity never hurt. Is that a little twitch of her lips, a beginning of a smile? Nope, crashed and burned. She has a solid professional look that drives out my poor attempts at mood lightening but I will keep trying anyway.

"Arms out at shoulder height, legs apart at hip width, please." She is walking round now, pen flying on her clip board. I comply, as failure to do so might lead to worse things.

"I don't need to cough do I?" I think I am funny, apparently she doesn't. She is looking at the love bites with some sort of red light. A magnifying glass mystically appears and she is peering at me, closely.

'These are from thirteen different mouths.' She isn't speaking to me as she starts writing. She is frowning a little and writes some more. The rubbing sound of her sleeve on the clipboard sounds loud in the silence that fills this room. I can't even hear the hum of the fan on the computers.

"What?" I try to sound unconcerned, but fail miserably. I know that this is serious and I have been lucky to escape their grasp.

"There are hypodermic punctures in each one. As well as the one in your arm." She walks to the stainless-steel trolley-tray thing and returns with a swab thing and starts swiping over the hickies. She is very efficient and there is no stirring as she works near my groin, thank goodness. I jump as she unexpectedly lifts my penis and swipes all over it. It is bloody cold. The peeling of foreskin and swipe around is dispassionate and I focus clearly on a speck on the wall.

"This will smart a bit." She is still holding my Penis and she isn't kidding. The heat from the insertion of a rod into my urethic opening is unpleasant and requires a deep breath. That was only half of it; the scraping of the little umbrella is intense.

"You will need treatment for all known STDs just in case, but this swab will identify any actual infections." Oh joy of joys, just what I need. Serves the little fella right; he has been getting me into trouble for years.

Anyway she lets go of my now brutalised member and stands before me, light test on my eyes and a few other doctor like things. I tune out as she concludes her examination, which involves a few utterly pointless pokes and prods. She brings a camera over and the flash startles me. I wasn't expecting that.

"I hope you got my good side and zoomed in." I try to be funny but fail, once more. I sound like I have body issues, which I don't but I don't want full frontals of my body being posted anywhere. Not even in her Occult Doctors Quarterly.

"I have zoomed in on the bruises for reference purposes. Your modesty is safe Father." She smiles gently with a little imp-like dimple. Not an Ice maiden after all. She is pretty and underneath I can feel her sympathy for my ordeal. She hands me a paper suit onesie to wear and points to the door.

"The Bishop will meet you in there soon."

In my white paper onesie, I make my way through a rather ordinary looking door into a stone hewn corridor leading to a private chapel. Who built this and when I have no idea, but it is old and the paper feet are doing nothing to keep out the chill. It is a holy place, and one where many have prayed (and probably received) divine inspiration. I hope so. It is here that I will begin the process of my cleansing. Upon the wall a crucifix, looks down at me and I can feel the emanation from it. Power, pure power for good. A few kneeler mats lie against the rough wall and the candles that illuminate the room are fat and white, proud on plain wooden holders sunk into the floor.

"Andrew." The bishop joins me. His voice filling my ears but not loud enough to be a shout. The tone is formal and serious. This is not a routine thing and we need this to cleanse me of their influence.

"Bishop." Great small talk. In fact I don't want to speak in here, it seems wrong somehow. This is not a room for idle chatter and pointless words. I turn round and see that he has brought a jug and cup. Obviously water. He hands them to me, genuflects to the Crucifix and leaves. He will be back at dawn, when the long night has been passed.

I will be alone in here, with water and nothing else until tomorrow where my excoriation will begin. I have time to reflect and time to come to terms with what has happened to me. I strip off the paper onesie and select a padded kneeler. I approach the crucifix with eyes downcast and position myself at his feet. The plain red kneeler, the colour of blood, in recognition of his gift of sacrifice will have permanent dents after this I expect. My usual irreverence is stowed away as I contemplate the sacrifice of our Lord and the ordeal of the cross.

The long night has begun and I silently begin to pray. I know that this connection and sanctuary will be vital in removing the enchantment laid upon me. It is only by reaching a purifying zen-like state that I will be able to move forward. The silence is crushing and my ears can pick out the tiniest flickering of sound from the candles as they mark the passage of time. The early onset numbing through my knees is another measure. I used to be able to stay kneeling for hours at a stretch but nowadays the discomfort sets in early. I will need to change position early and often. Middle age and all that. It isn't the age it is the mileage.

I hope that by silencing the worldly noise and bustle I will be able to find memories locked deep inside of what was done to me. By finding out what they did I will be able to work against them. So far the numb knees are pulling my attention and making that inner silence difficult to find. I wonder if I should lie down? Perhaps not. I drink the first cup of water from a pewter cup and wonder how often this is used or is it a special cup for those who need this place.

Everything slows and the silence becomes total. While I may indeed be an irreverent wise-ass, this place is one which truly removes any desire to be so. I reconnect my body, my thinking and embrace the power that has grown in this place over the years. Holy men have prayed here, and I am the least of them. The redemption of the sinner is for those like me. My acceptance is total but then again, I have proof everyday of the eternal struggle of Good and Evil, so it is a simple matter really. I try to roll back the steps and actions of the past few days, from arriving here and the journey over in the car to the discovery and hopefully I can extract something from this fog.

Sounds come to me, not pictures yet, and it is as if I am

muffled and only maddening little half word sounds are crawling out of my memory. Perhaps I was hooded? That might explain it. I try further back to find an image or a feeling. It feels like an age has passed when I am startled by an image. Vivid and sharp.

She is above me, masked, and riding my cock as I am held down. There are many hands holding me. Blonde hair spills past her phantom of the opera mask and her rather fantastic figure is a sight to behold. There is some chanting going on too. I jump, as if shocked to see this event of my recent past and then ephemeral it slips away from me and try as I might it will not come back. It wasn't Angela Brookes though, the breasts were totally different. Very nice, but different nonetheless.

Chapter 26

All through the night, I try and try to pull out more memories but there is a very definite hand brake there. A wall if you will, and only one look beyond this barrier was afforded me. Even then it was a fleeting, tantalising little glimpse of little real use in identifying any of the cultists. I hope it was a real memory and not a composite of fantasy. He isn't known as the prince of deception for nothing. I try not to fight to catch the image that is just out of reach.

The water is long finished and a drouth (as they say in these parts) is upon me. I am thirsty, sore and bloody knackered. The candles are guttering and making a racket. My heightened senses identified that the candle nearest the door has just gone out. All is now dark, or are my eyes closed. Who knows? It is the former as I try to stare around the room. What time or day it is I have no real idea, except that the Bishop will return at dawn for me. I hope he doesn't sleep in.

Often as one sense is denied another takes over, or so they say, I stare deep into the blackness of the chapel. Amazing what you can see when there is no light. Another little glimpse is coming, I can feel it. Tantalisingly close now, almost able to taste it. A thunderous noise behind me as the door is pulled open, jolts me back to the here and now. As loud as the rolling away of the stone that sealed the tomb of Our Lord. The flooding light searing my eyes ending my Long Night.

"Behold, I am the Light!" The Bishop's voice is strong and full of power. Who knew the old dog had that in him. "Andrew, return to the light. Night is passing. It is a new day. Walk in the light with the Lord.' His crook in one hand and his hand outstretched to take mine. Like a little lost sheep returning to my shepherd, I rise and stumble towards him. A rebirth, as it were.

Now begins the scouring and cleansing of my soul and the physical vessel in which it resides. Holy unction adorns my brow, the fingers of the Bishop making the sign of the cross, forever marking me as one of God's flock. The ring proffered to my lips is kissed swearing fealty to God and his church on earth. His benediction calls the blessing of the Father, Son and Holy Spirit on this poor strayed prodigal. I can feel the heat suffuse my limbs and fill my heart with joy. Who says there is no magic in this earthly world? It is here all right. We seem to have lost the means to find it.

I follow his crook as he leads me to another room with a massage table whose legs are set into the floor. Four Priests come forward and lead me to my position. Face down with manacles holding my naked body to the table. It is about to begin. My face can see the floor and the padding is almost comfortable. I know what is next so I am anything but relaxed. Excruciating it will be. The driving out of any evil ties to me will take time and involves making the host body so uncomfortable that the malice is driven out. In the middle ages whips and chains would have been de rigueur, thank goodness for progress.

Silence reigns for a second and then eight hands full of coarse grained salt start to rub all over my back, legs, shoulders and buttocks. Which might have been simply uncomfortable soon becomes unbearable as they scour and scrub my tender flesh. There are no areas exempt from this harsh handed rubbing and before long I realise it is my voice I can hear screaming in agony. There seems to be no stopping and this is only the back. My face and genitals will be subject to this too. I just want it to stop and stop soon. Sweat is running down my face and dripping off the tip of my nose. There are tears running just as quickly, even though my eyes are scrunched shut. Searing heat is running from my feet, all the way along my body as my feet are being treated now. I would have told everything by now, had there been questions to answer.

Limp as a dish-rag, I lie there whimpering, sobs racking my chest as I can't get a breath. For how long I lie there, I have no idea but I am being turned over and my respite is over. They begin again. I don't know if it is worse to see my brothers of the cloth rubbing and sweating as they labour over my flesh or to have had the view of the floor. I try to focus on the ceiling but soon I am floating on a sea of torment as nerve endings all over me scream in protest at the treatment of salt. Dead Sea salt, apparently, the only suitable salt for this job. Dark Magic doesn't like it, so rumour states. I know I bloody don't. All at once the restraints are loosed and I curl foetus-like and sob my way to insensibility.

Strong hands raise me from the table and carry me, unresisting and barely conscious, to another place. I am lowered into an ice bath that almost causes my heart to stop. My throat constricts and I cannot pull air into my lungs. Never mind the sensory overload that is assaulting my brain. A long silent scream passes my lips and my rigid body is held tight. The bumping cubes alongside my face are almost too much to bear. I am ducked under the water and I choke and splutter as my still open mouth fills with ice cold water. I am brought to the surface, cough and pull air in gulping like a landed fish. Under, again I am forced, as they hold me tight to the course. Thrashing and struggling in their grip, I am submerged again and again. The shivering is uncontrollable and I think my bladder has emptied. I am losing any connection to my body as the toll of the purging is paid.

I am pulled out of the water and the cold air feels even more so, as I am carried elsewhere. Chattering and chittering my teeth are battering off of one another. I will need dentistry if this keeps up. My neck and jaw aches from being clenched so hard. Actually there isn't a single part of me that doesn't register as being in pain. Even my hair hurts. I am a miserable wreck of a human being and I know we are not done yet.

After the cold, I am to be sweated. The steam room then sauna that the Bishop had installed is perfect for just this type of thing. You know, torture. While I am coming back to the land of normality from scrubbing and flash freezing, the steam room is almost unbearable and I know worse will come as I am taken into the hot box. Who knew removing enchantments was like treating a sprain. Hot and cold treatment until improved. The warming of my body is welcome as I stop shivering and the teeth have, in fact, survived. I am washed out and nearly catatonic. The Sauna is pulling sweat from my pores in rivers, making the salty fluid aggravate my sensitised nerve endings. I moan as my misery is complete. Would whips and chains have been better? If I have to do this again I will be asking.

It is bad enough to have been foolish and to have fallen between the sinful thighs of an adulteress. It is much worse to have confessed your actions to the Father Confessor, who looks like the very notion of any earthly pleasure, would be anathema. His disapproval really strikes home the levels of my stupidity and the need to be fulsome in my contrition is not in any doubt. My sins are many and the questions surrounding them are pastoral and about my relationship with The Almighty. No vicarious thrill seeking from this Priest, he is worried about my relationship with God and my self-destructive tendencies.

"Why do you resist the path that Our Father has laid before you? You have powers to use for the good of His flock and yet you rebel at every turn. You must seek the answer within yourself, my son." Buggered if I know might once have been my response but today after an exhausting night my witty responses have all vanished like a sale of Château Neuf de Pape in Tesco.

"The powers of darkness beset us at every turn and we aren't winning." I manage to mumble. My desolation after last night is almost all consuming. The building blocks of my Id have been disassembled and are now down to me to reassemble.

"My Son, the powers of the Enemy that assail us are as nothing before the power of our Heavenly Father. Your trials and tests are harsh and rightly so." His sympathy for my burden, is appreciated but I don't quite get where he is coming from. My silence leads him on.

"Faith, that is the difference." He stops, and waits. I am

meant to join the dots myself. It is a struggle. Maybe my ordeal has left me slightly slow. It seems that the lack of a need for faith, having proof already, is the root of my behaviour. I know that the Almighty exists, no doubt. Absolute knowledge. Most people struggle with uncertainty and that leads to undesirable behaviours. My problem is that I know I am already in the shit up to my ears so take a somewhat cavalier attitude in my actions. He tells me that I abuse this knowledge like a spoiled child. He is right but I don't really want to be told such. I will have, I don't doubt, hours of penance to do before I am absolved. I wait for the sentence and wonder just how many our Fathers or Hail Mary prayers will be needed.

"Ego te absolve a peccatis tuis." The magic words wiping my slate clean, once more. I am utterly stunned that he has decided my repentance is complete at this stage. There is more but I have paid my penance and now can be on my way. If only it were to be so simple. I have a couch session to go yet, more self analysis and a great big dollop of angst. Freud will be sitting in, analysing my bloody awful relationship with my mother.

Chapter 27

Dim light, a nice soft leather couch and another person in the room, not in my line of sight but I know they are there. Obviously it's time to talk about my mother. Or perhaps it's my childhood and my early fumbled sexual encounters. I have, what can only be called an overriding, contempt for psycobabblists, or whatever they are are known as. Psychoterrorists, or something like that. Analyse that. Fuck's sake there's elevator music coming from somewhere. Now, over the last 12 hours or so I have been broken down to my most basic level and wrung out. Stomped by a herd of theological elephants and scoured to within an inch of my sanity, and now I have to endure a session of this nonsense.

"You know that psychoanalysis doesn't work on the Irish, they are immune." Let's start with a joke and play nice. I try to take the tension from my voice.

"Father Andrew, it says here you are Scottish, from Fife. Not Irish." A humour bypass in action. A woman though, so all looking up a bit. I much prefer spilling my guts to a woman. Although she won't understand the half of it.

"Really? Who knew." I stare up at the ceiling anyway. If I am expecting some sort of inspiration from the emulsioned surface above me I might have a very long wait.

"Do you know why we are talking?" She asks gently. I wondered that very thing myself. As far as waste of time goes, psychoanalysis is right up there as far as I am concerned.

"Because silence is difficult?" I really can't be arsed. Let's see where that goes. I wonder if my notes say churlish and childish.

"'Is silence difficult?" Oh For fuck's sake. I wait, surly child time. She must have a great deal of patience or be being paid by the hour at an exorbitant rate to put up with this.

"We are trying to unlock your memories and see if we can discover what happened when you were under an enchantment." She is taking no shit from me, might just be calling her Ma'am by the end. It might be just what I need.

"Shall we begin?" Not really a question more a command, couched like I have a choice. The muzak goes off. A period of silence descends over the space between us. "What is the last thing you remember before the black out?"

"Locking up the vestry and heading back to my lousy travel Inn. Where I woke up later." I pause. So does she. I am to continue, obviously.

"No wait I don't think that's right." I am surprised because I am trying to remember and I think I constructed that from what I should have been doing. "I remember something else. A blue car that nearly rear ended me at the roundabout. He was shouting until he saw the dog collar. That was on the way back from Eucharist." Wowsers, how much has been wiped?

"OK, lets try something. It is a deep breathing exercise. It will create an environment in which we can dig deeper. Breathe in for seven counts and out for eleven counts. We will do this for twenty repeats. Begin." I presume the we, is so I don't feel a pratt. She won't be doing them with me. I start the count. I doubt I will manage to keep track. Twenty is a lot of fingers, might need to take my socks off. I start, as she breaks the silence, her voice probably no more than a whisper. She is close by and it is wholly dark. Have I dozed off.

"It's time. Let's walk our way forward from the car incident.' Her voice is soft and runs into my ears like desert sand.

"These are things that are passed and can harm you no more. Release the memories from the prison you have built to keep them from you." She slides on and lets the words sink in.

"I built the prison?" I am somewhat incredulous. If I wasn't so chilled out I might object. I feel that arguing is so not worth the effort and I let it go.

"It's your mind. You decide what you remember and what you forget. Open the door and look inside. These memories cannot hurt you. They are passed." She stops and waits again. The darkness and quiet seem somehow a comfort to me.

I choose to forget do I? Well that's a new one. I try to recall what happened after the arse in the blue car. Nada, zip, hee-haw.

"Imagine if you can a prison door, locked before you." She waits, assuming I am compliant. "Look down at your hand, see the keys. Put the key in the lock. Turn it and open the door." I try. A medieval dungeon door stands before me and in my hand I have a big fucking black iron key, I insert the key and turn. By God we are in.

I don't know if you have seen the matrix but like Neo I am flying like superman through a battery of mundanity that filled the hours of my day that Sunday Afternoon. For some reason, I wanted to check out the church that night. What was I thinking? No idea, but then again it might come to me sooner or later.

I watch in vivid HD technicolour the satanic working and the coven's enjoyment of their naked sacrifice. I remember passing out as the Celebrant splattered his jism all over the naked breasts of the willing hottie. I also remember the floor coming up to greet me as I passed out. What on earth was I doing waiting that long? What happened next?

"Can you recall anything since the blue car?" I hear her voice coaxing me forward. I am not inclined to explain the movie I have just watched, especially not the full on naughty bits.

"Yes. There was a satanic working in the church and I passed out." Minimalist stuff, eh? Would it be worth mentioning the oral sex or the hot sacrifice on the altar? Probably not needed this time. I am sure she really doesn't need to know.

"Then what Andrew? This next bit is important." Her voice is like smooth oil sliding across my skin under soft hands. Is she a mystic too? I wonder. It seems I want to tell her though. It is like a brain massage under gentle fingers.

"I am lying on the altar." It's pouring out now, I can't and don't want to stop it. Like a pus boil, it needs squeezed until it's all gone. This is the poison that was set in my system.

"They are all around me, chanting and I can't move. They

are holding me down. They are aroused and excited and even though they have masks I can feel their fervour." I am so coherent it surprises me. It is like I am detached and removed from these memories, dispassionate, almost. The censor has left the building, taking my embarrassment with it.

"I am unresisting, I think. They have undressed me." I feel it necessary to explain I am nude on the altar. "I am fondling the genitals as they circle past. I don't think I am in any sort of control. The actions are wooden and like I am a puppet." It seems as if I was the second course of sex magic on that evening.

"You have done nothing wrong. Focus on what was going on. Details, if you can." She prompts gently, and I want to deliver, her goodwill all that matters just now. It is like I need her approval and assurance that I am guiltless on this. I was the victim and it isn't a role I play well.

"They are caressing me, getting me ready for sex." I can feel my blushes starting even now. I know I was not in control but I am still embarrassed. I need to carry on with this.

"One of the fatter women has mounted me, rubbing her slick pussy all over my face. I am writhing trying to get away." I hope I was trying to get away anyway. There are so many of them and my body is overwhelmed as I am the object of their sexual attack.

"There are hands and mouths all over me as she is grinding on my mouth. I am being ridden too." I am not telling the half of it but I am sure she understands that. Like any regression therapy, I am reliving the event and the tent in my trousers is a source of embarrassment for the future. I am so glad it is dark in here.

"Go on." No inflection, just a request. The silence that fills up the space between us feels long but is probably less than a minute as I pull myself through the ordeal.

"They are using me, I can't see who but there are a number of them. The one over my face is blocking any sight of what is going on. My body is betraying me repeatedly. I have no idea how long it is going on." I know that those using my member have been both male and female and I feel sick at the thought.

"Move forward, what next?" She is getting me out of there

and I appreciate it. I don't need to dwell in that place. I let out a long shuddering breath that sounds shaky, even to me.

"They are sucking me, all over." I guess that this is where I got the marks that so decoratively cover my flesh. Bastards.

"I can see the many heads buried against me." I am disconnected from the event. I see a face. One of them looked up as I looked down. I will know him next time. Got you, you bastard.

"My head is pulled back over the edge of the altar, I can't see anything. It has gone dark, I think I have been hooded." I lie. I am not telling anyone of the use of my mouth and throat by their Priest. Revenge is a deal best served cold. I will be cutting off his cock if I get the chance; law or no law.

"What can you hear?" She isn't letting me off that easily. She knows I am holding out and she is probing.

"Laughter. Cruel and harsh." They seem to have enjoyed my degradation. Like I said, vengeance is mine and it is coming.

Chapter 28

The buzzing sensation in my pocket was an unexpected pleasure. If only it would vibrate for much, much longer. I pull it out to see that Angela is the caller. No surprises any longer with modern technology, oh for the old days when a phone call was a mystery.

"Hello." I speak quietly into the microphone. I am not sure that I should do anything with her. My skin still glowing from the massive exfoliation a few days ago. I am almost back to normal but don't need this right now.

"'You need to meet me now." Her voice sounded a little strange. I decided to be gentle with the refusal. I need to keep my distance.

"Tempting, as it sounds, I have a few things to do today.' Playfully rejecting the offer of a nooner; you know lunchtime sex. After all I have been cleansed and it wouldn't do to fall at the first fence. I want to keep myself out of trouble.

"They'll hurt me if you don't." There are tears in her voice; changing the scenario from salacious to dangerous. I can feel the fury building in me, my vengeance has not been wrought yet. Perhaps this is the first outing of my revenge on these bastards.

"Who will? Who has you?" I am already moving from the Priest's desk and on my way to the rescue, although I don't know where to go yet. If only I had a white stallion to ride in on.

"They will, you know who They are." Abruptly the receiver is pulled from her. The sound of force being used can be heard in the background. I feel my grip tighten on my phone, whitening my knuckles.

"Come on Priest, you don't want your playmate to feel the bite of my monster." A voice that spawned many sinister villains crawls out into my ear. This one sounds like the real deal, not the pretenders I have heard before.

"Where? When?" I spit into the phone. There's no point in denying Angela Brookes is important to me. I am asking myself how far will I go for her safety? After all she was one of MacPhail's partners too.

"Kirkcaldy. Old Sea-view car park. At the back overlooking the beach. We'll be waiting. Come alone." Cold, flat and obviously an utter bastard. What I will do when I get there I have no idea. It isn't like I can beat them up; not really my bag.

"I'll be there." I want to add 'you little shit' but Angela's muffled cry of pain distracts me. The line goes dead. My face contorts in that silent For Fucks Sake look. I really have no idea where we are going to go now. They have ratcheted up the level of threat. I must be getting closer to something. I have at best a tenuous grasp of what has been going on. Organ smuggling but a distinct lack of proof or a working hypothesis. Locking the church doors and extracting my car keys, I will soon be on my way to a dangerous liaison. Not the one I had expected just moments earlier.

Should I phone Brotherton? And say what? The Bastards have kidnapped my girlfriend and then have to cover all the disappointing details of my sordid affair. Fuck that. I will text him if I get into trouble. They aren't likely to kill me in broad daylight. Run me out of town maybe. I wonder what on earth they have in mind. Another knee in the nuts? A faint ache, as if in memory of the event, fills my stomach. I will be nice and compliant to get Angela out of danger. We can get even later. Revenge is a dish best served cold and all that. I am building up a banquet of paybacks for the future.

It is lunchtime so we should be fine, with other people about and using the car park. In a few minutes I am arriving in Kirkcaldy, birthplace of Adam smith and called the Lang Toun. It is so called because it is a long stretch along the coast looking across to Berwick Law and Edinburgh. I am summoned to the farthest end for a meeting that might just be fatal. I am hoping not, obviously. With a new link road the journey is a quick one and very soon I am cruising along the 'Prom' heading to the older, less salubrious, part of town. The sea-view car park is at the rear of a derelict old warehouse store, whose sign has long since been removed. As a nearly-local I know the way and don't need the help of a map. There has been a sprouting of little houses made of ticky-tacky for the young upwardly mobile professionals. These must overlook my meeting place and will be a source of witnesses if it all goes Pete tong.

I turn into the car park. Fuck it is deserted apart from one big black car at the far end, an SUV of some kind. I park slightly far away, deliberately. I don't want to get too close to them. A sunglasses-wearing, mean-looking, shithouse-shaped thug steps out of their car. He has been watching far too many mafia movies. He makes sinister, comical for me. He is glaring at me, I can tell. I get out and point my fob behind me. I take comfort in the noise it makes.

"You waiting for me?" I do my best Don Corleone but I don't think he gets it. Why is he wearing a polo neck sweater under a suit jacket? Maybe the shirt collars don't go up to his size. Of course he doesn't appear to have a neck, just a stump that is holding up his head.

"Get in Priest." Ooh that was so scary. I am all a-tremble. Well not really but I don't want to get in. After all once I do I am really in trouble.

"Let the girl go and I'll come with you. Where is she?" Movie scripts one-oh-one.

He puts a phone to his ear and waits. His stare, at least I presume he's staring, looks ridiculous with the sunglasses. He just looks like a walking cliché. We stand like a pair of gunfighters, waiting. A car pulls in to the car park behind me; the crunching of gravel as it moves towards us confirms its approach. It parks beyond the SUV.

The doors open and Angela is led out. Her usually well turned out appearance somewhat dishevelled. The creasing on her upper arms shows signs of being held by some grubby mitts. Her face is a little pale but no runny mascara marks. Waterproof obviously. I give her, what I hope is, a reassuring smile. She gets a shove towards me and manages a stumble but not a fall. Her heels wobble a little but she manages to throw herself into my welcoming arms. I hold her for a moment and fill my nostrils with her scent.

"Let's go Priest." Well he is nothing if not consistent; dull but consistent. I hand Angela my car keys and whisper in her ear. "Contact Brotherton, he'll know what to do." She nods, almost imperceptibly, and hugs me for what may be the last time. I bloody hope not. Feels good to be held by someone who cares. Even if I should never have been there in the first place. Letting go of her luscious curves, it is time to uphold my end of the bargain. I make my way to soprano-boy. Oh well, here we go. A meeting with the enemy

"Get in, Priest." He rumbles again. I resist the urge to say 'I'm getting in, Thug, flunky or whatever you are.' This is heading in the wrong direction very quickly. I get in. The blacked out windows prevented me from seeing Flunky number two. He motions me to buckle up. In his lap a black balaclava with grey patches stitched over the eye area. I will be wearing it I presume. It will mess with my hair.

Neckless, as I now think of him, gets in the front. The hair cover is thrown into my lap and a get-it-on waggle of the pistol gives me instruction. Where the fuck did that come from? I hate guns, they have one function; killing people. Fuck. Flunky two seems to have a better command of language and doesn't have the Mafioso twang. I do as I am told.

The car starts and we are off. I sit still counting and breathing steadily. I know the area and will perhaps be able to get an idea of where they are taking me. We are at the junction, right and we are into Kirkcaldy left and we are off down the coast. I hear the indicator clicking and we have turned left, the coast it is. Excellent, I know the coast road well. I will, hopefully be able to trace my movements later, Brotherton will be so pleased. I am presuming there will be a later.

So off we go, a few bends and curves and after a few minutes (reached 300 on my count) we are indicating. Must be taking the

Kinghorn loch turn off, it's the only turn off. Bumps and corners confirm it, especially the very tight left-righter at the far end. Soon we are entering Burntisland, a lovely seaside town with attractions in the summer and crazy golf. I loved coming to Burntisland as a child, great trampolines too. I can almost see where I am. He slows to meet the speed limit, Neckless is a careful driver; we will arrive at a roundabout soon. Left down into the town, right inland and straight on up the hill to Aberdour. I get distracted and have lost count but I will start again after the roundabout. We go straight on, heading for Aberdour. All going well, might as well not have the balaclava on. Oh dear, what a bonus this might turn out being. I should be terrified but I am not, I keep focussing on where we are and not on the what might happen to me. I am, as they say, living in the moment. In the moment there is no place for the little death, fear.

Up and down the hill, slowing and through Aberdour we go, not stopping here either. I am less sure of the next bit but I think we have turned into Dalgety Bay. Not sure but we are sitting in traffic and not moving much. Straining and having lost count again, I need clues, anything. A tannoy announcement, what was that ' The next train arriving at Inverkeithing' So we didn't turn off into Dalgety Bay, soon we are winding through the streets of Inverkeithing with turns, left, right and we are in a housing scheme. We went sharply downhill so I know roughly where we are. We are here, apparently, the roller door of the automatic garage closes behind us. I will be able to find this again I reckon. You amateurs are so toast.

"Leave it on Father." The first words spoken for about half an hour. I leave it. Inside I am exultant, we have a location. Sort of.

It isn't a big house, feels like an 'ex-cooncil hoose' because in short order I am into the arena and sitting on an office chair. Duck tape wraps my arms and I await the arrival of the big boss. I strain my ears listening for clues not that my hearing is that great; I hope I am never blind. I hear footsteps and an outside door closing. The Balaclava is yanked off and a bright lamp shines directly into my face. White spots and a screwed up face time.

"What are we to do with you, Father? Any sensible man would have left by now." A slightly effeminate, lisping voice fills the silence. The hairs on the back of my neck are standing now. I feel cold, this is it. I go for bravado.

"Let me go? Wash my car? Get me a coffee?" Infantile, I know. I need to try and get the spots off the centre of my eyes and I squint and look from side to side. It probably doesn't really work, anyway.

"Sadly, not this time. Tell me, Father, why were you sent to replace MacPhail? It was no accident." I wonder where he is going. You don't kidnap someone just for this.

"Just Lucky, I guess." Hopefully I can irritate a mistake from him. I, usually, irritate everyone, eventually. Sometimes it can be really quick.

"Do not play the fool, Father. We are serious men and you would do well to cooperate." His softly spoken voice is seductive and dripping honey. I feel a little change in the spiritual ambience, he is gathering his will.

"That's me, Mr Awkward. Name, Rank and serial number." I grin at my own joke. I might be being silly but it is buying me time. Time for what I am not sure.

"Answer me." No change, just a compulsion. My eyes feel like they are being sucked forward. I can't blink, Fuck. I can feel them drying in the lamplight. I really want to blink but it seems that pulling them together is impossible.

"Father, why are you here?" The voice again. I feel the power contained in the undertones. I want to answer. I can feel my mind forming the answer. I have no idea what will come out.

"To catch MacPhail's Killer." I hear my own voice say. Bloody traitor. He has the upper hand now. I have complied once and refusing next time will be harder.

"There has been a confession for that crime already, you will leave when the replacement arrives." His suggestion feels all warm and comforting. On another person, this would have gained agreement but he has pushed too soon. I know the confession is hinky and it jars in my head. I wait. Clearing the fog is difficult.

"You want to go home and leave the whole thing behind, don't you Father Andrew." Oh he is good, though. Do I play along or frustrate him? I can't help myself, time to pop his balloon.

"It's the paperwork." I pause and blink. "You know, the forms, the reports. It is never-ending." The utter randomness catches him off guard. The link has been snipped. I can feel the cobwebs melting away as I straighten in the seat.

"What?" No syrup in his voice this time. He is annoyed and incredulous.

"I said the paperwork is horrendous." Surreal, python-esque idiocy. Deal with that matey. He can't get a handle on the lack of connection; he needed me to concentrate on his topic.

"Silence." His voice roaring like a lion inside my head leaves me gasping. Oh fuck. Perhaps I have pissed off the wrong chap.

"My master commands you Nazarene. Forget us. Begone. This is not your affair." The rushing of blood in my head has reddened my vision and my head feels like two taloned claws are crushing my skull. I must resist. In my head I scramble my thoughts.

"18, 42, 17, 26, 3, 9, 17, Baa Baa black sheep, cock, bollocks, Sampras, Spain, Beckenbauer.'" I select utter randomness to thwart him. He has nothing to catch. I keep going with the randomness.

"You will obey!" Thunderous, painful and full of power. I scream in pain as the talons crush my skull, squeezing my brain. That is how it feels as his mind bears down on mine.

"Fuck you." I spit through tears of pain. Defiance my only weapon.

"Obey me! My master wills it." The current of his power is coursing over me. His anger is palpable and directed entirely at me. Why don't I have gifts like this? What did I get? Impressions and psychic shocks.

"Say please." I manage to grit my teeth.

"I command you, submit to my master." he is practically screaming in my face. His eyes bulging as he strains to dominate me.

"Never." Great dialogue eh? I wish I could have managed some thing pithy but I am drowning under waves of dark power. The air is charged. I wonder where the flunkies are, I am getting distracted. This episode may have been going on for minutes but I feel like I have been working out for hours. I am weary, already. A door behind us opens. The air clears as my enemy has lost his focus. I can feel a trickling bead of sweat crawl down my spine. My hair is plastered to my forehead. The clamminess holds my clothes against my body as I realise that the sweat covers my whole body.

"Let me." A new voice greets me, bland and quiet.

"Of course, Master." I can feel the expectant triumph in his voice.

Oh Fuck. I was dealing with the monkey not the organ grinder. This day has gone from bad to calamitous.

"Stop playing games Father." Nothing yet but I feel everything tense in preparation. He walks in behind the lamp. A little murmuring between master and apprentice, so quiet I cannot pick out the words. An incantation perhaps.

"'Your place is elsewhere but tell me Father Steel, what do you know of us and who have you told?" I am resisting and he knows it. The lamp goes out and all I can see apart from white-spots are two baleful glowing red eyes. They are coming closer. I cannot close my eyes. He has them in his control.

They descend towards me closer and closer. I feel cold hands on both sides of my face and a mouth covers mine. I try to scream but his kiss floods over me causing my resistance to shatter as my mind is ravaged. A hot sweaty hand fumbles with my zip and yanks out my, surprisingly, erect member. I am lost in a sea of tortuous rapture as a second mouth engulfs my cock, sucking and pumping tearing me to a climax I cannot prevent.

Sex magic is so very potent and this bastard is an expert. His tongue fills my mouth commanding my submission as his apprentice fellates me. The ecstasy overtakes me as he feeds from my memories. Spurt after of spurt filling the bastard between my legs. I am spent and barely conscious as the kiss ends. I throw myself backwards landing with a crash on the floor. In front of me, daylight creeps along the edge of the curtains. What a dodgy pattern, seventies classic obviously. I look round to see the master drink from his apprentice. I pass out, thank god.

Chapter 29

It is dark. I am cold and I have no idea where the hell I am. Sounds like I am waking up from another whisky induced bender. I haven't had one for years. No hangover just a tender ache at the back of my neck. My hands are cold and cuffed around a pipe, so I will be going nowhere anytime soon. I try to stretch my legs out and realise I am a bit stiff and sitting in a puddle, but otherwise I am whole. Waggling my fingers and toes to get some circulation to flow.

Being locked in a dark place with no recollection of how I got here worries me, more than I would let on. I shuffle myself about until I'm able to get on my knees and then stand up. Bastards have nicked my shoes I notice as the water soaks through the soles of my thin black socks. Without being a drama queen, I am uncomfortable and its unlikely to get any better. I shiver and my teeth are just this side of chattering and if I let them they would start. Like a blind dog humping a leg I try to feel in my pocket for my phone. Not there, but that's hardly a surprise. I still have my coat on, albeit a bit wet in places, so I doubt I am being left here to die.

A rumble of road traffic jerks me back to the present and I realise that I am near a road, not hidden away in the boon-docks. Maybe I can get someone to open the container. I start banging with my hands and shouting. Well it gives me something to do, I suppose. A drip just splashed on my head, I jump away in fright and fall arse over tit in the puddle. Pain races from my wrists to my brain and I squeak like a big Jessie. This can only mean that the pipe goes out through the roof. I pull myself to a more comfortable position leaning against the corrugated wall of the container. I wait, letting myself become one with my environment, letting my ears pick out anything at all that will give me a clue as to my whereabouts.

Well at least the container is stationary, and I am not headed for Africa like a load of organ boxes. We aren't rolling on down a road either, so all good on that front for now. I can hear the occasional rumble of vehicles passing but no sounds of people. Of course it could be the middle of the night. My watch has been misappropriated by the bad guys.

A loud grumbling escapes my stomach which is as empty as my pockets, so I know it must be night time. No bird sound either, so night time it is. Feeling around with my hands I try to estimate the extent of the wet patch in which I woke up. Obviously it's the man's job to lie on the wet patch. I snigger at myself. This puddle is just sufficiently annoying as to make it difficult to get a dry bit but with a stretch and lying with my arms above my head I manage to lie on a dry bit of floor. I drift off, uncomfortable, sore, wet, cold and miserable. No doubt the next time I wake up it will be even worse. That's me Polly fucking Anna.

Rumbling almost continuous in tone suggests that morning is with me. Traffic moving past at speed on the nearby busy road has brought me back to the land of the conscious. It is still dark in my prison but not the total inky blackness that I last awoke to. Some holes in the structure are letting a little light in and from above me dripping water coming down the side of the pipe. Around it a corona of light adds to how much I can see. The backs of my hands are smeared with what looks like soot. On closer inspection they are pentagrams that have been smudged by me. Shit!

Bad enough to have been taken but to have been locked in darkness and marked is a new low for me. I rub my hands clean in the water, and then scrub my face too. The black mess that covers my hands evidence of the mark that no doubt adorned my forehead. Bastards! Twice now they have worked on me, and twice I have been caught out. They are ahead of me on points but I'm not out yet. They certainly have the upper hand, and my sulphurous swearing reveals how much I am upset. I know what they are up to but have little proof and now I am trapped and at the mercy not of a dabbling bunch of sex-game playing crazies but real practitioners of dark magic. I wonder what they have taken this time? I am in over my head.

The opening and closing of the container door, filled the space with some light for a moment. Unfortunately two henchmen have arrived to make my day complete.

"Stuck your nose in once too often Priest." Snarly voice opens the show. As intimidation goes it was a feeble attempt. He's obviously not very good and must try harder.

"You dirty rat." I do my best bogey impersonation but it fails to impress as they are too far away to hear me properly. Snarly voice, thinks its fear. So he looks happy.

Of course, I should be afraid. Wakening up chained to a pipe inside, what I presume is, a container. I don't expect them to kill me, two priests in the same month from the same church. I expect a doing but little more.

"He'll talk all right. Look he's bricking himself.' A younger voice behind me added his wisdom. He seems to like the idea of my fear. He is practically chattering like a monkey.

"Wait till the master's friend gets here." Glee fills his snotty voice; triumphalist bastards. I slump against the pipe, no point in straining for now. At least I can find the master's hideout, then we'll see. Let's see how happy they are when Brotherton and his gang kick in the doors.

Evil henchmen one and two wander off down the container, their footsteps echoing loudly. Suddenly bright light covers the floor as the door to the outside swings open. Just as swiftly it is cut off and I am left in darkness, alone once more. I try to get some sort of descriptions for Brotherton. Although I will be able to identify them should our paths cross in the future. I won't need Brotherton then.

all, balding and wearing a San Francisco Forty-Niner's jacket. Should be easy to find in Scotland. After all not too many watch American football, do they. I am a Steelers man myself.

So much for dumb, the shorter nondescript is obviously Dumber.
I feel a giggle building inside and now I know I'm hysterical.
Dumb and dumber, Jesus.

Chapter 30

It must be getting near the time; I can feel a power gathering from all around. It's like a great big elastic band tightening around my head. If I don't get out of here soon, well I don't fancy my chances. At an appointed time, something will visit me inside this box prison and that, as they say, will be that.

The bastards will pay for this, even if I have to haunt them personally. I am getting a wee bit frazzled, no way of getting myself out of here and, worse, no way to tell anyone where I am. The headlines will be 'Priest murdered and left in a container. Police appealing for witnesses.' Will they start looking for a serial killer who bludgeons priests to death? I doubt it.

My arm is aching; pain apparently spreads up from the ends. Snapping my thumb to get the cuff off seemed like a good idea at the time. Beginning to reassess that now. I tentatively touch it, and howl in agony. Fucks sake. No point in trying to move it to a better angle, it's dangling like a limp dick. The pain is excruciating, not at all like poking a bruise. More like medieval torture. At least the cuff is off and dangling from the other wrist.

A car is approaching, one of those expanding cars, you know the ones with music so loud that all we hear is doof-doof-doof. 'Turn the fucking music off for fucks sake.' I scream. He'll never hear me otherwise. The bright LED light from his headlights is streaming through the many little holes and outlining the doors. The engine cuts off after a flourish of vroom as his no doubt just post-pubescent right foot flicks the accelerator. Thankfully the doof-doof has stopped. The light so briefly burning my eyes has been extinguished. Now I am getting the fluorescent dancing lights on my eyes, night vision well shot now.

"Help! Lemme out!" I shout and bang on the door hoping against hope that he's not one of the enemy. The metal of the handcuff making a piercing racket. I keep banging and shouting, this is my final chance; it won't be long now until my demonic visitor will arrive. My head is being squeezed, pressure building like a kettle coming to the boil.

The door mechanism is being fumbled with. I can hear two voices, one of each gender. The lights come back on and I keep banging and shouting like a big Jessie. Dear God let them hear me. I launch my body against the steel wall making as much noise as I can.

"It's padlocked, man." A muffled young man's voice reaches me from outside. He must be all of seventeen, practically a child. At least he is trying to help.

"Smash it quickly, please! Let me out!" I know I am hysterical but it is now or never. If he takes too long it won't matter. After an eternity of throbbing pain from thumb to shoulder measured in elevated heart beats, a hammer starts to bang on the padlock. The metallic ting like the chimes of the final clock striking my doom. I can't hear what they are saying but she's giving him instructions on what and where to hit with the hammer. Domestic avoided as her advice is followed and the lock is pulled away and the lever mechanism pulled. I throw myself out screaming.

"Run!" I stagger away from my erstwhile prison followed by the two teenagers. Their faces masks of confusion yet they follow me away from the container. They know what terror looks like and decide that I might know what I am running from.

A flash of red light and the demon arrives. The smell of brimstone is overpowering. It roars a voice filled with hate and disappointment. It has been cheated of its offering. The container rocks from side to side as the Demon storms around inside. Its rage fills the night and I am so thankful that I wasn't in there to meet it. It would have been bloody and very, very quick.

"What the fuck is that?" Spotty young saviour blurts out. His snogging partner screams a high pitched, near professional scream. The brief frozen moment we shared, well and truly over. They start to back away, slowly. It seems years of Hollywood horror movies have made a resilient population of young folk who aren't unmanned at the first supernatural encounter.

"You got a phone?" I take charge. Spotty hands me a rather nice one. He is staring into the container, and disbelief fills his eyes. He looks quite comical, she has buried her face in his chest. She's sobbing a little, what a little stereotype. I dial Brotherton two rings later and I am spilling the lot. In a stream without much of a pause.

"Where are you?" Brotherton asks and I realise I have no idea. Spotty tells me loud enough that the next village have heard him. The container stops shaking, silence has filled the night. The whimpering is all that remains. The Demon has gone; I can't feel it any more. The vice that was holding my head is gone. Only the pain throbbing up my arm is left to remind me of my ordeal. That and the cold, the wet and the growling hunger in the pit of my stomach. The Cavalry are on their way. I hand the phone back to my young spotty friend.

"Thanks man. You saved my ass." Not what he expects and his eyes alight on my dog-collar. I smile back, a little wild but coming back down a bit.

"Father, was that real?" His voice almost afraid to ask. He wasn't quite ready to trust his own eyes. After all, a Demon isn't what you expect to see when out for a snog.

I nod. It's about all I can manage. I am a wreck, knees out of my trousers, handcuffs hanging from my good wrist, limp-dick thumb swelling like a sausage, black eye, split lip, covered in dust. What a picture. I think he will be converted after tonight's experience.

Brotherton arrived three car lengths in front of the marked police car. The blue flashing light illuminates the scene, casting weird shadows all around. His dismount and approach of the container are very smooth and professional. He peeks inside then moves away. I hadn't noticed how big he actually is. I would want him on my side if we are picking teams.

"It's empty." I tell him. I really should say something grateful but I don't. I am too fucked to care.

156

"You OK? You look like shit." I know he's happy to see me too. He points past my shoulder and does the air hostess thing to his posse of police constables. You there, you that way. All efficient and cop-like. A well oiled machine in action.

"My rescuers are in the car." I flick my head in the general direction, "You better take their statements. This needs a lid kept on it." A little widening of his eyes shows he gets my drift. He pulls his walkie-talkie from somewhere and rustles up an ambulance for me. I must really look like shit. I need a seat so Brotherton's car it is. The seats will clean. I hope.

I must have zonked out. Some new voice is calling me sir. I just let my eyes close for a minute, the headrest felt so good. The throbbing pains around my body like a lullaby just easing me to sleep.

"Can you hear me sir? Wake up." I thought they were trained not to panic but it's there at the edges of his voice. "Father Steel, can you hear me?" He is persistent at any rate.

"I'm fine. I'm fine." I surface to see a paramedic, in his natty fluorescent green and yellow uniform, squatting in the open car door space. His face showing a concern I hadn't really expected over a broken thumb.

"It's my thumb." I don't move my arm towards him. After everything, I tell him it's my thumb. Perhaps I am not fine after all. Maybe I have had a blow to the head.

"That's the least of our problems, I think." He smiles as he looks into my eyes. "We are going to need to go to the hospital. We need to get you checked out." He signals his partner and speaks into his microphone thing. Do they all ave them these days? I want one next time, then I would be able to call my own cavalry.

"Let's get you over to the ambulance, can you manage that?" Like policemen, ambulance men are getting younger these days. I shuffle my ass out of Brotherton's car and stand up, I am suddenly light headed but he has a hold of my good arm and I womble over to the ambulance. Apparently adrenalin had gotten me this far and I am now utterly wiped. My legs are like

157

spaghetti and remind me of Bruce Grobbelaar and that penalty.

The place is swarming with policemen, yellow tape rings the scene and there is no sign of spotty and the girl. Don't see Brotherton either. The haven of the ambulance is close and in a few moments I am introduced to Steve and John, my paramedic crew. They are very thorough, checking all the easy things and lying me down. I notice a mood change as I start to struggle to focus. My lip is blue apparently and we are off. The trolley thing feels very comfortable, and my eyelids are so heavy. Fuck it I give in. Lights out. Steve keeps speaking to me.

Chapter 31

Having been somewhat busy for the last day or two, sitting in a none-too-comfortable hospital bed, one tends to be out of the loop. A loop that the bad guys are well and truly wired into. When I turned out not to be demon dinner, someone had to be, it seems. Being apprentice to a Dark Master can be a hazardous career choice. There, on the front page of the local rag, was the apprentice that had eluded me at the civic reception.

"Council Leader's special advisor found dead in Riverside Park" was the big black headline. Reading further words like unexplained and suspicious litter, what can only be called, pretty piss poor, copy. Add journalists to the list of getting younger these days. The story was littered with poorly constructed sentences and inaccuracies.

"I know why he is expired." I say out loud. Talking to myself is an age old habit. I wonder what Brotherton knows about it. Body was found bobbing in the River Leven, inside the park. It had been there a couple of days, so the press have informed me.

"Yer Arse." I know when he died almost to the minute. So my experience in the container reminds me. My ribs hurt and my red raw wrists, covered by pretty little white bandages, are reminders of a rather close call. The panda look is not my best one, a suspected broken nose and split lip very visual reminders to everyone else that I had suffered a mishap. A fall I am telling anyone who looks gullible enough to believe me. A doing would be the professional commentary.

So my enemy works through a proxy or medium, is cautious and, most definitely, not a fool. Summonings are a risky business. Calling forth a powerful, supernatural, extra-planar being requires sacrifice and iron control. Any loss of control and a life is paid. My adversary has lost a well placed tool. The game is turning and turning in my favour at last. Of course if this is winning then thank God we aren't losing.

"Brotherton." He answers on the second ring; I am impressed. He's giving nothing away. I hope he can talk.

"Steel. I see we have a new body." No point pissing about. I want to know what the inside track is.

"We? It's related?" He needs to ask? He is definitely in need of some Padawan training. Of course it is related.

"Yes." That's me, expansive as hell. What a poker player eh? I want to get him really focussed and not distracted by little mundanities like facts.

"In what way? There's no connection. Looks like it could be a drug overdose or something unexplained." Oh dear, he's backsliding. I had such high hopes for him too. I sigh, a little too loudly and Brotherton pauses feeling the sting of my disappointment. Or at least I imagine he does.

"He was the apprentice to the Dark Master." I pause, suspense and all that. "I felt him at the civic reception the other week. I recognise his face." Smug smart arse is kicking in now. I have been lying around for a few days after all.

"Right, well we'd better have a chat about this." Brotherton has obviously remembered where he is and is not willing to have this chat here.

"Brotherton, this poor sod took my place and was sacrificed to feed the Demon. The Demon that was summoned to kill me. A poor trusting fool, betrayed by his master. We are starting to win.' Okay winning was a bit optimistic but he needed a pick-me-up.

"The Post Mortem will be back later today. We'll get a cause of death then." All professional cop-like again. I am so disappointed.

"I'll bet on a rare cancer causing heart failure, undiagnosed obviously." I might as well strut. If only I could do lottery numbers.

"Rest up and I'll swing by later with the report." Oh he does care. The line goes dead. He doesn't care that much, apparently.

Seeing as I am stuck in my utilitarian lodge room, convalescing, I suppose I should give some thought to solving this case. The Bishop expects me to, after all.

"What do we know?'" I muse out loud. This won't really take long but it will pass the time and there is no way I am watching Jeremy-bloody-Kyle. Daytime television is a buffet of mental programmes and chat shows with as many unrepresentative people as can be crammed in. Whatever happened to Richard and Judy?

"MacPhail killed by a summoned demon. Why? No idea." This might be really quick; it appears I know the square root of eff all. I can't actually answer the why of the key question. Motive escapes me, totally.

"Cult in St Margaret's and organ trafficking in Africa." I suck as a detective, usually cases are attrition with a serendipitous ending. Called dumb luck, if the truth be told. I can trace organs and shipping; which is a start. I know there is a cult and a satanic disciple, expired, and a Dark Master. What is irritating is that I can't tie these together in a coherent narrative with evidence. I was kidnapped after all. Surely there is something. I can probably find the house too.

"One funds the other but why kill MacPhail? I can't see him as a willing sacrifice." My head is empty and my bladder full, so I painfully wince my way to the loo. I get a fright as the fluorescent lighting does me no favours.

"Why would you off one of your own guys?" I look in the mirror as I aim my bits. It is truly amazing where inspiration strikes.

"MacPhail wasn't a team player! What if he had gone native? Wanted to come out or seize power for himself?" I think I am on to something, and hopefully not a painkiller fuelled delusion. It might be part of the picture. They might not have been one happy family.

"A power struggle in their little cult of sex maniacs? Why not something basic?" It was getting juicier by the second and, like all fantastic theories of mine, not a fact to corroborate it in sight. Evidence? Who needs that? Let's just roll with it for now.

I flop back onto my bed, replaying and rethinking what I know through my new prism. So if MacPhail was a challenge to the Master, then what? It's not like they would get a ready made replacement from the Diocese. Can't exactly advertise, can they? 'Satanic Priest required for cult in new town.' I wonder if their reach is great enough to get a priest of their choice? Then I recall the selection committee that actually picks the priest is made from the locals. They approve the candidate they want. It would be a closed loop, perpetually placing their man in the manse.

"It's about the money!" I say it like it's a fact. I amaze myself, really. Was MacPhail greedy? Did he want a bigger cut? I'll bet the fucker did, or perhaps he had had enough. You know, got bored of the sex and power. Perhaps he wanted to retire with pockets of dosh to a warmer, happier, climate. Maybe, just maybe, it was good old fashioned greed. Perhaps he threatened to expose the operation and became a liability? Doubtful, but you never know. I can't wait to run my thinking past Brotherton. I can almost see his serious cop face 'Where's the proof?' Bollocks.

"Apparently he had a cardiac arrest while using the outdoor gym, trim-trail thing. Died and then fell into the river. It was brought on by an underlying, very rare and undiagnosed, condition." Brotherton was trying his best not to be sour. I knew he was trying though.

"Cancer was it?" I am unbearable, sometimes. That superior facial expression settling into place, I don't even practice. I am a natural. A bit like the crowing of Peter Pan.

"Apparently so, a very rare one in five hundred thousand kind of cancer that's almost impossible to detect." He knows I am going to gloat.

"He shoots...He scores!" The basketball air shot meeting my commentary. Juvenile but I can't help myself. They are hardly going to put the cause of death as 'Soul extracted by aggravated encounter with a Demon' are they? Although the millennium has

162

passed so who knows.

"Amazing how mundane demon induced deaths can be made to sound. Anyone see the myocardial-infarction?'" I pause, eyebrow cocked "I'll bet not. How long until he was discovered and by whom? Do they think us that stupid? How far did he need to stagger to throw himself in the river?"

Brotherton looks perturbed. He knows I am right but the case is closed. The body of our enemy discovered but no case to follow up. He looks at me, expectantly. What he expects I have no idea.

Chapter 32

I should get a frequent visitor award or a badge or something. I have been in the Bishop's residence more times in the last month than in the last year. I wonder if there is such a thing? Perhaps air miles could be awarded. I park next to the dark blue Volvo, not round the back as the doorman continually reminds me to do. I do it just to wind him up, and it does. Contrary, that's me. I crunch my way across the gravel giving the door time to open, and sure enough it does, just as I mount the first step. The step looks worn from the many feet that have passed this way and not one of them with a frequent visitor award; nor a card.

"Welcome Father." He puts out a hand for my coat. His resistance to being a doorman has been eroded and his acceptance is complete. I smile as I hand it over. "The Bishop is in the study," He knows I know where it is. "You are to go on through." He hides his disapproval very well these days, or maybe he likes me now. Not very likely, though.

In moments I am sitting in the corner of a red leather Chesterfield sofa looking at His Eminence over his oversize desk. Surely he isn't compensating. He waves me over to a coffee pot as he reads some official looking papers. He mumbled something about Jeremy, I am presuming it isn't Jeremy Kyle, so I will wait and be mother when Father Jeremy gets here.

It is a lovely study. French doors letting in floods of light from the terrace, fading the curtains, carpet and couches equally, creates a lovely ambiance. A wall of bookshelves, with many very old and unread tomes, stand along one wall and the fireplace with its large mirror above it covers the other. A smattering of religious art fills in the wall gaps. It should feel cluttered but it doesn't. Even I could work in here. Well more likely I would get distracted by the texts of the ancients and lose all track of time. His computer looks a bit out of place but don't they always. I wonder how much of this room is hand-me-down and how much is his aesthetic. I'm betting it has pretty much looked like this for ages. The wooden shelves and panels have that old, cared for, look and if there wasn't a bloody air freshener thingy I would be able to smell them. No nasty brown staining from cigarettes in here, I don't think anyone would dare.

Bishop Michael's brow is furrowing as he dislikes what he's reading. His lips narrow in disapproval completing the wasp chewing expression. I hope it's not about me. It looks as if I am about to find out as the reading glasses are removed with a weary sigh. He looks into his coffee cup and delivers another weighty sigh, finding it empty. The study door opens and Father Jeremy bustles in. He approaches, genuflects and kisses the Bishop's ring, which I neglected to do. What a suck up.

"Bishop Michael, Andrew. We have much to discuss." Like he knows something very important. His man bag looks full to bursting, so no doubt he will pull something out of it.

"Father Jeremy, please be seated." The Bishop has great manners. I just nod, thankful to have avoided a pre-meeting scolding. I am such a let down, obviously. I rise like a pregnant cow from the couch and venture to the coffee pot, delaying the inevitable. I probably can't be civil without the caffeine.

"Coffee anyone?" I try to sound upbeat, positive maybe. Nods greet me and the Bishop extends his empty cup towards me. I'd better fill it then. I'd better not drip on his desk either.

"The Sabbat is nearing." Melodramatic opening from Father Jeremy. I resist my usual snide replies. "And we are no nearer to knowing where it will take place." He looks worried that we'll miss it. Like buses I am sure there will be another one once the apocalyptic disaster has passed.

"Nothing yet." I intone. It is my failure, obviously. Bishop Michael frowns again. He picks up the paper he was reading. He waves it about, showing it has an imposing logo on it, Home Office apparently. Oh dear I am failing on a whole new level.

"The Home Secretary isn't exactly pleased with our progress on this one. It seems the press have gotten a sniff of something and needed warding off." Oh no, the press. Run. I keep that one inside, too.

"They have some lurid pictures of your abuse Andrew. Full colour, news of the world stuff. A total bloody mess." Disgust written large across his face, not directed at me I hope. I didn't actually agree to it, as I am sure he knows.

"I haven't seen them." Probably not helping with that one. I put on my neutral face. Blame the victim for getting worked over and being used.

"They are very explicit, do you want them for a scrap book?" I decide that one is rhetorical and decline to answer. No piccies will be forthcoming then. Although I might have been able to identify some of them in the future.

"We need this lot wrapped up quickly. Jeremy what have you gleaned from the book Andrew recovered?" The focus of his ire has swung away from me, thankfully. Father Jeremy needs to deliver or he will get 'the face'.

"It's a genuine Grimoire with details of rituals and the like. It matches with some of our reference texts. Some very detailed and downright depraved. How many have been performed, it is impossible to tell." Jeremy pauses for a sip of, frankly disgusting over-brewed, coffee before continuing. "Their calendar of Sabbats is consistent with ones we know already which worries me. This coming weekend they have a High Mass and can open the portal." He looks anxious. What is he not telling us?

"Without the Book will they be able to perform the ritual?" Bishop Michael looking for a crumb of comfort throws it out there. He needs some good news to relay to the Home Secretary; I have the feeling there won't be any.

"I believe their Master will have his own copy." Jeremy's face looks like he has finally tasted the coffee. "Midnight on Sunday and the Gate will be opened, letting something through."

"If we interrupt their ritual, will it stop the Portal being opened?" I hear my own voice sounding reasonable. Perhaps fervently hopeful would be a better description.

"I don't know. Maybe, maybe not. The details on the Portal

are very vague. It may not be contingent on the ritual. Perhaps all it needs is the sacrifice." Jezza confirms my worst fears. We might not stop them. Demon running amok, we are all doomed. Doomed I tell you.

"Andrew, we need the venue. The earlier the better. I will brief the Home Secretary, and he won't be pleased." He swigs his coffee which, going by his face, has cooled. It was bad enough when it was hot. Mine is largely untouched.

My phone rings, probably should have put it to silent. Oh dear. I make the excuse face and leave into the panelled hallway glad to be out of there in one piece.

Chapter 33

I know my life is like the Indiana Jones meets the exorcist but a whole host of proper priestly stuff needs to be done. I need to maintain the orderly running of the parish while I root out the bastards that have kidnapped and worked me over. Let alone the vengeance that is to be visited upon them for the sexual liberties they have taken with me. The congregation don't all know about the war being waged on their turf or rather on God's turf. This little family's problems must not be aired in public.

So far I have managed not to get back into Angela Brookes bed, she and I both need a break. Me to recover from the physical damages I have sustained and she to recover from the ordeal of being abducted and being unable to speak about it. I have answered her texts; I am not that cold but there has been little playfulness in them. I am hoping that the cleansing and confessional undertakings I gave can be maintained. It will be easier if I don't get in the same room as her too soon. Her vulnerable look was heartbreaking, last time we met. It was public so there was no physical contact either. I had struggled not to hold her and protect her in my arms. I had managed that at least.

Anyway, surrounded by a pile of utterly pointless paperwork, I am ensconced in the cramped little office, that serves the church building. A gentle knock at the door generates the automatic reply "Come in." The door opens quietly and I am surprised to see the rather pretty daughter of my erstwhile paramour. She is very pretty and looking very serious. She has the echo of her mother in her features and probably why she seems so much older than her tender years.

"Father." She does innocence, fatally well. I know now why so many men are burning in hell for thoughts that they had been unable to avoid.

"Michelle, how lovely to see you." Warning bells going off all over the place, danger. What was she doing here? She is dressed to get a reaction. Short skirt and satin blouse package her very obvious assets. She knows it too, having used this approach before I expect. Or perhaps seen it used by her mother.

"I came to see you, Father. I need your help." She seemed uncertain, and a little concerned. I waited. Let's see where this was going. What did she know? Worse still I was probably being set up again. Her lip being gripped between her white, flawless teeth. I bet years of braces were needed as a child and the pay-off is plain to see.

"It's about the celebration here on Sunday night. I don't want to mess up." Here we go, information about to fall in my lap. Either that or another trap. How deep is she in? I'm in over my head so no doubt she is too.

"In what way, Michelle?" Keep it simple and don't push. Festinare lente, as my old Latin teacher would have said. Hurry slowly it had meant and he used it about running in the corridor but it fit well here.

"I haven't, you know, done IT before." She managed to get it out. She was a virgin and she was involved or was about to be. Her cheeks had taken on a flush that put truth to her lie of seductive vixen. She was exactly what she was a girl on the brink of womanhood and subject to the worries that everyone has as they transition.

"I see." I try not to faint. Apparently there had been no need to lock her up in a tower to protect her from boys. Good girl. She had been very grown up about her body then. I found that sadly reassuring that her virginity was intact and she was involved with a satanic cult.

"Mum says that I should speak to you." I try not to choke as I drink my lukewarm coffee. Angela sent me her daughter to deflower? I doubt it. Was this an opening? Surely she knew what it would mean. Angela must know that I am here to break the cult and that would involve trouble for members.

"She says that you are the best person to resolve my

problem." Michelle had taken her mother's comments to mean that I should be her first. The look on her young face was one I never wanted to see again. Functional lust; wanting it done in a business-like way. Did she expect me to do her here? Now?

There it was. Coded and delivered in such a way as to get Angela and Michelle out of the mess they are in. Michelle perhaps has no idea of just how deep a mess it is. The child thinks that it is all a sexy, grown up thing with no threat to her mortal soul.

"I guess I am." I try to sound normal about it, "What else did your mother say?" I need to make sure that everything works out right. I need to make sure there is no misunderstanding that screws us all. For once I want to reduce the collateral damage and devastation that will occur if the Brookes family is exposed in the press or courts. David Brookes is a decent guy whose only crime is not seeing what was going on in his household.

"That Sunday night was a big event and people from all over would be here. I would need to be ready for my turn on the altar." She didn't seem too phased about that, apparently. Her acceptance seemed total. Was I too late? It sounded like she was discussing doing maths homework or prepping for an exam. The pain in my chest sharp and immediate, she so needed saving and I was probably years late to start the job.

"Has your mother told you what happens?" I try to see just what has been explained, and perhaps glean some insights. Hopefully I could shock her out of this and keep her safe. Probably a forlorn hope but I would have to try.

"Oh yes. The ritual sacrifice is there for all too see, touch and use." The last bit was a bit too enthusiastic. A gleam of something is in her eyes. A lust for something she hadn't yet had and that no one so young should have to experience.

"It sounds simple, doesn't it?" I keep my voice bland but want to scream Noooo! I try to pull her eyes to mine, away from the spot above my head that her eyes have found so interesting.

"I can do it. It's not like I haven't seen our local mass." Oh dear, innocence well and truly lost. She seems to be ready to step up, like a new player on the roster. Fresh meat for the fat, lumpy swingers club of the satanic coven. What a total sin to have embroiled her in this already. I wondered who to be more angry at; MacPhail or Angela Brookes?

"Local meetings are less imposing for a young girl like you. After all you know all the people, don't you?" I try to curb her zeal. I want her to think about the less than perfect people who will have their mouths and paws all over her body; not to mention the other appendages.

"Father, that's part of the problem. I don't want Mr Reid to be my first and he has been leering at me for ages. He's gross." Her distaste curls her lip. Not that I blame her, he must have been one of the fatter, wobblier celebrants last time. She has standards after all.

"You do not choose who takes you on the altar." I sound stern, but really I am terrified for her. She bows her head quickly. I need to stay in my role or we are all in the shit.

"I am sorry, Master.'" She says so softly. Master! Oh dear Lord this isn't happening. I must prevent her ultimate corruption if nothing else. I wonder if she is confirmed in their faith or if they have a different process.

"Michelle, Being on the altar is a great honour and not one given lightly." I pause; her head is still bowed so I have no idea what she is thinking. I wonder if I can simply say she isn't ready this time?

"Teach me Master, make me ready." Fervour fills her shiny, beautiful eyes. She would be irresistible had I been MacPhail; perhaps he had been saving her for a special occasion.

"Has your mother not told you what to do and how to do it?" I try for a disapproving stance. Like all mothers teach their daughters how to be a sacrificial fuck at a Sabbat. After all what skills does one mother pass on to the next generation?

"I know how to, you know, with my mouth." She says it like it is so ordinary. "But what if it hurts too much the first time? I don't want to be a failure and mum has told me that some can be quite big and rough."

171

I stare at her, trying for aloof not shocked into insensibility. "Yes they can. Did your mother tell you about the women too?" Let's try for another shock attack, might just put her off. Although that is looking so remote at this point.

"That will be okay, Hannah and I sometimes practice on each other and I don't mind." I try not to faint. Bloody hell, Hannah too. Which one was Hannah?

"I see. Then all you need is a practice or two before Sunday?" I make it sound ordinary. Lose cherry, get ready for orgy within the week. Almost like a to do list that hangs on the fridge door. You know; get milk, put bins out, lose virginity for gang bang.

"That's why I am here." She stands up and begins unbuttoning her blouse. Her flawless young skin exposed with each button. What a lovely white lace bra too.

"Stop." I raise my hand. "I will not rush this for you. We will do it properly but not here and not now. I have others to attend to." Whoa, Time out. Run screaming from the room before I have a seizure and give the game away.

Looking confused and, luckily she isn't feeling spurned, uncertain she waits. She starts to re-button. I think I see tears forming at the edges of her very pretty eyes. Better that she is upset now than the alternatives. I smile paternally to her, hoping to lessen the blow.

"Michelle, you are young and very beautiful. You deserve a very special initiation and not be squandered under the less than worthy hands of the Mr Reids of this world." I lift her chin gently, making sure her eyes meet mine "When you are finally laid out on the altar, you will be magnificent." I pray she is buying in to this. I kiss her on the forehead and send her on her way, lucky to have escaped this mess without imperilling my mortal soul. How to stall her for the next few days and keep her out of my bed might be a bit trickier.

More importantly I have the time and place of their Grand Sabbat. Father Jeremy will be deliriously happy. This will give us a chance to smash this ring of organ trafficking Satanists and more than that save Angela Brookes and her innocent daughter from the depravities that might lie in store for them. Innocent being a relative term, obviously.

"Brotherton." I speak quietly into my phone. No point in taking chances. "I have a real breakthrough. I know where and when. There is a little fly in my ointment, however."

"Excellent. We need to talk. You can tell me about your ointment problem." He has learned so much from our association. I am almost proud of him.

"Costa, twenty minutes. See you there." And we are back in the game.

Chapter 34

I always thought the police squad room thing was just Hill Street Blues fantasy but now I know better. In what looks like a modern lecture theatre, at Fife's finest Police HQ, the backchat and chatter is flowing. The personalities are a right mixture with jokers and pokers in equal mix. They do look a bit young though. I see the local inspector standing, all smartly uniformed, to one side. He looks anxious; he is one of only a handful of people who know what is going down tonight. Beside him, Brotherton stands all ready to go. His blue eyes standing bright under the lights. There has been a total silence on this operation and that is how it will stay. I scan the room looking to see if there are traitors in our midst. Unless the cop that kneed me in the nuts is here, my search will come up empty.

"All right people, knock it off." The inspector raises his voice and the room stills. I can't recall his name, I think it was Sunderson. Of course it might have been Sanderson but his accent was tricky. Some dialects of Scots tongue are indecipherable.

"All radios to be deposited in the inspection tray that is coming round. All mobile phones to go in, too." A buzz permeates the group, they know there is a big thing going down. All happy faces they are not. You would think that we had cut a few hands off. After all how can we manage for a few hours without texting or Facebook.

"Inspector Brotherton has command for this operation. This is operation porcupine. Over to you Brotherton." Sunderson moves away from the podium, he looks like a competent beat cop who has seen it all. The hubbub of noise is as expected after the choice of operation name; something about a bunch of pricks wafts across the room. The tittering and suppressed laughter follows. Like all uniformed services the banter can be a bit puerile.

"Good evening. For those of you who don't know me I am Inspector Brotherton, CID. I have been put in command of tonight's operation and we will be leaving soon to get into position. There is a comms blackout on this one so no-one and I repeat no-one will have any contact outside until after the conclusion of this operation." He paused and stared round the room, daring any comment. A pin dropping would have been heard. The phones and radios were moved to the front. Brotherton felt safe to continue. His serious mien transmitting across the faces looking back at him.

"Tonight we are going to raid a paedophile ring." The words fell like thunder on the room. This was what they had trained for. All humour evaporated and they were ready. I didn't want him using the words Satanic Cult, so paedophiles was the way we would describe it. If they violated Hannah they would be. Funny how crimes against children get men so angry; especially as most paedophiles are men. I wondered at the tension building in the room, how many of them have kids of their own?

"We will be securing a stand alone building in the Gleninch area, and will proceed only on receipt of a go order. There will be armed response officers standing by but I hope we will not require them." Brotherton, is actually very good at this. I was even listening to his orders.

"We want to ensure we gather up as many of them as we can so there will be a Transit per two officers. The processing will take place tonight in the main hall. There is a complete black out on this until the Home Office say otherwise. Nothing will be entered into your notebooks, all records will be taken at processing in the hall."

A hand went up, about half way back. Here comes the trouble. I could see the back of his head but not his face. There is always one in any crowd, like a heckler at a comedian.

"Will we have video deployed as we make the raid?" A dark haired constable projects his voice across the whole room. A sensible question, I suppose. Good for that tricky evidence thing.

Brotherton smiles, obviously ahead of that curve. Looking at the officer who asked. He obviously knows him and likes the man.

"Stills and video will be taken as the raid progresses. We will want to identify as many as possible should the net be less tight than we hope." His voice covering the details, no notes or aids.

"We will be leaving in 10 minutes to our muster point. Any more questions?" considering Brotherton has told them very little, they have no questions. The pairings are read out. A few jokes and groans are the response. Drivers are given keys. The officers move about finding their partners for the operation.

Brotherton steps away from the podium.

Brotherton, Sunderson and I are in a squad car, no transit van for us. As only Brotherton and I know where we are going, we are in front of a cavalcade of ten transit vans. No flashing lights, no sirens, nothing. An anti climax if ever there was one. I suppose it is better if we have the element of surprise. Inspector Sunderson looks less than pleased that he has no idea where we are going. I pulled a Home Office Carte Blanche and that was it really. He hasn't addressed me directly since he phoned to check my credentials. I think he might be in the huff. I think he is too old for that sort of thing but I have had my moments too.

The plan is that I get dropped off, sneak in to the church, witness the defiling of virgins and call in the cavalry. Simple really. What a plan. I would like to claim credit for it. That might explain why it will be a disaster, if my churning guts are anything to go by.

It is nearing Eleven o'clock about an hour until the main event. Where are we going to hide the fleet of white vans? We aren't. Brotherton is going to have them drive to a different area and wait. Less chance of a leak or any late comers noticing a congregation of coppers. He must have pulled cops from all over to get this many in one place; budgets have reduced the numbers of bobbies on the beat in recent years. No matter what the politicians tell us.

It's my stop and Brotherton makes me check that my phone is

charged and primed. We give it a dry run. The bleep emanating from Brotherton's device means text received. All good then. I am deposited on the pavement a few streets over from the target. The circus drives away, leaving me to go on alone. It is bloody freezing and I put up my collar, that's me cooler than Elvis. Hopefully I can avoid ending up dead and meeting him in person. God is a big Elvis fan, I believe. After all, who isn't?

The clicking of my footsteps on the cracked paving stones sounds like a parade approaching and guaranteed to give me away. The incessant need to look over my shoulder in the gaps between the orange fluorescent street lights is getting a bit old already. Apparently I am nervous. Wow, who knew?

Chapter 35

Superninja, that's me. It seemed a great idea at the time. After my last foray into St Margaret in the fields after dark went so well, you'd think I might have been a bit more circumspect. Apparently not. When Brotherton said that we need eyes on the event before we storm in, I should have kept my mouth firmly shut. Instead I heard my voice saying 'I will go.' Bizarrely no one tried to stop me. Sneaking into a black mass without an invite was beyond any level of lunacy to which I had ever descended.

Yet here I was, softly turning the back door handle (again) and expecting to sneakily infiltrate. Seriously? You couldn't make it up. There were no cars in the car park, so maybe we have the wrong venue for tonight's events. I'm not sure if I want that to be true. The consequences of this being the wrong place don't really bear thinking about. Mind you, they are hardly going to turn up en masse and fill the car park. Perhaps the curtain twitchers would notice that sort of thing.

However, the discrete path to the back door would be the way I would expect most of them to use. I have a quick look over my shoulder, you know that moment where you realise that you might get caught. Tonight, in about twenty seconds, there would be a power cut in this sector of Gleninch. A lights out to create a dark cushion to allow the forces of law and order approach without being seen. Nothing suspicious in that. The last power cuts in the town were during the seventies and the three day week. Do you think the Cult, preparing for their Highest Sabbat and event in Millennia might get suspicious? Of course not.

Power and lights out in ten, nine, eight. Or not, they are out now. Slow watch or excitable electrician? Who knows? Premature de-illumination. I enter quickly and restore the door and the curtain. Four steps later I am in the vestry office. I close the door behind me to a tiny crack. Just in time too, as two big beefy blokes move quickly to double lock and bolt the back door. Correct venue and they are too late. After a few moments checking the door and the kitchen they move off again, I continue my silent hyperventilating and perspiring session. I'll give it a minute. I have a 'GO' text ready on my phone. One button press is all it will take to get the message to the cavalry, all eventualities covered, I hope.

I can hear a low chant coming down the carpeted halls, a procession of sorts, I expect. It is in Latin, of course. Bloody copycats. My hair stands on end as they enter the church and the closing of the doors mutes their devotions. They have begun. I peek through the crack before venturing out of my haven. No one about. Quickly I unlock and unbolt the double-locked back door. Escape route or entry for reinforcements secured I make my way along to watch the show, and what a show it is.

From my vantage point, coming in behind the organ, I have an unobstructed view of their service. They are all robed and masked: the pale phantom of the opera kind not the rubber ex-president Nixon kind. The church has had a similar make-over to the last time but this time there must be fifty of them filling the pews. This is no coven but a gathering of coven. There seems to be a hierarchy with some in Red robes and not the standard black. It is one of these Red Robes that steps forward and begins.

His robe parts and flaps exposing pale flesh underneath, but not in an overtly exhibitionistic way. Just a by product of movement. I wonder what the view looks like from his side; the gaping robes exposing many breasts of which I can see the covered backs. It is like a restricted view ticket at the football; a bloody pillar in the way of the action.

"Tonight is a great night. We will celebrate the joys of our master. Our lusts shall be his, his lust shall be our sustenance and his power will flow into us. Do you hear Him?" He intones, his head bowing. He is a tall man, and the robe hangs dramatically on his long, lean frame. A glimpse inside reveals scraggly hair covering his chest.

"We hear." And they bow theirs in response. All very religious; sadly not mine. The responses are all well known and that doesn't bode well for the reach of these bastards.

"Tonight we shall share two delicate flowers. Two souls freed from the Nazarene, two bodies to fill with our secret powers. Two spirits to set free." His gaze moves to the far wall and I see two white-robed, slim forms kneeling with their heads bowed. A picture of demure subservience. I know who they are. 'They are the instruments of your doom matey.' I smile grimly, at that thought. You will be spending the rest of your days in Peterhead sex offenders wing. Sharing a cell with Big Bubba.

"Tonight Our Master will join us. Tonight, this High Sabbat, our sacrifices will be rewarded. Tonight the Void will open and we shall be filled. In our sacrament we shall hear His voice, His words and His will. We shall obey." His sermon voice fills the room. Nothing mystical happening yet. I have the host in both pockets, Holy water, Holy Unction, salt, crucifix- you know the essentials. So far so good. Can't call in the cavalry yet; no one has committed a crime. Well a crime against God, but he will take care of that in due course.

His arms outstretched in supplication, head thrown back, his Red robe parts exposes his stiffening member. A bell tinkles its pure tones in the church and from the front row a black robe ascends the two steps and kneels before him. The ankles look female and the bobbing of her head evidence of her action and role. I can feel the pressure build as they begin their offering. After a few moments she mounts the altar, her nakedness complete as her robe is untied. She must be the starter.

I hope I can avoid passing out before they commit the acts we will prosecute. I have seen this show before so it is much less interesting to me. However, it seems that due to numbers, impromptu sideshows have commenced. A veritable sex-fuelled getting to know you session. So this is how they Pax Vobiscum, it will never catch on. The red guys seem to be the busiest. Or rather they seem to be the busiest recipients. I keep my eyes peeled that neither Hannah nor Michelle are included. They are kneeling demurely, forgotten almost. Like pure little statues, untouched and unseen.

The circling of the altar and partaking of the offering goes on apace but somehow tonight feels different. There is very little build up of mystical pressure, it seems to dissipate as soon as it is generated. Almost like the valve has been left open preventing any pressure building up. Odd. I would think that they'd need it to build to a climax to open the portal. The pressure I felt making my ears pop has been replaced by a low thrum. This is amateur level of dabbling, although I know they are serious. I wait. I am a little uncertain; I have cavalry to call and nothing but a swingfest to report.

You've got to admire Red Robe's restraint. He has been sliding in and out of her throat for about ten minutes while the sideshows have all come to a peak; casting their seed and convulsing through paroxysms of pleasure. They are drawing breath before the entrée. He withdraws himself as his partner descends the altar, smiling and apparently honoured. Another chime of the bell. Its game time.

He turns his masked face to the white-robed and hooded pair. His index finger points and they stand. They look a little wooden as they move forward to the rail. Their robes, I notice, are of a very different design and very, very flimsy. They drape beautifully, skimming their delicate forms. Their arousal, or chill, very evident.

"Do you freely consent to giving this night?" His sermon voice reaching all corners of the church. I am sure he thinks that is a disclaimer that will keep him out of the deepest shit. Like hell it will.

"I do." They chime together, almost mono-tonal. I can tell them apart but I wonder if this consent, freely given, will be sufficient cover for these bastards. The law sometimes lets us all down.

"Then come, make your offering to the night. Make a gift of your bodies and feed our Horned Master. His gift of rapture is yours to receive and enjoy." His happy member bobs in anticipation as he waves them forward. I wonder which will be first. Hannah apparently, her face coming into view under the candlelight. She steps slowly up the steps as two black cloaked hand maidens rip the robe from her. The violent tearing sound is like a thunderclap in the silence. All eyes are focussed hard on her, now naked, body. Which from the rear is, no doubt, whetting a few, very undesirable, appetites in the audience.

"Make your offering." The command is clear – perform. She knows her role. Who has been priming her I do not know but she doesn't hesitate.

I press my one button and call for reinforcements is sent. Hannah on all fours presents to the room; she will be taken by those present. Faceless strangers who will enjoy her body as she supplicates the master before her. I am so not allowing this. I know its not the plan but too bad. Brotherton will just need to catch up.

"By all that's Holy, stop!" My voice is loud and full of reach. I call it my fear of god voice. Collective whiplash strikes the gathered Faithful. "This abomination is over." I stride from the shadows like an avenger. What now? I have no idea, stalling time. I sometimes wish I had a sword to draw like Michael.

I expect a running for the door type stampede as they are discovered but they are rather calm. Perhaps a few erections have drooped but not quite the response I was expecting. I might be in trouble.

"Take him." A contemptuous command as he returns his attention to Hannah. Four large habit-wearing heavies close in on me. Oh shit, time to make like a rabbit and try to evade them. It is a futile effort as their outstretched hands grab and pull at me. My hay-maker of a right hook connects with a cheek shattering the mask and causing excruciating pain to shoot up my arm. I recognise the nuts-kneeing traffic cop, who was so kind to me last time. He doesn't look too amused. My nuts ache at the impending reunion with his knee. I am now effectively smothered and held on the ground as he exacts retribution for my punch. His stamp on my crotch ends all resistance. I am rolled into the side as the show goes on.

Violence and sex are a powerful cocktail and I feel the band of pressure build around my head, squeezing my skull. I can see through my tears that Hannah is an athletic and willing participant. Her back is smattered with shining libations delivered by an enthusiastic front row. A virgin she most certainly was not. Dear God, Brotherton, hurry the fuck up.

"Enjoy the show, Worm." One of the gang of four smirks. I stare at his plastic covered face, knowing that I will be getting the last laugh.

"Fuck you." I manage to get out. My lungs are really not getting much to work with. The stars that twinkle around the edges of my vision tell me that oxygen might be in a bit of a short supply.

"Oh they will, just like last time. Your turn will come." His triumphant leer needs wiped off his smarmy face. I clench my eyes shut but the very vocal encouragement and pornographic soundtrack fill my ears. A guttural roar of release causes the room to quieten and all the sexual energy to dissipate. I see her raised to her feet, used and smiling. A cloak and hood of deepest black is placed around her shoulders. One more that needs saving. Those stains will take some getting out.

"The time draws nigh." They move into a close huddle near the communion rail. Kneeling, half exposed and faces upturned, as their celebrant walks along in front of them. Their kisses on his, now coated, stiffening member are well received. Their chanting is much more serious now. Its in pigeon Latin and full of the usual mumbo jumbo. Perhaps this is the start of Father Jeremy's portal spell. I can't feel the power, its like trying to hold fog. It is disappearing as soon as it comes into being.

"Master come among us." Is their chant, repeated over and over. It is a dull monotonous and unimaginative chant but there is something not happening.

"Tonight he will come among us." Red Robe exults, his eyes shining brightly. He casts his gaze across the assembly, his face exultant. His eyes alight on the only one in white in the

183

gathering. "Come to me child." He points and a fully compliant Michelle Brookes picks her way forward. I struggle, although I know it is futile. The foot pressing my head against the floor gives me a shunt, making tears blur my vision. For once I am glad I can't see.

Is her offering going to be enough to open the portal? I doubt it, even though she is a virgin. The power just isn't here to deliver. Fuck, blood and sex. Is she to be sacrificed? Has she been kept for a real sacrifice? A real blood opening of the portal?

"Watch Maggot, and savour your failure." Where do they get their lines? Is there a book of sinister and lame Satanist phrases? A satanic phrases for dummies? Hammer House of Horror circa nineteen seventy? Michelle Brookes is lying on the Altar, passive but still clothed. The Red Robed Priest is offering a libation to those present. I shudder to think what is in that chalice but the recipients seem keen to partake. I can feel my tongue curling at the thought.

He returns to the altar his robes hiding Michelle from sight like Dracula in the movies. When he steps away blood covers her chest in a crimson pool. "Oh dear God no." I whisper, He has stabbed her. Our failure is total. She is lost and I can do nothing about it.

"Behold our sacrifice." He holds his bloody hands high. "With my blood she is marked for our master." A cut across one palm, the source of the blood. Relief floods through me as I realise that the blood isn't hers. Where the fuck is Brotherton?

"With my blood, I mark you for my master." He parades among the flock, marking their foreheads. Blood bringing power, earthy and ancient, to this gathering. A thunderclap goes off in my head as I feel, a few miles, away a rift opening. Vincenzo, it appears, was right. A vision of the event sears into me. My body arching as if connected to electricity.

Another Altar, a small gathering and a different sacrifice. They have duped us. The real masters are not even here. They have completed the ritual and siphoned off the essence from here. The blackness of the rift sucks all light into it and I know It has crossed over. In a flash the image is gone. Leaving me gasping for air. Another dig with a heel and I lose my vision to tears of pain and impotent rage. Michelle is raised from the altar, alive and well but covered in his blood and marked for their master, who is on his way. She seems to be happy, the smile on her face is wide and beaming. She is the star turn. More so than Hannah. Young women are so competitive.

"Make your offering girl." His voice is thick with lust, and his body beginning to show that desire made flesh. "Our Master is coming. The world trembles at his footsteps." For once he is speaking the literal truth. I know that he is on his way, and we need help.

"My body is my offering.'" She speaks softly but in the expectant silence it sounds like a shout. I can feel the coming storm, like a tsunami charging across the flat sands. When it gets here and crashes over us, we are all well and truly screwed.

"Show us; be not ashamed of your beauty." Her dainty fingers untie the white robe letting it fall away and pool at her feet. She steps proudly forward for all those gathered to see. She has much to be proud of. A heavy crash as the portable ram bursts in the front doors. Brotherton has arrived before their master.

God must love a western. I wanted rescued much earlier but in the nick of time will have to do. The stamping of heavy feet and manly shouts are like the sweetest hymns ever sung. The black uniformed, body-armour wearing, night stick wielding shock troops fill the room. Brotherton is shouting and so are most of the storm troopers. Nut-kicker has given me a souvenir as he legs it. I retch, depositing my tossed cookies all over the floor. My misery is almost complete. Groggily I get to my hands and knees. I need to get up quickly. There is so little time. 'Breathe.' I tell myself. I can feel the rising tide. He is coming.

Brotherton is directing the traffic as cuffs are applied and the screaming half naked women are carried from the church to our row of police vans. I manage to cough out his name and catch his eye. He looks shocked but glad to see me I think. He covers the ground quickly and is solicitous of my health. Apparently I look like shit. Well looks aren't deceiving after all.

"There is no time Brotherton. We need to clear everyone out now." I must sound crazed as I cling on to him. I am unsteady on my feet and grab a pew with my other hand, anchoring me vertically.

"It's fine. We got them." Bless him, he has no idea. He seems to think we are about to close them down.

"Get her out." I point at the now covered and compliant Michelle Brookes. She is being comforted by a female officer. The lights are on and the place is in chaos. I need a drink; the taste of vomit is not my favourite. A tremor strikes the building. He is here.

"It is too late Brotherton. Get her behind us." His wide eyes tell me that he can feel it too. "Now!" I bark at him. "Move." And his limbs start to respond. We may be in deep trouble here. I step into the space between the pews directly between Michelle

Brookes and the entrance. This may be a last bastion to slow the devil that is coming. Sort of like Verdun. 'Il ne passeront pas'. If it gets to Michelle, all marked in blood, then she will be lost and we will be lunch. Failure will be total and devastating.

The house of God, no matter which denomination, is a powerful place. The fact that this one has squatters has an effect but doesn't totally remove the sanctity. It is still His house. I hope that tonight at this Sabbat, and peak of Dark power, there is enough to drive away our enemy. Now is the time for faith, the flaw in my character. Knowledge is not faith, and it might matter this time.

"Brotherton, light that fucking candle." I point to the 'God is in' candle that they have extinguished. He looks nonplussed. "Just do it." I shout. I see him fumbling for his lighter. Michelle and the female police officer are in the far corner, ashen faced and afraid. They have no understanding of why they are afraid but they are right to be. We are in peril. Brotherton is all thumbs yet getting there.

"In the name of the Father, and of The Son and of The Holy Spirit. Amen. Blessed is he who comes in the name of The Lord. Hosannah in the highest." I cross myself and pull myself together. Raising my crucifix to my lips, a kiss of my saviour and I am ready. The cold of the Otherworld floods the church. The chill crawls across the floor and washes over everything it encounters. A synchronised scream fills the air from behind me. The air ripples. It is kick-off time.

A heavy thump, thump, thump builds the fear ahead of the arrival. The violent thrust of the doors wrenches them from their hinges with glass and splinters cascading around. The boom of the exterior doors slamming shut tells me there is no escape. Hairy, heavily-muscled, otherworldly arms extend from a huge hulking form, half hidden by the shadows. The cloven hooves I expect to see are reptilian, clawed and vicious looking. Not a goat manifestation then.

"I am come." A voice like nails on a blackboard assails our ears. I wonder if mine have started to bleed the spite so vicious and malice laden.

"You have no place here. Go back to the pit from whence you came." All formal and clear. Its never a good idea to get in front of a devil-demon thing but tonight I have no choice. Red baleful eyes turn on me. I feel my skin trying to crawl away as it stares. I want to run, and keep running, but there is nowhere to go. If I fail, we four will perish and that I cannot allow. It steps inside. I can feel its discomfort. Good, we might not get munched after all. The sanctity of a church is hard to erase and our visitor will not bear its touch without discomfort.

"You cannot withstand me. I come to claim my own." It hulks forward, talons looking mighty sharp and cruelly curved. The smell of rot is overpowering, and if I hadn't already tossed my cookies I would be joining in the synchronised vomiting with the others. Their retching bringing amusement to the Demon before me. Humans are so weak before him. "I am the master here." It spits the words from a, very unlikely, many fanged mouth. That mouth was designed for shredding flesh not massacring the spoken word.

"My Lord, is the Master here. His light shines bringing light to his house and the world." I hope Brotherton has managed to light the candle. While not really necessary, it is symbolic. Symbols are often forgotten or misunderstood but there is much that is ritual that has its roots in magic and the mystics of early Christianity.

A buffeting wind howls through the church, carrying a cruel laugh with it, causing The draperies to flap wildly and causing the hanging lights to swing on their cables. All around the altar candles are extinguished by the blast. All but one, God is in the House; and right behind me. The tumbling padded kneelers careen across the floor like a snowstorm.

"In the Name of The Father, Son and Holy Spirit I abjure you. You shall return to the hells that were made for you. I abjure you in the Name of Christ. Go from here. Your time has passed." All very serious and laden with power. I feel it flinch before me. Words have such power and at times like this key phrases unlock real power.

Gobbets of half digested flesh and green ichors pours from its maw in a projectile stream, splattering around me and (no doubt) ruining another pair of shoes and trousers. The air is filled with the sweet stench of decay and saliva is filling my mouth, a precursor to my vomiting.

"I will feast!" it roars, and sadly I get the spray. Lead-lined stained-glass windows behind the altar shatter outwards under the percussive blast. I can hear screaming and hope it isn't me. There will be no way to hush this up; too many will be witnesses to this event.

"You will never pass. The Lord of Hosts is with me. His power compels you. Begone. I abjure you in His name." I reach for the lead crystal vial in my pocket, which luckily survived the kicking I got. The Beast thrashes left and right, splintering pews and scattering the hand-embroidered padded-kneelers that had survived the earlier blast. A lovely thistle adorned one sails by. With an ear bursting roar it surges forward.

You know that faith I was talking about earlier. Now comes its test. My damnation and evisceration are dependent on my faith. The certain knowledge of the existence of the Almighty is not the question. The faith being tested is in his redeeming my soul, in His having washed away the Original Sin and in his divine love and protection.

"I will feast on your sin-laden soul. I smell the carnal sins, you are covered in them. I will savour their flavours over a very long time, your torment will last for eternity." A triumphal sneer accompanied these words, and a snatch at my chest. Grabbing a clawful of fabric the Beast hoists me from my feet towards the fangs.

The blistering swish of Holy water, criss-crossing at close range forced the Beast to recoil and cast me away. Glad as I am to be away from those teeth and the smell I am less glad to crash into the rail and crumple in an agonised heap. This time the synchronised screaming has me in the team. The bass section is supplied by our Otherworld visitor, holy water sizzling and

189

searing putrid flesh. It seems to have gotten some in the eyes, which has got to smart some. The wild flailing of massive clawed limbs sends pews in all directions. Furniture piling and destruction for beginners.

I am helped to my feet by Brotherton who, bless him, still looks terrified. The hammering on the main doors outside are a mere counterpoint in the cacophony. We need to pray. It's a powerful weapon in fighting the enemy. I drop to my knees dragging Brotherton beside me.

"Pray. By all you hold dear, Pray!" I cough and a little froth escapes my lips. Worse still it is pink froth. Not the best sign at the moment. Breathing seems to be hard work and a bit gurgly.

"Our father, who art in heaven, hallowed be thy name." I start it off for him, maybe the female police officer will join in. Michelle is out of it, probably just as well. Brotherton is starting to mumble along and might even be getting some of the words right. The Beast is flailing and clawing the air as our words land heavily on it. They must feel like physical blows to the demon as it reels and sways beneath them.

"Keep going, it is working." I shout to Brotherton who is only three feet away. I stand and wielding my holy water, I advance. The roaring in my ears is getting louder and louder.

"With this Holy water, I cast you back into the pit. Like Saint Michael and his Angels did so long ago. With this Holy water I abjure you. Begone! I command you in the name of The Lord. He who is Lord of All. He who is with me and lends me his strength. I abjure you, Unclean Spirit. Go back to the Abyss and await your destruction." I manage to get the words out past the agony in my chest.

The Holy water drops bring a scream of torment as they land but it is running out, my words and Brotherton's prayer are heavy blows causing the Beast to flinch repeatedly. If I can drive it from this church, Michelle Brookes we will be safe this night. The alternative is not one to contemplate.

The last drops are gone and it is still here, screaming but still here. Fumbling in my pockets I feel the small ceramic jar of holy unction. It may be what I need. I hope so as we have not much else left. I feel cold and my fingers seem to be trembling. The cough erupting from my chest doubles me over. It seems that Beast and I are well and truly fucked. If there was a referee then this fight would have been stopped by now. The Holy unction has smeared all over my hand as I fumbled the lid and drop the jar. Worse than a butter-fingered slip catcher.

"You will be mine Nazarene." Snarls reach my ears. It is right next to me, the claws dig into my shoulders as it pulls me in for a kiss. I would scream but there is no air in me to do so. The agony so intense is ripping through me as the claws rend my flesh. I gulp for air like a landed, desperate fish. The snapping of my collarbone goes unnoticed under the searing pain of the claws gouging deeper. There isn't much left in me as I start to feel my life ebbing away under its claws.

"I abjure you." I manage a whisper as my unction smeared hand pushes against its sweat covered chest. I am too stubborn to give up and die. The blinding burst of white light and a close range detonation are all I am aware of. It is over, my lights are going out.

Chapter 37

Waking up on a hospital bed, with tubes coming out of me, is not a great habit to get into. I feel so heavy that I just wait, my eyes are as focussed as a Vaseline smeared lens. Soft focus, more like unable to focus but I hope that will improve. I do the check. I can move my toes. If nothing else that is a win. My tongue is thick and cardboard-like. I try my eyes again as I wiggle my toes but that seems too much for me, I have no energy. It feels like I am just empty; no fuel. My leaden eyelids resist my attempts to get them open properly. My ears are working fine. I can hear a button being pressed and a whispered 'He's wakening now' reaches me. I am awake, its not like I am dead. The footsteps seem quite hurried, clacking on the floor. The lights are so dim, must be part of the efficiency savings. Another budget saving for the national treasure that is the NHS.

"Father Steel, can you hear me?" A bright white light is shone right in my eye; oh that's nice. Thanks, not. My mouth is moving but not much is coming out. They fill my mouth with water, lukewarm plastic tasting and foul. It works though. Apparently very little can't be improved with a little lube.

"I can hear you." I manage to croak, "Now get that fucking light out of my eyes" I want to add but I manage to avoid saying so. There is an audible sigh of relief from my care team. It seems they were very worried about me.

"You are a very lucky man, Father Steel. That was a close call." He's doing his best to make me feel better. Aren't doctors getting younger these days? Add them to the list that includes policemen.

"Being that close to a gas explosion and surviving, basically intact, is a miracle." He whitters on. So we are calling it a gas explosion, oh aye that will work.

"You will be going for some tests, and I will see you in the morning. Rest now, you are in good hands. I will contact Inspector Brotherton and let him know you can see him in the morning." There, there now off to sleep. The drugs are great, I just let all his drivel wash by and not one sarcastic reply. Gas leak, for goodness sake. You couldn't make it up. I wonder what stellar genius thought up that excuse. It is worse than the dog ate my homework.

So Broken collarbone, broken ribs, punctured lung and severe lacerations to the shoulder counts for basically intact these days. Let's not add in the nut-ache and stamp mark on my head, the black eyes, split lip, stitches in my scalp and the bruising pretty much covering my body. Yeah I am a picture of health. I read my chart and the notes on the file that was left casually lying about, when I looked like I was sleeping. Bruising to the brain and swelling from a possible fractured skull also part of my pretty much intact. I hate to see what not intact looked like.

"Father." Brotherton, is standing at the foot of the bed. My grumpy, frowny face is in place until I realise it is him. I wasn't really focussing as I let my mind wander about in the sedated state.

"Brotherton, you made it too." I smile a little. I don't want to laugh as it will hurt like hell. He has not a mark on him. That is so unfair. How did he manage that?

"Gas explosions are so dangerous. I am glad you are still with us." I wince at the in joke. He can see what I think of the Gas leak. "Father, I have some updates for you. We got a good sweep of these guys. Organ trafficking money is being recovered and charges laid on a number of the group. As Hannah is sixteen there was no offence there as she consented but the drugging and coercion of a minor has a few more in the cells. They will be going to HM Peterhead with the sex offenders or Barlinnie for the general criminals.' He seems happy. He got his men. I manage a twitch of my lips, it looks like a smile sort of.

"Well done, Brotherton. Big promotion in the offing for you?" I try to be interested. We got some of them but not the leader nor his inner cabal. Still a win is a win, as they say.

193

"No chance, they are slimming down the upstairs posts anyway. I might be moving to a new unit anyway." He looks at me, it is a funny look. Fucked if I can be bothered to ask.

"Yes, it was real. Welcome to my world." I don't need to be psychic to know what he wanted to know. He knew the answer but just wanted me to say it. A little confirmation that he wasn't hallucinating.

"I'll bet the notebooks are very interesting reading." I wink and try to smile. How on earth are they going to keep that one quiet. Good luck with that.

Chapter 38

It's funny, waiting to go that is. It was bad enough being sent back to my home town to solve a murder but being reluctant to go now that my task is done is, somewhat, surprising. A definite touch of maudlin sentimentality. Who would have thought it? I am a cold, uncaring bastard I hear. It appears I will miss the place.

The replacement should be here soon. I hope he is prompt. I have completed the final walk rounds and tidy ups. The service of re-consecration has been completed, in private, and God's candle is proclaiming that the Big Man is in. I have cleansed the building from bottom to top and it is now, once again, the house of God. It is a shiny, clean spiritual haven. The building works were completed by the time I was fit to walk unaided and without the stick. The new guy wont be told everything, obviously, but I'll know. And that's enough. The Bishop, personally, recommends this guy, so that's him fucked then.

My little red sunny waits patiently to take me back to my salubrious digs in the Capital, commonly called the barracks. Actually it is the very well appointed seminary. Spartan might be the best description but as I have very little, what do I actually need? An e-book reader would be nice, a Porsche perhaps? Maybe if there was a performance bonus scheme?

A blue Volvo pulls into the car park, with a young-ish, dog-collared, chap behind the wheel. Aren't Priests getting younger these days? Must be an age thing. He hasn't noticed my lurking and he seems genuinely cheerful. I am sure that won't last. I've met the congregation. I wonder if Angela will tempt and corrupt him? A little smile turns up the corner of my mouth, I hope she's over that little kink. I have had a tearful meeting with her and we have managed to get help for Michelle in the form of a scholarship summer school where she will be 'helped'. I hope she doesn't need excoriated. David Brookes just thinks he is surrounded by moody women and no one will tell him otherwise.

He parks and makes his way towards me and when I step from the shadow I catch him a little by surprise. That's me the ninja-master. Much like David Carradine's Kung Fu.

"Father Steel?" His hand extends and a smile that goes from perfect white teeth tips to his sparkly blue eyes. A real smile with nothing held back. Shiny.

"Good to meet you Father Matthew, I'm sure you'll be happy here." I do try occasionally. He doesn't need to know how clean I have made his new building.

"I am sure I shall. What are the congregation like? Are they recovered from the death of Father MacPhail?" His question hangs a little as I decide which version of events to share. Better not share too much.

"They take some getting used to. Although it is amazing what you can get used to. I think they need a new hand to take them forward." I smile, well more a sardonic twitch of my lips but it's the best I can do. A dossier has been left for his bedtime reading. It's a page turner. Perhaps I should have left a bottle of Johnny Walker to help him get over the shock. Too late, now.

"Excellent." We look at each other, he looks like a Priest whereas I just look a bit crumpled. I hand him the keys to his little part of the Rock of Saint Peter. Symbolic but he is impervious, perhaps it would be better if he stayed that way.

"Right, I'm off. Good luck Brother." I shake his hand again and he nods, still smiling. Clunk-kitty-clunk and the doors to my escape pod are unlocked. A quick pre-flight check and I pull away, the scream of the fan-belt setting my teeth on edge. Better get that fixed.

The End.

In the Shadow of St Giles.

by

Altany Craik

For my Wife, who doesn't like horror stories but she puts up with me anyway.

Chapter 1

Hair is a strange thing. Why it holds on to a psychic impression I don't know but it does. In fact it sometimes works better than skin for my gift, it doesn't always but this time it does. The long hair I have in my fingers I picked off an iron fence that was thick with paint which was in the process of drying. It was waving there for me to find, catching the street light and screaming touch me.

Anyway, this hair, detached from the owner's head was like a full VCR replay without the snow and fuzzy bit at the top. The picture of the otherworlder's face (we are so politically correct these days, personally I call them demons) vivid and instantly frightening. The malice that it had exuded probably made this hair jump to escape. The deep black and red skin with sharp fangs would be enough to terrify most people. It had terrified her.

Somewhere around here it had struck. It was the third time. Somewhere around here a body would be found. Somewhere around here another memory highlight for the poor soul that discovers the body. I sigh, something I have being doing a lot these days. It seems to me that these events are coming closer together with fewer false alarms in between. Worse still, this is in Edinburgh where I live. Hiding in plain sight, or at least buried under the masses of people, it is effectively using the human noise to mask its presence and movements.

This one is a hard, slippery Bastard. Another name not in the Bishop's prescribed lexicon. I suppose I need to call him, the Bishop, not that he'll be worried about me. After all priests wandering darkened streets, at three in the morning, is so safe. Do I leave the call until the morning? A sane person would, I suppose. Perhaps I will wait until I find the body and answer the awkward questions that the nice policemen will want answered.

'How did you come to be here at this time of night, sir?' I can almost hear it, the serious tone devoid of humour.'I was following a hair.' Alice eat your heart out. Perhaps I will be able to think of an appropriate response, not including a swear word. I can feel her but not the demon. Her body is nearby, dead obviously, but very close.In the labyrinth of the Old Town the shadows and secret places are many and well concealed. Under the Cowgate, and below the busier sections, is where my aimless wanderings have brought me. It has a certain smell, quite unlike anywhere else, old decay and laden with memories. Layer upon layer of events, detritus and vomit give texture and depth to the olfactory assault. Add now blood and demonic ejaculate and the platter of scents is complete.

Human brains do us a favour; they hide horrors to give us time to look away. Sadly, I have to look; it comes with the territory. The discarded torn body, half hidden under orange commercial refuse sacks, is a real treat. The spray shows up, to me, all over the walls of this alley and looks like an explosion in a paint factory. Luckily darkness will hide the worst from others for a while. The shredding of her flesh is the result of curved talons and an orgiastic frenzy and yet her face is untouched. It is contorted in agony but still recognisable, although all life has fled the scene. This poor girl was picked from a Friday night herd and taken. Her parents will be devastated, their grief adding to the tears of the world.

Another sigh and I am working my slightly numb fingers on my smartphone screen. Now that it is unlocked I need to choose; Bishop or police? Probably best to alert the Polis first. A few taps and I am through to a rather efficient operator.

'Can you wait until the Police arrive?' The female voice asks, no pressure implied. Do they get training to be non-threatening to witnesses?

'Of course.' It's not like I will be going anywhere, anytime soon. So many people call and leave, not wanting to be involved. I would probably be called anyway, cuts out the middle man.

'My name?' I respond caught a bit off guard. 'Father Steel,

Andrew Steel.' Best bond voice and diction. I hang up, a little embarrassed at myself. This is no place for levity,something I often fail to recognise. Time to do my thing before I have any company and awkward questions.

A short prayer for the poor lost soul, whose body adorns this place, and I tip-toe through the puddles. I know that I will get a reaction and I ready myself. I touch her fingertips ever so lightly, giving me the chance to break the connection quickly if I should need to. The scream is like a sonic boom in my head causing me to jump away as her agony floods through me. Her last scream would have raised every house in the area. Why then did her passing go unnoticed? The psychic scream of Brenda Forth was like a red hot poker in my brain as I relived her last moments. The tears are sprinting across my cheeks and cascading onto the cold, dark stone. Another layer of pain laid on this psychic tapestry; not the first and probably not the last.

In the distance, and approaching fast, are the sirens. Utterly pointless now that the deed has been done. Waking up the neighbours for entertainment perhaps? The blue lights are soon bouncing off the alley walls; revealing and hiding the blood stains as they strobe round. The alley walls like the camouflage on the side of jeeps and trucks with the splatter patterns.

'Step away from the body, Sir.' Authoritative and polite; never knew it was possible. Aren't they getting younger these days? Fucked if I know.

I suppose I should be glad that it's not that cold and not raining as the young constable takes my statement. It is a long drawn out, pencil and paper, exercise. Full name, where was I born? Where do I live? Where was I going? It is this last one that stops the bus, as it were. Obviously he doesn't like my answer. Not really that surprising to me.

His brows furrow as he looks up from his little black book of tedious details. 'Sorry, where were you going at this time of night?' He repeats, changing my status in his head from body-finder to suspect. Small wonder that so few crimes are actually solved these days.

'I was coming here.' I know, I could have thought of something better but I have had enough with the charade.

'Why?' It gets out before he can stop it, his police face all confused.

'To find this.' I am being an unhelpful sod but it is late and I am bored now. He, on the other hand, is somewhat stunned. I dig out my wallet and extract my ID. God squad, my crime scene. I hand it to him and wait for the lights to come on.

'I'll get the Sergeant.' He manages and wanders a few steps away before realising I could wander off. 'Come with me, Father.' These city cops aren't too bad, it seems. I smile and tag along as he moves through the tape.

'Sarge?' He approaches tentatively. The Sarge looks like the one from Hong Kong Phooey – you know, a bit round and carrying his doughnuts in front of him.

'Yes?' Oh dear the walrus moustache makes him look fierce. My PC hands him my credentials, wordlessly. He obviously can't think of a better description than God Squad, either. I can almost hear the growl underneath the bushiest mouser I have seen in years. He gives me the 'I-have-seen-everything-now' look. He's not suitably impressed by me. What does he expect? Robes and the Spanish Inquisition?

He performs a perfunctory 'Check these out' over his radio-walkie-talkie thing. It doesn't take long for their authenticity to come back. His gruff look of disappointment is almost comical; I try not to laugh.

'Father Steel, Glad to have you. How can I help?' You could have knocked me over with a feather. He seems sincere too. This is not at all what I am used to. I usually find the territorial tendencies kick in and I am obstructed until I pull rank on the locals; Edinburgh it appears will be different.

'I will just try to stay out of your way, but we need to see where the blood trail goes. He will have been covered in it.' Blinding statement of the obvious. Best if I keep the surprises to a minimum for now.

'Of course, SOCO will be here soon. We are canvassing the

area for witnesses; someone will have heard something or if we are lucky, seen something.' He is so different from what I expected. He seems quite effective; a nice surprise at four in the morning.

'Excellent. Pretend I am not here.' I smile disarmingly, or at least I hope so.

'MacGregor. I am Sergeant MacGregor. I am sure the Inspector will want a word when he gets here. He's on his way.' I nod and shake the proffered hand. Two shakes, up and down and its over, like pissing in a public urinal.

I wander around like Inspector Clouseau but trying not to mess with the evidence. There is no real sign of a blood splattered trail leading away. Maybe in the daylight it will show up and that isn't all that long away. In my head I am rolling the VT of her last moments, horrible and vicious as it was, in the hope that I can glean something from reliving it. No streams of tears this time, fortunately. My grim set face seems to stop anyone from speaking directly to me but I overhear the little snippets 'Who is he? What is he doing here?' You know, the usual stuff.

Waiting for the Inspector is like waiting for a bus; no sign of one then two come along together. Actually one is a Chief Inspector and the other a Detective Inspector. The one with the shiny buttons is the Chief, apparently. The other one is in a crumpled overcoat. Oh my god, it's Rebus. I smile at my own, internalised, humour. Then wipe it off quickly as Chief Buttons approaches. He has been briefed it would appear.

'Father Steel, Chief Inspector Cushions. Terrible business.' I replay his words and find it was Cousins not cushions, would have been funnier my way. I nod and 'Rebus' sticks out a hand and nods. 'DI White.' He'll be the one doing the actual work.

'Good Morning, Don't let me get in the way.' I try self-deprecation as a way of getting them to bugger off while I think. This is the third murder in as many weeks and we are still fumbling about in the dark. This is the first time I have been on-site, as it were. There were no crimes against the church to call

208

me to but I invited myself to this one. A few more pleasantries, card exchanges and I am left alone again, just watching and thinking.

Now the Brass and the Boss are here, order seems to spring from the chaos. Everyone knows their role and gets stuck in. The media, unshaven and rumpled are beyond the black and yellow tape that flaps gently in the breeze. I try to do my fade into the background act and I hope they haven't noticed me. Bishop Michael wants no questions yet.

Chief Inspector Cushions heads down to give a statement as SOCO and the Police doctor enter the alley from the other end. Thankfully there are no snappers trying to catch neither an explicit picture of the murder scene nor the mortal remains of Brenda Forth. For that I am sure her family will be truly thankful.

I am caught off guard by DI White when he hands me a polystyrene cup with dark liquid inside, I hope its coffee not something stronger.

'It's black. If you need milk and sugar you don't like coffee.' He smiles a genuine smile that reaches his eyes. He is a decent spud, apparently and quite young for a Detective Inspector, probably past thirty five but not by much.

'Thanks.' I take a sip and try to look cool, but it is foul. 'Not that this is much like coffee.' White adds 'It's from McGregor's Thermos' He swigs and tolerates the foul taste. His eyes catch mine and hold them. He has The Question.

'Why are you here Father?' His voice is not a whisper but it does only reach my ears. He is discrete too, another blessing to be counted.

'To help.' I look over the white foam rim and see his face hardening, so I carry on, he deserves more 'Seriously, I am here to help. We need to stop these murders.' He isn't ready for the Big Truth yet.

'Well, we need all the help we can get. What do you think is going on?' He looks round the crime scene; he is keeping this between us.

'A vicious psychopath is cutting a swathe through the town

and leaving very few clues. He is careful and yet the killings seem to be frenzied. Where's the blood?' Say nothing and yet seem to say a lot is a neat trick. I should be in politics.

'He's a careful psychopath then. These look random but something is niggling at me. No decent lines of enquiry are presenting themselves and the connections between the victims don't seem to exist.' His frustration is seeping out and that look, you know the seen-too-much look, has crept into his eyes. It happens and lurks around the eyes; a something that screams a pain in the soul that will never truly be washed away. Many cops get it; especially those that care and deal with murders, it makes them old before their time. DI White's salt and pepper hair is beginning to thin and his gut is hanging a little over his belt but he seems to command the respect of the uniforms at the scene. Like I said, he's a decent spud.

'A fresh pair of eyes maybe?' I hope it didn't come out as 'Let me do it.' I really need to think first and speak second. Oh well, too fucking late this time.

'Good idea.' He means it 'Meet me at the task force centre this afternoon and you can dig away.' And with that he's called away. Stunned, I sip the disgusting sludge in a cup. This might be a pleasure, not a struggle, working with the Edinburgh Polis.

The Task Force Centre actually looks like one; you know desks, whiteboards, computers and cops running around like organised headless chickens. The Glossy pictures adorning the boards are a veritable collage of blood-splattered-TV-serial-killer-show-style scenes of carnage. Enough to make a hooker blush as they say or probably don't. I stand in the doorway, with my visitor badge on show, looking like a little lost sheep. Perhaps my hesitation is down to the lack of challenge or approach. I could be anybody.

I bimble with purpose over to the first board. Grizzly doesn't cover it. Grim probably does. The Victim's name is Annabelle Weston, that doesn't sound that local to me. It appears that I am right, she'd moved here from Manchester only last year. Discovered by the Bin men when they were doing the weekly uplift. No witnesses, no clues, no DNA and no chance. Slashed and eviscerated but no marks on her face. The look of terror will need brain bleach to remove it. A plethora of triplicate, typed forms cover the board and none of them are new. It seems the investigation has moved on to the next scene from serial killers 101.

I wander along, not quite aimlessly but, with an indefinite purpose. I have been to the next scene but the body had been removed by then. I saw the splatters and splashes of blood and they looked like a frenzy in the daylight; that was ten days ago. The home office pathologist report on the cause of death has stabbing in capital letters. I nearly snort derisively. I suppose disembowelled by demon claws wouldn't be in the drop down menu of choices. Massive blood loss incompatible with life in bold in the notes. You think? I shake my head at the lack of leads or viable lines of enquiry on this board. Drawing a blank would be overstating the progress. No witnesses on this one either. Not exactly the pattern I am looking for. Perhaps I need to touch the bodies? That will be a highlight to savour. The look of disgust must be showing as the 'worker ants' are beginning to notice my dog collar.

A WPC, if we are still allowed to call them that, approaches me. Just the right mix of 'Are you lost?' and 'Not another bloody brass visitor' covers here face. She opens her mouth and a clear concise and effective 'Good afternoon Father. DI White said you would be along' is delivered. And she never said 'I thought you'd be older.' I smile gently, almost like she might expect. Play nice is my new motto.

'Good Afternoon, just leave me to it for now.' I don't want to waste her time nor let anyone in on the fact that I know as little as they do. I am meant to be a help, after all.

She nods and does just that; leaves me to it. Obviously she has real work to do. Across the office a ringing phone is answered by a rather spotty, dishevelled young man not in a uniform.

'DC MacBride.' He rasps into the receiver. I can't believe he is a detective; he looks about twelve years old. The face he pulls as he tastes the, apparently very cold, contents of his mug tells a story. The coffee here is disgusting. I smile at his discomfort and turn away before anyone notices. This is not a place for levity.

Reading police-speak reports is a tiring pastime and I have persevered much longer than I usually do. The manilla folders have moved from one pile to a new one as I plodded my way through them. Witnesses are very thin on the ground and are proving that they saw and heard not very much. Only one nags at me and not because it comes from a prostitute. Her witness statement has a reference to being cold and uneasy. A possible lead for me, not much use to the polis though. I make a note of her name and address and her working handle too, well you never know when you will need something like that. A prostitute called Tiffany, sounds so much more exotic than Carol MacDougall.

'Tea Father?' The WPC is back and seems at ease with my presence. I smile again, getting the hang of playing nice.

'Call me Andrew.' I take the red mug catching sight of the 'keep calm and carry on' logo; so very apt for this place.

'PC Craig, Jill.' She smiles back and I notice her lovely eyes. She is pretty but she looks about twelve too. They are getting younger these days. It isn't my imagination.

'When will DI White be back?' Not that I really need him but I will want to talk to him now that I am up to speed on the pointless reports.

'He will be in around six. Is there anything I can help with?' She hooks a wayward lock of brown hair behind her left ear. It is an unconscious thing and probably takes place twenty times an hour.

'I need to see the bodies. Can you arrange it?' It is a matter of fact delivery and I offer no explanation as to why. She seems unfazed, as if expecting unusual requests from me. After all how many priests are included in a multiple murder investigation?

'Of course, I can take you over to the morgue after your tea if you'd like? I just need to make a call.' I nod and soon I will be off to a harrowing event, oh the joys of my life.

'Annabelle Weston.' The orderly pronounces as he pulls out the tray. The cold air rolls out like Dracula's fog. The ruination of her torso is profound and, although tidied up, is still shocking in the severity of the wounds. Her blonde hair has lost its shine and clings limply to her head. Thankfully, the terror has faded from her features, her face is slack and betrays none of the trauma she suffered. I let my fingers trace along her forehead. My audience seem scandalised that I am touching the body.

A rapier thrust of visions lances into my brain like a scalding. Almost instantly I need to be away from contact. I am hearing her screams and feeling the lacerations as they were being inflicted. Vivid, almost a re-enacting, I break contact and stumble away. The pains in my gut I know are echoes but they feel very real to my brain and I collapse in a heap. I would say I was writhing but more like a contortionist explosion as I rub my chest.

'Are you all right Father?' They are in my face, all

concerned and worried. My body is bathed in sweat that has miraculously coated me in seconds. I manage to pull air into my lungs. To their stares I expect I look like a landed fish. The gulping is steadying my breathing and I manage to croak 'I'm fine.' After all, doesn't everyone throw themselves on the ground after touching a body? They don't seem to believe me, if the looks on their faces are anything to go by.

Her, Annabelle's, experience was viciousness incarnate but more than that was the undercurrent of sexual gratification. The demon had taken her; keeping her alive and conscious as his barbed, engorged phallus ripped up into her insides. I could feel my gorge rising as I began to relive and feel the tearing in my gut. Luckily I was able to shut down the feelings and keep the contents of my stomach from presenting themselves all over the floor. A plastic cup is being thrust into my hand, and directions to drink are beginning to intrude on my brain. I drink it and sit for a moment; you know, recovering as if anyone really recovers from this.

'Why is there no mention of sexual trauma in the notes?' I fire out from left field. Their faces, at another time might be comical, are shocked. Apparently it was a secret. Not from me it wasn't.

'We haven't ascertained what caused the damage to her. It is almost like a medieval torture piece was used.' PC Craig manages to mumble out, her young features still not covering the shock she has held in about it.

'I see.' I don't feel the need to expand further. A little mystery never goes amiss. Anyway I need to get outside and I let Annabelle Weston's memories slip away for now. Memories that will lead me to her killer. No one gets away with this.

From her eyes, as she was torn and shredded, I caught a glimpse of where it killed her. Not where she was dumped but where it did the deed. Unluckily for the Demon I recognise the place. His trail may be cold but it isn't gone. I am coming and he won't enjoy that.

214

Chapter 3

'So Father, Jill tells me we had an episode at the morgue.' DI White, it seems, is a master of understatement. He doesn't seem too happy either. I thought he was going to be all right, too. I am sure the disappointment wont kill me.

'You might call it that; I couldn't possibly comment.' A Sir Humphrey response. I am being childish but I have an excuse. I can still feel the ache in my gut from having my womb ruptured. Oh wait, I don't have one; so why do I still ache?

'Talk to me Father Steel. What do I need to know?' Maybe he'll be okay after all. Maybe he's getting heat from above, now is the time I suppose. I sigh.

'DI White, I am going to tell you something. Something difficult to believe but is true none the less.' I pause for effect. His eyes have narrowed as his suspicion is writ large on his face. He doesn't interrupt, however.

'You know that I represent the Church and the Home Office.' He nods, unsure of where I am going. His face is schooled almost as if he has to regularly hide his thinking.

'This is covered by the Official Secrets Act and disclosing the things I tell you will result in prosecution and imprisonment.' I use my serious adult voice. The blue twinkle in his eyes is excitement not psychosis, I hope. He waits, leaning forward slightly.

'I am a psychic. When there are crimes that need my gifts I am sent to resolve them. Your murders need my gifts. Our murderer is a demon.' I wait for a beat. His breathing is steady and he seems to accept what I am saying.

'However, we can hardly go on the news with that.' I smile gently. Usually the recipient of my statement babbles a bit. Some times they have an explosive denial and outburst. DI white just soaked it up.

'So what happened in the morgue?' Damn he's good. No wasted questions; just right in. Damn, I like him.

'I touched the body and I got a full replay of her passing. It wasn't pleasant.' He nods as if he understands, Bless him. 'I get to feel it too.' He winces in sympathy earning some brownie points with me.

'I did get a lead, though.' I produce my rabbit from my proverbial hat. Although, to be honest, it's a very small rabbit and Edinburgh is a very big hat.

'This one?' DI white asks, hopefully. It's only the fifth set of flats that look exactly like the view I got. I shrug. It might be but, then again, I thought the last two were definitely right. We press the trades button and I let DI White push. The wave of psychic power that washes over us is intense causing me to stagger back. There is a sweeter smell too.

'This is it.' I manage to choke out a few words. My mouth is filling with saliva and my stomach is giving petite-lurches wanting to join in. I really don't want to hurl right now, not after the morgue performance. I want DI White to respect me in the morning. Why? I have no idea but I still do.

'Smells a bit fruity.' White sniffs the air. A penlight comes out and the super-strong cone of white light reveals a very dirty stairwell filled with detritus. The residents, apparently, don't seem to mind.

'Upstairs.' I step inside letting the magnetic door catch seal us in. The click-clunk feels like a prison cell door locking out the real world and keeping us in. The delights of a murder scene await us upstairs. The concrete stairs deaden the sounds of our footfall. Six floors up our prize lies. We pass a number of steel covered doors with polythene bags taped to them, inside there are papers.

'Evictions.' White tells me over his shoulder. I didn't ask, but thanks anyway. I trudge along trying not to wheeze. I need to do more exercise, I promise myself I will remember. The seminary has a gym of sorts that I have never used nor seen totally at odds with the current health and well being agenda that the Bishop is promoting.

'No wonder no one noticed. Are there actually any residents in this block?' I speak quietly and yet it still seems to ring out loudly. There are three doors on each landing and finally we stand outside our goal. My knees are giving me a warning that this type of activity should be avoided in future. I nod in response to DI White's look. It is this one and I can almost hear the screams of terror. She could have been screaming her pretty lungs out and no-one was here to hear her. I shake my head feeling her despair, trying to dispel it.

DI White turns the handle and sets his shoulder to the door. It groans as he snowploughs the crap on the other side. His light shines over a dry smeary trail of blood that coats, in nearly-dry splatters, the uncarpeted floorboards of the hall. The door to the living room has partially fallen off one hinge and the red rusty dots of blood clash with the old-nicotene-darkened orange gloss.

'Watch where you step.' White steps forward, carefully placing his feet. Of course, now I can't see what I am standing in. That is the least of my worries as the psychic screaming and demonic presence that once filled the hall are battering at my brain. I stand still; it's about all I can do without staggering. White murmurs into his radio, I presume he is calling this in. No doubt we will need to preserve the scene as they say on all those American detective dramas.

I flick the grimy light switch and, amazingly, the lights come on courtesy of Osram and the electricity board. I instantly wish I hadn't. I survey dirt and mess of frequent four-legged visitors apparent among the shredded take-away rubbish. The appetiser over the main course is yet to be revealed in, what was once, a living room.

The sofa, probably one of Ikea's finest, is against the near wall, an island of very dirty beige. A big red pool stain filling the middle cushion and more totally destroying the Swedish elegance and design. I scrunch my eyes closed to dispel the picture that confronts me, knowing that DI White cannot see the scene as it once was. A geometric, nylon based, seventies pattern carpet has soaked up some more of the liquids that her evisceration provided. Was the poor girl taken in her own home? A place where she should have been safe. How had it gotten in and why would be mysteries that we might never fathom. Although looking round, it is very hard to believe that this is anyone's home. A flop zone of desperation would be a more apt description. The waves of despair lying under the terror like undertones of a good wine are seeping into me and I try to keep the tears on the inside of my eyelids.

'This is where she was killed.' Someone has to state the obvious. I am not touching anything if I can help it. I don't want to re-live this again, the ache in my insides only recently forgotten. I need to remove some of the emotional charge in this room so that I can function. At the moment the maelstrom of memories blowing round me is making thinking and breathing a multi task too far. I start to dispel the energy in the room. It sounds like muttering but the words of Our Lord are incredibly powerful things.

The darkness of the room is lifted a little as I push away her pain and the debilitating terror. Her soul escaped from the torment of her flesh at the time but the echoes of her hurt remained until now.

The layers of despair that imbue this room are a problem for another day. I can now breathe and keep my eyes open; progress I think. My cheeks are damp, coated with my tears, remnants of the emotions I have just endured. The whole block holds more painful memories than any one place should have to bear. The waves of unhappiness, desolation and fear have been laid down by tenant after tenant. Grinding poverty and generations of lives devoid of hope have created this black pit. Did this attract the Demon? It's a theory.

'Was this her address?' I fire my question out of the blue as White does his cop poking around. Looking over his shoulder 'No she lived in Stockbridge somewhere.' He gives me an answer that helps and just raises more questions.

'A bit of a trek over here then eh?' An unspoken someone, or many some-ones, must have seen something. An appeal maybe? Might be worth a try anyway. How is this bastard able to move about unseen? Red skin, horns, claws and fangs are usually noteworthy.

The smell, at once unique and overpowering, fades after a few minutes until it is hardly really noticed. It's a bit like dog owners with the wet-dog smell. They don't seem to mind while we cat-people want to gag.

I decide to leave DI White to poke around until his heart's content. I will have a wander around. From here I should be able to follow our other-world visitor (the lexicon of political correctness) he will leave a very singular trail; a joy that will be, no doubt.

In less than forty-five minutes the white-suited, humour-bypassed mob arrive. The crime scene tapes a barrier to the other residential ghouls. I am allowed an access-all-areas-backstage pass. Uniform are on the stairs. While standing usefully about I wonder if Chief Inspector Buttons will make an appearance. A bit like the pantomime Dame, I snort as the Widow Twankie look fills my imagination. The radio bleeping and static are giving me a headache or perhaps it is the demon mojo and the smell. I make my way onto the landing, ducking under the yellow and black tape like a veteran.

The trail, which was the reason for this excursion leads

me downstairs. It is not new but now I can pick it out from the many other trails running over it; psychic bloodhound, that's me. The visit here seems like a one-off; not a habitual. At least I can only find one path to follow. Passing through the magnetic-lock door and reaching the clean air of the city, I suck in a great dollop. Urchins, hanging on the railings, are watching everything all excited and wide eyed. A muddy football, tucked under an arm, unable to compete with a murder. Personally, I blame TV. It makes excitement of tragedy; shows out of misery and shit programs out of good books.

The gaggle of whispering, nudges and staring at me as a result of my dog-collar seems to reach a frenzy among these unwashed little oiks. I make my way over to them and I swear they have stopped breathing.

'Awright boys? You from round here?' I pretend I like kids. I don't really though. They nod; it's a start I suppose. 'Seen anyone who shouldn't be here hanging around?' I ask gently, all cool like, with no inquisitional pressure.

'Are you wi' the pigs mister?' Oh the mouths of babes, revealing the worst of what they hear.

'It's Father and yes I am.' I smile as the gang tell Wullie to shut up. They might get in trouble. 'Did you see someone Wullie?' Kids aren't born bad, they just learn real quick round here. He shakes his head a little too vigorously to my way of thinking. He doesn't want to be a grass, I suppose.

I wear my gentle persuasion face, all friendly and Holy. I smile and get down to their level; on my hunkers. 'It's okay to tell me; they'll no bother.' I twitch my head in the direction of the uniform standing at the door. 'What did you see?' I pause. They might give up their information without the need for a bribe. The bumping and nudging continues as Wullie is prompted to 'spit it oot'.

'Ah saw sumfin.' Sniff 'It wiz getting dark and a big man came oot the flats and walked up the road. He walked funny.' Wullie had described every drunk and Jakey in Edinburgh.

'What was he wearing?' I try to tease out something useful from this illuminating interaction. Wullie, it seems, is on a roll, and there is no stopping him now.

'A big coat like him.' The dirt filled fingernail at the end of his grimy hand, catches my attention and I see that he is pointing at a Mac, worn by one of the many functionaries at the crime scene.

'Tell him about the smell.' One of the prompters whispers. No detail too small in this story that won't bear the retelling.

Wullie, struggling for vocabulary, blurts it out 'He wiz stinkin, like a dead cat.' Fingers plugging his nose as he recalled the smell, the gang all giggle at the pantomime.

'Thanks Wullie. Here, get yersels a sweetie.' I put a fiver in his grimy little paw. In the old days it was a few coins; that's inflation for you. I open myself to see if I can get an image of the Mac-wearing, funny-walking smelly suspect. My fingers bump Wullie's hand and I glean a clear, if somewhat fleeting, image to hold on to. Thank you my boy, you have been more than helpful.

DI White is a good guy to know. He has a few strings pulled and within twenty minutes a sketch artist is sitting with me in the back of a police transit van pulling the face of our suspect together. Obviously, I am describing young William's image not the demonic form that I am more familiar with.

'How's that Father?' The question catches me off guard a little as he turns it round. My eyes widen at the very lifelike depiction. It is incredible. 'Bang on' as they say.

'It is excellent, very much like our guy. We should show it to DI White and get it on the news.' The start of a plan forming inside my, usually empty, head.

After all if we make out that the suspect is a mass-murdering psychopath, the good people of Edinburgh might just spot him. It would certainly hamper his movements at any rate. DI white, as if in response to my thought, slides open the side door and climbs in. Outside, it is beginning to rain; a real surprise I don't think. He nods approval at the likeness and smiles a bit ruefully.

'David Gilroy.' He motions to the picture. 'I found a drivers licence upstairs. The sketch is very good, though.' He pulls an evidence bag from his pocket. There on the pink and white plastic is our man.

'Let's get him on the news.' DI White is looking forward to having a lead at last. Can't say I blame him. My way was better, though.

Chapter 4

I just need a deerstalker and a magnifying glass and my transformation to Basil Rathbone will be complete. I don't have a bumbling, portly Watson to look smart next to but I make do with a succession of modern Lestrades. A city is a wonderful place; full of mundane and mysterious places. Edinburgh is old and, to my sensitivities, a great many supernatural echoes are cast over its streets. It makes my blood hounding a little bit difficult at times. My demon has a head start so I might need a while. DI White is busy processing the scene and reporting up the chain of command. I suppose I should do the same but it can wait. Oh what a rebel I am.

You have to wonder about the people who designed these housing estates; they are a cluttered mess of curves and boxes. The houses like rabbit hutches and all in need of a good scrub, some of the gardens are nice though. Depressing cheek by jowl, crushed-in living and there is just no space to be. The resident's cars fill the streets on both sides almost to capacity. This working class area is not the modern, uplifting, post war utopia that was expected or promised. The Council can't even keep the weeds from the verges and cracks in the pavement. It is a demoralising mess.

It has been about ten minutes since I was certain that I had a trail to follow so now I am reduced to scanning from side to side like some sort of metal detector. Beep, Beep, Beep no psychic trail, Beep, Beep Beep. I must look like a bloomin' arsehole scanning the ground for coins. Not been mugged yet, so all good I suppose.

The reputation of this scheme is well known and not a good one. So no self-respecting human being should be wandering here once the sun goes down. Here I am, anyway, I am sure my dog collar will protect me. The orange street lights are coming on like an early warning system telling the non-local denizens to hurry up and leave. I am tough, so any hints are a waste of time. These mean streets are no tougher than the ones of my childhood. Aye, right.

It is getting properly dark and I have lost contact with the trail, so backtracking will be needed. That will need to wait as I need a pee. A middle-aged man issue that has made me an expert in finding a loo almost anywhere. I try not to think about it. Whistling helps, no really it does. So tunelessly I am keeping a tune going as I make my way along the less than friendly streets.

My pit stop is just around the corner. St Sebastian's Church; a modern utility space with toilets and thankfully it is open to the world most of the time and tonight is no exception. The minister does a great job with the dispossessed in his patch, you know, God's mission and all that. Buggered if I can remember his name; face yes, name no. Good job it is on the sign on the outside, written in nice gold lettering.

'Father Andrew, so lovely to see you.' His twinkling eyes, above a broad grin is, so sincere it is disgusting. I am conscious that my hands are damp after a lack of paper towels in his facilities. I wave as I cross the vestibule, ruefully trying to indicate my hands are not dry. He grabs one and shakes it anyway.

'How are you? I was nearby and needed to make a little visit to the boy's room.' I laugh no point in pretending otherwise. Honesty is the best policy is what we are all taught as children and forget as puberty strikes.

'We are a haven for those in most need. Glad to have been here for you.' His voice is a rich beast that probably sounds fantastic from his pulpit. He even looks godly; his hair has just the right mix of salt and pepper and good looks. His congregation will love him, I have no doubt. If

Carlsberg did Men of God, this is what they would come up with.

'What brings you here, apart from our facilities?' It is the most normal question in the world and I need to think quickly. Of course, he has no idea what I actually do and probably thinks I am a scholar or something.

'I am helping the police with some specialist knowledge support in their murder cases.' Nearly the truth and a pretty good 'don't ask any more because I am not able to tell you' response.

'That sounds fascinating. You must be kept very busy.' He is ushering me into his office and away from the exit. The group therapy people in his church hall need their privacy and he ensures that.

'It is all the excitement I can take and more.' I do self-deprecation and a rueful face. I am crap at small talk and sometimes conversations end up being interrogations or strained silences. Father Peter plays mother with the tea and it is obvious to me he wants to say something; perceptive or what?

'I have a few very worried young ladies in my flock. They are terrified about this serial killer in Edinburgh.' He looks over his cup as he sips. Perhaps he knows something useful.

'It is terrible. Surprising that there have been no witnesses coming forward.' That's me, Say Nothing Steel. A funny look settles on his face, not funny ha-ha more funny contemplative. Almost as if he's not sure how to put it.

'Some of the girls have been telling me about a strange guy that has a funny walk and smells a bit rotten.' He just blurts it out. Can I play him at poker on pay day? He'd lose the lot. He has just blurted out our only lead. 'And they are keeping off the streets. Might not be a bad thing all the same.'

He's worried and he needed someone to tell. I was his

someone apparently. There's more to come but he won't be using the big E word. Evil. We hardly say that these days. Oh if only he knew the half of it; Evil would be every other word he used.

'Where does this guy hang out?' I might as well ask , you never know. When serendipity takes me somewhere unexpected there's always a reason. I like to let it play out. Great process isn't it; if it ain't broke and all that.

'They keep seeing him down by the old community centre. It has been shut for years and is all boarded up.' Father Peter paused and swigged his tea. Mine's cold, so his must be too. The silence begins; he is trying to let it out.

'He sounds like our person of interest. I will get the police to check him out.' Listen to me all technical and official. What I really mean is that I will take a look and fumble about. If it is my guy it will probably be better that I just deal with it. I smile reassuringly.

'Of course he might just be some weirdo that creeps everyone out.' I add putting my unfinished cup on the table. I am not drinking cold tea on purpose, there are limits; cold coffee yes, tea no.

'I went to find him.' Here we go; more serendipitous clues falling into my lap from on high. I wait; not quite on the edge of my seat but I want to tell him to 'spit it out!'

'You know, to see what help I could get him. We have a great homeless program in the capital. Lost sheep and all that.' He's a little embarrassed at doing the right thing. Maybe it is I that should be feeling ashamed at my lack of pastoral focus.

'Anyway, I went to the community centre and didn't go in. The boarding has been opened up I think.' Father Peter has been looking at the wall as he spoke but now his eyes have caught mine. 'I was too scared to go in. Really terrified.' His words are almost hissed and his eyes are staring hard. 'I have never felt such dread, ever.' There, it's now out in the open.

Father Peter has stumbled upon my Demon's lair and is sensitive enough to feel and fear its presence. If he had wandered in I might have been looking at his corpse in the morgue. I look deeply at him, he'll do. I smile, gently. Help unexpected is a little miracle all on its own.

'Let us go together and we shall see what we see. When two or three are gathered together in my name, I am with them. The Lord will be with us.' I let my calming spirit roll over him and can see him visibly bolster. I imagine it like a little blue wave washing away fear and bringing calm.

'Father Andrew, I feel so silly.' He begins but I stop him. I give him a reassuring smile, I hope. His eyes have lost that wildness that was there only a few moments ago.

'No Father, when the Lord warns us, we must listen. Let us go now and see.' I am trying to get the tone right; firm but not mental. Usually comes out with psychotic undertones. He nods, accepting the call to arms with no further resistance.

A few minutes later we are a couple of middle aged priests wandering along the road. The rain has started and will just add to the experience. To the rest of the world all is fine but inside my head why can I hear the theme from the exorcist. We move through the raindrops and the pools of the orange street lights.

Chapter 5

Gordonstoun, this housing scheme obviously named after the school of royal patronage, is a utilitarian place reminiscent of the seventies films by Ken Loach. Depressing and dull you might call it; I couldn't possibly comment. The render is painted an off white and I am sure that helps break up the monotony. The street lights and drizzle just complete the picture and feel of misery. Joy seems like a very unlikely visitor to these streets.

Father Peter is tour-guiding all the way to our destination. So and so lives there, he had a heart attack last year. Mrs McBlah lives here, lost her son in Iraq. And on it goes; I'm not really listening. I can feel a growing pressure, an unease. We are definitely going to be having an event. The trail is like a shining ribbon of pain and dark despair. That might just be an echo of years of post-Thatcherite worklessness that has blighted too many communities in central Scotland. It's all her fault obviously. At least so the politicians keep on saying, and for once they might be right. Broken clocks are right twice a day so it shouldn't be too surprising if they luck out.

The hedges round here are bushy, vigorous beasts that encroach the footpaths giving a claustrophobic feel at best and cover for thugs at worst. Damp but undaunted we turn into Something street; I am sure it has a name but 'street' is all that remains of the sign fixed to the side of the houses. At the end, in the midst of some greenery sits the flat-roofed dereliction that is the John Thompson Community Centre. Named after the Celtic goalie, apparently.

Boarded up to keep the 'yoof' out; the sterling board panels have been adjusted to allow access to anyone who really wants in. Father Peter pauses as we pass the sign forbidding entry. I can feel the laid down dread, it would keep most folks away. They might not know why but they would not choose to go any closer. Well those with no God inside might not feel anything and stumble inside.

'Walk with me Brother.' My tone has changed. It happens when I stop being me and act like the messenger of the Lord I am. I expect him to follow as I move up the crumbling tarmac path. Perhaps I should have started a hymn; something uplifting. I feel my lips twitch at my own humour, but the near smile dies as I start to smell the decay that is our particular 'friend' from the hells.

The way in, of which there are a few, is well used and I probably could have found it anyway. Father Peter is tight lipped and anxious. He seems to be inching behind me, more and more. The board is loosely attached and can be encouraged to open with very little effort. The cavernous black hole that kills any light is like the throat of the beast. Inside, out of the rain, a darkness of more depth than is possible awaits us.

'Follow me.' I cross the threshold. If Peter crosses behind me, he is a brave man. He does and behind us the night is shut out. The immediate lack of the rain noise makes the silence loud in our ears.

'Let there be light.' The click of my mag-lite torch brings a white, clean cone to drive out the darkness. I try not to smirk but I know I am. 'Chocks away!' I might as well have said.

Where once there had been carpet tiles now only the outlines of old glue make the pattern. We have entered through a side entrance and the corridor leads ahead of us with doors to either side. Offices and toilets or changing rooms: I have no idea but behind any one of them a nasty surprise could be waiting. I stand for a moment just soaking in the silence waiting for my equilibrium to return when the rich baritone of Father Peter sounds out a wakey-wakey.

'Hello!' He calls out. I try not to jump in surprise and

fail miserably. Of course, it could have been worse had the effeminate squeak had escaped my lips. Is he expecting an answer? Might as well have rung the bell or booted in the front doors. There are reasons I prefer to work alone. Fucks sake.

Going by the empty Buckfast bottles and chip wrappers, this has been a favourite haunt of kids for a while. As we begin our advance I can feel the air thickening ahead of us. It's a bit like wading through soup. Behind me, Father Peter's footfalls sound much less assured. I press on. He must follow or be left in the dark. If he is feeling half of what I am he won't want to wait in the dark. He's keeping up.

The swing doors with glass circles, so loved by councils everywhere, are slightly ajar. Hinges jammed or broken, I have no idea. My white cone fills the space and sends a little light beyond. I peek inside and lightly push open the one on the left. A deep breath, filling my lungs with stench, was not a good idea. I cough and my eyes are watering leaving me temporarily vulnerable. Father Peter fills the corridor with the contents of his stomach. His retching, almost, encourages me to join in.

The sudden scuff-scuff and thumping footsteps means we have company. That company is charging at us with murder in mind. I can hear its spite clawing through the air at us. Shit.

Fighting in the dark is terrifying but fighting in the strobe of a waggled torch is even more so. You can see just enough to be terrified and not enough to do anything about it. Who's idea was this anyway?

The bellowing roar as the demon charges elicits a terror-filled scream and not from me.

Father Peter has seen enough in the torchlight to be properly unmanned. The thumping impact of a hard shoulder bowls me into a breeze-block wall; the cement unforgiving as I bash my skull. Seeing stars might be one description; agony might be another. In the fall I have released our only light; it casts a spinning disc of white across the floor like a seventies disco revealing the detritus and little strewn floor.

Father Peter has stopped screaming and it takes me a moment to realise why. Two hands wrapped around his throat are choking the life from him. I suppose I should be thankful, our enemy is still inside the human cadaver and not in its true form. Otherwise Peter's throat would have been ripped out already and he could have been on his way to Saint Peter.

Getting to my feet is a struggle but I manage it. Waves of nausea roll over me, worse than any whisky fuelled sickness. The dizziness is good though, people pay good money for this sensation. I wobble forward with my crucifix ahead of me. I lumber into the beast with two backs rolling on the floor.

Contact with our foe is like a huge static charge running over my skin but when my blessed crucifix hits home the surge of power is like holding bare wires. We are catapulted apart, Father Peter lying between us. A howl of pain-filled anger fills my ears as it escapes up the hall and away. All my energy gone, I slump down next to Peter. Remarkably, he is still with us. Groaning and gasping like a landed fish but still in the land of the living. Tears are running down his cheeks but I don't think he cares about that, though. His throat is all crushed, bruised and scratched but he'll live. He won't ever be the same again but he'll get over it, probably.

'Fuck.' The ubiquitous expletive is so apt at this moment. Peter nods, seems we agree on that then. I let out a long held breath that comes out in shuddering little gasps. I pull out my mobile and call the Polis. They will have to come in and get us, I am walking nowhere at the moment. I am sure DI white won't be happy that I went out to play without him. Anyway in the meantime Father Peter and I need to have 'The Talk' and get our stories straight.

They're no very quick, these Edinburgh Polis. Where else would an attempted murder take twenty minutes to get to? Maybe I shouldn't have said the attacker was gone. Perhaps a 'he might still be here' would have worked better. The rewards of honesty are, as usual, piss poor. Dropping DI White's name obviously made no difference either. After a protracted wait they are arriving; better late than never but heigh-ho.

Armed response officers make a hell of a racket as they cleared their way down the hall. High-power torches blind us poor victims as we put our hands up to block them out. We are like a pair of priestly vampires caught in the light. I need to get one of theirs, puts my mag-lite to shame.

'Father Steel. Father Steel are you alright?' What impeccable manners too!

'I'm fine he's gone.' I manage to make myself held over the noise. 'Father Peter needs the paramedics. Where's DI white?' I go into frustrated cop, TV cop mode, barking out orders. I don't think they are paying a blind bit of notice though.

Being assisted to your feet like a pair of old codgers is a bit much but they mean well. In a few quick heartbeats we are in the back of an ambulance being quizzed, questioned and poked.

DI White arrives just in time. He has headed off an outburst of irritation after my being asked the same question for the third time. 'Did I get my name wrong the last twice?' I snap.

'Father Steel. Thank goodness you are all right.' He climbs in beside us. Father Peter is being helped further into the ambulance. The paramedic is taking my blood pressure again. He seems concerned about something. His machine keeps bleeping and the screen resetting or whatever.

'I hit my head, by the way, you know the bit that's bleeding.' I try to be helpful but it is coming out like a diva.

DI white laughs 'barely a scratch.' It seems the paramedic has had the humour bypass and gives me the shut up look.

'I know but your blood pressure is very high.' He knows he's dealing with a child. So fucking what I want to say but manage to keep it in. I roll my eyes and White thinks it's mildly amusing. With friends like him, I see why monasteries are so popular.

'We need to go, Sir.' He speaks directly to White. It seems that when you are hurt you are no longer in charge of yourself. Still here.

'DI White, it was our guy. He can't be too far away. He's been hiding in there.' I pause as he starts getting out. Where the fuck is he going?

'I will come to the hospital as soon as I can.' He shuts the door and with a double thump we are off.

I lie back on the gurney thing as Instructed. Resistance is futile, it seems. I let my eyes close for just a minute. I am knackered.

Chapter 6

I was only out for a moment, honest. Well probably a wee bit longer than that but the persistent 'Father Steel can you hear me?' is bloody annoying and eventually I felt compelled to open my eyes and reply.

'Yes.' I managed without the attendant 'Now fuck off!' The sound of relief floods through her voice

'We'll be taking you for an X-ray very soon.' She's a nurse; things are looking up. What happened to the humourless paramedic guy?

Wincing through my partially opened and probably fluttering eyelids, I look up as I am wheeled along a corridor with lights above me. Now they're there, now they're not. Like the carpet in the Shining; brrrr, silence, brrrr, silence. The hanging signs pass in an infuriating blur. They aren't designed to be read from flat on your back. My head hurts like a son-of-a-bitch, by the way.

The babying talk continues as I get my head fried. Click, click, click. 'Roll onto your right side.' Click, click, click. 'Other side now.' You get the idea. Luckily for me I am on my side as I throw up. A quick splurge that splatters almost musically on the tiled floor. The blast radius will be spectacular I expect. I'm not proud; I just don't give a shit. I lie back for a moment and we are off again. Marvellous.

Dr Parker is worried about my x-rays and my blood pressure. 'Yours would be high too mate, if you had been fighting a demon this evening.' I want to point out. I don't but I want to. Would get me sectioned I expect.

'You'll have to stay for observation Father Steel. I will see you again in the morning.' He flaps shut my folder with a finality that will brook no disagreement.

'Fine.' I try not to sound grumpy but fail miserably. Moments later he's gone, white coat flapping behind him like superman. I notice a clock above a door as I am wheeled away. Three eighteen. FFS how much did I miss?

I have missed breakfast, or rather, it sits on my table but the lumpy, now solid, porridge has had it. Why did I ask for porridge? No idea but I did. Anyway I am not forcing that down. This comfy bed is trying to seduce me to sleep again and it has almost won when my room door opens. These are private rooms but this means anyone can walk in, apparently. This anyone is the Bishop. He can come in, I suppose.

'Andrew, how are you feeling?' He's worried about me, I can tell by his face not being in the usual disapproving pose. I try to scoot up but it is too much effort and my head is threatening to explode so I don't bother.

'Not great.' See, I can be civil. He sits on the plastic chair, scraping it closer across the floor. Thanks for that, the sound thunders through my head. His florid, bishoppy, face is too close and out of focus. Probably a good thing all things considered.

'What happened, Andrew?' He is talking quietly which I appreciate more than his usual booming tones. He is in discrete mode. Walls have ears and all that.

'I found the hiding place and we got jumped in the dark by the demon.' Succinct eh?

'I see. Why was Peter with you?' Surprisingly little recrimination in his voice, it appears he just wants answers.

'It's his patch and he had felt it already. He was sensitive enough to not go in alone.' I really can't be arsed. I am going to get a telling off and no doubt I will behave like a teenager. I know I am meant to tell very few people about what I do but I didn't tell Peter until after his up close and personal encounter. He would have worked it out anyway, he isn't stupid.

'That was foolhardy. Why didn't you get the police first?' Disapproval fills every word as they reach my ears. Here comes the telling off. Will I ever recover? I expect so.

'I didn't actually expect it to be in there. I was following its trail from the new crime scene.' At least I had something to report. Not exactly progress but a semblance of something that could lead to progress.

'At least we know what the human form looks like.' Silver lining and all that.

'It has been on the news.' The Bishop doesn't seem impressed by my version of progress. He waits. It must be my turn again.

'The Demon,' I begin and see the furrows starting on his forehead 'can take over human bodies. I don't know if they need to be dead first. The one he's in stinks and won't last long.' Best put all my cards on the metaphorical table.

'That should make it easier to narrow down which other-worlder we are dealing with.' His correction is as subtle as a brick. I didn't use the approved term from the lexicon. He can be such a stickler.

'He may have been in a few meat-sacks which might explain why we haven't had much luck finding him.' Meat sacks causes the eyebrows to shoot up and a frown to settle in full force upon his face. Besides I have had enough of this conversation already. Hopefully he will bugger off soon, he didn't bring any grapes or flowers.

'Andrew,' There is a warning of displeasure under the tone 'Why is it here?' This is the crucial question. A question, to which, I have no answer. There must be a reason; psychopathic murdering demons don't just appear on their own. I hope.

'Someone summoned it? An escapee from some prophecy? I don't know.' Not the answer he is looking for.

'I have people looking into The Writings but nothing yet. We will keep looking but we need some sort of direction.' He is trying to help, bless him.

'I will go back to all the scenes and see what I can glean. Besides, now I have been up close and personal, I might be better placed to make progress.' Of course, I need the Doc to let me out.

Morning it seems is a nebulous term to mean 'whenever I can be bothered'. In this case Doctor Parker meant two in the afternoon. I suppose it is still morning somewhere in the mid-Atlantic. Pissy? Me? You bet your sweet bippy I am. Lunch was pish, too, but at least I ate it. The only saving grace is my nurse; she is fantastic. She has kept an eye on me; fed me Paracetamol and tea and only taken my blood pressure four times. She has a beautiful voice and the clearest, shiny blue eyes anyone has a right to. No wonder they are often called angels. As if on cue, she pops her head around the door.

'Doctor Parker is on his way along the ward. He won't be long.' Her smile is a little ray of sunshine. The Bugger better let me out. I have been reading my own chart and my blood pressure is on the way down.

The entry swoosh, of a man on a mission, and Superdoc is in my room. He is scanning the observation notes and giving a running commentary for himself I think. It is like a pre-flight checklist. His eyes flip over the top of the clipboard.

'How's the head Father?' A question flying from amidst his muttering and luckily I was paying attention.

'Just a dull ache. The Paracetamol helps.' No messing about, I just want to hear a few magic words.

'Well your blood pressure has gone down to safer levels. However you need to see your GP and have it sorted out. It is too high to be healthy in a man your age.' Cheeky Bastard. 'You don't have a cracked skull. You were very lucky. You weren't concussed either which I find remarkable. Don't push your luck too often though.' He is trying to be helpful, I think. 'I would normally keep you for another night but I need your bed and I think you'll be fine. Is there someone who can keep an eye on you?' Yippee freedom is looming on the horizon.

'I live in the seminary. There are plenty of Brothers to look after me.' I try not to do a little happy dance.

'Good then, Father, you can go home and rest for a couple of days. GP for the blood pressure and take care of yourself. You aren't as young as you once were.' He is scribbling on my notes.

'Thank you Doctor Parker.' I say but feel an near overwhelming urge to tell him to fuck off. He has all the bedside manner of a pathologist. Still, I will be out of here and that is all that matters.

Chapter 7

After two days of molly-codling I have definitely had enough. The Bishop has been putting a few words out. Obviously of the 'look after Andrew' type because my room might as well have been fitted with a revolving door. The stream of visitors has been well orchestrated and unending. The fact that no one has brought a dram with them suggests a level of organisation that doesn't usually exist in the seminary. Even Father Ignatius (if ever a candidate for changing your name by deed poll existed) didn't bring me his hip flask of dubious whisky, which normally I'd refuse. It has led to many a black out and hangover from hell.

My headache has, all but, gone and I am able to move about without feeling that my head will explode. Apparently there has been a breakthrough in our case. I say our but DI White has been most inattentive since my brush with chummy. No Calls, no flowers, not get well soon card. Nada. Zip. Hee-Haw. Almost like a one night stand with a promise to call. That was until this morning.

The body of our smelly, decaying suspect has turned up at Cockenzie Power Station. He was clogging up an inlet valve or some such. DI White reckons he went in near the River Esk at Musselburgh. Tides or something like that. Anyway, I am up and dressed and raring to go. There is a car on its way. I am only a little bit moist and my shirt is helpfully mopping up the sweat that is leaking from my back pores.

As if by magic, like a taxi booked in advance, my fluorescent panelled cop car arrives to whisk me away to view gruesome remains. I am off to the morgue where, I hope, I have a better time than I did last time. I am sure the morgue technician will feel the same way.

By the time I am deposited at the Edinburgh body store, I feel like a criminal. Sitting in the back of a cop car with two silent cops up front will do that to you, you know, the silent treatment. I wasn't my usual chatty self. Yeah right. It takes a certain type to be a traffic cop and I have had a few run ins with their colleagues in other areas. My balls ache with an old memory. They are the raw materials for the SturmAbteilung.

So it is just me, DI White and the body. A private viewing of sorts. DI White doesn't want any further questions about my performance. 'It isn't pretty Father.' He pulls open the horizontal fridge. The clunk of the handle and smooth hum as the tray runs out on well lubed acrylic rollers the overture music to our visit. The functional, sterile environment of tiles and the smell of bleach masking the worst of the odd smells that waft out towards me.

DI white unzips the body bag. It is a real treat. The hard plastic teeth pulling apart to reveal a horror reel highlight. It's like a kinder surprise but no chocolate and definitely no toy. The first wave to hit is the stench. The rot has set in and it isn't recent. Then again I already knew that. Eyes have been removed by an ophthalmic seagull and other bits have been nibbled here and there by other denizens of the sea.

I hesitate, letting the psychic banquet wash towards me. Ordinarily I have to touch but this one is almost radioactive. I can see the aura, riven through with cords of black, and it is seeping towards me. Our demon friend has left his mark all over this one.

'Buckle up Buttercup.' I mutter to myself as I reach out to touch a hand that the last time I saw it was wrapped around a clergyman's throat. An instant stabbing sensation travels up my arm causing me to cry out like a big Jessie. I grit my teeth and hope they don't crack under the pressure. As he was already dead, I don't expect to relive his last moments. I get a set of highlights. A series of meaningless images fluttering like a swarm of butterflies – all very colourful and distracting – but very little to explain why him and how his life of drudgery had brought him to this place. I sigh as I let go of the hand. The stabbing pain is turned off like a switch but a cold dull ache remains in its place.

'Anything Father?' DI White is hopeful or expectant; I am not sure which.

'Not really.' I shake my head slowly 'But I will need a few minutes to pray for his immortal soul.' This one needs cleansed and any residual darkness washed away before it is buried in the ground. If not it can mess with the sanctity of the graveyard.

DI White bows his head, bless his little cotton socks. Maybe I should have said 'You need to piss off while I perform some magic shit'. I wait and eventually he gets it. Rather sheepishly he offers to get coffee. See, he is a good guy.

'In the name of the Father, Son and Holy Spirit.' I mark his forehead with the sign of the cross. The skin feels warm to me. It should be clammy and cold but it isn't. I touch my crucifix to the fleshy forehead and begin to start the Rite of Cleansing. I need to remove the darkness that infested this corpse. All at once the lattice of lines become visible like old Indian ink tattoos. The air around me begins to thrum like a singing bowl.

Torn, sunken eyelids flash open revealing sightless empty sockets. The fingers, all bent and broken, begin to twitch. The hold of the Dark is great on this one. The tattered lips begin to move revealing the ruin of teeth standing on blackened gums. I continue the prayer of cleansing, my crucifix firmly pressed to the skin.

'The power of Christ compels you to leave this faithful servant.' I, all but, shout as the body tries to roll over. It shudders at my command but it doesn't stop. The twitching, spasmodic hands have gripped the sidebars and are now giving leverage. The sizzling on the forehead is loud filling the near silence. Heat builds up on my hand as the darkness fights against my power.

'I command you, in the name of The Father, The Son and The Holy Spirit.' I practically yell at it. Him. It seems to have raised the cavalry. Footsteps are approaching at the gallop, that's all I need, witnesses.

A dark fugue is seeping from it, I am not calling it a zombie, eye sockets, mouth, nose. Running down it's face like exhaled smoke; just not in rings. The burning on its forehead is causing pain but it isn't enough to stop it. With its hands on the bars it pushes up and away from my glowing crucifix. A voice filled with pain slips words from a mouth that should no longer speak.

DI White crashes into the room, and almost comically slides to a halt beside me. This is not what he expected, I can assure you. 'Oh my God. Fuck.' Not four words I would chose as my last but perhaps I'm just fussy. DI White's mouth is opening and closing but nothing else is being produced. Our, not quite, peacefully dead friend manages to force out almost intelligible words.

'The Master is coming. The Master is coming. Death. Death.' Sounds that fill us with dread.

'Be Afraid. Be very afraid.' Is what is charging through my mind. DI White is staring, poor chap. There is no training for this in his handbooks.

The mouth opens super wide and a fountain of deep black-red blood flies through the air towards us.

Hitting like a water cannon, it drives us back. Gallons of it; more than could ever be in a human body fly through the air. The morgue is splattered and covered in a cone of deep crimson.

The body collapses with a soft, squishy thud back onto its trolley. Thank God, which I do. The attendant has just opened the door behind us; he missed the show I hope. DI

White is still rooted to the spot. The stench is horrendous and the vomiting starts behind me. Wimps.

Chapter 8

The Bishop's residence is very grand. Even more so if you get the full effect by walking up the gravel drive. Ordinarily I park my, less than new, red Nissan Sunny beside the sleek black Volvo but today I got the bus. After all with roads all churned up to put in the trams, driving in the capitol is so not a pleasure. Anyway, the solid stone seventeenth century manor house is a beautiful building. It is a hefty Episcopal statement about the permanence and importance of the church. Size, as they never say, matters in far too many things. Compensating much?

I ring the bell, set into a stone circle not a poxy plastic thing, and wait. I have been summoned, asked for lunch but what's the difference. The Bishop wants an update and that might not take long. I wait expectantly for the door to respond immediately and it doesn't. It gives me time to buff my shoes on my calves to get a wee shine. I am just finished when the dog-collared-butler opens the door.

'Good Afternoon Father Andrew, you are to go on through to the study.' So polite, it makes my teeth ache. No disapproving frown to set off my shoulder chip; so I need to behave. Removing my coat, I smile as I hand it to him. 'Thank you.' He isn't impressed at being treated like the help. I know I am being a bit petty but old habits die hard.

Anyway, the study is a veritable Aladdin's cave of very old and interesting books. The mahogany ocean-going desk sits in front of the French windows but nowhere is the bishop to be found. I should probably just sit on the chesterfield and wait but I love to peruse books. Too many haven't moved in years but the dust is removed regularly by the house elves. My eye stops on one I haven't seen or read before. 'The Dominion of the Earthbound.' It looks old.

Old enough to be serious and it is bound in light coloured leather. The lettering is black, which is what caught my eye. I sneak a peek at it; lifting it quickly before I get caught. Hand in the cookie jar as it were.

It is heavier than it looks, a satisfying heft and definitely a reading table book; not an in-bedder. The opening page is a lithographic print of the Great Casting Out of Satan and his gang from heaven. It is much stylised but beautifully done. On the next page the author of this tome is announced. No idea who he is but I am sure I should know. A flick of the very expensive paper pages and we are off on an illicit journey.

'The Kingdom of Heaven was purged of the followers of Lucifer and following their casting out, over the earth they gained dominion.' A gloomy start, if ever there was one.

'Andrew.' The boom of Bishop Michael's voice fills the study and I jump slamming the book shut. Looking round I try not to look guilty, fat chance of that. I fail miserably. 'How are you feeling?' He is crossing the carpet and can see the book in my hands. I hand it to him as he nears, contraband surrendered. He almost doesn't frown at my invasion of his things. The Dominion of the Earthbound is safely tucked back on the shelf. It will remain an unscratched intellectual itch for me until I get another itch somewhere else.

'Come, sit.' His hand waves like a traffic controller. He seems to be in a reasonable mood, although I am sure I can change that. The banalities pass without a hitch and he presses the 'go' button.   'How's the case coming along?' It is the give me an update demand.

'Slowly.' It's best not to overstate progress that doesn't actually exist. I wait a moment and I suppose it is still my turn. 'I had an event at the morgue yesterday that gives me concerns.' This is a new ploy for me, it's like asking for help I actually need.

'How so?' The vertical line that splits his forehead deepens a little but not the full on disapproval face yet.

'The body our demon friend has been wearing got up and spoke before showering me with blood.' I might need to provide some details but these can wait. Bishop Michael's eyebrows have shot up and are hiding under his hairline.

'Dear Lord.' His eyes raise heavenward. I manage not to smirk. 'What did it say?' He wants the details then.

''The Master is Coming!' a couple of times.' I pause and add casually 'And death a few times, too.' I manage to keep my face straight, now is not really the time for humour.

'That sounds ominous. Have you spoken to anyone about this yet?' I shake my head; no chance. His eyes are a wee bit shiny, he wants the gory details.

'The blood fountain covered DI White and myself; missed the morgue tech though.' More witnesses to give the Bishop nightmares.

'Oh Andrew this is getting out of hand.' A public relations disaster is looming, obviously. DI White and I will say nothing and the morgue tech knows nothing; so all will be fine. I have been wrong before, though. I can see a lengthy call to the Home Office for Bishop Michael this afternoon. A trouble shared is a trouble doubled I think.

There is a pregnant (though I'd call it lengthy) pause which looks like stretching on for eternity. It is interrupted by the tea-bearer bringing in the tray. The frown upon his master's brow gives him pause. Is it for the interruption? He'll never know. At least there is a plate of Hobnobs; not chocolate ones but still Hobnobs. Wordlessly he removes himself.

'Is there a pattern emerging? I hear that DI White is highly thought of.' The Bishop has his thinking cap on; and you thought it was a Mitre. I have a mouthful of biscuit so he will have to muse a bit longer. I try to crunch quietly.

Perhaps I should pour the tea and be mother.

'No pattern I can see as yet.' I manage to speak without spraying crumbs everywhere. A slurp of tea washes away any issue of full-biscuit-mouth, I can speak again.

'I don't like this one Andrew.' He is looking out the French windows. I make a face as it's obviously my fault. I hope he can't see my reflection in the glass.

'Neither do I. The bodies are dumped so I haven't discovered if where they died is significant. I will walk his trail again today. That might turn something up.' I swig my tea not letting it get cold.

'There's a ritual element to this Andrew. What for and for whom we may not find out but it is there. Do we need Father Jeremy's help? He is still in the Capitol.'

'It couldn't hurt.' I say out loud. My inner dialogue is more of the For Fucks Sake variety.

'I'll give him your number and let you sort it out. I have meetings in London for the rest of the week. Hopefully, between you, it will be resolved by my return.' He picks up his cup, doesn't skip a beat as he swallows the very cool tea. Was that a deadline? Sounded very much like it to me. I'd better get lost then. Sent out to find a demon and discover its nefarious plot. Stop the plot and avert any disaster by next Monday before the Bishop parks his arse back in that seat.

I can feel my face souring up as I am effectively dismissed. Happy bunny I, most definitely, am not. I take a handful of hobnobs; an act of rebellion that is probably a better idea than 'Fuck off!' No sign of lunch either.

Chapter 9

Edinburgh is a lovely place, full of culture, architecture and arseholes. Well, at least, this bit is. The Gardens, all resplendent and colourful being enjoyed by families and tourists, is the scene of a yob-a-thon. A host, nay a plague, of football-top-wearing-post-pubescent idiots is romping along making a racket. Their mono-syllabic, high brow, chants are such a great advert for a cultural hub like the capitol.

I manage to tutt loudly and shake my head; complaining in the true Scottish style. Say nothing, do nothing, moan later to anyone who'll listen. Oh dear they have spotted the dog-collar. The finger pointing and childish shoving of each other has begun. If only this could be an original effort I might be less irritated by them and their nonsense.

'Paedo, Paedo, Paedo-phile.' They chant in unison. It is like a hive-mind with a brain cell between them. They march off with their new tune; all gleeful and pleased with themselves. Their lusty and enthusiastic noise would shame many a choir in the church for volume but that is about as positive as I can get. I'm not sure if these are home-grown or imported eejits as they all look the same to me. Knuckle draggers of the lowest order and thankfully receding into the distance.

The peaceful reflection I had been enjoying is well and truly shattered leaving me grumpier than usual and my latte has long since disappeared leaving a foamy, lumpy dreg in the bottom of the recyclable cup. The FFS face is definitely on display to the outside world, a great advert for a caring clergy. After a sigh that has its roots in the soles of my shoes I decide to visit the National Gallery of Scotland, a wonderful place. I go, not for the paintings, but for a decent cup of coffee and the most delicious Viennese whirls.

Besides, it isn't that warm out here anyway.

Sitting in the corner giving off the 'don't bother me vibe', coffee and cake before me, I am irked that someone feels it is okay to park themselves in the seat opposite. A corpulent fellow with a belly that practically shelves over the top of his trousers makes me feel less depressed at my keg belly.

'Is this taken?' But his arse is descending as he asks. A presumptive possession of the limited real estate if ever there was one. I presume I have to answer with something less sarcastic that I want to.

'No. Go ahead.' I manage politely, my inner sarcasm kept well in check this time. 'Too bloody late if it is.' I really want to say as I pull out my phone. I am feigning a busyness that doesn't exist while my peace is shattered by my slurping companion. If people growled then we might avoid these situations.

My phone buzzes and squeaks causing me to drop it on the table with a clatter, a text arriving as I pretended to be busy. That'll teach me. I manage to not exclaim my surprise with an expletive but only just. Father Jeremy, apparently, has sent me a text. I look ruefully up at my table sharer. He has a wee grin on his face and I try to prevent a sour look appearing on mine. It seems that Jezza wants to meet now. I suggest we meet at the foot of the Scott Monument and a few buzzes later, it is a date. I am not bloody going up it though.

It is not warm and the slightest wind seems to steal all the heat out of the day. I see Jeremy moving along with the flow of humanity, just one more face in a sea. Unfortunately he has seen me too, and now he is waving like an idiot. Not a discrete hand up, here I am. No, it is more a Donkey from Shrek waving about like a demented ecstatic. A village somewhere has lost its idiot.

'I see you, you arse.' I mutter to myself as I wave back, once. I have definitely descended into middle-aged grumpy man. Still, Father Jeremy ought to be a help and Lord knows I need it.

'Andrew!' He is almost breathy in his excitement or perhaps it is the exertion. His cheeks are flushed just below his little glasses, almost cherubic looking, and he looks so neat and tidy. We must be playing opposites; neat priest and crumpled priest. Oh well.

'Father Jeremy, lovely to see you.' I manage to fake enthusiasm. Our handshake is brief and functional. I stuff my hands back in my pockets, too cold for no gloves.

'Shall we get a coffee? I have much to share that might be useful.' Good old Jezza, overstating his usefulness before we start. I wonder what dusty, crusty old scholar can tell me what is going on. Still the offer of a coffee is never a bad thing; for some folks it is a pint but coffee is a good second choice. I am on a hat-trick of lattes and will probably get a little hyper; might need to be a decaf.

'Sounds good, let's go to Jenners. It's just over there.' I offer like a proper host, after all Jeremy is a visitor to our fair city. Jenners is a beautiful old-fashioned department store for the well to-do. The building is gorgeous and the price tags are remarkably reasonable. They do a lovely cream tea in their café on the fifth floor, too.

I love the inner stairwell, all open to each floor, and the railings of carved wood and iron decoration. Opulence delivered from another time making it feel just a little bit special. They even have a bra fitting department, not that I have availed myself of that service personally.

In no time at all we have passed the clouds of expensive perfumes and ascended (using the lift) to the refreshments. The soft lounge seats in the corner are discrete enough, I hope. I have barely stirred my Americano (the latte was unavailable) when Father Jeremy begins.

'It's a ritual. Or at least there has been one.' That

explains everything, obviously. I don't interrupt as I have an urge to sarcasm bomb him.

'The other-worlder has only 28 days to complete its task, whatever it is. It has one lunar cycle to be exact.' His glasses have slipped a little and he's peering over them like a mad professor. Maybe I am meant to be more appreciative of this kernel of information. A mini pause has begun but I crumble to avoid a comment to regret.

'Okay.' I manage to say without giving myself away.

'We need to know when the first killing took place. That will tell us when the time runs out.' He looks at me expectantly and I am caught on the hop.

'I don't know exactly when the first killing took place.' Best be upfront about my deficiencies. 'But it was found on the third. So no more than a day or two before that I expect.' I can ask DI white for details and pull out my phone to text.

'That doesn't leave very long. Whatever is going on will come to a climax on Sunday. Five more days.' Jeremy helpfully reminding me it is Tuesday. I don't snigger at his climax although the image almost twitches my lips.

'How many killings will there be?' Maybe there will be some good news. I doubt it but one can hope.

'It depends.' He begins and then slurps his chocolate. A grown man drinking hot chocolate with pink and white mini-marshmallows, I was almost embarrassed for him when he ordered it. 'There may be four for cardinal points or five if it is a pentagram.' The little mallow residue on his upper lip is distracting.

'So one or two more then?' I know we have three already. If there has been another one during my convalescence then the Master may already be on his way.

'The last one must take place on the final day of the lunar cycle, probably under moonlight.' At least that is useful to know.

'Is there a manual somewhere I've missed?' Sorry, it

slipped out. It's probably called Summoning for Dummies, I can see the yellow and black cover right now.

'Not exactly, Andrew.' He smiles and slurps. 'I have gleaned these from the archives over the years. The details are scattered across texts and witness accounts. Some are very old.' Smugness fills his voice and face. I want to growl again.

'Any clues as to where it will happen?' I'll bet your tomes don't tell you that Jezza.

'Not really. However, it will be somewhere within the confines of the summoning perimeter.' He is winging it, I can tell, as he is waving his cup about in a vague airy gesture. Never play poker Jeremy the bad boys will steal your pocket money.

'So Edinburgh then?' Thanks a fucking bunch.

'It needs to be on holy ground, too.' Jeremy adds to the mix. And the hits they keep on coming. I wonder what else he will omit to mention. No doubt I will find out when it is most critical

'Edinburgh, church, Sunday night under moonlight.' I smile but want to scream. 'He's as good as caught.' Jeremy is serious, for fucks sake. And he's on my side; with help like this who needs hindrance. My Americano is finished too. I look at the empty cup and sigh.

Chapter 10

I suppose I should be thankful; after all it confirms what I suspected. The killings have been taking place elsewhere and the bodies dumped. Well, apart from the last one, I know it happened in the alley. Small wonder the pattern won't fit and the cops have no idea how to fit them together. It is the same killer though. That's something at least of which I am certain.

Plan of action is to find the actual sites and plot them on a map of Edinburgh. That way I can find the point where it will culminate on Sunday night. Thwart the demon plot and kill the baddie. Simples as the little meerkat on the telly would say. DI White will be so impressed. I am not surprised that every case seems to end in a complete disaster and an extended stay in an NHS bed.

Edinburgh is a great place. No really, it is. However, it is old. Old towns and cities have lots of one thing, churches. It was the hobby of choice for centuries for the wealthy when times were boring build a chapel, if it got really dull build a big church or a Cathedral. They are lovely and the tourists flock round the bigger ones clicking their cameras. For me though, the truly vast list of churches, cemeteries and possible sites is a real pain. Add to this the list of 'newer' religions and my list is getting longer and longer a bit like Santa's naughty list.

I need a bigger map. So far mine looks like a massive spot the ball with lots (and lots) of little crosses on it. I wonder if the police have a decent map they would let me deface? Looking back at my handiwork (an hour or so of effort) and I conclude that it tells me nothing. I need to find the first site and go from there. That might just be the key to finding the others. A needle in a haystack springs to mind.

'DI White.' He sounds tired to me, poor sod.

'Steel here. I need a map, a big one of the city, if you have such a thing.' Probably should have done the small talk thing. Oh well, too late now. This playing nicely is such hard work.

'No problem, what are you thinking?' DI White is such a helpful fellow and he never seems to be too upset at my demands.

'Churches are the key to this. The murders are taking place in churches or church grounds. It's part of a ritual.' I might as well give him the full picture. It will save time later. Of course, that's about all I have to contribute.

'There are lots of churches, synagogues and mosques in the city. It will be a big list.' No shit Sherlock.

'We can start with the ones near where the girls were dumped. He can't have carried them too far.' I attempt to minimise the size of the task at hand.

'OK. Come on down and we can look at it.' He sounds resigned to a long day. He doesn't know the half of it.

'Oh White,' I catch him before he hangs up 'we are missing a couple of bodies. There will be four or five culminating with a last one on Sunday night.' Bombshell dropped and bomber heading for home. I can feel his grip on the receiver tightening.

'Dear God.' He whispers. I can almost picture a head in hands moment.

'Exactly and the last one was a recreational kill; not part of the pattern at all.' I like to share good news early and often.

'We need help. The Brass are going to be so pleased to hear this.' There's an accompanying rustle of papers coming from his end.

'I'll be there as soon as I can.' I hope he finds that comforting.

'Finding the bodies is not important just now.' Direct

but true, so I keep trampling on. 'The sites of the murders will help us stop the last one on Sunday night.' Spelling things out to rather pedestrian thinking plods seems to be my Sisyphean task.

'Yes, Father, but the bodies will hold vital clues.' Chief Superintendent Nitwit wants a body search for an unspecified number of corpses and in unspecified areas.

'Like the ones we have in the morgue?' I lob my grenade into his argument. He gives me a look. I get it a lot; it's a cross between 'Fuck off' and 'you are disrespecting me.' I might be immune to it though. Chief Stupid-intendent Cousins gives a little mini-sigh and capitulates. I can always play my 'I am in charge' card but I save that for emergencies.

'All right Father, I take your point. How do you think we should proceed?'

'We need to check as many churches and their grounds for blood splatters. If we identify a possible site then DI White and I can check it out and see what it tells us.' Just a simple, little task obviously.

'That's a lot of churches.' Cousins doesn't look happy but that's life. I wonder if this is what the Bishop calls playing nice? Probably not.

'Sooner we start, the sooner we will get a lead.' I try to be upbeat; there's only so much he can take in one go. I could have said 'Let's turn that frown upside down' but I didn't.

DI White hands me a coffee in a proper cup too. It even looks the right colour; the coffee not the mug. PC Jill is bringing one for the chief Super. A packet of Hobnobs appears as if by magic. Cousins is a biscuit man; a double dunker and his deftness at consuming the oaty-goodness of Hobnobs is a well honed skill. A few biscuits in and he speaks, his face and tone much friendlier.

'We have ten uniformed officers available now and we will be able to pull in some traffic guys later this afternoon.

That will make a start.' He's thinking out loud and I let him continue as I stuff my face.

The frown on DI white's face is getting deeper. He is thinking, I hope. 'It'll still take days we don't have sir.'

'We don't have any more juice to do it, I'm afraid.' Cousins is scanning for more of the disappearing biscuits.

'What if we ask the Clergy to do it? We could get each of them to check their grounds and church buildings. Might give us a start?' I hear myself uttering such helpful suggestions and am surprised. No hint of sarcasm tainting them either.

'Let's get on with it then.' Cousins has decided in his evaporating-post-biscuit-glow. To hear is to obey, said no one ever.

What do clergymen and women do on a midweek morning? I have no idea but not many of them are answering their phones. I might be on a few blocked lists but I doubt I am on them all. PC Jill is having the same sort of luck but at least she has managed to contact a few. I swig my cup of tea-substance and find it all but empty. My face is a mirror of my inner unhappiness and frustration and I plop it down a little more firmly than I really meant. Another voicemail box. I manage to articulate a message and leave the contact number.

'Dear Father Campbell there is a demon running amok in town. Please check your church and grounds for blood splatters as it may have been the site of a satanic summoning.' Is screaming around in my head and, I hope, not the words I actually say aloud.

Next on the list is the attractive sounding 'Light of the World Church of the Lord.' I snort in derision, I am such a snob. No bugger in there either. I put the receiver back and decide to make the tea. PC Jill has at least got someone to talk to.

I waggle my mug and mouth the 'Tea?' question. Her

bobbing ponytail confirms the yes. It'll be the first useful thing I've done in the last hour. DI White waggles his too; my promotion to tea-boy has been made official. Years of study to end up making the tea; I have peaked, obviously.

DI White and I are the flying squad. As soon as we get a possible we are going to swoop down upon the site with all sirens blaring and lights flashing. The Sweeney would be so proud; I am Reagan and get to shout a lot.

Uniformed officers have been sent to the closest possible sites (based on where the bodies were found) but we have heard nothing yet. How hard can this be? I thought we had cracked it with my genius suggestion but apparently not. We have some traffic cops to use this afternoon. I hope they have been briefed properly as the list of churches and suchlike is a long one and we aren't there yet.

My efforts at tea may prevent me being given the task ever again. The tea looked fine at the kettle but is probably a bit on the strong – undrinkable side. Better that than the milk with a hint of tea in it. It is hot and wet so it will have to do.

Next on my list is 'Magdalene Chapel, Morningside', it sounds delightful. It is ringing and I have just burned my tongue on the tea. A silent bout of swearing ensues, fuck-fuckitty-fuck.

'Good morning, Father Andrew, how can I help you?' How on earth did he know it was me, I nearly laugh.

'Good morning, I am calling on behalf of Edinburgh Police. We need your help.' I pause, gives him time to say 'of course' or something like that.

'We need you to check your church and grounds for anything out of the ordinary. We are particularly looking for blood splatters.' I pause again.

'My Goodness.' He sounds camper than a row of tents. The shocked tone tells me he might need some assistance.

'This is a murder enquiry and you need to check as

soon as possible and confirm back to the task force here.'
Better get him to do it before he needs a wee lie down.

'Oh my,' He splutters 'of course, I will. Right away.'
He'll be running about like a wet hen and will probably
faint if he finds blood.

'Thank you. As soon as possible, if you please.' Get
off the phone and move on. How people manage to work in
call centres I don't know. Nobody answers their phone and
when they do they are unhelpful. I have been doing this for
ninety three minutes and I have had enough already.
Chapeau to those who have to do this all day every day.

Chapter 11

'We have a hit.' DI White calls over to me. I am under whelmed. I was expecting a ghost-busters-esque lights flashing and siren. Oh well. I didn't get a pony for Christmas either.

It seems Father Andrew at Magdalene Chapel has found something, so forgive me if I am sceptical. I'm betting this is a false alarm. He was such a drama queen on the phone he would be desperate to take part in the enquiry. It would give him something to gossip to parishioners about; how he helped solve the murders. I can feel my face looking sour.

Traffic in the Capitol is really just an exercise in clutch control. Movement is sluggish like, I imagine, the turgid Mississippi river. Moving through the traffic like a big catfish, slow, slow then zip through a gap to the next bottleneck. Luckily for us DI White is a catfish and hasn't used his lights yet. I would be sirens and lights by now but there are rules I believe. Who knew?

'Won't be long now.' DI White states it like a fact. He has said that very same thing four times now. His credibility has taken a knock.

'No worries.' I manage to be civil but my sour puss is looking out; so hopefully he will believe me. I want to scream 'Use the fucking siren!' but I'll keep that in for the next nearly-there-a–gram

It turns out that not long was less than a minute as a beautiful little Gothic chapel heaves into view. A well tended gravel car park welcomes us with a reassuring crunch. Like Crockett and Tubbs we dismount the car. Wish I had my shades on; we are so cool.

I can feel the power of God through my feet. This chapel is very pure. It isn't often I can feel it outside. The sun is playing across the stained glass, showing their

craftsmanship to any who care to look. The tableau of
Mary on one side and Saint Michael on the other is an odd
mix. My frown, as I can't put my finger on it, gives away
my grumpiness. They are very lifelike, not stylised
representations, and that is even more unusual. Curiouser
and curiouser, as Alice might say.

The Oak studded door with black iron hinges shout that
this door will keep all comers out. For a heartbeat White
and I look at it then both go at once for the iron ring handle.
I let him do it, a little push and the house of God is open.

I am getting goosebumps as I cross the threshold, not
creepy ones, good ones. It's like the loving caress of a
recharge as I feel the tingles run through me. I try not to
purr as we move into the church and avail myself of the
holy water in the silver font. I genuflect and cross myself as
we turn to face the high altar. The dark stained wooden
pews are dust free and have seen many a pious buttock.
This is a Holy island in a sea of amorality. I will keep this
stored away for future emergencies, one never knows when
a real emergency may present itself. Lucky is the Priest
with this charge.

As if on cue here he comes, practically mincing,
towards us. I school my face trying for bland. Hopefully it
doesn't just show sour. What is it with the camp prancing?
Buggered if I know.

'Father Andrew? DI White.' Cop takes charge, I nod
not trusting myself yet.

'There's some blood behind the church, in the
graveyard. It is just terrible.' No prelims just a near
hysterical panic and the only thing missing is the flapping
hands.

'Take us there, please Father. Time is of the essence.'
See, I can be polite. A firm hand is usually what is needed
with the highly strung in the priesthood. I can do firm.

It is like a switch. Halfway down the tidy graveyard
pea-gravel path the Holy switch goes off. Holy – not holy.

Consecrated – not consecrated. The back of the graveyard isn't part of the church. There must have been some enlargement that was never consecrated, probably part of the various local government reorganisations where land often changed hands. I'll bet no one thought about ensuring the ground was claimed and consecrated. This might be the place after all. The boundary wall of the church is a good twenty feet further on. There are no yew trees for the Unforgiven to be buried beneath.

'Over there.' Father Andrew points a shaky looking finger. Does he manicure them? 'Near the Angel at the back.' He stands rooted to the spot, obviously not wishing to get any closer.

'Thanks. We'll take it from here.' I try to sound sincere but his uber-campness is really irritating. DI White has moved on, not waiting.

In an accidental pincer, we surround the angel looking over the dearly departed resting place of Alexander Lothian and his clan. Going by the list and dates, this is a family plot. The Angel is a thing of beauty. Well sculpted and very smooth; a very expensive piece. It has withstood the determined efforts of Mother Nature and Father Time. I want to run my fingers along the surface but remember we have an audience.

'There's blood all right.' DI White is snapping on his gloves as he scans around for a source. I might have missed the large pool and splash of blood bright in the daylight or perhaps I would not have spotted the lovely spray up the back of the plinth being blind and all. It isn't new blood, I can tell that by looking. It isn't that old either.

'There's more here.' DI White is moving to the wall. I suppose I should go look but it is just more blood. If it is our guy why didn't anyone hear anything? There are houses not that far away. There isn't that much cover either; the graveyard isn't polluted with trees like many are. This one is open to the sky on this side. There could be some cover from the larger monuments and crypts, I suppose.

A grim look has settled on DI White's usually professional cop face. He stands with his hand on his radio thing.

'The trail leads to the wall and over. Is it our guy?' He looks expectantly.

I am caught a little off guard; I was looking at the headstones nearby. Dawdling, you might say. 'What? Oh right. I will know in a moment.' I am so not looking forward to doing this. Father Andrew is standing on the path as far away as he can be but still claim to be taking part. Obviously, I was too subtle with my 'piss off' earlier. He looks like the last kid to get picked at the football. He is so uncomfortable being near to a crime scene. I'd best go behind the Angel and out of sight. I wouldn't want him to faint after all.

I'm not squeamish, at least not any more. Today, however, I am reluctant and I am not sure why. I wonder if it is because I know what I might experience. Evisceration of the victims has been horrible and once seen is there for permanent recall at random times and places. I take the deepest breath I can before I let my hand slip across the blood on the plinth steps at the back.

I almost smile as I get a pleasant surprise. No jolt of pain and savage re-living the event. She is walking hand in hand with it. The Demon has her within its thrall. I don't recognise her from our incident boards. This is a new one waiting to be found elsewhere. We are further behind than we knew. She feels calm, the skinned knees and grazed shins from the climb over the wall are ignored. I can feel them even though she didn't.

I hope she took a good look round before he kills her. The actual site may hold evidence for DI White, whatever he can make of it. I feel sudden sharp stabs into the back of my hand and realise his claws have just extended burying themselves in her soft flesh. A puzzled, foggy moment as she looks down to see his scaly talons submerged in her hand and the red blood running freely over them.

The scream she tries to get out is lost as he clamps a crushing fist around her throat. Very little sound escaped her after this. The hypnosis is gone replaced by a terror that mankind should never have known. I feel my face contorting as hers did, the tears running over my face only this time they aren't thick with Avon mascara. A brain numbing thudding blow echoes through me as her head collides with a nearby gravestone.

Then he took her. Roughly and with a level of rapture that is sickening in its intensity. Luckily she is barely conscious, as his frenzied thrusts take him over the edge. He casts his seed onto the holy ground, attempting to defile the consecration that has lain for centuries. I am unsteady and my gorge is rising I lean against a handily placed chunk of stone.

With barely a post-coital hug the demon carries her behind the angel and guts her. I manage to shut out the act of his talons twisting the intestines and feel only an ache. Her life passes quickly as her blood pulses out. It doesn't take long. 'Mum.' A plaintive last little whimper escapes her lips. It is over.

Like the flapping end from a projector reel, I take a moment to stop trying to watch. There is no more. My eyes open again on the real world and a few blinks clear away the tears that I shed with her.

The ache in my core and the pain in my soul are reminders of why we are here. DI White is looking at me in an odd way. Father Andrew looks a bit horrified and ghoulishly fascinated too.

'You all right?' DI White breaks the moment. He knows something happened but he just has no idea what. He doesn't try to touch me, which I appreciate. It is obvious I am fine, isn't it?

'I need a moment. It is our guy.' I am still leaning on a headstone it's solidity and permanence a godsend. I wipe my nose, which has twin streamers and I realise that I must look a fright. I often forget about the tears, as they come so often. I have a hankie somewhere and the patting of all my pockets until I find it, is a ritual in itself.

I hear White on the airwave (or whatever they call walkie-talkies these days) our find is a new scene and the circus will be on its way. I wonder what her name was. Everyone who is killed leaves a hole somewhere in some other life. Someone will be waiting or looking for her. Someone will miss her voice and smile, I can feel tears building. Do they really need to know she was raped and then slaughtered? Does anyone ever need to hear that?

I look over at Magdalene chapel and feel my anger rising like a tsunami. My grip on the headstone is painful but I need something to hurt. A nail on my index finger splits giving me a pain to cherish. Getting angry at God is like shouting at the sea; utterly pointless. I can feel the heat of my anger like a spike of bile burning in my gut.

'Father Andrew?' DI White approaches, gently, timid almost.

'What?' I snap like a total diva. His face is a picture. I just kicked a puppy or killed Bambi. I just want everyone to fuck off and leave me alone for a minute. Is it too much to expect?

'Father Andrew has put the kettle on. You should take a few.' His kindness is misplaced but appreciated. I would have told me to go 'fuck myself'.

'Sorry. Thanks I will.' I pull my spikes back in and attempt rapprochement. 'She is a new victim. Raped then killed.' And with that joyous news I walk like a man who has shit himself towards the chapel and the reviving tea.

Chapter 12

'It's all about the sex, Jeremy?' I am being patient but I really want to scream down the phone. He's convinced the consecrated ground is the key and I'm not. It might be but the sex is definitely important to this whole thing. We are dealing with one sick Mo-fo of a demon. I can feel the grip on my phone tightening and my jaw clenching as he twitters on.

'I hear what you are saying but can you look into the rituals with sex as part of the buffet. It brought her a long way to rape her; if she wasn't needed awake he would have knocked her out.' I try to point out the obvious but I can feel a 'For Fucks Sake' itching to be added to my comments.

'Thank you. Let me know soon as. Cheers, bye.' I get off the phone before those milling about in the white suits start to pay me any attention. Their onesies with hoods look ridiculous but then again trying to track a raping, murdering demon might seem ridiculous to them so who am I to cast aspersions.

I am standing on the consecrated bit of the church grounds; it usually helps me to get my equilibrium back. Today, however, not so much. Father Andrew's tea, though sweet and hot, wasn't much of a restorative either. I feel emptied. Like a big spiritual vacuum cleaner has been inserted and sucked me dry. It is a bit like finding yourself running on empty because you missed breakfast and lunch and it is four in the afternoon.

'Fuck.' I let it out. Only in Scotland does one word say everything quite so efficiently. It is the ubiquity of the word that has made it the punctuation of choice all across the central belt. Sentences can often be littered with it; this time it is the summative use.

'Couldn't agree more Father.' White heard me as he approached from my blind side. His face is pretty grey. We are miles behind and the race ends on Sunday night. DI White knows we need a miracle.

'How many more are we missing do you think?' I catch and hold his eye. He looks a little wild around the edges.

'I thought you said there would be four or five?' He isn't accusing but it is there just beneath the surface.

'It's not an exact science but it looks like the worst of our nightmares may be on its way. Demons like killing. Perhaps this one is just running amok. I hope not but who knows.' I might as well state the obvious. DI White needs to know that we might be in for a larger body count.

'Fuck.' He joins me in the shortest and most effective sentence in the known world. A moment of perfect misunderstanding hangs in the air between us. I need a pee; don't know what he's thinking.

'It's on the news. They're calling him the graveyard slasher.' PC Jill informs us as we return to the incident room. It's like a whirlwind has been through. A new board with our newest discovery and lurid (sorry glossy) pictures and reports cover its surface. The flat screen television on the far wall has rolling news coverage and a reporter from the scene of 'this latest gruesome murder.' A ticker along the foot of the screen stating in big letters 'Murder.' My face twists, I can't help it.

'Thanks for your help, ya bunch of useless bastards.' I growl and plank my arse on a desk. I start a mental countdown 5,4,3 and my phone buzzes in to life. A look at my screen confirms the caller. Bishop Michael.

'Steel.' Even though I know it's the boss I pretend I don't. It lets me sound all gruff.

'Andrew 'The Graveyard Slasher'? This is a nightmare. Where are you with this?' His deep voice is filled with anxious undertones.

'We have found another site but no body. This one likes the killing.' I pause, letting him absorb the news. 'There could be a whole raft of them out there waiting to be found.' I let the unfolding mess land in his lap.

'So much for Father Jeremy's four or five then?' He seems a bit put out. Luckily it isn't my fault this time.

'That might be a little on the low side.' I am trying to be helpful but that didn't come out right at all. Around me the police officers are all busy so totally ignoring me.

'You need to find it Andrew and bloody quickly too. The Home Secretary's office has been on the phone three times in the last hour.' He sounds exasperated but not angry at me, at least not yet.

'I will do my best Bishop.' I mumble into my phone. I am watching the rolling news coverage and reading the subtitles. They are basically saying they know nothing and that we know nothing either. The square root of nothing would be closer.

'Andrew this needs stopped. Get Jeremy to hurry up and help.' His tone is the one that says just do as you are told. He's obviously forgotten that Father Jeremy is already helping but I won't remind him of that. A scholar will be a real help, obviously.

'Yes Bishop, I have to go.' Best get off the line before he gives me other things to do.

'Keep me posted.' Another non request and he is gone. No take care or see you later. Not like him to be so abrupt. I bring out the best in people.

'This stuff brings out the crazies. So far it is just the serial confessors but it can get out of hand.' DI White informs the team, of which I am one. 'Uniform are taking up the slack with statements and chasing off the idiots. We have more crime scenes than we can cope with and I am bringing in help from Fife and Glasgow. They'll be here in the morning.' A few groans from the gallery, I am not sure if it's the Fife or the Glasgow bit.

'That better be for the soap dodgers.' I mutter Soto Voce. There is a tension breaking giggle from the guys. Even DI White cracks a smile. The soap dodgers an affectionate term for the Glasgow contingent.

'All right, settle down.' He pauses leaning forward on the lectern 'This will climax at the weekend, I am reliably informed. There is a ritual element to this that concludes on Sunday. Our focus will be on predicting where it is to occur and catch the Bastard in the act.' He has his audience. They are all focussed and ready now. It is more than I would have told them but DI White knows his guys.

'The lang spoons and the soap dodgers will be picking up the slack as we make the collar.' His smile has a hint of the wolf or maybe maniacal would be closer. He pauses for effect 'Well? Why are you all still sitting here? Get on with it.' Mister Motivator in action.

So we have seven scenes and four bodies; including my close encounter in the community centre. One of the bodies is a recreational kill in my opinion but DI White thinks it counts. Jeremy does too, apparently.

I am staring at the city street map with the highlighted religious establishments, there is no discernible pattern. No ordinal points, no pentagram emerging; no bloody clue. I know it sounds off but if I were trying to hide a pattern it would be carnage with many extras. As well as a few recreational hits. Then again I could be a sociopath or a psychopath or whichever one it is. One thing is certain, we need more data. Data would mean bodies, so I am careful what I wish for. A sigh escapes my lips. I feel old and tired.

'We have a body.' DC MacBride shouts across the room. The effect is instantaneous, with a collective lurch into action. 'Just down the road from the Morningside Church from today.' Spotty, it seems can't recall the church name.

'Father, you are with me. MacBride, make sure the morgue get their ass on this as soon as. I presume uniform are on the scene?' DI White is barking as his overcoat gets pulled on. MacBride is nodding and writing the commands down. It wasn't that difficult to remember.

'Uniform are on their way, two minutes away.' DC MacBride sings out across the room. I am good to go and DI White is two steps ahead of me as the dynamic duo head for the bat mobile. What a strange pair we make; it is like a cop show in action.

Chapter 13

Casually dumped in a, big grey, household waste bin our other-world friend really has no class. Caroline Forbes, identified from her purse helpfully left in her jacket pocket, is our poor soul from Magdalene Chapel. The indignity of her disposal seems extreme, even to me. The uniformed officers standing guard within the tape perimeter seem particularly discomforted by it. White is busy speaking into his radio as I scan the houses around us. No one is forthcoming with anything useful. I can see the steady progress of two officers as they go from each green-painted council door to the next. An exercise in futility but one that needs to be completed and added to the evidence log.

These big omnium bins, with their little roller wheels have revolutionised the handling of domestic waste. Long gone are the days of the bin man carrying the bin out to the scaffy truck; now we put our bins at the kerbside and a few button presses later they are tipped into the compactor wagon. At least the body wasn't tipped inside the truck. It had been left untouched as it was the wrong bin. Today was green bin day; plastic recycling not general waste. The bin men had just rolled on by leaving the gruesome contents undisturbed. The woman from number 29 had gone out to retrieve her bin and looked at the offending wrong bin. She was sitting in the back of the ambulance, having taken a turn.

I am always surprised that people these days are able to walk past anomalies and not feel even a little bit curious about them. Two days that bin had been at the kerbside. Two days that no one noticed the reek. Two days that little red drops on the pavement had been missed or ignored. Two days that no one even peeked inside. Two days of tutting and moaning to spouses about the inconsiderate sod who had put out, and left out, the wrong bin. A disgrace no doubt. Community? It seems to be seeping away under the onslaught of modern life. Hundreds of little personal castles with little connection or care for the castles built in the same row.

'Mum' had been her last thought. Her last word of choice and one that said so much. Somewhere her mum would be receiving the worst news that would ever reach her ears. The cruelty of a random event in the cosmic battle would leave little possible comfort for her maternal soul. A peace that even our victory and justice would never return to her. Forever her heart would be broken, shattered by a cruel fate. A wrong place, wrong time that would never be understood and a 'Why?' would haunt her all the days of her life. I hoped that there were siblings of Caroline Forbes that her mother could hold tight to her breast.

The prickling around my eyes was my own, not a recollection of past horrors. My heartsick sorrow for a woman I have never met who would soon be called on to visit the viewing room and identify a cleaned up yet still ruined body. I let out the breath that was making my chest hurt and looked round the ordinary street. I needed to do something. Anything. The twitch of a curtain revealed a face that held something. It wasn't ghoulish interest; it was terror. My eyes had caught the looker. The witness that had seen something. I marched straight towards the door, there was no point in her not answering.

'I am Father Steel. I am with the police.' I spoke firmly watching her face take in the dog collar and the reference to the police giving me the authority to compel her obedience. Her housecoat was clamped around her like a suit of armour against the world. The flowers a bit faded and worn but not shabby though, her hair that silver grey that old women get rinsed with blues and pinks.

'Come in, Father.' She hurriedly closes out the world as she leads me into her sitting room. The room with the view of the street, a view I am sure she has watched evolve over the years. Her husband, bed ridden, upstairs took so much of her time that the seat by the window was a regular haunt for Agnes Thomson. The crucifix hanging on the wall spoke of religious observance and a devout adherence to a God who had left her in a hard life full of pain and duty.

'A terrible thing to happen.' I open with a starter to get her speaking. I know she needs to tell me something. If I make it easy for her she might just spill the lot quickly. At least she never felt the need for the mandatory tea offering. She shifted uneasily in her seat, looking once more at scene unfolding outside. The bin would be removed, body and all, with the extraction taking place in private at the morgue. It would eat up resources and tell us little more than I already knew.

'It is terrible.' She shook her head slowly from side to side, disbelief that this could be happening at her front door. 'I heard the bin lid banging down two nights ago. I had just given Bob a drink of water and was sitting here for a moment.' She looked over at me, deciding how much to reveal. I let her find my eyes and hold them, willing her to trust me with what she knew.

'He was a big man and he stomped down the street, a big dark coat pulled up with a hood. I couldn't see a face.' She looked away, screwing herself up a bit. 'I saw his hands dripping and I know now it was blood.' Her hand balling over her mouth as she realised what she had seen. 'I should have called the police then.' She seemed ashamed at her lack of action.

'We will find him. Thank you for telling me.' It hadn't been that much of a help but it did confirm the sequence of events. I patted her hand gently ' A police officer will get a proper statement soon.' She looked up at me, and pulled a deep shuddering breath inside to fuel her last snippet of information.

'When he got to the end of the street, I swear he looked

round and could see me watching. His eyes flared red in the dark. He was evil Father. And then he was gone.' She was terrified thinking he would return.

'He won't be back. Perhaps it was the light but I think you managed to see the evil that was in him.' I hold her hand, comforting her that she hadn't been seeing things. She was a devout soul and I was sure that faith would keep her warm at night. She had seen my demon but not the whole picture, luckily. The buzzer from upstairs told her that Bob needed her now.

Chapter 14

'It takes a great deal of strength to force a body in that space. I couldn't do it.' DI White was filling me in on the medical examiner's report. He had seen plenty in his time with the police but this was a first for him. I could feel the shock of it seeping from his pores. Sitting in his office, surrounded by folders full of paper on the cases on the whiteboards in the main room, I looked at him letting him continue. He knew we were chasing a demon but he still didn't really get it. His head was moving side to side in little micro movements as if his brain would not accept what he knew to be true.

'The Demon will be very strong and I doubt that it took much for it to snap her into that bin.' I had to remind him of what we faced. I suppose I could also have reminded him that there will be at least one more to be found and of course the final one on Sunday night. I decided that he didn't need that added on top of his shock. The medical examiner's report had included a line about the spinal injuries allowing compression into the space. That and the lack of internal organs. DI White nods; he's a little distracted.

The desk phone rings, pulling us back to the here and now and away from our own images playing in vivid colour in our heads. It might be easier if we could just project our thinking onto a wall or screen. I would bet on my show being the goriest. We look across the desk at each other, a moment where neither of us wants to pick up the phone, is this another scene discovered or someone upstairs demanding action. I raise my eyebrows, 'On you go' I might as well have said. A deep, sole of the boots, sigh escapes White as he lifts the handset.

'DI White.' A neutral, if a little tired, voice giving away

nothing. His hands tightening on the handset the only clue of his feelings. The scrabbling hand finding a pen from the debris covering his desk and in a few seconds a terse 'go ahead' had him writing on a scrap of paper. The frown lines deepening as he made slashes with the pen. It was an address, apparently; I can read upside down. A skill that has surrendered many a secret to my eyes. I can do reflected, too, a man of many useful little skills. None of which are often that useful. I waited, the cool substance that covered the bottom of the Styrofoam cup was unappealing, until DI White caught my eye. He didn't really need to tell me that there was another body waiting for us.

'We have to go.' He managed to whisper. He was so close to defeat that he couldn't really summon a fight. I hoped he would recover from this. Cops see too many things that just hang around in their heads, waiting for a repeat like all the programmes on Dave. He looked up slowly finding my eyes, looking for a reassurance that I couldn't give him. This one might be as unforgettable as the one detailed on paper before us.

'We will get this bastard.' I tried to be confident but so far we were managing to lumber around in the Edinburgh traffic like a pair of drunk, blind men without a white stick between us. I don't think DI White was fooled. He stood up, pushing the chair back on its little castor wheels, it seemed that a huge bench press was needed to get upright. The weight of the world indeed.

White is getting the hang of this 'Flying Squad' thing; the blue lights and siren were deployed straight away. The interminable trips of stop-and-go were now replaced by a heavy right foot and the 'get-the-fuck-out-of-the-way' siren and lights combo. I didn't comment, I just held on to the handle for the afraid. The cars in the capitol seem to know how to make spaces that don't exist. Judicious use of the pavements to make a path between the tightest two lanes of traffic allows the emergency services to get through the old town in record time.

'Where are we going?' I ask, although I read the address, upside down, I had no actual idea where Perseus Crescent was. White needed to be distracted from his black fury that emanated from him, the crushing of the steering wheel looked almost painful.

'Leith.' He let it out and that was it. No other details. He seemed to be taking this personally, which might make him very volatile if we ever got our hands on the demon. It might make him dead. I couldn't have that; he was one of the good guys. I tried to remember the churches that were down Leith way but all that sprang to mind were the pubs and hookers that plied their trade there.

'St Thomas Aquinas.' I managed to pull one from my memory. It was a sturdy beast with a decent view over the sea. I couldn't recall who the Priest was; I could tell you who scored in the cup final of years gone by but the names of local priests was too difficult.

We were very nearly there and the abrupt halt and screaming of tyres caught me off guard, throwing me into the door as White had to swerve away from the arse end of a white transit van that didn't seem to hear or see our approach. DI White had obviously passed the advanced defensive driving course or had spent far too long racing karts at the indoor circuits. The collision that I thought was imminent was avoided with flicks of his wrists and fancy footwork.

'Get out of the way ya fucking arsehole!' He screamed at the top of his lungs as he swerved back in front of the startled van driver. I was holding on tight waiting for the crunch of metal but it never came. Our lights clearing the way as up ahead I could see the bell tower of St Thomas Aquinas. The grey skies beginning to offer the usual Lothian weather; a little moisture to help the grass and weeds grow.

The road ahead was full of police cars, an ambulance and a load of spectators trying to get a view over the yellow tape. We arrived just like the Sweeney, all screeching tyres and slamming doors. A Uniformed constable raised the tape quickly to remove any delay. We were needed inside quickly. The clicking of cameras just one more noise in the cacophony. I was vaguely aware of a guy trying to ask DI White if this was the graveyard slasher.

Inside the church the milling about of white onesies meant that this was the crime scene. We moved like Moses, parting the red sea, and progressing into the vast church and taking in the High Altar and the stained glass that allowed multi-hued light to fill the space at any time of the day. I could smell the sweet, cloying smell of rotting flesh. It was nearby. The flash and clicking of a camera told me that a body was lying to the right but it was the body mounted on the cross that held my attention. It was like no one wanted to take him down. The gouges across his back a parody of the whip marks that adorned the back of Jesus as he bore his cross. The pile of rubble scattered all around witness to what had happened to the original cruciform of Christ. Hanging there now was a flesh and blood resident and from the shreds of clothing still clinging to him, it was the local priest. Father Francis, I recalled his name. I stepped up the central aisle, I think White was behind me but maybe he didn't want to approach the body hanging over the top of the cross. I couldn't really blame him.

I genuflect as I approached the rail and realised that it was probably not the right thing to do, after all the Crucifix had been defiled. The drips of blood that had made their way down the length of Father Francis back, thighs and shins were still intermittently adding to the pool below his blood covered feet. The splintered ruin of his shins showed that his killer had taken the time to torture him before he died. I moved around to see the front view and wished instantly that I hadn't.

Flapping from the ruin of his throat was his tongue. The black blood congealing and covering the purple shirt and white collar leaving a dark wet stain all over his chest. The mouth open in an eternal scream of pain and terror ringed in blood and home to a set of shattered teeth. Worst for me was the empty black and bloodied sockets where his kind eyes had once lived. I managed to avoid throwing up at the rivers of ichor and blood that had run from these sightless sockets. The destruction of Father Francis had been comprehensive and done as cruelly as possible, This was a killing for the pleasure of seeing another suffer.

A blurring of my sight as I stepped forward to touch his foot was due to the tears of genuine sadness for my brother in Christ. I let my finger tips touch his ankle, I am sure the onesie wearers were scandalised that I touched the body. I am ready for a hideous re-run of the last moments of Father Francis and the demonic fiend's orgiastic frenzy of cruelty. I let myself open to my gift. I feel the warmth travel up my arm as the waves of pain course through my body, echoes of the torment that Francis endured.

I often wish that I could fast forward past the pain, hurt and emotion like a DVD but I have to feel it all. The eyes, although removed are still allowing me to see and feel the wounds as they are inflicted. The end is pretty much as I expected and now I can see the scaled face of my enemy, his claws and his sharp incisor filled mouth. The cruelty in the eyes is like a blow with each glance. I watch as he entered this church, still wearing a human form. The body collapsing off in a heap as Father Francis stood screaming at the sight of the Demon emerging.

As it stalked slowly forward Francis had been unable to back away, frozen in place by the red eyed glare that held him. The disbelief of what was happening before him overwhelming his mind. Nothing really prepares you to see a demon peel its way out of a walking corpse. We have all seen the films but the actuality is much more shocking. I wondered what the medical staff would make of the remains, discarded in the pews.

DI White was moving towards me as I stepped away and let go. I must have looked awful, prompting him to ask if I was all right. I didn't want to explain that I had just felt a shadow of what Father Francis had, and to complain about it seemed disrespectful. I nodded but he guessed otherwise. He moved up towards the altar; he had to look. He was the commander on the scene now. I left him to it and sat on the front pew. How had the demon crossed the threshold and entered this house of God? It should have been enough to keep it out. Was it gaining in power with each death? Was the coming climax bringing it power? I had no idea.

I took out my phone fully intending to call the Bishop when he beat me to it. I almost dropped it as the vibrations pulsed in my hand. I quickly shut off the noise; I was sitting in a church after all.

'Steel.' Habits die hard, even though I knew it was him and I needed his help. I still wouldn't give anything away.

'Andrew, are you at St Thomas Aquinas? The media are all over this.' His voice sounded hurried and a little frantic. I took a deep breath.

'Yes Bishop and it is carnage. Father Francis has been tortured and mounted on the cross by our demon. How it managed to walk in here I have no idea.' The peeling itself from the corpse could wait a few moments.

'There are television cameras on the way but there is a clip on the internet from a mobile phone.' That most certainly isn't my fault. I wondered what it had captured.

'What does it show? The demon left here in its own form I think.' Maybe Bishop Michael had watched it all.

'The video is a peek inside after the event and is moved on by a policeman. Still the fate of Father Francis is now circulating in lurid detail. The Home Secretary is most unhappy.' Bishop Michael passed on the dissatisfaction with aplomb. I think I am supposed to give a shit about the

Home Secretary and his unhappiness, I don't.

'I have to go, DI White needs my help. I will call later.' I end the call before I get any more orders. I look up at White, he looks a little green about the gills. 'You all right?' I return the favour.

'We need to get Father Francis down from there and the remains bagged up.' I twitch my head over my shoulder. DI White signals a few of the onesies over and points at the body. They will have the logistical task of getting the body down. A blazing high power light has been set up outside, probably from the television crews, and it seems to flood the church with colours. The stained glass panels causing rainbows and patches of different coloured light to dance around us. I look sour but that isn't really a surprise as the Chief Superintendent stomps his way into the crime scene. The big outer door is slammed shut cutting off the hubbub from outside.

'DI White, update me on where we are.' Buttons tries not to bark but he manages not to stare at the body hanging over the cross. He fixes his gaze on White who starts to recount the very limited amount we know and makes it last longer than I could have done. Maybe White has a career in politics to look forward to.

'The press are out there like a pack of hyenas. I need more than that.' The Superintendent is as impressed with the long version as he would have been with my short 'Fuck knows' response. He has a funny puce colouring and I think he will look a bit flustered in front of the cameras.

'Right, we need to get the story straight. Is this the Graveyard slasher or is this a new psychopath?' He is barking now, and that never gets a great response. DI White looks to me to answer that one. Thanks mate, thanks a lot.

'It is the same person.' I manage to make it bland and give nothing away to the 'Brass' so that the more awkward questions are avoided. He hasn't been told the half of it and

I doubt he could cope anyway. He's a square peg in square holes kind of guy.

'It seems that he's moved on from young women then. Are we sure?' We both nod, no point in pretending otherwise. 'White we will go out and give a holding statement. Father Steel you had better stay out of sight. We don't want to have you part of the circus. White, let's get this done. Formal briefing at Duke Street station in an hour or two.' Chief Superintendent Buttons knows how to cover ass and make the cameras focus on the right thing. He might as well have a 'nothing to see here sign made.' I doubt our brothers and sisters in the media will obey though.

Chapter 15

DC MacBride is left to provide any assistance I might need and to prevent my screwing things up. He is a decent, if somewhat spotty, cop and doesn't try to over reach. He takes a lot at face value from me and I expect that is more to do with the instructions from on high. He makes sure I am always within sight too, even when he is scribbling in his notebook. Perhaps he has been left to keep an eye on my unconventional activities and report back. Anyway as I walk around the church his eyes seem to be a constant companion.

The bodies have been bagged and taken to the morgue and will be examined tonight. I am still working to a Sunday night climax but my faith in Father Jeremy's predictions has taken a bit of a beating as the body count starts to rack up. So much for four or five. This demon has been a bit busier than that and we still have very little to go on. The patterns and randoms are inextricably tied up and we have no idea which is which. I wonder how the press briefing is going and how well DI White is managing to say we are devoid of clues,leads and the only thing we have a pile of is dead bodies.

'How did it manage to walk in here? It should never have managed to walk under the shadow of the Crucifix.' I realise I have spoken out loud. DC MacBride looks in my direction, as if wondering if it was aimed at him. I wave him back to his note taking as I walk around, letting the church speak to me. It isn't really saying much. I walk to the sanctuary lamp, its red glass diffusing the flame within, expecting something like inspiration to strike. It doesn't.

I sit on a smooth, varnished pew and let myself pray. Well, not exactly prayer, more a case of looks like prayer as I slip into a trance of sorts. I ease my will out into the church. It should feel sanctified and holy but this one feels null. Nothing. No spiritual energy; no holiness laid down over the years and years of delivering the sacrament to the Faithful. There is no feeling of faith suffusing the ground beneath our feet and no feeling of the enemy either. It is as if this church is not a Holy place at all.

'Jeremy. It's Andrew. I am in St Thomas Aquinas in Leith. It doesn't feel right. Can you look into the history of the place.' I speak quickly knowing that he will have a long set of questions to illicit my 'For Fucks Sake' response. I am hoping for a quick dismount and escape.

'Yes it is the place you are seeing on the news. Our friend walked in here and killed the priest. Bold as brass. I have to go. Let me know.' I click end call. I am getting too like Bishop Michael. Aye right.

It is like an itch on the inside of my brain. The need to know and I has left me in serious trouble at times. I walk to the entrance vestibule and start my walk from there. The oak doors, so solid and studded with iron, at my back keeping the night out as I step forward on the smooth grey flagstones. They are well worn and old, not some modern addition or laminate flooring that seems to find its way into modern churches. The font ahead of me, beautifully sculpted, with a decent level of water in the bowl. I place my hand on the stone, letting my mind open to the holiness that should emanate from it. It doesn't give anything. No power of the Lord in this font. It might as well be a thirty quid sink from Homebase.

I know I am looking grumpier by the minute. I start to recite the Lord's Prayer, bringing something holy into this empty place. I speak softly so that my words fall in a shroud around me, no one else needs to hear me. The words tumbling in a stream from my lips fly straight to God's ear; or at least that is what we tell people. The rites, repeated every weekday and twice on Sunday have been washed away. The footsteps of this demon have cast years of devotion aside. How it has managed this I have no idea but I am afraid. The Priest who stood before the demon was afraid and it seemed to embolden the beast. Memories of his screams of torment rattle about inside my head as I walk the stations of the cross.

This isn't a case of satanic squatters and a front of a church; this is a case of the church being totally wiped of any sanctity. I continue on, praying and blessing at each cardinal point; praying at the little side shrines, Hail Mary-ing and Our Fathering repeatedly as my fingers run over the beads of the rosary. There is no resistance to my words or deeds and that is heartening. Standing at the altar, I open my spirit and 'feel' my way over it. The blood splatters have not been cleaned yet and, while it looks a bit gory, it is just a block of stone. The whole church will need re-sanctified and reconsecrated, the Bishop will need to arrange that once the furore and circus moves on.

'I have to head back to base Father. Do you want a lift?' DC MacBride calls to me from about as far away as he can be. He is uncomfortable being in here and not because of the bodies that have been removed. He's seen too many exorcist movies I'd bet and knows what happens to the sidekicks and help.

'I will be fine here. I have some thinking to do and I will see DI White in the morning at the task force room.' I don't look over my shoulder. The crazy priest is staying and he is glad to be going. To be honest I am glad he is going too, his watching me like an informant was becoming a little tedious. I notice the television camera's are still here but they aren't lighting the church up any more, just a hubbub and smaller individual spotlights for the 'live from the scene' pieces. They will be running this all night and tomorrow I expect.

A thought, you know the creepy undermining kind of 'what if' thoughts, struck me. What if it didn't leave? What if it was still here somewhere? I wonder what the first on scene officers did by way of a check? Shit. It wasn't in here but I couldn't tell if it was still hiding on the grounds or in the bell tower. This place is such a null, I can't feel very much at all. I need to find out. The oak and iron studded door is shut and I know there is a uniformed policeman outside but I really don't want to be caught on camera opening the door and calling him in. Discrete the Bishop had said; this might not be discrete at all if it is still here.

I pull the door open about three inches and peek around the edge like Harold Lloyd, ridiculous and silly but I spy the uniform and psst him over. He takes a moment before he gets that I want him to come inside. Maybe I needed to wave at him or something, so far so good no action from the camera crews. I slip the door closed, quietly.

'Officer was a full search of the building done on arrival?' The puzzled and not very helpful look tells me that maybe full and search didn't take place. I try again. 'Can you radio in and find out?' I don't want to scream but he really isn't keeping up. My terseness can get out of hand if things don't go my way, escalating into a full strop and toys out the pram behaviour. I wait as he radios through my question. We stand together waiting on the reply. A noise from far inside reaches our ears. I don't need to wait for the answer, I know.

'Get DI White and back up, now.' I shove him towards the door as I head past the font of totally normal water and into the tennis court sized playing field that the Demon has already played on. My footsteps ringing out as I stomp across the stone floor, I am coming and it knows it. A fury building in my chest as I recall the cruelty visited on Father Francis a reason for my headlong pursuit of a demon that might just rip my head off and spit in the hole.

'Flee as you will, the vengeance of the Lord follows you.' My voice like a sergeant major's as he roars commands to recruits on his parade ground. The sounds of flight fill the church ahead of me, the scrape of talons on the stone steps of the bell tower, telling me that my enemy has no where to run. My crucifix presented boldly before me as proof of which side I am on and the only weapon I have with me. That and Faith, obviously.

'Run ya bastard, I am coming.' Not very ritualistic but I want to get my hands on this one. The brutal murders of Brenda, Caroline and the rest making the red mist descend, and caution well and truly a long forgotten thing. I start to mount the bell tower steps, my knees pumping as the first few corners pass in a blur but the tightness in my chest starts to slow me up as oxygen isn't being sucked deep into my lungs. At this rate I couldn't catch the thirty nine bus let alone a demon fleeing the wrath of God.

The last few turns are abject agony as my knees scream at their treatment and my lungs burn from the abuse I put them through. There ahead of me is an abomination that should never have been in our world; a scaled red and black skinned murdering bastard. The sharp rows of teeth that have been buried in human flesh so vicious looking, a warning not to get too close. The snarl on lizard like lips and the hiss of warning as I step on to the bell platform, it is wary. It would be better if it was afraid, then I might have an advantage.

'I abjure you, in the name of Our Lord Jesus Christ.' I step forward, my arm steady and the silvered-iron crucifix boldly presented. The flinch away from my words and symbol fill me with a hope that warms me to my core. The demon moves in a blur of movement swinging the bell hard on the rocker. In a second I am bowled across the small space into the stone wall, crucifix falling from my fingers as the numbness travels down my arm and causes my fingers to spasm in pain. I stare up at the demon, relieved to see the back not the descending teeth that might have ended my life in a bloody fountain as it ripped my throat from the front of my neck. The shattering of the louvre slats under a heavy fist making a portal through which it was about to depart.

The wings unfurling as it flew into the darkness of the night.

'Aye run ya bastard.' I manage to mutter before the coughing and wincing commences. What on earth was I thinking? Rambo I am most certainly not.

Chapter 16

I know that I should have waited for back up. Really though, how would have back up been any use in the bell tower? If White had been with me he might have been the victim of a slash of wicked talons leaving him bleeding to death as his arteries pumped his life's blood all over the walls of the bell tower. The pain in my shoulder is a small, but worthwhile, price to pay to get close to the enemy. I can identify it now to Father Jeremy, whom I expect to have a rogues gallery to interrogate and thereafter a solution as to how to defeat it. After all, he is meant to be the fount of all knowledge.

'Father Steel.' An unknown voice is yelling up the stairwell. I presume it is the uniformed cop from the front door. He sounds a bit panicked. Maybe they were told to protect me.

'I am up here.' I manage to shout back and start the process of getting up from my supine position lying where the bell left me. I doubt anything is broken but that doesn't mean the groaning and wincing is any less. I hear him climbing the stairs and he doesn't sound like breathing is a problem, even with the kevlar vest and the tool belt bigger than batman.

His head appears round the corner and he scans the platform, seeing nothing but a smashed out louvre and the priest trying to rise from the floor. He moved up into the small space, his night stick a pointless implement in his hand, what he thought he would do with it is beyond me. He helps me to my feet, muttering concerned sounds and not commenting on the, rather impressive, coating of dust that has transformed my black uniform.

'Let's go.' I don't try to explain what has happened. One less person to swear to secrecy and one less for the

Bishop to berate me about. The lack of comprehension covering his face is comical and if each step down the stairwell hadn't been a juddering pain I might have found it humorous. As it was, I was in a great deal of discomfort by the time I had parked my sweaty ass on the front pew. I sent him back to his post outside and I waited for DI White to appear to be told how much of a fuck up, we had contributed to.

I sent a text to Jeremy while I sat there, recovering. I could almost see him ecstatic at the news I could identify the 'other-worlder' and had a decent description. Almost like donkey in the kids cartoon Shrek, jumping up and down almost wetting himself.

The beep was a little too quick, Jeremy had replied. A few flurries of thumbs and we had arranged to meet at the seminary tonight. The joy of joys that was my evening to come. I would need to imbibe if I was to avoid committing a crime with a lengthy prison term.

I was on my second glass of Château something-or-other and reclining on my bed, letting the ache in my shoulder ease away on a raft of alcoholic anaesthetic when Jezza opened my door. He managed to look excited and bookish at the same time, an arm full of folders was trying to escape as he tried to shut the door. Almost with a final bid for freedom the four shiny black plastic folders slipped from his grasp and fell on to the foot of the bed. A look of relief on his face that they hadn't cascaded to the floor spilling their contents as the ring bindings popped open.

'Father Andrew, how are you this evening?' He was trying to catch his breath after his exertions with the folders. I poured him a glass of wine and let him get settled.

'These folders contain pictures of Demons through the ages and are compiled from many different sources. I thought that you might be able to pick out the one most like the adversary you fought tonight. It might give us some clues on how to combat it.' He swigged his wine a little quickly for my thinking; maybe he was fortifying himself.

I opened the first cover and looked at the depiction; a five year old with a crayon could have produced better. It was going to be a long night if the artwork was going to be like this all the way through. Jeremy said nothing helpful as I tried, and succeeded, in not snorting derisively. The pictures carried on in a similar vein for a while, all being extracted from very old looks by the look of them. Soon though they started to improve a little and I am sure I passed one that looked remarkably like Milton's paradise lost. The first folder was finished and I didn't think there was much to say about the contents that wouldn't sound like a churlish teenager so I started the second after refilling our glasses. I would need to open another bottle on the next round.

The second must have been more recent, if the nineteenth century is more recent, and the lithographs were much better. More detail and much more realistic. Gone were the childlike representations and instead the images were obviously authentic. Little details and feelings that left me in no doubt that those making these images had seen them not just imagined and fantasised about them. Some of the artists had caught the malice in the looks too, which made them seem to leap of the page and would have been frightening to those of their time.

I look up at Jezza, a bit grudgingly perhaps but I meant it 'These are good, much better than I expected after the early ones.' He smiled and nodded, his wine coming dangerously near to spilling for my liking.

'Thanks, it has taken a while to compile. I have kept all the really speculative rubbish out and focussed on the ones that are authenticated or match other texts. I have an identikit pack that we can use if the gallery doesn't work.' Jeremy was prepared for the eventuality that I couldn't pick out a likeness. Bless him.

The pages turn more slowly now as I start to pick out

features and likenesses that bear some resemblance to what I faced tonight but nothing is quite right or even that close. I wondered if the search would be like trying to identify one sheep in a flock of thousands; I know they say shepherds can tell each one apart but I doubt that is really that true. I lift my glass absently to my lips and a disappointed sigh escapes as I realise it is empty. I put it down again and am pleasantly surprised to see Jezza fish a bottle from his man bag. It looks expensive and not a cheap one from Tesco either.

'I brought a little refreshment. Looking through these folders is thirsty work.' He smiles and deftly opens the bottle, handling the corkscrew like an old hand. As he pours he tells me that there is a great little vintner (off licence to you and me) just around the corner from his lodgings and some real bargains can be had if you know what to look for. Who knew he was a connoisseur of the fermented grape? I taste the luxurious red liquid and decide that his shop needs a visit.

An hour passes until my close encounter fills a page before me. The picture is black and white but there is no doubt that this is my guy or at least one of is relatives. I look up at Jeremy.

'This is it. The one I chased was red and black but this is our guy.' I pass the folder to Jeremy letting him peer down through his reading glasses to get a good look. It also freed up my hands to refill from the very tasty red wine that had my name on it. I sat back, pleased that the whole exercise hadn't been a total bust and that Jeremy had been decent company too. He was reading the three pages of notes behind the depiction and muttering to himself as he absorbed the bio of the enemy. I was a little too fuzzy to do that so I waited to be told the highlights.

'This bad boy has been around.' Jeremy swigged his glass obviously enjoying the taste before carrying on. At least he didn't swirl, gargle and spit it out. 'He has been recorded a number of times in the last two centuries but the image comes from a body of work by a parapsychologist in Paris, Pierre Tourand. He has had regression therapy patients produce images very like this on a number of occasions. They have been remarkably consistent to be honest.' He pauses for effect and carries on with the background. 'It is unusual for multiple patients to describe the same thing in isolation, lending authenticity to their stories. They are each independent of each other and have no contact.'

'That is all very well and good Jeremy, but I need to know what to expect when I meet it again and, more importantly, how to banish it from here.' I try to keep him on track with his musings. I know that it is real and not an imaginary demon encounter having been close to it now on two separate counts.

'We think it is summoned for a short spell to complete a specific task lasting a whole lunar month. The notes suggest that it makes recreation of its time in our world delaying completion of the task until the last possible moment.' He looks over his glasses at me, all serious and scholarly. 'That might explain the extra kills and seeming randomness. It also means we have some surety that this spree will end on Sunday night at the latest.'

'Does it have a name?' I ask, not really sure why it matters but it might. Jeremy seems surprised that I asked.

'There are a few names listed but none are authenticated. The most occurring is for Basomel.'

Chapter 17

Ideas that strike at three in the morning are generally not the greatest and should, in the cold light of day, be discarded. This one was probably no exception. I had been thinking about how to find the demon's lair, or rather Basomel's lair, and had struck on the idea of the tourist bus that flits around the old town of Edinburgh. The bus is a hop on, hop off arrangement but I planned just to sit on the open top deck and feel if there were any traces or spots that needed more attention. I would sort of zone out and see what turned up. I did, however, need company and Father Jeremy had agreed to meet me and be my chaperone. I think he just wanted to be involved in the hunt for the Demon.

Starting at the world famous Scott Monument we climbed aboard and paid the twenty quid for the experience. Unlimited travel for the day on the route which seemed bloody steep to me and would probably be mostly unused. If we didn't find it today then we were screwed for tomorrow night the mission, whatever it was, would be completed and Basomel would be on his way back to the pit that spawned him. We were on the clock, as it were.

Father Jeremy had brought a Thermos and some sandwiches to 'keep us going' but I doubted the contents of the flask would be any more drinkable than Murdoch's coffee. I had pre-stocked myself with two Danish pastries before meeting Jeremy. The paper cup of rapidly cooling Costa latte was keeping my fingers warm and making me regret the lack of my gloves. We sat at the front of the double decker bus, enjoying the shield of the windscreen but still outside in the fresh air. I wasn't cold yet, but I was sure I would be before too long. The incipient hangover was threatening to return as my early morning paracetamol was wearing off.

We were off, and the smooth ride advertised was relative to being in the back of an army truck. The juddering stop start of the capitol traffic was down to the tram building project and not the driver's fault, or at least so he said. I put it down to his lack of clutch control and a past it, old bus. However, the slow weaving through the Old Town was what we wanted and soon I had slipped into my waking zombie routine. The coffee, long since finished, left me holding a soggy paper cup that needed to be disposed of.

I waited, open and receptive to any trace of our quarry but nothing much was forthcoming. Maybe being on the bus was too far from being able to feel him. Usually I would be able to pick it out of the tapestry of the city. After all I had danced with him twice now and relived his finest handiwork repeatedly; there should be a stronger link.

Crossing over the North Bridge on our way to the Royal mile and the Palace of Holyrood, I felt a vague unease but that could have been anything and I made a mental note to probe more on the next pass over the bridges. The Train Station sits below with the mass of people and buildings nestled under the main arches. I like the cobbled Royal Mile as it passes all the twee Jockanese shops selling tartan everything and tat imported from China and they sit cheek by jowl with traditional pubs and kilt makers. It is a real hotch-potch of shops and experiences. The street performers earning their meagre crusts attract tourists in crowds and the locals even stop to watch, occasionally. It is all part of what makes Edinburgh so much more appealing than Glasgow. Cultural festivals are embedded now and it has begun to pull in visitors from all over the globe. Although if we don't catch this demon then perhaps the tourists won't return.

In what seemed like a blink of an eye we were down to the Palace and the new, over budget, parliament building that had just needed even more work done on its security.

After all the main chamber was right over the entrance and a car bomb would have been particularly effective. Of course, when the design was approved we didn't need to worry about that sort of thing. It is an interesting building when viewed from the air, or Arthur's Seat but from the street it was totally underwhelming. Four hundred and fifty million quid not so well spent I think most people felt. Anyway I felt nothing down here and we had a ten minute halt.

'What's on the sandwiches?' I spoke without preamble and scared Jeremy out of his skin. He would be a great help if we got into a scrape. He smiled nervously and handed me a cheese, tin foil wrapped, sandwich.

After an hour and a half we were going round again, sandwiches consumed and the beginning of a need for a comfort break was becoming more insistent. Then it happened. I was trying to pay attention as we crossed the North Bridge and I felt a pull that could only mean below us. I got up and dragged a startled Jeremy from the bus at the next available stop; the junction of the Royal Mile and the Bridges. We had a lead. It seemed my crazy tourist idea had turned out to be not so daft after all. Well hopefully I could pinpoint the location of Basomel and we, Father Jeremy and I, could deal with it.

In my pockets I had three vials of Holy water, my crucifix and some dead sea salt; Jeremy was similarly tooled up. We would be well equipped to meet Basomel; especially in the daylight. We walked down the knee killer Fleshmarket close and its stone steps worn down by years of revellers. The Halfway House pub would need to be missed this time, although I had been in there on more than one drunken occasion.

With a little regret at missing out on a pint and a growing feeling of going in the right direction my aching knees carried me down through the dim alley to the main road below. I am just pleased to be going down the steps and not up. Although I have gone the other way more than once and needed oxygen by the time I reached the middle let alone the top.

Market street and the back of the train station lay before me the chill wind and noisy traffic made me pull my coat tighter; I was cold and I hoped it was just the weather. Jeremy was buttoning his coat too, at least his looked substantial, mine was a bit thin. Out of season and pretty much useless for the frigid air of autumn Edinburgh. I felt the pull to my left The high North Bridge above us to the right, all sooty and showing signs of the years of train emissions.

'Let's go.' I muttered to my companion as I stepped smartly across the road between little gaps in the slow moving traffic. I hoped Jeremy knew how to cross the road and not get run over; if he wasn't a city boy he might struggle.. He followed me closely and that might be a good thing at some point. Moving on past a few galleries and boutiques I saw where I was being led.

'You've got to be kidding me.' I stopped abruptly causing a neat body swerve from Jeremy. He was looking round a little confused. 'Look.' I know I sounded sour but I couldn't really help it. Ahead of us on a black sign the words in dripping blood red 'The Edinburgh Dungeon' was our destination.

A theme park of the macabre history of Edinburgh with full sounds, sights and smells to make the visit authentic feeling. Well, if my senses were right, it would be a very authentic experience. I doubt that it was hiding in here all the time but it might explain why no one reported seeing something on the streets.

Jeremy laughed, a little too shrill in my ears, before he asked 'What do we do now?' I am pleased he thought I should know and a bit irritated that I had no clear idea on what to do. My bladder was sending me a warning that the cold and coffee had contributed to its need to be relieved.

Being cold isn't my favourite thing and needing a pee isn't high on the list either, I shrugged answering my bladder and Jeremy.

'Lets get a coffee and think about this. If it is in there, we can't have it being publicly exposed and causing pandemonium. The Bishop would have an aneurysm.' I start moving back to the train station making sure that Jeremy is right beside me. If I get too close it may know I am coming. It might feel our approach and bolt. We wouldn't want that now would we.

Chapter 18

Stirring my latte and enjoying the post bladder relief sensations had given me time to think. Jeremy was on the phone to the Bishop and I think he was finding out that his news was not well received. Bishop Michael did not need, nor did he really want the details. He wanted us to solve the problem and do it discretely. It was the discretely bit that I usually failed on. I could hear the 'yes Bishop, No Bishop, three bags full Bishop from over here.' We weren't in uniform but I doubt anyone was fooled by Jezza's disguise of being a normal.

I have been in the dungeon, years ago, and it wasn't a great idea. The effigies of the macabre gain their own power as more and more people look at them and feel fear. Burke and Hare were fine but some of the other attractions were beginning to absorb and would need some attention in the future.

The torturer and his set are particularly authentic and I could hear screams and echoes of a past that hadn't really happened just been acted out time and time again. I wasn't looking forward to going inside. The tours have a guide and take you through the various attractions as a group which might make dealing with Basomel a bit tricky.

Of Course, I am assuming he is hiding in plain sight, like an exhibit he could be hiding in the back or in their storage areas.

'Bishop Michael has left it to us to deal with. Discretely.' Jeremy is a bit breathless as he sits down. I'd bet his Americano with hot, skimmed, milk is cold and undrinkable but that's his own problem. I'd have had my coffee first, before beginning to check in with his Eminence.

'Of course he does.' Sarcasm is seeping out again.

Jeremy swigs the cold sludgy coffee and his face cheers me right up again. He is deciding if spitting it out is better than swallowing it. He has such good manners he swallows it, keeping his complaint internalised.

'Here's my plan. We buy two tickets and join the tour. When we find him we hang back and, in the gap between the tours, we drive him off. Simples' I pretend I am the meerkat from the insurance advert. Great plan I think.

'What if he..' My hand silences him and again when he tries to restart with another question. 'But..' He isn't buying into the plan.

'Jeremy, we can't plan much more than that as we have no idea what we will find in there. If the tour doesn't reveal him then we need to see what our options are.' I am condescending, talking to a child who understands nothing and worries too much.

'What do you have with you? I have Holy water, dead sea salt and my crucifix. You?' I speak quietly, not wanting to draw any more attention than Jeremy's call to the Bishop did a few moments before.

'Holy water, the Host, a jar of Unction and my Crucifix.' Jeremy is seems is packing heat or hunting demon bear. I wonder if I am a little underprepared or lacking in weaponry. Too late now. We will just have to manage; two holy gunslingers heading to the saloon.

It takes less than five minutes to be standing in a queue of tourists waiting for the next group tour. It seems to be very busy and the queue moves so slowly. Groups of twelve are being led away at ten minute intervals and we will be in the next one with eight far eastern visitors and two Americans who seem rather taken with my surly Scots accent and Jeremy's plummy one. They have lots of cameras slung around their necks let alone the number of smartphones, if things get a bit hairy keeping things under wraps might be a bit difficult. Oh the Bishop will be pleased.

'Next group, move forward please.' A polite costumed tour guide, who must be an acting student, theatrically waves us forward. Jeremy and I gravitate towards the back behind Sam the American and his wife Tanya, they are nice people to be fair but I want them to give us a bit of room. We are moving towards the famous pair of grave robbers Burke and Hare, hearing of their heinous crimes in lurid and gasp-inducing details.

I can feel 'our friend' has been in here, more than many places but I have no real idea if he is here now. It isn't an exact science and sometimes I just feel something that is from the past more than I expect. We are heading into another exhibit about cannibals in caves I think, I wasn't really listening but the cave constructions are very realistic and perhaps I need to wander round the corner away from the area subtly lit by floor and ceiling coloured faders. I pull Jeremy back with me as we let the others move on a bit. His eyes are looking a bit wide and wired, no more coffee for him, as I pull him into the shadow of the glass fibre cave stone. A finger to my lips in the universal shut the fuck up' and I lead us into the shadows.

In a few steps the darkness is nearly complete as the mock cave turns a corner, taking us away from the main path through the planned historical attractions. I let my eyes get used to the near darkness, if it is here we might be in trouble if we can't see. I have my little mag-lite torch in my pocket and as I can still see absolutely nothing I decide to get it out. The cone of bright white light shows an empty corridor leading to a fire exit. I click it off and we turn to catch up with the group.

Our guide has come looking for us and is none too happy at our dalliance with the way out and not having been rapt in his delivery about the sinister side of Edinburgh history. He urges us to keep up as we make a move for the next bit. I wonder what he thought we were doing. I wonder if he thinks we are a couple? You know, like the

Birdcage or something like that. He manages to stay in character, spinning out the fake 'auld scots' that nobody has uttered seriously for decades; I wonder if I suffer from the Scottish cringe. I don't think so; I just have no tolerance to shite and am a grumpy old man in training. Anyway we mince back to the rest of the group and their disapproval for holding up the fright-fest.

The interminable nonsense continues as we parade through an eighteenth century operating theatre, a court that ordered some woman to be hanged and apparently they heard her banging on the coffin after the event and decided the sentence had been carried out and she was allowed to go. 'Huaf hingit Mary' or as the guide explained it was 'Half Hanged Mary' and the understanding dawned on our tourist friends from the land of the rising sun. Personally I thought it just showed that the council was piss poor in those days too.

We were past the worst, or was it the best bits, when I could feel him. He was close by; I doubted that he was in another body it felt so raw. I knelt down to tie my lace, letting Jeremy move a step past me while I let my mind wander around us. I slipped my hand into my pocket and slowly removed a vial of Holy water. 'He is very close' I whispered letting Jeremy know that the action was about to kick off. I stood up and turned round looking behind us. I could feel him, watching, waiting and hoping we would walk on by.

I waved my hand in an arc splashing a little sizzling rain of Holy water across the space I thought was where he was hidden. His scream, like a rasping howl across a violin, filled the tight space we filled. He had managed to mask his visible presence but not the essence of his being. The Holy water had dispelled everything racking his body with searing pain. The light in this transition corridor was low and the red and black skin, fangs and red eyes were less distinct, fortunately. I criss crossed another two slashes from my vial causing agonised screams to fill the air as he turned and fled.

Jeremy and I were in hot pursuit as we tried to corner the beast although it moved faster than an Olympic sprinter. I heard the push bar fire exit clatter open as we turned the corner. The screams filling the corridors behind us would need to be sorted out later. We emerged from the caves into a storage space and cafeteria which had a trail of scattered chairs and tables telling us which way it had fled. It was outside and getting away. There are many shady alleys and passages in the Old town area of Edinburgh and if we didn't catch up soon it would disappear right in front of us.

'Jeremy call White, we need him down here as soon as he can.' I shout directions over my shoulder as I burst out into the street. Chaos has descended on the street. A taxi is at ninety degrees across the road and the traffic is a total shambles. There are screamers and a few stunned looking pensioners as well as a few kids with their phones taking it all in.

I shout 'Which way?' my crucifix is in my hand as I try to sprint. The alley is dim at best and dark in many places but I doubt it has stopped. It is fleeing the scene and no doubt has a few places to hide around here.

A scream from the end of the alleyway tells me that I am behind but the daylight is slowing it, or at least I hope it is. My arms are pumping like a madman and I don't think I can keep running at this pace for much longer. I am a middle aged man not made for running and my shoes aren't exactly helping.

I charge out of the alleyway and see the stunned surprised faces looking to my right so I head right. After all a large, cloaked red and black skinned beast has just run up the street and into another alley (they are called closes here) and I am trying to find breath to tell people to get the fuck out of my way. It comes out a little like 'Excuse me', it is that good mannered Britishness that infests me at times.

The close is downhill a little making it easier than an uphill one, but there is no sign of the bastard, I am way behind and I am soaked with sweat. There seemed to be little real surprise or panic among those who were witnesses to the demon; perhaps they thought it part of the Fringe or something. Certainly no screaming and panic. What is wrong with these people?

Chapter 19

Red faced, breathless and bent double trying not to throw up is how DI White found me at the end of the close. I had the presence of mind to put the crucifix away so that the nice people of Edinburgh and their tourist friends were not alarmed by a man charging about brandishing a cross I front of him. My breathing was slowly beginning to work and the pain in my knees was almost unbearable.

'You okay?' I recognised his voice or I might have just waved him off. I looked up through my sweaty fringe and nodded, wasn't it obvious that I was just peachy? I nodded again and pushed up from my knees and leaned back against the wall. 'What happened?' He asked, I just wondered what Jeremy's message had been. A garbled mess most likely.

'It was hiding in the Dungeon.' As if that should be explanation enough. Or perhaps that was all the breath I had to use. DI White needed more than that though, after all the chaos caused by the initial part of the chase took a little cleaning up. The police switchboard had gotten a little busy about a large cloaked figure being chased by a middle aged man.

'Father Jeremy and I found it and caused it to flee. I chased it but it can run faster than I can. Fucker got away. It could have gone to ground around here or kept going.'

'We need to search the area. It could still be here. The place is mobbed and it could be carnage.' He is taking it seriously, which is good, discrete it will not be. What is he going to say? We are looking for a large bulky demon in a black cloak with jagged teeth and red and black skin?

'We need to be discrete. These things are best done quietly.' I try to stand straight but it is a challenge. 'It would be better to call it a stunt by students or something. It isn't beyond the realms of possibility'

He doesn't seem at all convinced but we will keep the search to a couple of uniforms and White and myself. Oh yes and Father Jeremy.

'Andrew, I have just seen video of you running up the royal mile with your crucifix waving about. What on earth is going on? The Home Office are having a fit.' Bishop Michael is on the phone and unusually his manners have slipped. He seems a little put out. I can't imagine why.

'I was chasing the Demon up the street.' I am being childish and I am sure he knew that. I wait for the outburst before I continue, an outburst that doesn't come. I can almost see his pursed lips and frown deepening as he sits behind his desk.

'What about being discrete? I expected better from you.' His disappointment attack would work on most people but not on me. I don't really worry about being a disappointment; I am immune these days having disappointed so many on so many occasions. My mother probably over used the approach when I was a child building up my resistance to it.

'It was hiding out in the Edinburgh Dungeon when we discovered it. I splashed him with Holy water and it fled the scene.' Oh dear I have been hanging around the police too long; next it will be proceeding along the road. 'It was better to chase it than to let it run I thought.'

'In the Dungeon? Really? That is remarkable. Well, yes you probably did the right thing driving it out of there but waving your crucifix in the air and shouting and swearing at people to move? That was not acceptable Andrew.' A demon is running loose killing priests and young women and my swearing is unacceptable? I count to ten because I can feel a 'Fuck off' rolling on my tongue and it had better not get out. I take the necessary deep breath and let it out before the safer response of 'Yes Bishop' escapes my lips.

'We could always say it was a tester for a film? Most people seemed to think it wasn't real anyway. They stood and gawped rather than flee screaming.' Limiting the exposure on this was going to be vital and I thought this was better than the student stunt but it isn't really my area.

'I think I could get that to work Andrew, that's a good cover. Is Father Jeremy still with you? Tell him well done on identifying the Other-worlder. Keep me posted.' And just like that I was dismissed.

We were still wandering around the upper section of the Royal mile when DI White handed me my third paper cup of coffee; it must have been my round but I missed it. We were cold and footsore and it was dark. The lights made up for a great deal, being so pretty and everything however our overwhelming failure to find hide nor hair of the enemy was frustrating. The area around us was filled with marks of its passing and there were many of them. This must have been the centre of its activity, if the frequency was anything to go by.

I swigged and scalded my tongue and managed not to swear but I saw DI White smirk at my misfortune. I rubbed at my tongue and I suppose that made me look even sillier but it seemed to work. DI White did an update on his radio and received two negative responses from our uniformed helpers.

'If I wanted a showy finale to my mission where around here would I do it?' I mused aloud. Sometimes I ask decent questions when I talk to myself. Jeremy turned to look at me as if I had sprouted a pair of horns, an odd look on his face. Well, an odder look than usual.

'Basomel is a show off so that is a good question. Tomorrow night he will complete his mission at midnight. He will need holy ground and this area is right in the eye of his storm.' Jeremy was getting scholarly and all excited, bless him.

'I think you are right but where would he chose?' I wanted an answer not a lecture. I was still trying to get my scalded tongue to calm down so I could have more coffee.

'Behind you.' DI White spoke quietly between non scalding sips. We both looked round at him like he was speaking gibberish. He flicked his head to the building right behind us. St Giles Cathedral standing proudly ignored behind us. It was resplendent in the lights of the Royal Mile. After years of grime and traffic soot build up, it had been shot blasted clean and looked relatively new.

'Would it try there Jeremy? What about the Tron just down there or that one up the road?' It was Edinburgh and I could see churches round almost every corner but St Giles is the Cathedral, so maybe.

'The Cathedral would be the ultimate desecration and two fingers.' Jeremy nodded and DI White seemed to be willing to take him seriously. It was thin and based on a random question that I asked myself, very thin.

'Wouldn't hurt to take a look. I can arrange it for tomorrow.' DI White was right, it wouldn't hurt but I thought it might be a total waste of time that we couldn't afford. Would he strike again tonight, it being his last hurrah before the climax? I doubted that he would after all the criss cross of Holy water would have seared to his very soul.

'Lets do that. We need to make sure that we have enough eyes out and about tonight though.' I was unsure that having more uniforms patrolling would make any difference but at least it would keep the Chief Superintendent happy. Something must be done and all that.

'It must be my round. Pint lads?' I make the universal pint swigging gesture and I get two takers for my offer. This being Edinburgh, the one thing we have an abundance of is pubs and luckily they are always close to the churches. Is there a causal link there? I believe that there might be. I always need a pint after church and it seems that the men and women of Edinburgh feel the same.

Chapter 20

Waking up in a strange bed and not being too sure about how I got there is not a usual thing for me. I know I was with DI White so I doubt I got into too much trouble. Father Jeremy left early in the evening citing a need to do some research but I think he was struggling to keep up. We were talking shop for most of the evening when PC Jill and MacBride turned up and kept us company. I look over and a half dressed DI White is lying on the other side of the double bed, I can smell bacon cooking and when I move my head I am a little fuzzy but not totally defeated by a hangover, so rough just about sums it up. Not the rough as guts, just rough.

I pull myself to my feet finding my socks still on and my trousers over the chair. I am a middle aged man and the morning after sight is not a great one. I pull my trousers on and stagger to the bathroom. I look in the mirror, a little bleary, not too bloodshot and after the mandatory cold water facelift I feel much more human. I rub some toothpaste in my mouth and swirl with the tap water, thank goodness the foul taste has gone.

'Morning.' I shuffle along the corridor to the living room and find Jill has slept on the couch, giving up her bed for the two old boys. She pops her head out of the kitchen and smiles.

'Morning Father, Would you like tea or coffee? The bacon wont be long.' She is such a bright morning person she is making my head hurt. I am grateful though.

'Coffee would be great. Paracetamol would be good too, if you have some.' The need to clear my head is taking precedent over any other function. Caffeine and painkillers are always a good start. DI white shambles in to the room, much more worse for wear than I am. He looks terrible, serves him right for getting us both pissed. I am ensconced on the couch sitting on the quilt that had been used last night by the very generous PC Jill. She had let the pair of drunk old blokes pass out in her bed and made the use of the couch, which felt very comfortable.

DI White is a groaner. Every movement is accompanied by a little noise and a subsequent holding of his head. He is a bit of a scratcher too, although his hand doesn't stray to his bollocks. A fact for which I am eternally grateful. He shuffles on to the couch and catching my eye, gives a chuckle of embarrassed camaraderie. Now that we have gotten pissed together there is a bond that can't be broken; or at least that is the drunken theory.

Jill hands out coffee and didn't even bat an eye at the state of semi dress that is her senior officer. The pain killers are consumed and plates of bacon rolls appear; either she is truly a generous hostess or she wants us to get lost. I don't get any feeling that we are being booted out. I wonder what her boyfriend would think of two colleagues crashing at her place after an extended impromptu session.

'Is Sandy coming over Jill?' DI White asks her round the side of his buttery bacon roll. He obviously knows more about Jill than I do, I never thought to ask last night or if I did I promptly forgot.

'About ten, we have church this morning. There's plenty of time though so don't panic.' She sipped her mug of tea. She started to tidy up around us as we started to return to the land of the living emerging from the Sunday morning clan of post-binge zombies.

'I need to go home and call in. The Bishop will want to know what we will be doing to resolve the problem. Tonight will be busy. Can you get the men to stake out the targets?' I slurp my coffee like a truck-stop cafe customer; following it with a chunk of bacon roll.

DI White is nodding in agreement, so all will be well then. I leave the details to him to sort out with the Chief

Superintendent. A key turning in the front door causes us to stop talking and look at the hallway. A young woman comes bounding in to the flat 'Jill' She calls down the hall hanging up her coat. She is another disgustingly cheerful morning person as she has a smile that positively glows from her face. She walks in and straight in to Jill's embrace and a good morning kiss. I am cool and nothing shows on my face.

'Good Morning Inspector, Father Steel.' She smiles in greeting but their arms are loathe to let go until Jill gets another coffee.

'Morning Sandy, How are things at the Royal Infirmary?' DI White is speaking with his mouth still working the bacon round his teeth. He obviously knew that Sandy was a girl and never let on to me. What did he expect? Tutting and disapproval? So twentieth Century and passé obviously.

'Bloody bedlam. I have nurses nearly hysterical at the graveyard slasher. Can you not catch him or something? It is a madhouse with girls calling in sick instead of doing their shifts. Bad enough that there is a shortage of doctors but nurse numbers are critical anyway.' She's shaking her head about a subject that must rankle each and every day. Her frown is a deep one liner. Apart from that she is pretty.

'Father Andrew is helping with the case and we are hopeful.' DI white brings me in to the conversation with a nice segway. I nod without giving much away as my mouth is full of coffee.

'Well I hope you catch him quick. Are you some psychologist or profiler Father Andrew?' Her eyes narrow just a little; maybe she has had a less than satisfactory encounter with a Priest or a psychologist. The line is still there, and probably a little deeper.

'Something like that.' I smile, taking the sting out of my words and add 'I hope we can get the bastard soon.' I swig my coffee again, for emphasis.

'Well getting pissed and hungover isn't a great start to catching the bastard is it?' She laughs at our discomfort and wraps an arm around Jill's shoulders. Their happiness evident in their ease together. Love is love, as I want everyone to accept.

'I suppose not but it was supposed to be a pint; not ten pints.' I shove DI white playfully, making him, almost, slop his coffee. I manage to stand without a groan and make my goodbyes. I need a shower and a shave and well, you know the rest. DI White is a little bit away from being ready to move so I will have time to think on my walk back to the barracks.

There's a note on my door, a pink post it seriously, and it is from Father Jeremy. I peel it off and decipher his perfect handwriting. He wants me to call him the moment I get back. I wonder if that means his tipsy research last night brought some joy. I decide that my shower is much more important if I want to function properly. The walk back through the Meadows part of Edinburgh has cleared my head letting me think about the Demon. Would it really try to finish in the Cathedral? Wouldn't the consecration make it impossible for it? Perhaps because the Cathedral is open as a tourist attraction that could lessen its power over evil? I had lots of maybe type questions.

Jeremy it seems couldn't wait and, standing in my underpants, my phone rings. It is the bold Jeremy. I sigh as I answer 'Steel.' I sound tired not pissy for once. Jeremy is a bit breathy as he launches straight in with his news.

'The Cathedral is very likely. It has been done before and Basomel was the culprit.' I am pleased we know and shocked at the gall of the beast, in equal measure. Jeremy pauses for effect, or maybe it was the dun dun dun music.

'How sure are you? Last night you were only a little bit convinced.' I hate to rain on his parade but I am freezing my bollocks off here. I climb into bed to keep warm.

'Almost certain Andrew. It would be too coincidental to be an accident. I have redrawn lines on the map based on activity and project where he might have committed crimes. We are missing one but the lines cross very close to St Giles. We need to contact Bishop Michael.' He ends with a flourish or maybe it was a ta-da.

'I agree, you need to contact the Bishop.' I can hear his questioning voice now 'How sure are we? What about the police and how can we be sure? What about the public?

Discretion is paramount.' I think Jeremy will be best placed to answer those directly while I have a shower. Bishop Michael would phone me right after Jeremy's call ended.

I was shaved, showered and dressed in uniform waiting for the call. The coffee I had made myself was almost gone when my phone sprang to life, Bishop Michael.

'Good Morning Bishop.' I greet him as if I am a happy morning person. It is a total change from my usual grumpy flat 'Steel' and catches him off guard. I hear the little pause and I smile to myself; I know it is childish but the small pleasures are the best.

'Good morning Andrew. I have just had a call from Father Jeremy who thinks that we have a location for tonight's denouement.' I didn't expect him to say climax.

'He believes so Bishop. I am not entirely convinced.' I let my doubts out so that if it goes wrong then I am not left holding the bag. An alibi for the future as it were.

'He seems very sure after consulting his books and historical events. I think, unless you turn up something better today, we go with the St Giles Plan.' He concludes, his tea cup clinking as he put it down.

'Plan?' It was out before I could stop it. What plan? We had a tenuous location and now there is a plan. Not a Jeremy plan please.

'Jeremy thinks we should stake it out and between you manage to dispel it. Salt and water are the best weapons he assures me, for this one.' Bishop Michael is a big picture, broad sweeps kind of bloke and this plan has more holes than cheese. I snort derisively.

'I will work on the details with Jeremy during the day Bishop.' With help from friends like these I don't fancy my chances. Fucks sake.

'As for yesterday's fiasco, I think we have that story contained.' Bishop Michael isn't finished with me yet. I probably shouldn't have snorted but you couldn't make it up.

He wanted to rein me back in a bit.

'How did you manage that Bishop?' I decided to ask rather than fence with him. After all this had gone on longer than most of our phone calls and I wasn't in the mood to set a new world record for pointless conversations with your boss.

'The Home Secretary got a film director to say it was a reaction test for his next movie that might be set in Edinburgh. Secret cameras were following the action and all that. It was a stunt with actors, he was on the BBC last night doing the piece.' I am supposed to be in awe, obviously.

'That should play well with the footage that will be all over the internet from the phones. Hopefully everyone buys it. I need to go Bishop was there anything else?' I need to get a hold of Jeremy, maybe literally, and retrain him on how I do things.

'Nothing more Andrew. I will be back at the residence tomorrow afternoon, we can catch up once this little problem is resolved. Be careful Andrew and discrete if you can.'

'I will Bishop.' I make a face like a teenager. I am back to my usual sour expression as I end the call. Fuck. Fuck. Fuck.

I phone Jeremy while I am still irritated and I am even more so as I get his voicemail, not a great start but I leave him the call me message with no hint of my desire to rip his head off. Plan? He has absolutely no idea. He will have us waiting outside in Spanish Inquisition robes or hiding round the corner waiting like the keystone cops. I have two zip-lock bags full of Dead Sea salt and six little crystal vials of Holy water lying out on my bed as I check my weaponry. I have a little jar of Chrism, which I sniff, I love the balsam smell. I always feel better afterwards.

'Jeremy.' I answer the buzzing phone without swearing

which seemed a racing certainty just a moment or two ago. I wonder what he will say his cunning plan comprises of.

'I have spoken to Bishop Michael and he thinks we should presume that St Giles will be the location of the event tonight.' He pauses for effect, to which I don't respond. 'We should get DI White to stake out the Cathedral and we should be ready nearby.' He pauses for breath.

'I think we need to go to the incident room and talk to the Chief Superintendent and explain your great plan.' I wonder if my finely tuned sarcasm has reached him. His next comment proves that he is immune or stupid.

'I think you are right, we will need his permission and resources. I will meet you there. I will leave now.' He seems a little excited and that might just get him killed and if that happens I, probably, will be likely to join him. If I get him killed then the Bishop won't be best pleased. Life is so unfair.

I will be a while before I get there to sort out his mess. I have an appointment with the Father Confessor.

Chapter 22

I dislike Confession, or Penance as we should call it these days. I bet that I am not alone. Over a billion Catholics worldwide probably dislike it just as much as I do but I know that if I am to fight on the Lord's behalf tonight I need to do it with a soul cleaner than a brand new Kleenex. Any little chink of sin or darkness lingering about me will make me vulnerable. The need for purity is not one I used to consider all that important but I figure that it certainly might keep me alive tonight. Afraid? Me? Probably.

My enemy has a name and centuries of form at this sort of thing and what do I have? Father Jeremy of the dusty old tomes and some salt. Seems like a fair fight is in the offing although I still can't see that we can destroy the Demon. Drive him off, maybe but destroy? I think we will need more than salt, water and Faith. A flame thrower might be a more appropriate weapon or maybe a more effective one.

I am a little early and I can feel the serenity of the chapel as the late Autumn sun slants through the windows. Although it is a modern building of low quality seventies build, the feeling of peace in this place always works for me. I can really descend into the inner place that prayer facilitates after the 'God bless Mummy, God bless Daddy' are past and real worship begins. I am sarcastic, caustic even, but when I give thanks and beg forgiveness I feel the emptiness of my soul and it is a humbling place. It is then that I know what hell would be.

The tinkling of a little bell telling me that the Father Confessor is in and my sacrament of Penance is about to begin. I move to the booth, letting everything temporal fall away and the need for spiritual cleansing is all I focus on. I pull the curtain closed and hear the slot slide back as I sit in the near dark of the confessional booth.

'In the name of the Father, the Son and the Holy Spirit. Amen.' His deep rumbling voice fills my ears. Now it is my turn to begin.

'Bless me Father for I have sinned. It has been some time since my last confession. I am a sinner who does the work of the lord and my weaknesses and frailties are many and manifest.' I begin, slightly formal but I always feel that my words are heard by the Holy Father so I try not to be informal.

The Confessional Seal is just that, sealed and the sins I beg forgiveness for range a cross a wide range of small medium and large. The problem I have is that I know I will probably commit them all again and again and my contrition is suspect at best. I suppose I am contrite and would in an ideal world retire to the scholarly pursuits that the wonderful libraries could offer but I am the sword in the hand of the Lord and I know that in the progress of swinging that sword I wander through a trough of sin and I add to it frequently.

The Father Confessor is listening intently to my words and I have frequent pauses to gather my thoughts, he doesn't do much more than encourage me to find the root cause of my behaviour. It is hard questioning and he has no idea what I actually do here and why I am so problematic and self destructive. I feel totally wrung out at the end of our session and I think he realises that there is little left uncovered and unexamined.

'My Son, go and make your peace with Our Lord. Your sins I absolve but you need to absolve yourself and let the grace of the Lord flourish within you. Stop fighting his plan for you and accept. Go in peace to love and serve the Lord in the Name of the Father, The Son and The Holy Spirit, Amen.' The words the final act in our conversation. From my lips to God's ear indeed and his encouragement is exactly what I need. I return to the pew and reconnect myself with why I am what I am and who I am working for.

By two thirty I am in the incident room drinking tea and waiting on DI White to get off the phone. PC Jill has looked after me while I had to wait. Of Father Jeremy there is no sign at the moment and, for that at least, I am glad. The walls of pictures and notes tell us the square root of heehaw and I feel sorry for my colleagues in the blue uniforms. This was a crime series they could never solve and never protect the populace from. Some things just don't fit in the tick box forms as to why a case remains unsolved.

DI White puts the phone down and waves me in, he is smiling a little. Is he punch drunk or pleased to see me? I smile back and sit in the soft seat opposite his desk and watch him swill down , what I presume is, sludge in the bottom of his cup.

'I have the Chief Super's permission to set up a perimeter of uniformed officers in the area, discretely, and a flying squad to make the swoop.' He pauses expectantly and carries on as I nod. 'The plan is a simple stake out and wait. If Chummy arrives with a victim we pounce and effect an arrest.'

'An Arrest? Seriously? We will have to banish the bastard. There won't be an arrest.' For Fucks sake. I had such high hopes for DI White too. It seems his police training is very hard to overcome.

'Well I suppose not. We need to stop it from taking any more lives and as you say banish it. Father Jeremy wondered if It would take over another body for tonight.' DI White was a little embarrassed at his back sliding, for which I forgive him.

'I am not convinced that it will show up at the Cathedral. Father Jeremy is working on slim pickings in terms of clues. Logically it sounds fine and meets the expected behaviours but I am just not sure. We need to be able to move if it turns out to be a bust.' I am frowning, I can feel it.

'How many men do we have to brief? Obviously the Home Office want this kept quiet. What shall we tell them?' I am thinking out loud and trying not to put problems in front of us but we need to plan better than the fag-packet plan that we currently have on the table.

'I can keep it down to a small reliable core who will keep their mouths shut but you will need to do it. They will think I am just winding them up.' DI White looks longingly at his cup of sludge, probably jealous of my fresh hot cup.

'Four will be enough the rest will be on crowd control duty, stopping it getting out but they probably won't see anything. We can do a wash up and debrief at the end before anyone leaves for the night.' I try to sound like I am an old hand at this. I wonder if DI White is buying in to the image.

'Okay four it will be. Jill, MacBride, Murdoch and Anderson. They are all reliable and my team.' I nod, I think he knows his people better than anyone.

'Perhaps a proper briefing including the Chief Super will be a good idea. Where is Jeremy?' I want to get things ready and then get a little sleep before tonight's main event. Although at this time of year it will be dark soon so night is a long time in Scotland. The streets will be dark and shadowy soon allowing the enemy a little bit of cover and an opportunity to carry out his plan.

'No idea. He said he needed to get some provisions for tonight. He was pretty vague, if you know what I mean.' White's shrug speaks volumes. He doesn't understand Jezza either.

The phone on the desk springs into a fit of violent ringing and gets snatched up as a self defence mechanism. 'DI White, how can I help you?' He is such a professional. A quick conversation with a few 'yes sir's thrown in tell me it is the brass upstairs. It is a mercifully short call.

'We are wanted upstairs. The Chief Constable wants a word with us. It seems the Chief Super isn't happy about our progress and didn't like the lack of detail about the case.' DI White straightens his tie, trying to look less crumpled than usual. I am in uniform, a fact that is guaranteed to get me the respect I need. Probably not.

'While I understand your frustration gentlemen, the Home Secretary has made my presence here a need to know and I am unable to go much further at this time. We will have a resolution tonight, that is all I can tell you at this point.' I am reasonableness incarnate and playing like an adult. Two things that happen only very infrequently. Must remember to write it in my diary.

'Dammit man, I am the Chief Constable. If I want an answer I will have one. There will be no use of my men and resources until I know what is going on in my own force.' He has gotten a little bit purple at the refusal, however polite.

'No one is more aware of that than I am, Sir. If it would help you could call Bishop Michael or the Home Secretary and ask them to give me dispensation to break the Official Secrets Act.' I was pushing it a bit. I could just tell them but his attitude pissed me off. He was one of the 'Do you know who I am?' brigade and they get as little as I can give them. His spluttering at my use of the Home Secretary is warming; good to know my trump card still has its uses.

'I am not happy Father Steel. There are bodies filling up our morgue and no sign of a collar. And now you tell me it will be resolved tonight. I am sorry if I sound sceptical but I have a responsibility to the people of Edinburgh and this need to know is frankly not acceptable.' The purple is fading and now he wants to be reasonable. I decide that these two might as well get the talk, there is no way forward without it. I look like I am wrestling for a moment on the horns of a dilemma before looking at them in turn.

'Very well Chief Constable. I will, of course, need to pass on the details of this conversation to the Home Office but I will tell you what I can.' I look him square in the eye. He nods accepting my threat and I can see a little triumphant gleam in his eye. He has banged his desk and gotten his own way. 'I am empowered by the State and the Churches to investigate all matters that are supernatural in origin. This case is one such matter.' I put my hand up to stop the blustering interruption that is forming on his lips.

'You have a demon stalking the streets of Edinburgh. Why it is here, who summoned it and many other questions are unanswered but we know where it will be tonight. When we catch it, I will destroy it and there will be no more killings from this one.' I say everything gently but with a 'you asked' underneath.

'That is ridiculous.' The Chief Constable lets it out. He thinks I am now just pissing him about. He leans forward all lurking body mass and thinks that will intimidate me.

'Ridiculous or not it is true. My credentials and authority are before you. I am sure you could have them checked out again if you are uncertain. This demon has been a busy boy and we are on the verge of resolving the issue. I am sure that is paramount in this matter is it not?' I hold his gaze with mine. I could have said 'Do as you are fucking told' but that apparently isn't in the play nice section.

'A fucking Demon.' He is struggling with the concept. Well, I suppose it does sound unreasonable to the Head Plod. I'd bet he came through uniform or traffic; never had an original thought in his life I expect.

'Yes a fucking Demon, with whom I have been up close and personal three times now. We will be able to finish the job tonight and that will be the end of the matter. The stunt out of the Dungeon was the Demon and it took some covering up.' He looks at DI White, looking for him to refute my claim and doesn't get one.

'Fuck.' There we go, he seems to be catching up as he flops back into his high-backed leather executive chair.

I look at him and let a little hint of a grin grow on my face 'Exactly Chief Constable.' It seems we are on the same page now.

I look to the Chief Superintendent and he is a little pale. He might need his hand held. I doubt the advanced leaders course prepared him for this kind of thing, he might need to man up.

Chapter 23

'That was fun.' DI White is smirking all the way back to the incident room. I try not to encourage him but the cheeky grin just won't stay off my face. The Chief Constable was very accommodating and didn't need to call the Home Secretary once he was on the right page. The page that said Demon running amok. I don't think the Chief Superintendent is going to recover quite that quickly. Especially after my dire warnings about losing his pension and suffering possible prosecution. I'd bet they are having a little fortification in the Chief Constable's office, they both need it; poor things.

'Well they did force me to tell them. So I am totally blameless on this one. They didn't babble too much did they?' DI White and I are at the elevator waiting for the doors to open when I hear a breathy foot slapping approach, Father Jeremy has caught up with us. He seems all agitated and will need to be calmed down.

'Jeremy, lovely to see you.' The words and tone sound reasonable but the inner dialogue is less charitable and probably just reeks of irritation.

'Father Andrew, Inspector.' He nods as he pulls oxygen into his lungs. It appears the silly sod may have just run up the stairs in time to go back down in the lift. 'I have been reading and have a suggestion for tonight.' He is about to launch into an explanation right here, in public waiting on the lift.

'Jeremy' I cut across him a little abruptly perhaps, 'We can cover that in the incident room.' The fact that I had to tell him was irritating enough but the fact that his discretion bypass had kicked in meant he hadn't thought about the consequences of his blabbing mouth. I am glad he doesn't take Confession, he would be hopeless at keeping it private.

He is bursting to tell me something and the whole three minutes until we are back in DI White's office must have felt like an eternity to him. I shut the door and almost get my arse into a seat when Jeremy draws a breath to expound his pearl of wisdom.

'Salt.' Obviously the looks on our faces make it clear that we understand totally and he continues 'Basomel cannot tolerate salt.' Well that cleared everything up. Or rather it didn't.

'And?' I need to prompt him because if I don't he will stand there like we should applaud his amazing three point shot. Although I doubt he has any idea what a three point shot actually is.

'We should cross each threshold with salt leaving only one for him to pass over and then we should pounce.' I wonder if he has been imbibing but maybe he is just a bit mental.

'Would that work?' DI White asks, he hasn't learned yet to not encourage Jeremy but I expect he will learn soon. Religious scholars are great at advice, plans and theoretical ways that should work but usually they fall apart in the crucible of doing.

'No.' I butt in but Jezza is on a roll.

'Yes, theoretically. If Basomel cannot pass the salt then we can contain him.' He sounds so sure.

'Tell me about that pouncing thing?' I wonder if he realises that I speak sarcasm like he speaks English. I must be bilingual. The stunned look on his face has just unearthed the bit of his theoreticals that he hasn't gotten to yet.

'Well, I , well....I thought that would be your bit.' He stammered along wilting under my direct gaze.

'How do we banish him Jeremy?' I think I need to know if I need a ritual or just to beat him to death with salt and holy water. So far he hasn't really been much help on this front.

'Well, as I said, he cannot tolerate salt so we would need to use salt as our main weapon.' He is fumbling along, searching for a lifeboat.

'The salt will be fine for driving him where we want him to go. I am just a bit concerned that once I am between him and escape what I can do to stop him. He is a powerful foe and just winging it will get us all killed. Or at least some of us.' I have my, now legendary, scowl settled on my face.

'You have your faith and the salt should be enough.' The sanctimonious prick has that look on his superior face that makes me feel like slapping him until my hands can't do it any more.

'Where do we come in?' DI White is looking for sensible instruction, he has obviously come to the wrong place.

'You will need to pull the victim to safety and then seal me in with the salt. You know Thunderdome style.' They both look at me like I am talking in tongues.

'Fucks sake! Mad Max three, Thunderdome? Two men enter one man leave.' I shake my head, what a pair of cultural pygmies. Who can forget Auntie in that chain mail vest?

'You will need to keep it from getting out. No matter what, if it cannot finish the ritual by midnight then it will return to its place. If it completes the ritual something bad will definitely happen. We don't want that now do we?' I am in full sarky-bastard mode.

'We still do not know exactly what the culmination of its ritual will herald. It is very difficult to know what the outcome could be.' Jeremy has returned to saying he has been able to find out very little that is of any real use.

'Sealing the Cathedral with salt is actually a decent shout but we can't do that until it is inside; otherwise he will know it is a trap.' I had to grudgingly accept that the salt trap sealing the entrances and windows might just be a good idea.

'So you need to be inside waiting then?' DI white has picked up on the crap bit of the plan. Or at least it is the crap bit as far as I am concerned. Wait inside a Cathedral for a seven foot plus black and red skinned, fanged, clawed demon who wants to rape and eviscerate a human sacrifice to complete a ritual. Why wouldn't I be happy to be the one waiting to interrupt its coitus with a stinging shower of salt? Maybe I just need to lighten up.

'That sounds dangerous. I will wait with you.' DI White drops his bombshell like facing almost certain death and imperilling his mortal soul is nothing. It is the most amazing gift to his fellow man a man could give.

'I think you need to be outside controlling things and making sure nothing goes wrong.' I try to put him off but I am so proud of him. I hope the moistening and tightening around my eyes doesn't let a tear escape.

'It'll be fine. I will be inside, on the scene and I have deputies for dealing with the outside. The matter is settled.' DI White is a great human being. Obviously mental but great nonetheless.

'Okay then but we will need a few rules.'

The four of them were sitting there in the interview room, waiting. The banter was flowing when DI White and I strolled in. The tables were impromptu seats as they looked at us, wondering what needed privacy. Wasn't the incident room private enough? Of the four, three I knew and had seen about the place the fourth must be Anderson. He was from vice or cyber protection and had come up with DI White. He could be trusted, apparently.

'Okay settle down. This won't take long.' DI White interrupted the back and forth piss taking that was still flowing and I think MacBride was losing badly. He was taking it well though. 'Father Steel needs to brief you for tonight's operation.'

'Thanks. Tonight will see the end of our operation but I need to brief you on a few salient, if unusual points before we start. What you are about to hear is covered by the Official Secrets Act and doesn't leave this room. It will mean much more than pensions and careers. It will be a closed court and indefinite detainment.' I pause looking at the blood drained faces. This they did not expect. I smile gently before adding 'So far it hasn't come to that. You have been chosen by DI White as people I can trust and rely upon. So I am about to share secrets that are difficult to accept on first hearing but believe me when I say every word is fact.' I pause again, the imperceptible nods of agreement ripple through them, with a few glances to DI White who is ignoring them and focussed intently on my delivery.

'I work for the Home Office and the Church and whenever a crime against the Church takes place I am called to take a look. I only deal with cases involving supernatural events. These murders are one such event.' I wait for the disbelief in the supernatural to show on their faces but there is nothing so I soldier on. Murdoch doesn't even have his heard it all now look on.

'The murderer is a Demon summoned to complete a ritual tonight by Midnight.' I stop and look at them. Anderson flashes a look at DI White which may have had a subtext of 'Thanks mate, thanks a lot' or something like it.

'How do we fight a Demon?' MacBride is in first bless him. I like practical but for my first group briefing I had hoped for a little more awe and much more babbling. Neither of which seems to be forthcoming.

'You don't. I do. I have certain advantages and abilities for this sort of thing. Although fighting Demons is anything but straight forward.' I smile a little by wryly. Usually after fighting Demons I have a long rest courtesy of the National Health Service.

'What do we need to do?' Murdoch's deep voice

rumbles out past the moustache and the others look at me, expectantly.

'I will be inside with DI White and you, with many other officers will be outside. DI Anderson will be a proxy for DI White and will run the plays. The other officers will know nothing but will need corralled when things kick off. You will make sure that the others do as they are ordered and keep them away from seeing anything sensitive. We need to know that outside the Cathedral we have people who know what is going on and will follow the plan.'

They all look suitably sober and contemplative and I wonder if religious observance plays any part in their lives. Well maybe it will in the future. Jill is a church goer but that might be out of habit or an attempt to lay the ground work to marry her girlfriend.

'One more thing, Father Jeremy will be outside with you. He may be able to give important information if things go in an unplanned direction.' I can't believe that I just told them to ask Jeremy if things go wrong. Although if things go as wrong as they might then DI White and I won't care. We'll be dead.

Chapter 24

We have adjourned to eat and rest, now that the
planning is done. DI White has a big team and our
specialists. Over thirty officers will be in holding patterns
nearby and a few will be working near the Cathedral to
make sure that Jeremy can seal the box, as it were. He
seems to have decided that we only need to seal portals and
not every window, and there are lots of them. I hope he is
right about that. I don't want it flying through a window
and off up, or down, the Royal Mile. I doubt we could use
the same hush story a second time.

I have had a Big Mac and fries on the way back to the
Seminary, a very modern last meal if ever there was one. I
nearly had the Quarter Pounder with cheese but decided to
push the boat out. Anyway on the way back to my room I
have been thinking about a weapon. Something I can use
on Basomel if he gets a bit frisky or close. Or Both. I
decide to phone Jeremy and see if he has any suggestions
that might work but his Faith answer earlier doesn't really
fill me with hope.

'Jeremy, I need a weapon for tonight. Any
suggestions?' I miss out the introductions and foreplay
getting straight to the nitty-gritty. I can almost see his
eyebrows dancing up into his hairline.

'A weapon?' He seems to forget that I will be up close
and personal while he will be outside surrounded by
policemen.

'Yes a weapon. Something to fend him off with if he
gets too close. Do we have any sacred daggers or
anything?' I have seen loads of films where the hero has a
special weapon to defeat the enemy. A sword would be
better; well bigger anyway.

'No we don't but salt will hurt him while you do the rite

of banishment.' He seems not to get it.

'And while I am ploughing through the words what is to stop Basomel ripping my throat out?' It has obviously been on my mind all day. I await a pearl of wisdom to flow from his lips. I might have to wait a while.

'The salt should bind him to the earth and you can always scald with scripture.' I am sure he believes that. However, when a large fanged and taloned demon is coming towards you with an unhappy look in its eye reciting scripture gets a little tricky.

'Thanks Jeremy, thanks a lot.' I hang up and think about possible weapons that might work for me.

After an hour of snooping about I have found a whip. I am not really all that sure how to use it but if I soak it in Dead Sea salt then maybe it will work. There was a set of darts sticking in the common room board but I didn't think they would be up to much. I also considered a sock with a couple of pool balls and salt as a sort of club but I ruled that out too.

I set to prepping the whip and try to get it as wet and salty as I can. I am pretty pleased with the result and I think I am on to something here. My new found idea will need to be run past the Bishop if tonight goes well. A patent to follow, perhaps.

I practice a few sweeps and realise it is all in the wrist. The swish and snap is pretty loud and it appears I am a natural whip wielder. Maybe all those hours watching Indiana Jones at the cinema have paid off. I am getting there in terms of hitting my door, every time from about nine feet. Armed now I can set to learning the ritual that I might need to recite by heart. I need to know the structure of the Abjuration and Dismissal, any set out of sequence might allow Basomel to escape the utter destruction he so fully deserves.

The time is marching on and after a period of reflection as I prayed, I am ready. The police car waiting for me at the seminary steps is like a prom night Limousine, ready to carry me off to a place I have never been; deliberately locked in a Cathedral with a Demon. I will need to add that to my CV and highlights reel.

DI White is briefing the troops and while very efficient and police speak; it has nothing on my secret briefing earlier today. The glances from Jill, Murdoch, MacBride and Anderson are knowing and somewhat terrified. I smile back trying to give them a level of assurance that all will be fine not exactly what I am feeling inside. The positioning and call signs are allocated and the hands for questions are going up.

DI White is covering them with his full police Inspector training. He is using his professional, no nonsense voice that is totally at odds with his slightly crumpled outfit.

I wonder that his wife lets him out like that and find myself wondering if he is divorced like so many of the senior policemen are these days. It seems to have a high attrition rate and I suppose I shouldn't be surprised that the hours take their toll. I suppose that it is hard to go home to normal things after looking at a body stuffed in a bin. I know he has kids, he mentioned them a few times, Kevin, I think, and Alison. A little weary light came into his eyes when they came up in conversation, teenagers I think.

'Father Steel and I will be based in the Cathedral, we expect chummy to turn up there.' I am pulled back to the now by the saying of my name. It is funny how we always seem to pick our names out of any room full of conversation; a bit like a radio scanner, locking on at a few syllables. A few heads turn in my direction and I try not to flush at the attention, it's not like I can help it. I am rescued by the entry of the Chief Constable, can't remember his name, and the standing to attention of everyone in the room.

'Carry on Detective Inspector.' He stands to one side with the Chief Superintendent following him like a house elf. I smirk at the idea of Dobbie following the Chief Constable.

I notice everyone sitting just a bit straighter in their seats and eyes a bit more focussed on every word of DI White and not a smart arsed comment forthcoming. They are all so professional and taking instruction from the Gold Commander, DI White, and making sure they understand what is expected. The Sergeants are now detailing the pairs and vehicles and expected station points and confirming call signs.

The Chief is making sure that DI White has this under control and has just informed him of something unpleasant, or at least going by the clenching of the jaw. I wander over, a spare prick at this wedding for now. The Chief tries not to glower in my direction as I approach.

'Gentlemen.' As if I should be included, I don't need to draw my hall pass do I? They look at me together but no one wants to say 'piss off' so I wait like a bad smell. They will need to continue.

'Chief Superintendent Saunderson will be in the control room managing communications and despatch options.' The Chief wants his flunky in control and DI White most certainly doesn't. Neither do I but I doubt it will make a difference as we will do what we need to anyway.

'Have you thought about managing any story leakage? Any plans for preventative messaging to prevent the online spreading of police concentration in that area?' I fire this in just to be an awkward sod, seems that they haven't even thought of that. That will give them something to do while DI White and I get ourselves sorted out. I lead him into the office where his piles of paperwork are almost like a chaotic work of art.

'You need to be protected so I have a few things for you. Firstly this.' I hand him a bag with salt in it. He is impressed, I can tell. 'It is Dead Sea Salt and if the Demon ever gets its hands on you throw it in its face and run for it.

Although if it gets to you that means it already has gotten to me and we are truly in the shit.' I smile in a way that is meant to be funny but he isn't all that sure. I hand him two vials of holy water.

'Use these as a spray or as a grenade. Same as the salt, if you need them we're fucked.' I laugh and he joins in. Good lad. It is like demon fighting kit for beginners and I am not sure that they will help that much.

'Finally, I will bless you and mark you for God. Are you baptised?' He nods again, weighing up the salt and water combination I have given him. I pull my jar of Chrism from my pocket at taking a tiny fingerprint worth stand before him.

'The Blessings of God the Father, God the Son and God the Holy Spirit be upon you. With this unction I mark you as one of God's flock. His Love within you, His protection around you. Amen.' I mark a cross on his forehead, leaving a little shiny cross that no one will notice. If they do they will take the pure piss out of him, colleagues can be so cruel.

Father Jeremy has the job of organising the sealing of the Cathedral, he will be meeting us there with enough salt to do the job. I wonder if road grit would do the job? Probably not. Salt as always been a tool of the Lord, ever since he turned Lot's wife into a pillar of it at Sodom. She watches over the Dead Sea allegedly. Who am I to argue?

We agree that we will be in position from nine o'clock making sure that we don't miss Basomel and allow him to complete his mission. The victim will still be alive when he gets to the Cathedral. The tricky bit will be separating him from her and making sure he can't consummate the act that will bring the, proverbial, roof down. If we get the timing wrong then we will be the dessert. The power that will flood through him will make him almost indestructible and our little tools will do little against him. I worry about the nullification of the consecrated ground of the Cathedral, if

334

Basomel can pull that off again the game will be, well and truly, a bogey.

'Have you done this before?' DI White asks as he drives the unmarked police car through the streets of the Old Town. I wonder which this' he means and decide I'd better answer the one I think he means, you know, the Demon slaying.

'Yes. I have dealt with a demon before. They are vicious and dangerous so don't get in its way.' I look across at him and realise I don't want anything to happen to him; he is one of the good guys. I'd better keep him safe.

'That's good to know. I'd hate to think I volunteered with a beginner.' He smirks, humour being the best antidote for fear.

'The last one left me in hospital for a while but you should have seen the mess of him.' The laughs fill the car, not that it was that funny but the need to let it out and embrace the lunacy of waiting in a Cathedral at night for a horny, psychotic demon to turn up with a victim and interrupt it.

Chapter 25

The Royal Mile is still a busy place at nine o'clock on a Sunday night; revellers, students and tourists enjoying the bars and restaurants that are numerous on both sides of the cobbled streets. The grey stones shine, slick with moisture from the drizzle, giving the street a magical look. The overhead street decorations of fluorescent reds and greens bringing a smile to lots of faces. Don't they know about the murders? Probably not, they all seem to live with such a relish of life that I am a little jealous. Was I ever happy? When did life stop being a good place if it ever was? Buggered if I know.

We pass a couple of marked cars that don't look out of place in the street. The fact that the weather isn't great should see most of the possible witnesses inside and not in the street, although going by the shortness of skirts the local girls don't feel the cold. Their clothes more suitable for the balmy summer evenings not the late Autumn ones where cold is in fact an overstatement. Scotland's weather is the single biggest contributor to the miserable bastard syndrome that infests the totality of the male population, that and the performance of the national football team.

Luckily the women are not so infested. DI White parks in the City Chambers reserved parking, as if he cares that it states permit holders only, The buff sandstone arches look really grand as you drive under them and on to the cobbles where the Lord Provost of Edinburgh parks his car. The building is beautiful too, if you like architecture. Location is everything, City Chambers next to the Cathedral, next to the Courts of Session and just downhill from a castle.

We make our way across the street to the Cathedral and along the long wall, the main entrance is facing the castle, we pass the old side doors and a busker has set up his pitch there. He is giving it all he has with John Lennon's Imagine, and I am sure he will be arrested for the assault he is committing on a great song. His caterwaul has attracted a few umbrella wielding spectators. They seem impervious to the low quality delivery and even part with a few coins. Maybe they feel sorry for him.

'He's not one of ours is he?' I nudge my partner, laughing at his 'Fuck no' response. We turn the corner and stop to spit on the cobbles. The mosaic of the Heart of Midlothian sits on the site of the old prison, cheek by jowl with the courts and the church. It is tradition to spit on it although I suspect the Hibee fans really enjoy giving it some gob. In Edinburgh we have two football teams Hearts and Hibs; although I don't care about the pointless beautiful game, I know that the undercurrent of religious sectarianism makes their rivalry ugly. Not quite as ugly as the soap dodgers from Glasgow rivalry between Celtic and Rangers. Still it exists in the capital.

Jeremy is standing in the rain like a plonker, if he had waited in the lee of the arch he would have been dry; maybe he likes to be miserable. He waves as we approach, it doesn't look too out of place, after all priests wave at each other all the time. Just not like a hysterical lunatic.

I wave back in a decorous for-fucks-sake-stop-being-an-arse kind of way. DI White nods and tries not to encourage him, I wish I had thought of that. In no time at all Father Jeremy is ushering us inside like we didn't know the way. I have been in this Cathedral many times and I doubt it is new to DI White either. Jeremy is getting all excited and breathless, again. Heaven help us.

'There are four possible entrances and only the front door will be open. When he arrives we will be waiting ready to seal the entrances. Jill has the back, Murdoch and MacBride have the other two. DI Anderson and I will seal the main doors.' Obviously Father Jeremy and the rest will be pivotal tot he success of trapping DI White and myself inside with a demon. He had better get it right.

The inside of St Giles sits waiting like a bride waiting for her groom, so serene and silent. The feeling from the flagstones is one of centuries of penitence and piety, I can't imagine that Basomel will find it comfortable touching the stone. I look at the high stained glass panels, so intricate and lovely in their colours and symbolism. I bask a little in the whole sanctity before White coughs gently.

'Where should we wait?' He asks quietly, the reverence obviously reaching him too. I look round, I hadn't really thought about it really. I suppose the high Pulpit will be the best place; near the middle and give time for the doors to be sealed behind it. There is also a little bit of cover, making us less obvious in the first instance. The high Altar is still some way behind us, giving us an interception chance; always making the assumption that it will come through the main doors. After all it is a supremely arrogant and showy demon.

'This used to be four churches, you know.' DI White adds some local tour guide knowledge. He seems embarrassed to know something about the Church. I look at him, waiting fro him to go on. 'We did it at high school. About twenty years ago now. John Knox used to rant and rave from up there.' He waves his hand airily across the Nave.

'Four churches?' This is news to me. If that's the case would this be the place for the final sacrifice? We might be waiting here for an event that will not be happening here. I wonder if the knowledgable Jeremy knows this.

'Yeah but I can't remember the names though. One was the Old Kirk. It is the main Church of Scotland church anyway.' He isn't feeling my worry.

'It is called a Cathedral but I wonder if that is a modern affectation?' I frown, I need to know. It is old but not ancient and has been restored in the last hundred and fifty years or so.

'Jeremy. Did you know the Cathedral was four churches originally?' I speak quickly into my phone. 'It might not be the site. Would any of the other churches nearby be better options for Him? Find out quick. We don't want to be waiting about with our dicks in our hands while he does the ritual elsewhere.' Fuck.

'Go and find out.' I practically hiss at him, I know I am being unreasonable but how the hell did he not know this. Just because it is a big religious building, it doesn't make it the most likely. I can feel a chill running all over my skin. I know now we need to check the other churches nearby.

'Can you task some officers to check the other nearby ones we talked about yesterday. The Wee free one and the Tron. Tell them to look for signs of entry or anything suspicious.' I am getting a bit edgy. I stomp up to the Altar, letting the stained glass panels calm me before snatching my buzzing phone to my ear.

'It was four churches.' Jeremy starts with the obvious. I think he might be a bit upset with his own stupidity; well add him to the club. 'It was a Cathedral when it was Episcopal but has been seen as the High Kirk since the Reformation.'

I practically snarl down the phone. 'I don't need you to read Wikipedia to me. Find out if this is the likeliest site or if we are in the wrong place.' I cut him off and shout to DI White. 'This will be the wrong place. Have you got people looking at the others?' He holds a finger up to me making me wait as I approach him. He nods as he passes instructions. My phone buzzes again.

'What?' I snap without looking at it. I really should have looked first. If I had I might have avoided upsetting the Chief Superintendent who is all concerned about the possible change of plan.

'Sorry, I thought you were someone else.' I try to row back my tetchiness but I don't think we will be on Christmas card lists this year.

'This is turning in to a bloody shambles.' I turn to DI White as we have that moment where we both know we are fucked. Individually and collectively. 'I don't mind my own fuck ups but I don't need any help.' I state, the sour look on my face would curdle milk.

Chapter 26

I have always been, what you might call, volatile. It's not as if I don't realise I am over-reacting, I do, but I just can't stop it once the fuse it lit. My mother used to tell me it would cause me problems in later life. I don't know if she meant a heart attack, stroke or just no pals. Probably meant all three. I am stomping about like an elk in the Rut and filling this hallowed Cathedral with under the breath swearwords and not so under the breath swearwords. I wonder how many fucks this Cathedral has heard over the years ; well I have added a great many and regrets I have not a single one. Father Jeremy comes in looking like a kicked puppy and he is lucky that my spleen has been well and truly vented.

'This better be good news Jeremy.' I growl as he approaches. His face is tripping him, a wonderful Scottish description for looking like he is going to cry. He stops out of punching distance which seems an unnecessary precaution.

'This is probably not the site. I have made a few calls and the split nature of the consecrations wouldn't make it a prime site for his needs.' He is staring at a space past me, where DI White looks much more forgiving.

'Probably?' I spit, incredulity filling every fibre of my being. 'I think we need a little more than that. If we go chasing around the city centre to find the site of this cosmic event and can't find him we might all be seriously up shit creek.' I know I am being unfair but we need a little bit of definite information.

'He might still choose here as it would be suitable but just not the key prize we thought he might seek.' Jeremy is chewing the inside of his cheek like an eight year old who hasn't done their homework. Basically we have no idea and

Jezza is carrying that can. It doesn't matter how many 'we' statements he slips in. Collective responsibility in action; no it will end up being my fault and I am less than happy about it.

'No sign of entry at the other two local churches.' DI White feeds back the information coming through on his radio. Well that is something I suppose; although it makes us even more clueless.

'Jeremy, we will continue with the plan for now until we know otherwise. I can't think of any older churches near here. Can you?' He shakes his head telling me what I really knew. We are well and truly in the shit, right up to our necks.

'Call the Bishop or someone who can help and find out where the nearest churches are by age. DI White and I will wait in here. Who knows maybe Basomel is as utterly clueless as to the history of this Cathedral as we were.' I flop down into a pew and look to the high altar for some divine inspiration.

DI White sits on the other side of the aisle and fiddles with his phone; texting someone. I want to be angry but I feel it all slipping away as the loss begins to strike home. It looks like we will lose this one. I don't actually know what the hell I am actually trying to prevent, I just know it would be bad. I look a my watch, it helpfully reads cowboy time; ten to ten. I smile as the tune of bonanza plays in my head. It is the smile of the desperate, I need something to go right tonight and so far it has been a series of cock-ups.

I laugh and it startles DI White from his smartphone and it turns out he was playing candycrush and not texting. He looks guilty thinking that his playing was the cause of my mirth. 'It could be worse you know? We could have been sealed in here with a Demon.' I grin and he grins back. Two clowns laughing in the face of adversity, so very British..

'You were a little hard on Father Jeremy. He might just

have saved both our lives by being useless.' DI White leans back and stretches, tension has made him stiff and tense.

'Probably. It will cost someone else theirs though. Our good fortune has a price, one neither of us wants to pay.' I go from cheeky grin to morose bastard in nano-seconds, another wonderful trait inherited I am sure. 'I need to pray. You just amuse yourself and don't let us get sneaked up on.' I wink to tell him I am joking.

I need to think and the act of kneeling with my eyes closed and letting my mind de-clutter itself is the way I know best. Everyone would assume I am praying but it is more a mental exercise of clearing all the crap from my mind and letting the solution to my pressing issues come to the surface. I let my mind drift away from this here and now and try to feel my way around the four churches I am knelling upon. It feels holy but a bit messy, like the energy is confused and basically an ineffective barrier to the powers of the Dark. I wonder who did the consecration; Presbyterians are a bit different and lack much of a ritual to call the power of God to sanctify the whole of this lovely building.

The power of prayer to invoke the almighty is a powerful tool and I am sure that as the masses took part in the service of consecration there was a great deal of power laid down and tying in the essence of the Hermit Saint Giles. I begin to pray in earnest hoping that my words fly straight to the ears of the Almighty and that he deigns to listen to me and give me some sort of answer. Of course, he doesn't usually reply and I certainly won't be holding my breath waiting on a direct response. It isn't like a hotline although it would be handy if there was one.

'Hi God, Sorry to bother you but Jeremy has made an arse of this; can you just give me a clue. Not even a big one. Just a clue or pointer to get us moving in the right direction. Thanks. Much appreciated.' I play this ridiculous musing in my head as my inner voice wanders like an irreverent teenager that thinks it is funny and it patently isn't.

I let myself slip into an open kind of state. I don't know what to do nor what to expect. Divine inspiration is a bit tricky to predict and accounts for the Stigmatics and the ecstatics and the collapsing in tongues brigade. I am lucky that my symptoms are a little more normal and not the most extreme end. After all bleeding hands and feet must be very inconvenient and unnerving. My breathing slows and I can feel the lightness that may be my meditative state or the lack of oxygen to my synapses. I wait.

The wash of power flowing towards me seems to emanate from the west, it is like a ripple on a still pond of psychic energy. Like someone dropped a bloody big boulder into a deep still pool. The shudder that passes through me brings me back to the here and now. My eyes flash open like the spooky fright bit from a horror film. DI White jumps like a big Jessie, he was staring at me apparently. How long he has been waiting for me to come round I have no idea.

'Father, it is ten past eleven.' He seems to be concerned that time is short and I have been sitting on my ass doing nothing of any value.

'It is west of here and it has begun.' I can feel the formality capture my tongue and the diction and pace of speech is different. He looks at me a little differently. 'Let's go. We will need a car.' I am back in the here and now although I am unsure where we will be going exactly. Perhaps I will be able to feel him when we start moving.

'Jeremy, we are heading west. Find out the nearest old church in that direction.' I speak quickly into the phone, he needs to deliver or we will lose the vital moments that might be the difference between an innocent slain and a battle lost.

I start striding up the Cathedral flagstones and out into

the night, I can't wait on DI White to find a car and I am drawn off up the High Street, or Royal Mile as it is called; he will just need to catch me up. The pull at me is very clear I am heading in the right direction. It feels like a chord being plucked on my spider's web of psychic energy. The pressure is building as the ritual is begun and I know that time is growing short. I cannot afford to miss this confrontation, Margaret needs me her name coming unbidden to my mind. Her terror is like a cold wet blanket clammy and chilling to me and yet arousing and gratifying to him.

The night is full of people, revellers out for a few beers and some carousing for the lucky ones. A few speculative glances in my direction at the crazy looking priest stomping up the street. The jeers of the drunkenly stupid reaching my ears causing my cheeks to flush hot with anger. I feel the need to retort but keep marching on. Where the hell is DI White? How long can it take to commandeer a police car? The answer isn't long in coming. He screeches to a halt beside me and I get in. He sets off, his heavy right foot causing a wheel spin on the slick cobbles that are exposed to the tyres. He doesn't fishtail the car but it causes a few of Edinburgh's denizens to get the fuck out of the way.

In seconds we are passing the Free Church of Scotland Church, St Columba's, and we are on the road down past the Castle mound. The high walls of the castle forbidding above us, perched like a black shadow scowling down at us. I am glad not to have had to attack that rampart. The feeling is changing as I feel the energy building to my right and now behind us. There are no old churches behind us on that side, just the castle.

'The church is on the other side of the Castle. Probably St John's on the corner of Lothian Road or maybe St Cuthbert's?' I know both of those having spent many an hour there. They have great coffee. White punches the siren and the lights begin to strobe. The road goes past the kings stables and the exorbitant car park that was built deep underground. Everyone obligingly pulling over as DI White mounts the kerb and makes a path that will take us to the lights and Lothian Road. He is driving like a madman and I hope we will get there in one piece; although with what awaits us at the other end I doubt we will be in one piece afterwards anyway.

Screaming tyres as we swing across the cross hatched yellow junction have me hanging on for dear life. The force of the turn throwing me against the door and it is then I regret the lack of the seat belt. Too late to put it on now, we will be stopped in a minute. The thrashing of the engine sounds impressive as do the screeching brakes telling everyone that this is a police emergency; as if the modulating siren and bright blue strobes didn't tell that story already.

'Less than a minute Father.' DI White has a solid grip on the wheel as we bounce and slide up on to the pavement along side the black metal railing that lead up to the massive spired church of St John. The slippery pavement caused the car to scrape along the railings leaving an interesting smear of paint on the iron and stone. The dents in the door and quarter panels pretty impressive, he hasn't missed any on his side. The headlight might be buggered as well; a full house. We get out like Starskey and Hutch sprinting towards the doors.

Chapter 27

I run up to the old wooden doors, re-varnished and pale in the street lights. I shove hard with my shoulder expecting them to open under our arrival. The solid thud and numbing of my shoulder reminders that I am not superman. DI White is on the radio calling for keys and someone to open the church. I notice he wasn't dumb enough to try the doors. Obviously it is a rookie mistake to make; well too bad I made it.

There is another door facing on to Princes street and I slip and slide around the corner before rattling the old heavy metal ring handle. Locked and no sign of anything happening inside. I can feel myself getting a bit frantic as I charge back to DI White as he stands outside the front doors. We are drawing a crowd of semi-interested onlookers, some of them with phones pointed in our direction.

I catch my breath bent over with hands on knees, adrenalin making me breathless. DI White 'Fifteen minutes for the keys.' He has had an answer and it doesn't present much chance of being in time.

'There is a door on the terrace that might be a better chance. Come on.' I drag him down the worn steps ignoring everyone and everything else that might be around us. I wonder if the car will be nicked by the time we get back. I stumble along my shoes slipping on the traction free flagstones causing me to slip and slide like I am Bambi on ice. I wonder if the terrace door is susceptible to a kicking in. One look at it tells me that I'd need a battering ram and a team of burly soldiers to have any chance. Churches sometimes had to hold the mob outside and generally the doors reflect that level of sturdiness.

'We will have to wait for the keys.' DI White is rattling

the handles like he expects the door to just open under his touch. It doesn't, obviously.

'We will be too late then. I don't feel him here. Perhaps St Cuthbert's is the site.' I look from the terrace down into the darkness of Princess Street Gardens. The church is the dark shadowy shape overshadowed by trees. It has it's own graveyard and is pretty old. I have no idea if it is or isn't suitable, all I know is that this isn't the place. I can feel nothing at all from inside or even having been here. There is still about twenty minutes until midnight and the culmination.

'We need to go down the park steps to get to St Cuthbert's. Are you sure?' DI White is looking at me, worry beginning to pinch his features. We are so grasping at straws and he knows it.

'Give me a moment.' I try to gather myself, if I can't get some equilibrium it could be happening behind me and I would feel nothing. I take a deep breath and ignore the fire in my knee joints. I open my spirit to feel around me and aim my thoughts at St Cuthbert's with its pretty spire and cupolas visible above the darkness of the trees. I feel nothing from there either.

'Where the hell is he?' I can feel sod all and time is running away like sand through my fingers.

DI White is looking at me with horror, or is it revulsion.

'Are you all right? Your nose is bleeding.' Bleeding doesn't really cut it as I wipe a black bloody sludge from my nose. The smell is of rot and I throw up spectacularly over the terrace railing and the splatter patter of it landing on the stones below would have impressed me had I been watching. Snorting and coughing to get the gloop out of my nose causes a secondary round of retching and vomiting that coats the old iron railing that I am hanging on to. All the way down the lower half of my trousers is a viscous bloody smear that has them plastered to my hairy legs.

'Keep your nose out, Priest.' Reverberating in my head.

A message from the enemy and he has given himself away. The attack pinpoints him where before I could not find him under some sort of spell. I grin at DI White.

'I know where he is.' I look up and high above us is the castle. Edinburgh Castle, world heritage site and unconquered it is in great condition; housing all sorts of artefacts and more importantly the Chapel of St Margaret. The Chapel sits inside the inner walls high above us, it is very old and perfect for Basomel. I snort out the last vestiges of the bloody snot like a professional footballer, one blast from each nostril.

'It is in the Castle.' I start running for the car, DI White doesn't ask any questions and gets to the car ahead of me, shouting at the spectators to get out of the way. Leaving the blue lights on attracts a crowd apparently.

'We need the castle opened.' DI White is shouting into his radio set, I am struggling to get the seat belt to stop locking and decide it will just get in the way anyway. I stop fighting with it and we are moving, lights and siren filling the night and causing everything to get the hell out of the way. The engine sounds so loud inside the car and I realise that the last set of kerbs we bumped over may have ripped off the exhaust. Looking out the rear window tells me a story. It isn't exactly ripped off just being dragged underneath and causing spark showers and a racket.

'Nearly there.' DI White is weaving all over the road as the car becomes a little less happy at his driving. The hard left turn at the mini-roundabout bounces his side against the tiered stone kerbs on that side of the street, they create a bumper that throws us back into the road. The cobbles all slick and slippery are for tourists and marching soldiers not half wrecked police cars.

'Thank God.' I want to be funny but I am clinging to the door handle and am braced into my seat ruing the lack of the seatbelt after all. The street leading up to the castle is old and narrow. The violence of the siren and blue lights driving everything ahead of us like a panicked herd of cattle. People squeezing into doorways and screaming in terror. Not just the women either, I joined in as we near-miss a crowd of revellers walking arm in arm down towards us.

In what seems like an eternity we burst out on to the esplanade where they have the Military Tattoo here every year. It is a huge space and White just guns the engine harder as we speed towards the drawbridge and the huge gates scattering the temporary barriers like skittles and dragging them along under the car. Naturally the gates are still shut.

The Chief Super better deliver or the mad driving will have been in vain. The screech and grinding noise as we pull to a stop is impressive as we throw open the doors and run for the gate. The headlights like two on-stage spotlights, creating fantastic shadows against the old oak and iron gates.

'We need this gate open now.' I shout at DI White because it is obviously his fault. He is already speaking into the radio. Professional call sign and requests for action and not a 'Get the fucking door open' anywhere in the conversation.

I am banging on a bit of door without black iron reinforcing studs, I would like my hands to work for the rest of my life, however short it might be. 'Fuck.' I roar in frustration, I look round and am temporarily white-spotted by our headlights.

'Garrison Sergeant on his way down with the keys, ETA less than a minute.' DI White is repeating the message I can hear perfectly well coming out of his radio. I can feel the growling in my throat as my impatience is getting to epic proportions. I stagger back as if a blow has just landed on my chest.

In St Margaret's Chapel the sacrifice is awake. I feel her terror and I know that Basomel is loving it. It fills my head, her screaming 'Noooo' and the view from her of the sharp fangs and red scaled skin. She is so young, probably eighteen but maybe not. I can see through her eyes the talon rip away the white spandex top barely caressing her skin. The little red lines not yet yielding blood. Basomel stills her with a stare, her bladder empties all over her legs and short skirt. I feel him swell with power and the burn of lust.

The rumbling of the heavy lock brings me to the gate once more. Slowly it opens enough to let us through and I sprint inside leaving DI White to tell the Gatekeeper something. He can tell them whatever he likes I am running up the steep flint-like cobbles and find that the years of avoiding exercise might just cost this young woman her life.

Puffing and panting and every ounce of oxygen feeling like a knife in the chest, I manage to make most of the first climb emerging from a tunnel onto the main path behind the battery terrace. I have been here many times and Mons Meg sits there like a monster cannon, the newer one-hundred-and-five-millimetre field gun delivers the percussive one o'clock salute every day. I wonder if I can use it to destroy the Demon. I can bet that has never been tried before.

My mind drifts as I try to avoid the agony of the ascent, knowing all the while that I may be too late. The sweat clinging all over my body is chilling in the wind and completes the discomfort my flesh is enduring. Past the museum and on to the inner ramp and under the inner Bailey gate. I am almost at the flat bit of the interior when my knees collapse and I run my face, chin first over the ground. The ground coming up to meet me so fast. The chain that keeps visitors from restricted areas invisible in the dark the cause of my fall, not exhaustion; although it must have been very close as to which would get me first. I groan and hold in the desire to squeal in agony.

DI White is helping me to my feet, probably because he

doesn't know where the Chapel entrance is. Up the steps and along the high wall to the end. I can't actually force any words out at the moment, so he will have to follow me. I notice the knees are out in my trousers; another uniform destroyed in the line of duty. I doubt the bloody mucus and vomit would have come out anyway. I stumble using hands and almost on all fours to get up the flight of uneven, worn steps to the wall. The battlements look out over a twinkling city below, full of beautiful well-lit monuments and architectural wonders. Tonight I just need some air in my lungs.

DI White has no requirement for oxygen apparently and he is running towards the Chapel of Scotland's Saint, Margaret not Andrew. There is light from candles twinkling in the pebble glass panels that have filled what was once an open window. The screaming has commenced again and I try to make my knees bend and move but it is a struggle. White has kicked open a very heavy door, which is impressive but foolhardy. He throws his salt inside, in one go. I know this by the scream that erupts from the lips of our salt averse Demon. He charges inside, bravery seems to be built in with duty to protect and serve, and from what I guess was a demonic backhand, he flies back out through the doorway and off the walkway onto the grassy bank below. On the inside luckily, if he had gone over the battlements he would be a posthumous holder of whatever commendation policemen get.

I advance as fast as my tortured limbs will allow, Basomel can feel me approach and I can feel his uncertainty. The air as thick as soup as I choke on the heady power cocktail of fear and blood that Basomel so enjoys.

Chapter 28

The door slams shut before me. The diagonal strips of
very old timber and the regularly painted black gloss
diamond shaped iron studs prevent my shoulder being used
to force my way inside. I grab the handle and push, the
door grinds open slowly, something metal is scraping over
the grey flagstones. I see inside, everything etched
permanently in one flash. This little chapel, at the top of the
fortress, would have been an austere place to come to pray.
The chill from the stones would pass all the way up your
legs making them ache. Suffering for faith before a
beautiful little stained glass window that would be backlit
on sunny days. Although these are few and far between in
Scotland.

The altar, although in reality not much more than a
block of basalt on which the castle sits, is covered in
candles. Thick candles that smoke and reek telling me they
are tallow not wax; and the tallow used is probably human.
On the altar a number of offerings, bloody and dried out
organs ripped from the victims of his spree. The final
offering lying stunned from a blow to the side of the head,
is before the altar. Her pale flesh bruised and abused; legs
bruised and grazed from being dragged along by the hair.
Her young face swollen on one side where a slap has been
given, a slap like no man could ever deliver. The power of
the blow has probably cracked her cheekbone.

Between her legs, his back exposed and his haunches
moving forward is the enemy I seek. Luckily she is out of
it, the pain would be excruciating and he is not gentle. The
echo of a previous recipient jars my insides recalling the
wreckage he wrought inside her. The folded wings
protecting him from me, like a leathery armour. The stench
of his ardour and flesh filling my nostrils, not making me

gag but spurring my hands to action. The casting of salt brings a scream that shatters the glass pictogram of the cross. I have air in my lungs and God is with me.

'I cast you out, foul spawn of the other-world. Go back to the pit made for you and your Master. In the name of Christ I abjure you.' The criss-crossing of the salt scarring and scalding the wings on his back causing them to spasm. The candles are buffeted and their light extinguished in the blink between words. In my hand the salted whip, I don't recall pulling it from my pocket. I pull my arm back and swing, in the dark anything could happen. Indiana Jones I am not and the first blow slides across the enemy causing pain but not much more. More like a pointless slap but causing pain due to the salt I soaked into the leather.

'In the Name of Christ I command you. The blood of the Martyrs condemns you and the power of God compels you. Return to the abyss and trouble this world no more.' My voice is like thunder in such a small place. I feel my words land like blows driving him back towards the altar. His hulking form flinching before me and recoiling from my whip. The whip that I am flailing about in spasmodic flicks. One flick lashes across his cheek landing like a deliberate blow, bringing a screaming roar of pain. I close in with salt running out but still scalding him. His rising scream suggests that some coated his sticky phallus and has got to smart. His frantic rubbing at the area would be comical in a different setting. A smile of grim satisfaction fills my face.

The girl lying on the floor chooses that moment to close her legs and roll away causing me to trip and stagger into the wall. Basomel flees past me towards the door. Escape his only thought as his inner cowardice in the face of the Lord comes to the surface. He reaches the door, staggering under the pain of the salt and the lash. His taloned hands ripping the door from the frame, so great is his desire to get away from me and the power of God. The discarded door clatters on the floor louder than a thunderclap in such a small place. The path to his freedom and the outside now clear.

I throw a vial of Holy water as hard as I can smashing it above his head on the stone lintel, its contents cascading and sprinkling the Demon. His cowering under the shards and burning, hissing liquid gives me a moment to get back to my feet. The girl has rolled away and is in a curled ball to the side of the Altar as far as she can be from the demon. I don't blame her. The ritual disrupted we need to destroy him before he escapes into the night.

'You are going nowhere ya bastard.' I hear DI White's voice from outside, as he tries to prevent the murderous fiend from escape. He is brandishing a handful of salt like a talisman. He needs to throw it straight in its face. His hesitation I hoped wouldn't prove fatal. I stumble forward, slipping on the scattered candles rolling about in the dark under my feet. Making my movements like a trainee stilt-walker on the wet cobbles; all legs and stumbles but I managed to keep upright enough to see DI White backhanded by a heavily taloned hand, launching him from the battlements once more.

Basomel jumps up on to the crenellated wall and in a moment of smug triumph, screams defiance in my direction. My whip hand flying forward, the salted leather wrapping around his neck as he threw himself from the wall. The biting salt causing Basomel to plummet on the far side of the wall. In that split second I know I should have let go. I didn't and the law of physics caused me to be dragged over the battlement like the tail of a roller-coaster, plunging over the inner wall onto the grass-covered rock below.

A thirty foot drop onto padded rocks is not something I would recommend but thankfully I had a large, taloned and fanged landing cushion. The whip entangling both of us; trapping me and burning him, has us rolling over cobbles and gouging at each other like a pair of pub brawlers. I am trying not to get my throat ripped out as his talons start to shred my coat. His fist glancing a blow on my shoulder causing me to slide across the slick, damp, cobbles and making me finally release the whip. His wings are hanging like a pair of limp curtains, not having survived the fall intact and his movements tell of other injuries. I am glad that I am not alone, because my body is one big throbbing ache.

I groan as he gets to his feet and staggers away from me. The steps to the Gun Terrace leading him down and out of sight, I know I need to follow him. This ain't over yet. Turning on to all fours I manage with a wince or two to get to my feet. I can't let him escape. His time all but over as far as the ritual is concerned and he has failed in that as far as I can tell. If I can't get him now then he will litter the city with corpses until he is destroyed. Only the ritual sacrifice was time bound, or at least to Jeremy it was.

I slip down the slippery steps catching myself on the handrails and avoiding another fall in the dark. Ahead of me Basomel is looking over the parapet for a means of escape. A bell chimes the first of midnight's tolls, at the sound his head spins round to glare at me. I smile back grimacing through the pain.

'You are fucked.' I whisper, before pulling myself upright 'The power of Christ compels you to his will. This water, blessed and pure, casts you from this earthly realm. A place that is yours no more. I abjure you, foul fallen spirit of Hell.' I am advancing with each word, Holy water in one hand and presented crucifix of Our Lord in the other. My pains falling away into the background of my consciousness. I can practically feel its fear.

'I close the door that opened to let you walk among the living, thou O cast out and damned spirit. I am the word that seals the gate, the word that pronounces the sentence on you and those that seek to escape the Pit. I am the light that the Lord sets before you. I cast you from the lands of the living.' I cross the Holy water over the chest of the Demon. The screaming in my mind and in my ears like lancing talons of fire. His talons bury themselves in my back as I sear him with the Crucifix on his chest.

The blast of power released throws him backwards driving his curved claws deeper into my back. I don't know which screams are the loudest as we are catapulted over another wall, higher this time. An embrace that will be the destruction of both of us.

Chapter 29

Falling together, like Gandalf and the Balrog. His talons hooked deep into my back like a cat that is desperately trying to avoid a bath, so agony inducing and deep I am in a Zen-like state. The pain washing over me like a purifying heat, leaving my mind wandering at speed as the rocks of the castle mass race past us. I find myself wondering about DI white and if he survived. I am wondering what spin and story the Home office will put on this and how much video will leak into the social media streams of conspiracy theorists. A laugh, probably hysteria escapes my lips.

The futile flapping of ruined wings accompanies the fall of two mortal enemies in the eternal struggle. Is this one going to be a win for either of us? A score draw, so prized on the football pools of years gone by. The spite and malice of my dancing partner are like blows all of their own, his snapping fangs not quite reaching me as we fall. The smell of charring flesh surrounds us, the smoke making my eyes water, as I press deep the blessed depiction of Our Lord on the cross. The heat making it impossible to release my hold, burning my hand too.

It isn't the fall that kills you. The shuddering impact with the jagged rocks below the castle walls would normally be fatal in almost all cases. In my case I land on the sturdy, muscled body of demon flesh and as we fly on to the next impact am thrown clear of his talons with an agony filled scream. The sailing through the air a blessed relief from my enemy's caress and hold. I am sure he isn't too upset to be free of me. The crucifix is no longer in my hand although I am sure that won't matter as I find a birch tree slowing my progress to the ground. I fall the last few feet onto a muddy path that must be a short cut round the castle foot that the local kids probably use.

I am alive, and surprised beyond belief. The tolling of a bell somewhere dragging me back from a moment of lying face down in the mud, and to the present. Groaning as I move is becoming a habit but I can barely lift my head to see where Basomel is. I hope he is as wrecked as I am, or there won't be much of a contest in round three. This was a classic rumble in the jungle but, sadly, I think I am George Foreman looking up from the canvas.

Escaping, the fucker is still moving, that is what he is doing. He is scaling a wire fence that leads over the tracks to Princess Street Gardens. I say scaling, it more or less crumples under the weight of his body. A dragging leg, bloody and scaled, showing his injured state. One of his wings has been ripped from his back by the black rocks of the castle, and the streaming ichor flowing from shoulder to hip gleams under the fluorescent orange street lights. I push my body a little further, getting my blistered hands beneath me to get me on to all fours. Crawling after him seems like the right thing to do but unless I get upright I will never catch him. It would be easier to lie here and wait for help to arrive.

I never really do easy, too stubborn I suppose. Amazingly I get one foot in front of another and zombie walk along the path towards the fence. I see Basomel entangled in the briar that fills the space past the fence. He is frantically trying to get through them and down on to the railway tracks. I start to feel in my pockets for anything that I can use in this fight. The salt is finished, scattered all over the chapel and his dick. The Holy water is gone, two shattered in my pocket and others already splashed on his hide. Crucifix, gone, was embedded in his chest and might be there still. My Indiana Jones whip is between the upper walls I think.

I have smelly unction in a little jar but that's it. The prospect of getting up close and personal with Basomel again does not fill me with happy feelings. I trip as I near the fence. A green bottle, a Buckfast bottle to be accurate, a high caffeine-alcohol mix that is a staple of kids these days, causing my trip. In my day it was Diamond White cider but this is now the fortified wine of choice that is consumed all over the central belt. I scoop it up, my intentions to bottle the bastard.

Basomel is nearly free of the grasping thorns of the briar patch, and will be able to jump the last five feet down into the railway cutting and the tracks below.

I manage to get round the side of the tangle and am going to catch him one more time. I feel a rage burning in my chest, making me forget the agonies I will feel later. I charge, more a lumber but you get the idea, crashing the monk-made empty bottle on the Demon's head. It shatters spectacularly leaving me a jagged stabbing weapon that I force deep into his chest. It shatters into his flesh and mine. We have a synchronised screaming moment before I shoulder him as hard as I can, knocking him onto the tracks below.

I manage to avoid the last little fall, hanging over the wall edge topped with dress bricks, I am done. There is nothing left in my tank for this night. I bottled him like a street thug but he is still moving, the bastard just refuses to die. He stares up at me, we are both fucked. Is he considering ripping my head off, I hope not because right now all I could do would be to watch. We have a moment of understanding; the eternal battle rages on and we are just expendable meat sacks that are the proxies.

I pull in a hot gasping breath and realise I shouldn't have.'I abjure you, you fucking scumbag.' I manage a whisper but it might have been a shout as he flinches away from me. 'In the name of the Father, the ' I start to cough before I can finish. A rumbling noise fills my ears and a screech of hard metal filling the night as a very startled train driver tries to halt his Scotrail diesel-electric hybrid engine and the two carriages, that constitute the last train to Dundee, before impact with an unexpected object in the tracks.

The driver fails and Basomel decorates the front of the train and is dragged under the wheels that finally finish his time in Edinburgh. The screaming face of the driver is muted by the thick glass and the juddering halt of the train causes the lights to flicker on and off before going out all together. The emergency lights come on and I can see a number of faces pressed against the window trying to see what is going on. Bugger, one of them is pointing at me. I hope they can't see my dog collar or it will be more press for the Bishop to suppress. Although, to be honest, I don't really care any more. I need a rest and the brick wall feels so comfortable.

My phone is buzzing in my trouser pocket. It takes me a few moments to realise that is what the noise and vibration is. Groaning as I reach down, every inch a torture of fire on my back. I dig it out and look at the screen. The black blob obscuring the caller and cracks all over the screen tell me that it is as wrecked from the descent from the castle as I am. I press the button and press it to my ear. Speaking is a bit of a stretch at the moment so I wait.

'Father Andrew? Where are you?' Jeremy sounds frantic. He really isn't cut out for this type of excitement.

'I am having a lie down at the train tracks below the castle. Basomel just stopped the train.' I manage a whisper and I hope heard me because I am not repeating myself.

'I will send help. Are you okay?' He manages to gush down the phone and pissing me off. I am really an ungrateful sod. He is going to have someone come and save my ass and I get pissy.

'Not really. Hurry up.' I lie back watching the stars above the castle. The are so clear and sharp, I hadn't really noticed them before. I am cold.

'Make a hole.' I hear a voice in the darkness. There are lots of noises but I can't seem to really get a grip on them. I can't make them into a coherent picture. 'He's lucky to be alive. People jump off that part of the wall to kill themselves.' Another voice but I can't summon the energy to be arsed to respond. A few jolts and a slamming of doors and it is quieter, thankfully.

'Can you hear me Father.' Firm but not shouting in my face. Obviously I can as I am not deaf. It seems that my body is basically inert and a cause for concern. My eyes are so heavy that I will open them later. I so want to be left in peace.

'Father can you hear me?' Again with the urging. I am sure he means well but, frankly, he is getting on my nerves. My eyes flicker, involuntarily as I try to sleep, causing him to prattle on about Lord knows what for what feels like an eternity.

We are nearly there, or so he says and has been saying for sometime now. It must be an Edinburgh thing; nearly there is very elastic in these parts. A cough escapes me and the pain lancing me hurts like the devil, causing me to groan inarticulately as the ambulance pulls to a halt. The cavalcade of medical staff and porters wheel me away to the innards of the hospital. Why do they keep peeling my eyelids up to shine bright white lights in? I am being assessed, apparently. Poked, prodded and stared at by worried faces, if they match the worried voices that   I can hear. Hustle and bustle surrounds me but I am not really with it. I have no idea what they are doing to my body but I know I don't like it. The words are less distinct now as the team prepare me for something. I feel a bit spaced out, not in a bad way all things considered. The pins and needles sensation on the tip of my nose is a weird sensation and I smile.

'Father Steel, glad you are still with us.' A woman's voice speaks quietly near my ear 'You have had a fall and we are a little worried about the bump on your head. We are heading to theatre in a few moments. Just relax and we will take care of you.'

They say nurses are angels, well this one's voice had power and I believed her that everything would be all right.

'Special Branch. Anyone that doesn't need to be here; Out.' The barking of orders second nature to the owner of that voice. I can't imagine too many times when immediate compliance doesn't occur either. I manage to open one eye, a little like winking but really because it is too much effort to open both. Four burly, armed, Special Branch officers have moved to take over.

Hustling everyone out; except a nurse who is next to me and a white-coated young doctor with fuzz on his chin. He is objecting but they are ignoring his ineffectual demands to stop. Of all the times I have wanted to call in Special Branch and this is the one I get; I can't even enjoy it. I manage to keep watching from my restricted vision seat.

Enter stage left a middle-aged, little woman in green coveralls and head cover; a mask dangling below her chin and her clogs clattering on the floor angrily. 'Get your guns and stupidity out of my theatre.' She snarled like a pit bull causing everything to halt mid-step. I would have laughed but that was a stretch. In moments I am wheeled away missing the eyeball to eyeball that must have ensued. The soft angelic voice reached my ears just as they started the anaesthetic.

'You'll be fine. She's the best neurosurgeon in the country. Relax and I will be here when you are done.' I try to smile or at least I would have wanted to. I was out as her words finished feeding through to my brain.

Chapter 30

'You should see the other guy.' DI White makes light of
the swollen, purple face mask he is wearing on one side.
He does look frightful but I suppose I don't look great
either. He eases himself into the visitor's chair, moving
looks difficult for him too. The dynamic duo, that's us, got
our asses handed to us on a silver platter. I manage to
twitch my face into, what might be construed as, a smile. I
am actually pleased that he is here and in one piece, more or
less.

'I did, he wrestled a train and that didn't end too well.' I
go for dry sarcasm because laughing hurts too much and the
draining tubes move if I do. I have a lovely set of punctures
in my back, a full set of ten, that have taken some
explaining and have been problematic for the medical staff.
The cracked ribs are a minor problem by comparison.

'I don't remember anything after I got this.' He points to
the contusion on his face. He had a brief fall and a collision
with the courtyard so I am not surprised that he recalls
nothing.

'I decided to fly off the battlements attached to a demon
by a length of leather. I am never using a whip again.' I
grin, trying to make light of the life flashing by in an
instant. The look on his face is comical.

'Then, because we had so much fun, Basomel and I
decided to jump from the Gun Terrace in a suicide pact.
Luckily I landed on him. Not many people survive that fall
I hear.' Dead pan delivery minimising the terror that I felt
and the fact that I was lottery-winning lucky to survive.

'Dear Lord, that is incredible. You are so fortunate that
you aren't a smear on the path. How did the train get him?'
He really wants to know. I don't blame him, I think he
expects magic or something. He will be so disappointed by

the last bit.

'I bottled him with a buckle bottle and shoved him in front of the train.' That pretty much covers the details. I look straight in his eyes daring him to disbelieve me. He erupts in a welcome laugh. He believes me and yet can't believe that a Priest Buckie'd a demon or that I might know how.

We look at each other, veterans together and both sure in the knowledge that this isn't over. The Demon has been vanquished but that doesn't end it. We need to find the summoner and cut the head off this particular snake. A snake that I have, frankly, no idea how to find. The snake might not even be in Edinburgh. I let myself lie back on my padded back, feeling a little twinge as the stitches are compressed.

'How do we find out who caused this?' DI White asks after a few moments of easy silence. It is good that he can cope with silence because often I lapse into it as I try to find out what is going on. That and the fact I have pretty piss poor social skills and often don't try very hard.

'Jeremy and his books are very useful, allegedly, for this sort of thing. He will be able to find some obscure snippets that will help us just enough to stumble on to a resolution.' I wince as I lever myself round a bit. The light-weight plaster cast on my left wrist supporting another of my falling injuries. 'One thing is for sure the enemy will get a head start on us. I am going nowhere for a week at least and you look like a few days would be a good idea.'

DI White nods his agreement before making his goodbyes. I doubt he will be off work for more than a day, after all what else does he do? It isn't like he makes model air-planes is it? His movements tell me just how hurt he is, falling twice on to flagstones, and that he will be a little slow for a while. He was lucky all the same.

Hospitals used to like to keep injured people in the

wards for days at a time but that has all changed. The ward sister was in my room just a few hours after DI White telling me to get up and move around. Doesn't she know how injured I am? She took no nonsense either, dragging me out of the bed and taking me down to the common room where other patients gathered. All on the pretence that she needed to have my linen changed and I needed to be ambulatory. Apparently that's the same as walking about with my stand thing with the drain on it.

I am shuffling along like a geriatric and finding the lifting of my feet a trial. I feel the sweat beginning to bead on my brow as I struggle with the effort. The aches and pains trying to tell me to stop and go back to bed but my care-provider is having none of it. I groan like a sick goat a few times as I mince along the corridor.

'You need to keep moving or you will seize up and that'll take much longer to recover. Just take your time and we'll be fine.' She is trying to be helpful and professional so I don't tell her to piss off and leave me alone. We reach the common room with chairs tables and a television. More importantly there are newspapers and no other patients, yet.

I stand next to the table, abandoned by my nurse for the moment and look at he front page. 'Deer menace causes train disruption.' I almost laugh out loud but I know that will hurt so I hold it in. Deer? Which rocket scientist dreamed that one up. Like a deer is seven feet plus with wings. Anyway it seems to have had good coverage on all the papers.

'Princess Street Gardens to have deer cull.' I mutter a little under my breath, I didn't think there were any deer in the gardens or anywhere in the city centre. People will believe anything I suppose. Anything more reasonable than a demon was finally destroyed under the wheels of the late train to Dundee.

'Terrible isn't it.' A younger female voice wafts past my shoulder, obviously referring to the impending cull of

Bambi and his family. I turn my head slowly to see a student nurse, I think, peeking past me a t the headlines.

'Absolutely.' I agree with her although I suspect there will be no cull, ever. I am too tired to really play nice but I suppose that I should at least try to be civil. 'The deer caused an inconvenience so the council decides they need to be exterminated. Ridiculous, isn't it.' I manage almost a coherent viewpoint.

'Outrageous, they could at least just move them somewhere else. It can't be that difficult. Do you want tea or coffee or something?' I mumble back coffee and she leaves me to look over the rest of the paper. Not much of any real note inside the tabloids apart from a bit about 'The Graveyard Slasher' and continuing enquiries. The story will slowly wind down until we find a suitable patsy to pin it on. Preferably a dead one or a made up one. The facts are certainly not going to get in the way of tying that one up at a later date.

The hot steaming cup of freeze dried granules arrives as I am easing my ass into a comfortable looking high backed seat. I can get a good view out the window and also get a decent view of the television. I'll bet this is a popular seat among the inmates. Although I am not turning on daytime television. I don't think I could take a nuts and sluts production, ghoulishly watching other peoples dysfunctional lives played out in front of an audience. Who thought that would be a source of entertainment? Some heartless bastard in a suit, I expect.

'Do you need anything else?' She smiles at me again, leaning forward to make me comfortable when a pendant swings into view. I wasn't looking down her top, which on another day I might have. The silver and onyx twinkling caught my eye. I have seen one like that before. I know I have and I know it is important, I just don't know why.

'A lovely necklace, where did it come from?' I blurt out, hopefully she doesn't think I was perving her and sneaking a peek. She smiles and rolls it between her fingers.

'I bought it at a shop in the Grassmarket, it sells all sorts of unusual things.' She seems at once pleased I noticed and embarrassed that it was from an alternative shop. Does she know I am a priest? Is that the source of her discomfort?

'It looks lovely, does it mean anything?' I wonder if it is sold as a trinket or as a symbol of something or other. She is still running it along the silver chain and thinking about her answer, as if trying to recall what she was told at the time.

'I think it is some sort of good luck charm but I bought it because it looked nice.' She lets it drop back behind her top. She dismisses any importance of the pendant as she has settled me and is moving on to her next charge. I sit back and sip my coffee.

Having something to think about is probably a good thing for me. It will stop me just sleeping the time away in a fugue of boredom. The necklace intrigues me the Grassmarket has a number of 'Alternative' types of shops and our enemies might be hiding there. Shops where the more mainstream alternative lifestyle things come into the light of day. In the past it would have been bondage or adult products or seedy sex shops but nowadays New Age religious paraphernalia can be found. Everything from singing bowls for Buddhists to Wiccan and occult things. Mostly just harmless tat but sometimes items of significance can be bought. The rare and antique book shops are a particular source of interest and can be an afternoon stealer as I have found on more than one occasion.

I wonder where I might have seen one before, and after a good twenty minutes of racking my brain for anyone who might wear one that I might know, I resort to thinking about the women I have associated with recently. It is a short list and it pulls up nothing at all. I can feel my irritation rising when inspiration strikes. I shuffle back to my room, dragging my stand with the drains attached, I need to phone DI White. I am blissfully unaware of the arse-hanging-out nature of the hospital gown until I feel a cold draught caressing my downy cheeks.

'White? Steel here. Did any of the victims have a pendant? A silver and onyx pendant?' I forgot the small talk stuff again but if I am right then we have a lead. A possible line of enquiry as he might say. He is shuffling papers about and scanning the boards. I didn't think it was that hard a question.

'Jill is nodding at me. A squiggly shaped thing? Black and silver?' He is looking at the picture of it I bet.

'Sounds like it. I have a clue as to where it might come from. Can you check and see if any more of the victims have one? It may be the thing that links them all together. I think they may have been picked for slaughter.' I am stretching a bit but I'd bet I will be proven right. I need to sit on the bed all the nervous energy used up leaving me wobbly.

'Father Steel, you need to rest.' I have been rumbled by the nursing staff, no doubt I will be removed privileges of a phone.

'White aren't you meant to be at home?' I realise he is at work while I am incarcerated. It isn't fair.

Chapter 31

I am not good at recovery. Although these days I seem to be getting a great many more opportunities to practice the art of lying about and groaning like a sick pig. I get bored and then I get a bit cranky. Maybe that should be crankier. I have found that the quickest way to escape the nursing sorority is to be generally pleasant to them and then offensive as possible to the doctors. It seems that being crabbit to your nursing staff can result in unpleasant little experiences like hairs plucked by adhesive tabs. The bloke in the room next to me complains at the nurses all the time and has a less than pleasant time of it. His bed bath isn't nearly as warm as mine, I know because like all scamps we compare notes.

Badgering my doctor has been an effective ploy, he has had enough of my shenanigans and has sent me home to finish my convalescence so that my bed can be used for someone more needy. I am the picture of cheerfulness after his capitulation. Being back at the seminary does mean that I need to return each morning to have my wounds cleaned and checked. I am starting to move more freely now, like an eighty year old but still progress all ends up.

Bishop Michael was pleased that I survived my encounter and that the story of the deer on the track worked so well. He is less pleased that we had no idea what was going on. I have omitted to tell him of my current theory and my line of enquiry with DI White. We even have progress to report but I want to look for myself. PC Jill has been sent in on a couple of occasions to peruse the offerings and eliminate the stores that don't sell the right trinkets. We have narrowed our search and have been having the store, 'Bed knobs and Broomsticks' if you can believe it, watched.

Two weeks have passed since we had our tango on the

terrace and DI White and I are going to have a look ourselves, his face is fully recovered and only a little yellow staining remains at the corner of his eye. I am much less recovered but my heavy coat hides my extra padding and my tentative movements suggest that I am a little bit fragile. I want to see for myself if this is the harmless front of trinkets it purports or if it is something more. DI White has been suggesting another week of convalescence before we do anything but I am too bored, or stubborn, to wait any longer.

The shop front is a natty red colour and the window is full of pagan symbology as well as the ubiquitous candles and gemstones. The black velvet covered window display furniture looks plush and the Athame (symbolic daggers) and crystals stand out clearly. The prices on little stickers are enough to make my eyes water, thirty quid for a small amethyst geode? I am obviously in the wrong line of business. The beaten copper singing bowl, small, has a price tag of nearly two hundred pounds. I feel my face twitching in disgust at the gullible nature of the customers of the shop. DI White whistles at the prices on the silver goblet on the right of the window display.

'Let's go. Don't break anything, we can't afford to pay for it.' I grumble as I reach out and push the door open. The tinkling bell sounding as we step inside. There is an open wood fire blasting heat into the main sales area, a black cat curled on the hearth sets off the tableau. It opens a lazy green eye and looks at me, I look back daring the little bastard to hiss. It doesn't, going back to sleep.

'Welcome to Bed knobs and Broomsticks, how can I help you today?' The cheery young man is full of sincere teeth arranged into a disgustingly wholesome smile. He is tall, taller than me at any rate, and good looking which must help with the middle aged lady-desperadoes that no doubt are the core of the customer base. The younger goths will be interested too as will the rather omni-sexual dark masters, if any such frequent this place.

'We are just looking for inspiration for Christmas presents.' DI White lies smoothly as we start the wander through the sections of the small shop. The healing crystals and Moon charts all seem pretty tame but as we move into the bookcases we can tell the more serious aficionados would spend their time here. The books have very interesting titles and the price tags seem to grow exponentially as we go further.

I run my fingers along the spines of the books, just casually feeling my way around but there is nothing brewing so far. Paraphernalia of a variety of fashionable alternative religions and sects cover the shelves, themselves decorated by silver pen squiggles that mean absolutely nothing at all, and we come to the more recognisable occult items. Pentacles and chalices made of a range of metals adorn a bookcase; shabby chic I think they call the worsted veneer.

A glass cabinet is mounted on the wall with a selection of, what must be, more expensive pendants and chains. I scan the offerings recognising the one that looks familiar; silver and onyx and drawing the eye. I wonder if it is enchanted to draw a certain client group. It doesn't work on me but it might give me an idea if I could touch it. Three of the victims it turns out had similar, unique, pieces that may have come from a shop like this. One definitely came from here, paid by credit card, but the others may have come from here but proof is difficult. We didn't search each woman's home for a necklace, nor did we explore the fact that our demonic friend may have taken the pendant on the ones that didn't have one.

'Can I look at one of these pendants please?' I motion to the young man who is trying hard to ignore us and read his phone. I am loud enough to get him over and soon he is opening the cabinet with a small key that is pretty fiddly or he is nervous. I reckon it is the second of these reasons.

'These look very interesting, you must sell lots of them.' I try to sound enthusiastic and unknowing as my fingers tease and examine many other pendants before nearing the one I want to test. 'I think Jill might like this one.' I say casually as my fingers lift the onyx and silver item from the velvet backing. I feel a tingle like a static pulse, trying to make me not want it. Presenting a negative impulse that would be a minor enchantment. This pendant is for young women alone I think. I let it drop back. 'Maybe not, it feels heavier than I thought. Thanks for showing me.' I make it clear that I don't want to buy it. Was that relief flashing across his young face? Or maybe I just want him to be guilty and involved.

'Do you have a website?' DI White distracts him as he fiddles with the cabinet and soon our server is off to get a card with the details. Once we have a moment alone, I nod telling White we are on the money. This is our place.

'Do you buy in your jewellery or is it made by yourselves?' I ask as I look at some pewter chalices and Wiccan items. I look up trying to see if there is any dissembling by the mouthful of teeth.

'We buy it in from local craftsmen and women. The details are on the website if you are looking for specific items. The bowls and such are bought in from farther away. The owners would be better placed to help with any specific enquiries, I just mind the store.' Another attempt to disarm and divert us. He wants us out for some reason. It is not as if we are in uniform, although maybe priests and coppers give off a vibe all the time anyway.

'Okay thanks. I will have a look online and see how we get on. We are local so I can always pop in another time.' I am getting into the role maybe I should be on the stage. We are back out the door and into the street wandering away casually across the road towards a rather busy looking cafe. I casually glance at the windows above the shop seeing a tell-tale twitch, we have been watched and probably rumbled. We head inside to formulate a plan based on what we know. Which isn't much.

'The pendants are the key.' I start with the main thing, again no small talk as DI White puts our frothy Cappuccino mugs in front of us. I suppose I should have let him sit down first. Oh well, too late for a do-over.

'I thought they might be. I thought the one you wanted to check looked an ugly piece and I can't see why anyone would actually buy one.' He sips his mug, getting the inevitable froth on the end of his nose. You can't bring culture to a laddie from Oxgangs, you shouldn't even try.

'They are enchanted to be attractive to young women, I'd bet. When I touched it, it made me not want to buy it, a general negative reaction to it. It seems that these pendants were used to select targets. Maybe the beast was sent after the women wearing them. Why? I don't know but I am pretty certain.' I wonder if I should tell him about the nose froth. I sip mine, avoiding the adornment and I wipe my nose anyway, DI White surreptitiously wipes his realising he had been dipping his beak.

'It makes the shop a front and the toothy bastard an accessory to the murders. I think he would fold like a cheap card table if you lifted him.' Not that I am telling DI White how to do his job, well I am but I am being subtle about it. I slurp at the chocolate covered froth on the top of my coffee, culture Fife style.

'I doubt I could get a warrant for a search but we could ask him to come to the station to help us identify a number of items of jewellery. We could see if he denies they are from the shop.' DI White is being way to police-like for my liking. I want to just kick in the door and drag him away, Spanish Inquisition style. He is a minion and would probably lead us to the next step in the chain.

'We were watched as we left the shop, from the upstairs

window. Do you think they didn't believe we were customers?' Hard to believe but I wonder if my acting career is in tatters after one bad review.

'I think they could tell we weren't just looking. People can usually spot cops a mile away. Probably picked you out too, your disapproval at some of the items might have been spotted.' He is gently suggesting that my face tells the world what I am thinking. What a shocking revelation that is.

'We will need to move quickly then, or they will be gone before we know it.' I swig my cup and avoid a runaway drip, seeing it hit the table and not my trousers. The aches in my back seem to be less now that I have an enemy to hunt.

DI White, pulls his phone out and starts dialling the station. No sooner the word than the deed, and he is planning to have this shop watched. DI Anderson being shanghaied into action to use his team. Possible drug ring running out of the shop is the excuse. It always gets the police to act if there is a chance of busting the supply chain. I decide to call in a favour as I get mine out, as it were. We are the picture of modern conversation both on our phones to someone else; first world problems eh?

'Jeremy, Steel here, How are you?' I start off a conversation, I surprise myself at times. Father Jeremy is a little bit down on himself after the Cathedral farce and the strip that Bishop Michael tore off him for his error, I have long since gotten over that mess. After all I had an interesting flight and my life flashing by was a great in flight movie.

'Fine Father Andrew. How are your wounds?' He sounds a little bit nervous, like I am going to bawl him out for being wrong. If that was the case I would be on the receiving end ad infinitum. Never kick the puppies, they grow into great big wolfhounds with slobbering jaws full of teeth.

'Good Jeremy. I am well. I need a favour. Can you tell me if a pendant could be keyed for a demon to hunt? I have a picture that I can get sent to you? I have just been in a little shop of alternative religious artefacts and have discovered the enemy, I think. I knew what I was looking for and it felt like it was telling me not to buy it.' I know I am a bit garbled. It might just be easier for him to meet us.

'I am not really sure I know what you are asking.' He is hesitant, the Bishop must have really chewed him out. I have had that one and it ain't pretty.

'Can you come down and meet us? It might be easier, I need your expertise.' See, I can be nice. He needs someone to be on his side it seems. DI White is looking at me like I have grown horns. I frown at him as I end my call with Jeremy.

'What?' I look at him, not appreciating the little grin under his coffee cup. It is like I need to be a bastard all the time. He is laughing at my softer side; I'll never hear the end of it.

'Better not tell the Chief Super that Father Jeremy is on the case. He demanded that 'the useless twat' be kept as far away as possible.' DI White is openly grinning now. I know my face is a picture that would curdle milk.

'Tough. I need his input and the Chief Super can suck it up.' I am openly grumpy now, probably because I know I will have to buy the next round of frothy artisan coffee at capitol prices.

In less than an hour we three middle aged technophobes are huddled around a pretty dodgy laptop looking at the website of 'Bed knobs and Broomsticks' on the free Wi-Fi from the cafe in which we are ensconced. Jeremy brought the tech and as such is the one touching the buttons. I can tell DI White is itching to get in and go much faster but he is managing to resist at the moment. I am bored watching their efforts and am keeping an eye across the road. The shop is still open with a very limited footfall. It can't be profitable, surely. It is as if people are encouraged to walk past, perhaps a minor enchantment to keep people away this afternoon.

'The pendants come from an artist in Mid Calder, apparently.' Jeremy has another tab open and another website slowly loading. The pictures would suggest that the artist is definitely on the alternative spectrum if the site décor is anything to go by. It seems to be all black and red and symbols of Goth persuasion, the artist is a young woman with those big ear spacers making big loops of skin from her earlobes; looks stupid if you ask me. She is adorned with pentacles and the usual stuff that those trying to be different all wear.

'It proves nothing really. She may have made them but whether she puts the enchantment on them is another thing.' I mutter quietly enough for my other two amigos to hear but not any further. DI White nods in agreement.

'It does give us a reason to visit, though. We could go out this afternoon and shake the tree?' He seems keen to get something happening and to get someone into the interview room. Something we agree on.

'This looks a bit interesting.' Father Jeremy is peering into the corner of the screen. I am at the wrong angle and can't actually see a damn thing. DI White is doing the peering thing too. It seems when they do that their brains and mouths stop working. I keep my irritation in check but it won't stay there forever.

'You are right, I thought it was just a mark on the screen.' DI White is pointing as he leans forward 'right click it.' They are disappearing down a techie rabbit hole and opening a new tab or something. I still can't see and decide that I might have a long wait if I don't move round; not that I expect to understand what I am seeing anyway. I decide that I might as well get another set of coffees for all the help I will be about a mark on the screen.

Twelve pounds eighty for three fucking coffees. Granted they are specially hand crafted, lovingly tended and blended by a barrister of impeccable skills and deft touch. It is still twelve quid for three coffees, I feel that I have been fleeced and I am smiling like a village idiot as I pay for them. Jeremy, I notice, has deep pockets and short arms as it never seems to be his round.

He and DI White are doing the heads together geekfest thing, a little club I will never be a part of. I try not to bang the coffees down like my mother used to bang our dinner plates down on the table, especially after she had been arguing with her boyfriend of the day. Passive aggressive sort of thing, or at least that's what the psychobabblists would call it.

It seems there is a little bit in the very corner of the screen that those in the know would know to click taking them to a special site, a portal Jeremy called it. He went on at length about some technical stuff that White seemed to follow with ease, I was lost at the Darkweb statement. I think they knew my nodding along was for show and that I had no idea.

'It is like a secret internet Father Andrew.' Jeremy is being patient with the child in the team. I nod but how can there be a secret internet? Wouldn't everyone just log in to it or something? What would stop them? Is there a special handshake? Like the online Masons? I think he has me rumbled as he carries on 'The more unsavoury characters hide on the Darkweb. The drug dealers, the pimps, the Satanists, arms dealers and the like.'

I think he may be exaggerating for effect but if I were any of those guys I would want to be on the secret web thing. It seems that the tracking is harder on the Darkweb than on the internet we all use. Surely the police are all over the naughty one? Going by the look on DI White's face it would appear not. He looks like a kid in the proverbial candy store.

'What are we waiting for?' I ask as they salivate over their discovery. Shouldn't we just get right in there?

'We need a login.' Oh that makes it clear then. Whatever a login might look like, we do not have one. Sitting here across the road from the bad guys nest of vipers and we are looking for a login or logon or something.

'Should I just go over and get one? Just kick in the door and terrorise the toothy twat in the shop?' I know that won't work but staring at a screen that says username and waiting will achieve eff all. Fuck my frothy coffee is cold. I drink it anyway, after all I paid for it.

Chapter 33

The head scratching continued until we were evicted from the coffee shop and had to decamp to the incident room. The room was still looking fully functional but the caravan of resources has moved on to another more pressing case and, while the cases remained open, the knowledge that the demon had been destroyed by the late train meant that the brass had redeployed everyone except DI White, spotty MacBride and PC Jill. We were huddled round a laptop with a tech support from central services that had been pulled in as a favour. He was a friend of Jill's and was only too happy to help her and, by association, us.

He had brought some electrical stuff and his pilot's case of tools but I think that was just for show as most of the time he was clicking his mouse and tapping the keyboard. He looked very young for this sort of sensitive work. I thought. Still, we would have been looking at the login screen all night with no progress if we hadn't called in some help. The Darkweb, would have remained dark and we would have been arrhythmic due to the consumption of coffee.

DI White and I plan a little visit tomorrow to Mid Calder to beat the bushes and see what slithers out from under them but we need a clue as to what to expect.

I think my two wannabe geeks are getting in the way of our imported one and I can feel my boredom threshold being threatened once more. I have busied myself with making coffee and reading meaningless reports but the make work has died off and now, watching three animated heads clustered around a laptop has lost the limited appeal it had in the first place. I resort to google to look at the artist's website and am randomly clicking on pictures for expanded views when I get a chat box open on my screen. I yelp like the kid who has just been pinged in class with a rubber band, all very manly.

'How can I help you today?' It reads and is simply the artists way of interacting with a client, probably on the website so long that it sets off alerts.

'Guys I might have something.' I try to sound casual but their interest was piqued at the yelp, I expect. Young David, as I think of him, moves quickly to put his finger over the webcam and turns off the speakers on the desktop. He puts his finger to his lip as he slips a piece of Duck-tape over the camera lens freeing up his finger. He is taking this seriously but I know he wants to tell me why this was important 'Webcams and speakers can be operated remotely over the web and any Darkweb criminal might have that capability.' It is like an episode of Spooks.

'What do we type back?' DI White asks and the blank stares all round suggest that coffee hasn't stimulated too many brain cells in our little group. I begin to type. It is a conversation after all.

'I am looking for a piece of jewellery, something unique and different. Special.' I speak as I type it, you know in that slow I am typing it type of voice. I have the keyboard so I am doing it. It isn't fast typing either and I can feel a number of itching hands wanting to take over. The amateur finds a lead where the techie brigade got nowhere.

'Is the piece for a man or a woman?' The little text box pings back at me quite quickly. I type quicker this time, 'Woman' but the keyboard is a bit crap so my woman has two 'M' in the middle and I resend without the typo. I know I will have to give in to the inevitable and let someone else type.

'Let Jill answer and see if they are trying to lure her in. This may be part of their targeting scheme. We might be able to set them up.' DI White speaks quite loudly, being only a few inches from my ear but he is right. Jill might just sound like the perfect target.

The little box has a lol in it as Jill gets settled in and David the techie disappears to his laptop to do something that I don't understand. Jeremy follows to watch the other screen as DI White and myself wait to give our, obviously, expert opinion on what the answers should be.

'Did you have anything in mind? Earrings? Pendant? Bracelet?' The artist can smell money or is it something else. Jill starts to type a reply, and her fingers are flying over the keys.

'I am looking for something for my girlfriend and myself that will be special to us. Pendants and bracelets maybe? Matching but not the same. I like silver.' Jill is good at this, or maybe it is just what normal people actually do. I would have been hard pressed to answer that with much more than a few words. This feels like a real conversation.

'So his and hers complementary pieces?' The artist is trying to elicit the details so that she can make a recommendation. Trying to narrow down where to point her in a bid to present something appropriately expensive.

'Hers and Hers complementary pieces.' Jill drops her own relationship right in to the mix without batting an eye. From the stifled sounds and looks at the other screen neither of them were aware either. Maybe they think she is just playing a role.

'Okay that makes it easier to manage. I don't do a great many pieces for men sticking mainly to women's jewellery. Silver you said? For both?' The calm acceptance of the different relationship mix seems genuine, after all it is the modern world and marriage will soon be more than just between a woman and a man. Love is love, as all the churches should be proclaiming but aren't.

'Will I play along and see where she leads me?' Jill speaks directly to me then looks round at DI White, who is her actual boss. He looks to me to answer.

'Play along and see if she offers the kind of pendants

that I think are key, and see where she wants to go. Who knows she might invite you out for a fitting or viewing or something. You are doing well.' We should let her get on with it in peace, David says he will be watching on his cloned screen, whatever that is.

DI White and I move into his office to plan the next steps and options. That and have another cup of coffee which he starts the process off by filling the kettle from the bottled water dispenser. There are no actual taps closer than the toilets but the chilled plastic bowser is right outside his door. I don't think it is meant for coffee but needs must as they say.

'Can we have MacBride pull the shop assistant in to identify some pieces of jewellery tomorrow as we go on our field trip to Mid Calder? If we keep them both busy then they may be less able to react to what we are up to.' My planning skills coming to the fore in a blinding glimpse of the incompetent.

'We can, but I doubt we will discomfort them too much. After all there will be other staff to cover the shop and if there isn't we can't force him to come to the station.' The cold water rains on my parade delivered from a smiling assassin with a coffee cup. Luckily he has found some biscuits to soften the blow. I feel the frown settling on my face but we are making progress.

'Lets see what the artist throws up. If she is enchanting the pendants she is an accessory and a witch. If not she is just selling pendants to the shop and we can eliminate that line of enquiry.' I am learning this police lingo and sound like I belong here. Soon I will be proceeding along the road instead of going but that might be a while yet. Baby steps.

'I think you are right. This Darkweb portal bothers me more than a little as this could lead us into the lands of Serious and Organised Crime. They get a bit protective of anyone poking their nose into their turf. They won't want us buggering up their operations for a few pendants at an occult store.' He slops his coffee on his side of the desk and manages to restrain the expletive that almost got out.

'I hope David can get us inside and we can get a peek into their secrets. It might give us an edge on all sorts of things.' I think I get the idea of this web thing, but I might be a bit fuzzy on its usefulness. I doubt they have membership lists and a schedule of satanic events lying around.

'I hope he doesn't bollox it up. We will be in enough shit if we are caught tramping about where we aren't wanted.' He manages not to slop his coffee this time. The desk phone rings. We both look at it like it has grown spikes. It is after seven and no one would be expected to be here. I catch his eye, 'Brass?' I whisper as if they can hear me.

'DI White, incident room.' He turns on the professional I am in charge' voice and I almost feel myself sitting straighter in my seat. He seems to be sitting straighter too.

Chapter 34

I am pretty crap at hearing one side of a conversation. It is a failing of mine and the unhelpful contributions from DI White are about as illuminating as a torch with flat batteries. He isn't happy at the conversation but he is stoutly resisting the giving up of information. I don't think it is DI White's brass, just a generic brass trying to tell him what to do and like a good cop he is defending his turf. I huff a bit louder than I need to and DI White sends me the warning look, no one needs to know that I am there. Although I can pull my 'Do you know who I am card' if the caller starts to get shirty. I wait, badly, as DI White accedes to a demand to meet.

'Serious and Organised want to visit us. They are on their way over.' DI White doesn't look happy either, a pair of grumpy bookends we are. Will we have to put on happy smiles when they arrive? Fuck that I have aches that give me a pass. That and a cast on my wrist that marks me as walking wounded.

'What do they have to do with this?' I can't really see that this has anything to do with them. I am trying to catch a satanic demon summoner; serious I can agree but organised crime I sincerely doubt.

'Nothing but they know we have been poking at the Darkweb portal on our system and got an alert. We will tell them as little as we can and get them to piss off.'

'Seems like a plan. Do we need to hide Father Jeremy? Perhaps in the cupboard at the back?' I keep a straight face and wonder if he knows I am almost joking.

Our friends arrive in less than ten minutes which makes me wonder if they used their sirens to get here. They are an odd pairing, one like a great big shithouse of a man and the other is a slight framed spectacle-wearing bloke with a fine fuzz on top of his head. The odd couple they are probably described as by everyone who meets them. They seem to have had the humour bypass that afflicts many who work in specialist departments containing the word 'serious'. I give them a bland look as they make themselves at home, proprietary bastards and not even a 'pleased to meet you' or a 'hello' to fill the air as we get ready for a less than cordial meeting.

'Special Agents Johnson and Johnson?' I ask, they won't get it but it gives me a little warm glow. I might need to give them some clues as to my humour. My face is in the blandest setting I can find that isn't hostile.

'DI White, thanks for meeting us at such short notice.' The little one is doing the talking, which isn't a surprise. He still hasn't introduced themselves to me; I am chopped liver apparently.

'Father Steel, these are DI Wilson and DS Baxter. They are from Serious and Organised Crime.' DI White does the introductions smoothly, giving nothing away to our new chums. I nod like I know which is which, although I don't really care. They look in my direction and barely a nod between them.

'DI White, why are your guys poking about on the Darkweb? We have a load of sensitive investigations that could be compromised if someone lumbers around too much.' I am sure that he is trying to win friends and influence people; straight out of Dale Carnegie.

'It is an active lead for us in a multiple homicide investigation.' DI White is totally cool and professional, he hasn't offered them coffee though. I decide that keeping quiet might be the best option for now but I doubt that will last long.

'Of course. We need to just make sure you won't get in our way. After all, we are all on the same side.' He smiles, well it was an attempt to be friendly but came across as condescending in the extreme.

'I am sure that your way is not anywhere close to our way so we should be fine.' Another bland statement from my boy, giving away nothing and still keeping the peace. I can feel a get stuffed building but I am holding it in. I focus on the details as they play the 'show me yours and I'll show you mine' game of cat and mouse. Wilson, the little one, is wearing cufflinks and not cheap ones either. His police-work doesn't involve poking about in grotty flats or dumpsters. His suit is a few cuts higher up any pay grade than I could afford and looks well tended and his shoes hand stitched leather. He is very well presented. We are the Crumpled Brothers by comparison.

The back and forth has brought us no closer to any meaningful discussion and I can feel my face hardening into the familiar frown lines, it won't be long before something escapes.

'White, we both know I can call your boss and get you yanked off this area. Tell me why you are poking about.' DI Wilson plays the 'my dad is bigger than your dad' card, which is my last straw.

'I can call mine and you wouldn't like that DI Wilson.' I let it float out across the room. The spinning exorcist heads of our two visitors is almost comical. They can't work out which boss I mean and need a double take.

'I'm sorry Father?' He tries to get a replay in his head and can't decide what I meant.

'I forgive you, DI Wilson. I said you don't want me to call my boss. Why don't you tell us where your active investigations cross over with a possible Satanist?' I manage to keep my voice even. Their faces look so comical though.

'Father I am sure you mean well but this is a police matter.' He tries some more condescension, which is probably the worst option he could have gone for. His day is about to go in a whole new direction.

'Why do you think I am here Inspector? I don't mean well. I am here to catch a killer and our killer is a Satanist.' I feel my irritation getting the better of me. DI White gives me a warning look, it might be play nice or something like that. Too late for that, they are wasting our time and need to fuck off.

His face is a little flushed now, the unimpressive dog-collared spectator has teeth and attitude and he didn't expect that. He straightens in his seat, all pretence of cooperation and civility evaporating like the reek off a turd. His eyes narrowing as he turns his full attention on me. He doesn't know where I fit into this pantomime and he is a little unsure how hard to push his authority. One thing is certain he is not used to being challenged in his domain. A beat or two passes as he tries not to sneer at me. I wait, a little like a staring contest between five year old kids in a playground, until he has to speak.

'I appreciate your candour Father, but the police force has wider concerns to consider.' He begins. Apparently I am an idiot so I decide to let him continue; after all it is his career. 'DI White is not the senior officer here and I can have this investigation back away from any Darkweb entanglements and he knows it. Now Father, if you don't mind, we will resolve whether I let this little circus continue.' His arrogance is colossal and needs a little adjustment.

'DI Wilson, I will decide where our investigation goes. Unless, of course, you can convince my boss that you should be in charge. The Home Secretary always takes my calls. Should I call him?' The look on their faces is priceless; you can't buy this with MasterCard.

'I'm sorry?' DI Wilson has a wonderful level of incredulity in his voice. He is looking from me to DI White and is about to mount his response when my hand comes up cutting him off. I hand him a card. It will make his night I am sure. His gorilla is glaring in my direction which is meant to be intimidating.

'DI Wilson, I am here at the command of the Home office and have overall say in where our investigation goes. Crimes against the Church are my jurisdiction. If you feel the need have that checked out, go ahead but you know it would be a waste of time.' I pause letting my words find their way through the fog of his indignation. His face is turning that lovely blushing pink on the way to puce I expect. He is staring at the white card I have just handed him. After a moment he hands it to the gorilla, he doesn't say much either.

'So about this Darkweb thing.' I have given them as long as they are getting to catch up. 'In what way might you be encroaching on our investigation?' What a turn around for him to grasp. DI White is a great straight face player, he just waits letting the silence fill the space.

DI Wilson is trying to pull some coherence from his foggy brain, and is not really getting it together. He keeps looking at me and the card in sequence without making progress. He wants to check out my credentials but doesn't dare. He has no idea if I am a bluffer or not and that confusion is written large all over his face.

'DI White will keep you up to speed, Gentlemen. After all we are playing for the same team, are we not?' Wilson knows a dismissal when he gets one and the odd couple head on out, unhappy and unloved. I smirk at DI White who can no longer keep the grin from his police face.

'One nil to us, I think.'

Chapter 35

Mid Calder, as you might find out from Wikipedia, is not exactly a metropolis. It is one of three Calder villages which I almost never drive through on my way to Livingston and the mega shopping experience that is the Almondvale Shopping Centre. I always drive along the motorway and avoid all the little villages clustering near Edinburgh that once had coal mines and factories nearby. The stop-start nature of traffic light main streets make a simple journey tedious and almost interminable and that is why DI White is driving as I complain, not quite, incessantly at the time taken to get there. I am a little too old for 'Are we there yet?' but I can feel it coming. DI White doesn't seem to notice how long our drive into the central belt is taking. We have a sat-nav to take us in the longest possible route and the unmarked car is not in the greatest of condition inside. Hygienically speaking.

The winding route takes us out of the village to a farm track, with a road designed for bigger wheels than ours if the ruts are anything to go by. The intermittent scraping under the car suggests we might end up leaving the exhaust behind. The bouncing around is fun too until finally we each a better bit of gravelled road leading to a cottage with a few outbuildings. There are plenty of trees and hedges around making this very secluded. Perfect to prevent the nosiest of neighbours.

'We're here.' DI White with a blinding glimpse of the obvious. He parks the car on what looks like a solid flat bit but there is a great big puddle on my side. Bloody typical; I hope I don't have to wade too far. Luckily it isn't deep and I don't end up with wet socks.

The cottage looks well kept and has an arch at the gate, almost like a grannies cottage in little red riding hood.

Roses without flowers are waiting for the next summer and the foliage has died back a bit. A sign on the gate tells us we are at the right place. The red painted door is all glossy and shiny, somebody cares to clean it. I wonder if the designer lives alone or with a someone. The little fence around the front garden is wooden but not painted white, a cliche avoided thankfully. I let DI White open the gate and I wander up behind him. The passing of the threshold tells me that this is definitely our place.

'White, this is the place.' I speak quietly letting him know that something might go down very quickly. After our last tag team efforts against a demon we need to be careful. It is daytime so I am less worried although I have an itch under the cast that is irritating me mercilessly.

He nods and knocks the door knocker. It is a brass fox head and paws that gives a loud rat-a-tat-tat as DI White knocks. We wait for what seems an age before DI White starts the peering in the windows thing that people do.

'Maybe in the workshop at the back?' I try to be helpful, sometimes. Anyway we can see nothing through the net curtains that obscure everything inside. At least we haven't started chapping on the glass going 'yoo hoo'. I wander back along the path noticing the mixtures of herbs and plants in the cottage garden. Companion planting it is called, where one plant protects the others by attracting the bugs and pests. Only in this case I think the planting is a bit specialised and may be more of an active herb and spell garden.

Moving like a pair of nonchalant delivery drivers looking for a signature we make our way around the back to the three outbuildings. They are decent sized former cow sheds and farm buildings and all look used, if the doors and windows are anything to go by. I lead us over to the first one, no particular reason to do so, and try the handle. I am done with knocking and pretending we aren't here on my business. I have my hand in my coat pocket; a reassuring vial of holy water meets my fingertips. Locked and no sound from within, DI White is ahead of me to the next one.

Before I can warn him to be careful he has turned the handle and opened the door. I can't see inside but am moving quickly forward when I see him stagger out into the yard. In his gut a dark handled knife is lodged and the growing stain moving through his fingers and coating his trousers is not a good sign. He falls to his knees a few yards away and is groaning into his radio.

'Bastard.' I shout as I make my way into the doorway. The dim interior is a workshop to make jewellery and has a wide range of tools covering the benches. Perhaps I should have shouted 'Police' but it is too late now. The view I have of the long hair flying behind the enemy as she (it might be a he) passes further inside through a small door is fleeting at best. I snatch up a hammer like implement on my way past the bench. I have watched a load of action films and kick in the door that just slammed. When I say kick in, it flies in and off the hinges, maybe I have been a bit enthusiastic. The crashing and splintering of the wood sounds like a sound effect on a movie but inside is a little chapel of horrors.

A pentagram of silver on a black background, probably made of velvet, hangs against the far wall. The silver gargoyle-like faces holding it in their fanged mouths look sinister and vintage. The altar table is laden with the Satanists one-oh one-set, available from mail order in three easy payments of fifty pounds including post and packaging, and probably the booster sets too. The stone floor is swept to within an inch of its life, no doubt a regular chalking surface.

A young woman, maybe thirty, with long hair and a snarling disposition is chanting something at me. I am presuming it is a spell of some kind. She wasn't expecting the door to be in bits, I am sure and expected even less the hammer flying straight for her head. It seems to take her a few words to realise that the heavy lump of metal is aimed at her head. She stops mid stream to duck away from the missile that, incredibly, would have connected.

The tall floor-standing iron candelabra with fat black candles atop them gets the kick over treatment as I charge forward. I am going for a direct physical assault on this bitch. I have no idea whether she is a witch, priestess or dabbler but either way I am going to take her out.

A thick purple smoke starts to emanate from the floor as I scatter all the crap from the altar top. She is shouting words again, sounds like Latin to me but she is close by. The air is acrid and brings a watering to my eyes that is unhelpful if I am going to get her. Laughing, sinister and bitter, reaches my ears and a solid thud in my back throws me off balance, the smoke is coalescing into something solid. That something solid has just hit me.

The smoke filling the room like a gas canister escaping into space is making breathing impossible. I hold my breath and scramble away and try and remember where the door was. Another thud, this time on my shoulder helps me stagger through the space I made by removing the door. At least now I can get a breath, even if I can't see shit. I manage to get to the outside air and suck a huge lungful hoping to clear my head and stop the aching in my chest. I turn around, light behind me in the doorway, and realise the smoke stops at the door of the inner sanctum. A stand off of a kind, I cannot get in but it doesn't seem to get out either.

I look over at DI White, he seems to be holding himself together, the knife still buried in his gut. The red stain seems about the same size which I hope is a good thing. I retreat to where he is resting against the back wall of the house, my eyes focussed on the workshop as I make my way over.

'You all right?' I ask, not looking down at him just in case anything changes. He coughs and follows up with a groan and grimace combination.

'Peachy. The cavalry is on the way. Get the bitch.' He snarls a little giving a level of anger to his words. He points with his head, urging me to get back in there.

'They better hurry the fuck up.' I stand up and, taking a deep breath, cross the small courtyard to the doorway. If I seem a little less than enthusiastic it is because I have already been inside and know what is waiting for me. At the doorway I stub my toe on a bright red fire extinguisher, you know, the inconspicuous kind. I must have knocked it over in my escape moments ago. I manage to keep the swear word behind my lips but I notice a black one and a blue one too. I know the black one is carbon dioxide, having set one off in school as a dare. It has an explosion hazard sticker on the side.

'Come out, you have stabbed a police officer and there are more on the way.' I wonder if that will work, she might surrender. A demonic face coalesces in the purple hued smoke, a soundless snarl forming on its face. I am taking that as a no. I pull the vial of Holy Water from my pocket and find it has broken and the contents are soaked into my jacket. Bugger.

Chapter 36

I am not of the faint hearted brigade but I am not going to try and charge through demonic smoke to get at the witch within without some tools. It would be like turning up at a gunfight with a butter knife. A healthy regard for self preservation is how I would describe it, much better than being cowardly. When I need inspiration I find it comes in the form of words.

'Fuck. Fuck. Fuck.' I snarl as I look round for something, anything. The place is a workshop full of stuff that looks totally bloody useless, I have used the hammer that was lying about. A few craft knives and chisels scattered about but not much that will do much good. Like a demented springer spaniel I am spinning around looking and finding fuck all. The second bout of swearing is nearing the front of my lips as I start yanking drawers open in a fit of hope not expectation.

A cruel laugh rings in my head, was it the smoke demon or the witch? I have no idea but the red mist descends.

I used to have anger management issues as a child, you know stomping off in the huff when getting beat at football, cricket, tennis, monopoly, tiddlywinks you know the thing. Bad loser and flash temper. The mocking tips me over the edge a rage so visceral that I haven't felt the like for decades. A taunting sound that destroys my ability to rationalise. I find myself roaring and charging towards the smoke face in the doorway, unarmed.

The ground comes up to meet me in a split second and the air filling my roar is expelled in an explosive cough. The stars spinning round my head like a cartoon character a result of my collision with the stone floor. I would like to go on record thanking the Factories Act and the Health and

Safety Executive because they have just saved my life. Something they have been doing for workers all over the land for years. The red fire extinguisher, a requirement for workshops, had rolled into my path and tripped me up. Saving me from a fatal charge into the waiting arms of the demon.

I groan, the agony of my fall seeming to engulf my whole body. I now realise what the Doctor had meant when he said you really need a long period of convalescence after my flight from the battlements. The pain is good for me this time as the taunting laugh ringing in my head is no longer having the effect she wants. I know I am hurt because I can't even summon an expletive; mentally or verbally. I sit up, and it was a stretch to get that far, and notice the knee of my trousers is shredded and the underneath is an interesting red colour.

A moment of light-headedness passes as I try to get my shit together. My hands are shaking like a post bender detox session and I can't really do much more than glare at the face in the smoke. The modern fibreglass cast has shredded the back of my hand just adding insult to injury and a bloody stain to the cotton underneath. The ringing in my ears subsides a little to be replaced with a whispering 'The Master is coming' over and over again, undulating in volume in pitch like a bad sample. The hysterical undertones of religious fervour playing a counterpoint to the message. The witch has lost it, if she ever had it. The face glaring back at me has that arrogant cast that just gets on my nerves. I grunt as I get to my feet, it ain't over yet.

If I wait until the cavalry arrive there will be other casualties, policemen that are not equipped for this kind of situation. This one is mine to deal with; no one else's. I am leaning on a wooden rack still clueless and scanning for inspiration. The fire safety regulations for flammable chemicals, laminated, hangs by the doorway. Why would a jeweller have that posted so prominently? What chemicals do they use? I scan the room and see a chest-sized steel box, with stickers denoting hazards all over it, against the outside wall.

A painful, wincing and somewhat pathetic, few steps later I look inside to see bottles of dangerous chemicals and one I recognise. Acetone. It is perfect for my needs. I am going to burn the witch, medieval yes but with a modern twist. Fire consumes and purifies and has the added benefit of being my only option. The bottles are about the size of a wine bottle and perfect for throwing. I wont need a burning rag in the end. General Molotov would be so disappointed in me.

I throw the first into the face of the Smoke Demon, and it passes through leaving no sign of its passage. A second and a third are sent in the same direction. I don't have, what you might call, a good throwing arm and the third one smashes dramatically off the door frame. I throw the remaining bottles underarm, ensuring that they almost all get in. I can feel her uncertainty, as the voice in my head has stopped. She knows what I have thrown into her inner sanctum. If there isn't a bolt hole she is had it, and she knows it.

The Swan Vestas matches lying on the work bench strike easily and, resisting a quote from my favourite Christmas movie, I set the flame to the chemicals. The speeding aurora of flame seems to slide across the surface in a graceful wave heading for the grey smoke filling the doorway. The 'whoosh' sound as it gathers pace seems to suck the air before the bright flames start their consumption. I can hear the frantic activity from inside and know that there is no bolt hole. I move back, as the chemical heat starts to build, outside to wait for the cavalry. There is nothing left to do now.

'Master.' Her scream fills my head and my ears as she panics, the flames must be closing in on her. The power of her sanctum seems to have diminished in the flames, perhaps it has been cleansed too. I flop down beside DI White, he is still groaning a little. I smile at him, as a grim expression settles on his face, 'Better get a fire engine as well I think.' I wink at him.

'White to control. Fire service required on site. Workshop fire.' He presses the call button on the mic. I don't hear the response and neither does he as a concussive explosion blows out the windows and fills the courtyard with noise and debris. The screaming in my head is cut off as if a switch has been flicked. The shards of glass seem to land all round us and none find us. The flames are pouring out the windows and through the roof as the fire starts to eat everything that it can.

'Good luck putting that out.' DI White whispers, his lips beginning to look a little blue. The sound of the 7th Cavalry can be heard in the distance like a bad western. Well sirens, but unlike the cavalry they have missed the action and are arriving like British Rail, late.

'The building will be gutted by the time they get here. They'll be able to piss on it by then.' He needs to stay with me for just a little longer. 'You won't get a claim you know. Should have had your stab vest on.' I give him a nudge as the grin splits his face. The Ambulance swings in to view, thankfully. Some bloody cavalry.

Chapter 37

It is usually me that wakes up with some one else sitting in the seat watching. Tonight it is my turn. DI White has been lying inert for hours after the surgery. The stab wound was a little tricky apparently and luckily he didn't pull the dagger out at the scene or I would be sitting beside a coffin swigging his whisky. The ambulance guys were superb, no panic no fuss just a quick retrieval and blue lights all the way to the nearest hospital. I didn't know that Livingston even had a hospital but fortunately it did. The paramedic in the back was talking a stream of detail into his mic as we bounced along the farm road and so when we pulled up at the Accident and emergency door the whole NHS swat team took charge of my guy.

My patting his shoulder obviously helped as I tried to be there for White, the driver seemed to use the Edinburgh clock for our arrival time 'a few minutes' seems elastic around here. Anyway they whisked him inside and I was left to hobble after like a geriatric until a nice young nurse took care of my knee and the other scrapes. I should be thankful that the sticking plasters adorning my hands aren't smiley face ones. The paper stitches on my cheek make me look like a proper casualty. My knee is bound up with all sorts, looking much more impressive than a skinned knee has any right to look.

My mind is wandering like a vagabond tinker as I watch the steady rise and fall of his chest. The tubes leading in and out of him would worry anyone who doesn't frequent hospitals but I know what each one does. I have had some of them and I asked about the others. He is going to be all right , or so they keep telling me. I am waiting until his lights come back on before I am leaving. Is this how the Bishop feels when he waits for me? It feels awful.

I feel myself alternating between reminiscence and tears. The memories not really about DI White but the peaks and troughs of my life and those around me.

'I bet the Bishop just reads the paper' I say aloud, quietly. And the happy sadness fills me for a moment. I shake myself like a dog coming out of a pond and know that too much thinking time is dangerous for me as the string of losses of the past tend to surface over and over.

I get up and totter round to read his chart for the tenth time in the last hour. I read it like a professional, flicking the pages and reading what is in the bags hanging on the stands. Waiting is murder. I pace quietly, like a tip-toeing tiger in a cage. The door opens and a middle-aged, matronly figure enters and tries hard not to glare at the muddy shambles standing at the end of the bed reading the charts.

'He won't be awake for another six hours or so.' She speaks quietly as she checks a variety of settings and writes on the chart which I have relinquished to her care. She checks him once more and makes sure he is as comfortable as he can be, even though he will never know. 'Go home and change, get some rest and come back in the morning. I will take care of him until then.' I wonder if she means you stink and are in the way but her eyes radiate kindness and an unexpected empathy. My stubborn refusal to leave evaporates as I accept that she is right.

I take his hand and whisper to him 'Don't die ya bastard. You don't have permission. I'll be back.' His eyelids flutter a little bringing a smile to my face. He's in there. I let him go for now, and let myself be ushered from his room.

Bright and early, clean and uncrumpled, I open the door to his room. The bag of grapes and three newspapers in one hand and Costa coffee in the other, I am prepared for a wait. He is still sleeping, I can tell by the small movement under the coverlets. I managed a few hours of sleep and the rejuvenation of the shower was like magic.

I feel like a weight of years has fallen away with the culmination of the case. For a little while the technicolour recollection of demonic murders will leave me alone as I sleep, until the next one.

I read his chart again, checking the times and events that took place while I was away. They are like clockwork and the initials beside each one telling of bag changes and medication must be of the Sister that sent me home. Funny how nurses are called Sister. I have a sister and she kept an eye on me loads of times, probably why the name has stuck for the group of women that have looked after others through the years.

I sit in the chair that, I hadn't noticed was uncomfortable last night, will be my guard post for the day. Time passes like dripping treacle, slow and dead slow. The newspapers, not worthy of the name, don't last long and the grapes last even less time as I pick and pick at them. The coffee a distant memory and the quiet passing of time draws me back to the case and what was going on. There was so much happening that the why has been lost in the noise, pain and deaths. I roll my mind back to the start and begin my search for the golden thread that will make some sense of the things that we have endured.

I can feel my face contorting to a heavy frown and frustrated crabbit mask as I trace the steps and cannot get it straight in my head. Why did she summon the demon in the first place? Why target young women with the jewellery? All through it 'the master is coming' is irritatingly replaying and interrupting. Father Jeremy will need to find out what that actually means because I have no idea. Something big is going on and I just don't know what. I almost growl at my lack of progress and I wonder how I explain to the Bishop that this one is over but a bigger wave is coming. The dark tide is rising.

I pick up the local paper, an early edition has our fire on

the front page. A chemical accident and fire in a workshop resulting in the sad and untimely death of a jewellery designer. I feel my sneer develop as I read a story that says they know nothing but takes a few hundred words to say it. More inside will mean more guesswork and supposition. I turn to the page anyway. A picture of the cottage and an inset of the girl who died in the fire and more words detailing the tragedy. No mention of White or myself, so all good I suppose.

A moment, you know one that we sometimes miss, tells me to look again at the photo. I am looking but not really seeing the anomaly. Like an Escher or Rossarch dot splatter thing, I can't really see it at first but when I do it sticks out like a sore thumb. Standing on the hillside is a figure. It might be a local shepherd but I know it isn't. I can feel the malice emanate from him. 'I'll get you Matey.' I snarl to the paper. A cough from White calls me back to the room and I move to his side. His eyes slowly manage to open and focus on his surroundings. I am probably too close as he tries to see. His mouth moving a little, probably as dry as a sand shoe, and no words getting out.

'Good to have you back.' I smile to him as I get his water with the fat bendy straw. I feel the relief wash through me, utterly unexpected and I can feel my eyes a little moist. Luckily he doesn't notice as he drinks using all the energy he has to do just that. I remove the straw and watch his eyes close again. He will be back in a few minutes I expect.

'I ate your grapes,' I say quietly.

The End.

Printed in Great Britain
by Amazon